Grapes of Fortune

A Severn Family Saga

Lisa Absalom

To Richard, Martin, Amanda, Emily, Katie and William

Sylvia, Alison and Anthony

Well, it *might* have happened like this!

ACKNOWLEDGMENTS

Nottinghamshire History Resource nottshistory.org.uk

"Wine and the Wine Trade" by André Louis Simon, 1921

And
Huge thanks to Jackie for being my Editor

The Severn family are real, their personalities and lives, largely a figment of my imagination. Other characters are purely fictitious and any resemblance to actual persons, living or dead, is purely coincidental and not intended

THE SEVERN FAMILY

Grandfather Martin m Grandmother Martin

THEIR CHILDREN
Martha Martin m John Cramp
Boy Martin marries A.N.Other

OUR FIRST GENERATION

MARY CRAMP b.1731   Daughter of John & Martha Cramp
WILLIAM SEVERN b.1723   Marries Mary Cramp

SARAH MARTIN   Daughter of 'Boy' Martin
JOHN CROSLAND   Marries Sarah Martin

The Eight Children of William and Mary Severn

William known as BILLY	b. 1754	m. Elizabeth Hextal
John known as JACK	b. 1755	m. Ann Gadsby
MARTHA	b. 1756	
Mary known as POLLY	b. 1758	m. John Crosland
BENJAMIN	b. 1760	
JAMES	b. 1762	
GEORGE	b. 1764	m. Betsey Tebbutt
JOSIAH	b. 1766	m. Bessie Smith

Son of John Crosland and Sarah Martin

FRANCIS   b. 1755

The Next Generation

Jon Severn	b. 1779	Jack and Ann's son.
Beth Severn	b. 1781	Jack and Ann's daughter
John Severn	b. 1789	George and Betsey's eldest son
Mary Severn	b. 1793	George and Betsey's daughter + 8 others
Mary Ann	b. 1795	Josiah & Bessie's daughter

CHAPTER ONE

He stood, feet rooted to the ground. Petrified. Captivated. Excited. He could never have imagined this scene before him. His cheek was brushed by the gentle whisk of a horse's tail and the large, brown, calloused hand that was holding his own, pulled him sharply to one side as the rim of a towering cartwheel bowled past within an inch of his shoulder. Looking down he saw his crude, leather shoes half submerged in a sea of filth, unrecognised, the stench all around him was not from the cows or pigs he knew from home. The air was heavy with smoke, filling his lungs with an acrid taste and smell. The strong, familiar hand began to pull him along the street. His ears were ringing with an unfamiliar, unbroken din, the creaking and clanking of carts, the loud voices of street sellers crying their wares. There were harsh, masculine, strident voices calling, "knives ground here, bring your knives," "chairs over here, new legs and backs mended," "hot beef pies, two for a ha'pence." He heard softer, feminine, melodious voices, "sweet oranges, who'll buy my oranges," "flowers for sale; a farthing a posy; bunches two a penny," the rattling of a pail performing a metallic overture to the sweet, sing-song cry, "milk below, milk below." He was engulfed by an army of legs. Breeches and stockings and brass buckles glinting as feet sidestepped or skipped over the patchwork of stinking detritus abandoned there on the ground from the beasts and humans of Nottingham alike. The warm, comforting hand stopped leading him. He stood still in the awakening morning light, shivering a little in his thin, threadbare coat and looked up at the hand's owner.

"Here we are lad," he heard his father say, "this is your new home."

"So this is 'The Town'," five year old William said to himself his eyes wide with wonder, "this thrilling, awesome place is where I am to live. 'Town' must be what our minister at church on Sundays, calls heaven."

§

Nottingham 1728 - 1743
In 1728 Nottingham's population is around 10,000. England's
population is around 5.25 million.

William Severn had been born in 1723, towards the end of King George's reign, and his family moved to the town of Nottingham as part of the growing migration from the surrounding villages, leaving behind their life of hunger and despair to seek a better living, attracted by the burgeoning hosiery industry and the prospect of regular work. As hundreds of other families had done, his parents rented a knitting frame and set it up in the attic of the tiny dwelling they had found in a Yard to the rear of Middle Pavement. They shared this narrow, tall house with another, larger family, strangers to them but who also worked at a frame in the attic. From here they toiled for as long as the daylight lasted and then toiled longer again by candlelight, producing the fine woollen hose so much in demand for the fast growing population of fashion conscious men and women. The work was hard, dangerous to the fingers, paid for by the piece, and with onerous overheads to be paid to the Master Hosier, including rent, new needles and repairs to the frame, the family had to work long, long hours just to keep from starving.

Plucked from the wide open spaces of the countryside and planted in the noisy hustle and bustle of the thriving town, he was the second youngest child of the family. The oldest, a daughter had already married and moved away the year before, two of his surviving older brothers had stayed in Kimberley village working on the land and the baby, a sister, had come to Nottingham still in arms. William's days, young as he was, were spent working in the attic. For hours he would wind the wool ready for his father to load onto the frame and knit the straight pieces which his mother would seam and finish, turning them into stockings. He saw little daylight in spite of the large windows and he became as pale and thin as his parents.

When he was seven years old his life changed dramatically. His father, an uneducated man himself, was sufficiently influenced by the text of a Sunday sermon at St Mary's, that it was only by education together with hard work that his son could prosper, decided to send William to the charity Blue Coat school recently moved close by to High Pavement. From now on, his little sister would take on the responsibility for the majority of the wool winding.

School transformed him. Always a curious and interested boy, he now thrived, absorbing his lessons as readily as the sponges his mother used, soaked up vinegar. He quickly learned to read, write and do elementary arithmetic. He applied himself during school hours with enthusiasm and vigour and paid great attention to the many hours of religious instruction which formed the major part of every day.

One fine September afternoon a few days after he had started school, lessons finished, he was kicking an old cabbage down the street thinking he might risk not returning straight home but go to the Market Square and look at the stalls on the fringes of the annual Goose Fair. Another boy was walking in the same direction and they teamed up, going along together in companionable silence as boys will, taking it in turns to kick the cabbage. The time ran away with them and when William finally arrived home that evening he was soundly beaten by his father, but the memory of the crowds, the geese with their feet tarred to protect them on their long walk from the Fens, the acrobats and tumblers, the smells of the food stalls and greatest of all, the knowledge that he now had a 'best friend', raced around his head providing salve for his stinging buttocks and dulled his instinctive sense of remorse for his disobedience. His new friend, John Crosland, was only a few weeks older than William and whether by dint of his attending the grammar school or of him standing, when they carefully checked, a good finger's width taller, he had simply assumed the role of an older brother. A position William never questioned nor resented. It was a rare day that they could meet up after school, their free time being confined to Sunday afternoons after church, but they spent every moment possible, together.

About three years later, William went straight home as usual one afternoon, took off his blue charity school coat and found his father distracted, in an uncharacteristic mood, "Off you go boy," he said gruffly, his voice sounding gravelly and strained, "come back in two hours." Not wishing to question this unexpected good fortune William left the house and disappeared to spend the precious hours in the town, hoping to meet up with John to roam the streets, maybe collect up a few buckets of horse dung to take to the tanners in Narrow Marsh to earn a farthing, to look in the shop windows and to day dream.

The reason for his father's generous mood became all too apparent on William's return to the house. He learned his little sister had died of influenza that afternoon and, alarmingly, his mother was lying on their sparse mattress, wracked with fever, her face drenched with sweat, her emaciated body shivering with a deathly chill. Her eyes were shut and her breathing rasped loudly round the room. His father, feverish himself, huddled in a piece of woollen cloth was sitting on an old, hard wooden chair at her side, a jug of weak beer clutched in his hand which he held to his wife's lips from time to time, finding little response.

After an interminable and sleepless night, William was ordered to attend school as usual, "You must go lad, learning is the only way you will drag yourself out of this sorry state," his father's voice was hoarse and weak, "I shall look after your mother."

When he returned home, she was cold to his touch, her gaunt, grey face revealing in death, a glimpse of the happy young woman she might once had been. Lying next to her, his father's bony carcass, outlined beneath the threadbare blanket, was shivering uncontrollably, his chattering teeth pulling his face into a premature rictus grin. William kneeled and took hold of his hand, "Thank you Pa, thank you for sending me to school, thank you for giving me a better start than you ever had. I promise you I will make something of my life, I will not let this happen to me, I will not suffer in poverty as you and Mama did." He felt the slightest squeeze of response from his father's burning fingers, "I love you Pa."

Sitting on his cot at the side of the room, he heard the church clock strike midnight, the twelfth chime accompanied by his father's death rattle. He was ten years old and scared but he had used his time sitting there in the dark to make a plan. Knowing what was to come, he understood he had to leave. He was quite certain of what happened to orphan boys like himself.

"I'm not going to my brothers in Kimberley to live a life of poverty again and I'll not let the Parish bind me to some stinking tanner in Narrow Marsh. I have learned enough at school to know I can make something of my life, I shall rise up out of this despair, I have promised my father and I owe it to myself. One day I shall have a family of my own, we will love and fear God as the Bible says, but we will not be downtrodden, we will be strong."

He left the sad, fetid room, crept stealthily down the stairs, careful not to wake the other occupiers of the house, opened the door and concealed by the darkness of the moonless night made his way to John's house. Once there, he stole round to the shed at the rear, held his breath as he pulled open the old door, the top hinge had long fallen away and he flinched as the grating noise penetrated the calm. He tip toed across the room and curled up on a bed of straw and his back against their milk cow providing warmth, exhausted, he slept.

Hunger woke him up early. Heavy hearted in the knowledge that his parents were gone and his school days were over, he had hidden all morning, skulking in the alleys by The Shambles, hoping to cadge a broken pie or piece of bread amongst the crowds, but by the afternoon, ravenous, he chanced returning to his home to look for food. He should have guessed, the meagre stash of bread and meat had gone, consumed by other famished children. Walking slowly away from the house, not a bite to eat or a possession to his name, wondering if he could dare go back to John's, he was held up by a gentle voice, "I heard what happened lad, your mother and father gone," and looking up William saw strolling towards him, old Absalom Partridge, the publican of The Grapes, "I'm looking for a new pot boy," he said, "it's hard work but I'll give you a roof over your head, plenty to eat and maybe a farthing or two. I haven't got a boy of my own else I'd use him."

This act of mercy was the beginning of William's career. He worked all the hours The Grapes was open, collecting and washing the beer and gin pots, polishing the pewter till it gleamed, cleaning the floors, running errands and all the time, observing. Watching Absalom and his wife, watching how they poured the drinks, watching what went into the cellar, watching how they took the money, watching and waiting. He took note which of the customers were more influential than the others, who of them came to do business, he took notice of the wines they chose to drink, and he listened to their conversations as best he could as he scurried about, in and around their legs. He helped fill the jugs or pails with small beer collected from the back door of the house to be drunk at home, he helped throw the drunks out onto the street and all the time he was learning.

When Absalom came up to him and asked, "You're a bright lad, can you do any reckoning?" He was ready.

"Yes sir, I can reckon in my head as fast as anyone, I don't need a stub of chalk and a slate."

"Cocky young sir aren't you. Tally this up then. A noggin of gin, a jug of small beer and a quart of ale." William stared ahead, his eyes as blank as a rabbit's caught in the flare of a poacher, then just as rapidly focussed! "Gin 1d, small beer ¾d and ale 1d, "That's tuppence three farthings."

"Right lad, I'll be wanting you to start helping out with the serving when me and Mrs Partridge have to go out or the barman can't cope."

When his time came, Absalom Partridge gave up The Grapes, went to the magistrates to change the name on his licence and handed it over to the son he'd never had. William was now twenty years of age and the legal publican of The Bunch of Grapes. His heart rejoiced, this was the beginning of the life he had dared to strive for.

The tavern was a half timbered building about a hundred years old, the wattle and daubed spaces between the wooden framework having long relinquished the rich burnt amber colour they sported when new, were now a rather dull shade of cream. To William it was his home and his castle. He threw himself into the new venture, he was a good landlord and ran a respectable house in an often disreputable business. He kept tight control of any of his regulars who enjoyed a disorderly night, he neither gave, nor let his barman give, short measures, he never charged more than the legal price, he did not keep late hours and he most certainly did not serve anyone during the church service hours on Sundays. He was affable, a good conversationalist, treated his staff well and most importantly, he encouraged business men to come to The Grapes and never complained that they might sit at his tables for hours, discussing the issues of the day and talking more than drinking. William had plans for the future and in order to put them into practice he still needed to look and learn.

CHAPTER TWO
Nottingham 1750 - 1752
George II is on the throne, England's most recent war with
France ended in 1748

One late summer afternoon some seven years on, William had walked through town to put in his regular order at the brewery wholesalers on Goosegate and was making his way back home deep in thought, when he bumped, almost literally, into his great friend John. "Good heavens Will, you're miles away, I'd watch out where you're going or you'll end up under a cart."

"It's just as well you're here to save me then! Good afternoon John," they shook hands, "you're just the man I wanted to see, come back with me to The Grapes for a jug of ale, I want to talk to you about something."

"Sorry, no time I'm afraid. Aunt Martha and cousin Mary are visiting mother for the day and I'm expected to be on parade, just about now!"

He threw a covert look at his friend. This last remark was by no means as innocently casual as John made out, he was well aware that William was in love with his cousin Mary and always grateful for the chance to spend time with her when she came to visit.

"But she's exactly who I wanted to quiz you about! You know I really am in love with her, do you think she would accept me? I'm sure she likes me well enough, but more to the point, do you think there's any chance her old man would allow me to marry her? I'm twenty seven, I've been running the tavern for seven years and business is going well, so I'm not as bad a possibility as I might be."

"Well, her father is a bit of a tyrant, but I can't really see why not and as for whether Mary would want you, well old friend," John put an exaggerated frown on his face, "that would depend on whether I was willing to perjure myself and assure her that you were a decent sort of fellow with good prospects!" He ducked to miss William's hand as it veered towards his hat, "If you can leave your man in charge of the tavern a bit longer, why don't you come along with me now?"

"You know damn well I'd leave the pot boy or even the dog in charge of the place if it meant I could come and see Mary, but I think I should speak with her father first, so just a normal social visit, not a word about my intentions please." Laughing together they made their way to Weekday Cross and tea with the ladies.

Never destined to be tall, William was luckily content to be a compact, broad shouldered man, who when standing next to Mary's diminutive frame, gave the illusion of being a giant. He was pleased that today he was a tidy giant, his clothes were clean, he had been well shaved by the barber that morning and his sometimes unkempt, dark brown hair was pulled back from his forehead and tied neatly in a queue. His features taken individually, promised ugliness. Large ears, a prominent nose and pale blue, deep set eyes but the combination, surprisingly, resulted in a countenance which always attracted rather than repelled. William's only regret was his round cheeks would burn with a bright red blush the moment he saw his love. In his eyes, Mary Cramp was the loveliest girl in Nottinghamshire, and in contrast today, was completely unruffled. Her hair, the dark red colour of conkers just before they fall from the trees, was pinned up at the back and from under her little white linen cap, delicate corkscrew curls fell forward to frame her face. A few faint freckles were painted over her nose and her hazel eyes were flecked with olive green. Eyes which, when not lowered demurely as convention dictated, regarded you with a sense of determination belied by her stature. William thought of her as a little doll that he longed to hold and protect and Mary admired this big 'bear' of a man who would perch on the edge of a cane chair in her Aunt's parlour, awkwardly sipping his tea, looking at her adoringly and, if not completely tongue tied, entertain and amuse both her and her mother.

They had first met some months before at a gathering in Thurland Hall, where wealthier tradesmen, their wives and families would meet once a month for dancing, conversation, cards and general merry making. That evening he was standing with John at the side of the room. Dressed in his finest white, linen shirt, light brown, woollen waistcoat, dark brown breeches and calf length coat, with below that his finest hose and best leather shoes with the brass buckles, he was trying to loosen the fearfully tight stock strangling him at his neck and feeling very hot and uncomfortable. Until her saw her! Mary appeared to glide across the floor towards them, wearing a pale blue, fine calico dress embroidered with tiny rosebuds, seemingly covered with ribbons and bows, and held out on all sides by a fan hoop. Somehow, her glorious hair was defying gravity in a profusion of curls piled high on the top of her head and she bore just a hint of a mischievous smile on her face as she came up to her cousin John and, seeing full well the effect she had had on his friend, was introduced to William.

It was fortunate that William's overwhelming desire to dance with such an exquisite creature overcame his nerves and when their hands touched briefly during the minuet, he felt a thrill of excitement rush through his body and very nearly turn his knees to jelly.

Mary was not to learn of William's honourable intentions that late summer of '50 after all. His resolve hardened after his conversation with John, he had taken his courage in both hands, hired a horse for the day and ridden to Langar, a village some twelve miles south east of the town, met with her father John Cramp amid his flock of thirty sheep and had been soundly rebuffed for his impertinence in asking for Mary's hand in marriage.

In The Grapes the following day, the melodrama was playing out with John, as usual, our hero's faithful audience, "I cannot live without her, she is my reason for living. I shall die, I know it! I could ask her direct, she is after all twenty five and of age to decide for herself, but I know she will not go against her father. She is such an angel!"

"Come on Will, it's not the end of the world, only a temporary setback, here let's have another jug or two of beer. Drown your sorrows and then for goodness sake, think of something, get on with improving your chances."

"Of course, my dear friend, that's what I must do," William stood up smartly, slapped John on the back, and pushed his tankard away, "I must improve my chances. No more beer for me thank you, I must make plans!"

§

John Crosland's father had become a successful butcher owning livestock and properties in the town and since his death last year, as the only son, John had taken over the business and was running it well. He was an enthusiastic man with a cheerful disposition and lived at present with his widowed mother Agnes, above Crosland's butchers shop in a substantial house in Weekday Cross.

"We are so lucky to be in business at this time Will, look at all this," he held out his arms as if to embrace the town as they walked together down Middle Pavement, "the opportunities we have are vast compared to our fathers' generation. Just look at the numbers of country folk leaving the land to come into the towns to work in manufacturing, well, your family of course."

"Not that their move turned out well," William gave a wry smile, "but I agree with you, my few years schooling has made all the difference to my life and that wouldn't have happened back in Kimberley. I promised my father and myself when he died that I'd make the most of my time here on earth, I've been lucky enough to have a better start than he ever had, and I'll not waste it."

He pushed open the heavy oak door and the two young men walked into The Grapes. Immediately, William scanned the room. It was pleasingly busy for a late afternoon, a few of his regulars were lounging on benches round a long table, their cards in disarray, the game forgotten and the men absorbed in conversation made all the more voluble by their wine. A table of merchants in a corner, were upright and alert, sheaves of papers before them and the strong, bitter aroma of their coffee drifted through the smoke filled air.

Calling to Amos his barman for two tankards of beer, William drew John over towards the window, and looking back into the room said, "I think I should turn this area into a dining room, from here over to the fireplace and to the right, up to the bar. I could put six, maybe eight tables in and that would give me about thirty meals, twice a day. What do you think?"

"It's certainly a big enough space but will it still leave room for the drinkers? They'll lose their tables by the windows."

"I think so, and there'll still be the long bar for them. These tables and chairs can be moved over to the side, they're all spread out now just because I've got the room. The thing is John, at the moment nearly all my sales are beer and gin, only a small amount of port wine, and that's sold to people like those wool men over there."

John pushed a sleeping dog out of the way with his foot and sat down at an empty table, "What, the ones drinking coffee, is your port that bad?" Smiling, he raised his beer, "Cheers!"

"Cheers! I'll ignore that last remark. I'm sure I could make more profit selling food, what do you think?"

"I think you would, because then you'd sell more wine and probably more expensive wines."

"Exactly! I knew you'd understand."

"Where do you buy your port from at the moment?" John asked.

"James Ashby on Stoney Street, do you know him? I'd trust him to recommend which wines to start off with until I get to know more about the subject."

"I do know him, he was a good friend of my father's and funnily enough, I remember going to his shop for the first time, years ago now, when I was a child. I didn't realise it at then but later father told me the cellars were full of French and German wines as they still had customers from the old days who thought claret far superior to the port we all drink now."

"Those men will be long dead and gone and just as well. I've never made a secret about my views on the French, we've been at war with them for ever, they're our enemy. I couldn't bring myself to think about trading with them, let alone drink their wine. Queen Anne hoped the Methuen Treaty would ruin their economy and I must say I agree with her." William tensed, their views on France was the only source of friction in his friendship with John and they usually tried to avoid the subject.

"You know what I say, there's always a place for pragmatism in business Will, stick to your principles by all means," John rubbed his hands together, "but maybe leave the door open a crack?"

"Well the taxes on French wines are still the same as set by the Treaty, £55 a tun and only £7 a tun on Portuguese, so patriotism or no, it would seem our government still doesn't want us to trade with them either. Some claret does come into the country of course, Ashby has a little even, but it is very expensive and not for the likes of us, or my customers." William raised his eyebrows at John who nodded and he signalled to Amos, " A couple more beers please when you have a moment."

John drained his first tankard and asked, "I've only been drinking port for a year or two so I can't tell from my own experience, but my father told me that the quality went down dramatically over the past couple of decades. Is that true and the only reason people drink so much of it is the lack of anything else and the fact that it is so cheap."

"I think that used to be the case John, but what's exciting is the quality is really on the up now and given that every true born Englishman has come to believe that port is definitely better than any other wine, I think it's an excellent time for me to get really involved. The taste in England is for really dark, sweet wines and vintage ports fit the bill perfectly, and of course it's more expensive. I've always encouraged the traders to come here to hold their meetings and I reckon if I could feed them I could persuade many more, it's too good an opportunity to miss."

"It makes a lot of sense, you've built up well on Partridge's sales, and you're right, there's more money to be made from selling wine than beer and gin."

"You do know I'm not going to be a publican for ever, I'm going to open my vintners shop as soon as I can and right now this dining room is the first step. I think Ashby is third generation in his family merchants, he was apprenticed to his father and that's what I want John, it's part of my promise to my father, I want my and Mary's first born son to take over from me, I want continuity for my family."

"Steady on, you're running away with yourself! Are you thinking about asking Mary to marry you again now."

"No, I'll wait until this gets up and running, it will only take a little while and I've waited all this time, so I can wait a few weeks longer."

"Of course, I've just had a thought," a grin spread across John's face, "if you are going to provide food, you'll need a butcher to supply the meat for your roasts and pies."

"Yes, that's certainly a problem," William chewed on his bottom lip in thought, "The Lord alone knows where on earth in Nottingham I might find a decent butcher."

"Very droll, seriously though, you'll also need a cook who can turn out a decent plate of ordinary for a shilling and my mother might be able to help you there. All those years as a butcher's wife means she knows just about everybody in the town, and more embarrassingly for me, she appears to know all their circumstances and gossip too."

CHAPTER THREE
Nottingham 1752 - 1758
The Seven Years War against France begins in 1756

In October, William could wait no longer and two years after his first attempt, he made the trek to Langar to speak again with John Cramp. This time permission was given, a modest settlement agreed, and with great happiness, arrangements put in place. The banns were read on three Sundays in December and William and Mary were married in St Nicholas church on January 1st 1753.

On their wedding night, after a jolly party in The Grapes, Mary's 'big bear' of a husband proved to be a gentle, considerate man, tender and loving and for this Mary was very grateful and her admiration for William turned very quickly to a deep and abiding love. They settled rapidly into a happy married life.

Mary was accustomed to helping her mother with the domestic side of life. She had been taught as a child, as all girls were, that her only purpose before her own marriage, was to make life as comfortable as possible for her father and five brothers, and she transferred those skills easily to looking after her new husband. The living rooms above the tavern were quite small, one living room, a tiny kitchen area and two bed chambers and they proved easy to run with the help of Fanny their new general servant. The few pieces of furniture had been bequeathed by Absalom Partridge and were well made but unfashionable. The dark brown rug under the table had been his old dog's comfort and was frayed from chewing in one corner and his favourite chair, now William's seat of choice, was an old oak, open armchair, with intricate turned legs, the seat and back upholstered in a brown floral tapestry and the tips of the scroll arms polished black from generations of hands. Mary's own contribution, a sturdy oak bedstead, her gift from her parents, filled the main bedchamber leaving scant room for the plain wooden chair and small, walnut linen press brought from her room at home.

The overall impression of her home was shabby, but Mary was happy and she made plans to improve their condition as soon as decently possible.

As a young wife, her days were busy, the dining room was recently completed and Mary gladly took on the supervision of Mrs Jackson, the cook who had been found, as anticipated, by Mrs Crosland. Together they met each day to decide on the meals to offer their customers and enjoyed choosing the ingredients, agreeing how they were to be cooked and Mary often accompanied Mrs Jackson to the markets and to King's the grocer to select what was needed. The meat of course came from Crosland's, which was a most satisfactory arrangement for the family friends and John's old carter delivered the orders three mornings a week. Mary also employed a young maid, Ruth, and applied herself diligently in training her to be their new serving girl. With Mary's attention to detail and Mrs Jackson's excellent way with pastry, The Grapes began to attract many diners and their trade began to expand very satisfyingly.

It wasn't just trade that was expanding satisfyingly! At the beginning of March when Mary and William had finished their usual breakfast of tea, bread and butter, before the day's work began, Mary left the dining table to kneel at the side of his chair, "Dearest, I have some wonderful news. I am expecting a child, and I'm sure it will be your first born son."

William choked back an oath of surprise and looking deep into her beautiful eyes, he stammered, "Oh my love, how wonderful. I am so happy, I have dreamt of this moment, it is the start of our own real family." Sunday, attending the service in St Mary's Church on High Pavement, William gave especial thanks to God for his good fortune.

On the 31st of October, Mary gave birth to a fine baby boy. It had been a long and hard first labour for her but it seemed even longer and harder for William! Banished from the bedroom he at first refused to leave the passageway outside, accosting Mrs Adams the midwife each time she left the room. "Is there any news, has the baby come, is my wife faring well?"

"No, it's not time yet, it's still early days. Your wife is coming along well." The words exchanged so frequently they became a mantra. Inevitably, after some hours, William found the sound of his wife's cries so distressing that he forced himself to retreat to the rooms downstairs and try to apply his mind to his work.

When Fanny came later to find him, "Sir, Sir, the baby has come and the mistress is calling for you," he bounded up the stairs two at a time and risked the wrath of Mrs Adams by bursting straight into the darkened bed chamber. "Mary, are you well, where is the child, have we a son or a daughter?" he babbled, staring ahead looking for all the world as if he were a simpleton.

"You have your son and heir," said Mary proudly, "We can name him William for you, but I should like to call him Billy."

"Yes, yes of course. Billy. Why, he's perfect. My son. Thank the Lord for his goodness." At which point, he was unceremoniously ushered out of the room by Mrs Adams who told him she had, "Things to tidy up!"

Billy thrived and was baptised at St Mary's within the week. Mary grew strong again quickly, was churched just a month later and life carried on much as before. Now though, Mary had the help of an extra servant to help Fanny with the home cooking and laundry as she, Fanny, taking great pride in her elevated status, spent time helping Mary with the baby.

§

William was always waiting for the right time to move his business on and now, at the beginning of '58, with five years of running the dining room, he had grown in confidence and knowledge, was providing a secure and comfortable life for his family and had some modest savings.

The family had also grown and Billy had been joined by a brother, Jack, now tugging at Mary's skirts still in his petticoats, and in Mary's arms, baby Martha. They were awaiting the arrival of their fourth child in October and, of necessity, Mary's life was now very different from those early days of marriage. She still loved to organise the dining room at The Grapes and shop in the markets, but found the family occupied many more of her hours and most of her time was spent happily, and certainly ungrudgingly, nursing her babies and talking to Billy. When he had reached four years old, Mary had finally agreed with William that the boy was ready to come out of his baby clothes and dressed in his little breeches and jacket Billy looked a miniature of his father. He was a rather serious infant, interested in everything around him and was utterly devoted to his mother, disliking intensely to be separated from her for whatever reason.

The friend Mary saw most often was a cousin on her mother's side, Sarah Martin, now married to John Crosland for five years and whose joys she celebrated and whose sorrows she shared. Sarah had suffered a miscarriage in their first year of marriage but after this sadness, had carried to term a boy, John, who seemed to cling agonisingly to life, as precariously as a drowning man would cling to a straw. Their next child was born weak and frail and the little boy had died within hours. Joyfully, only a few weeks ago in January '58, Sarah had given birth to a healthy, almost robust, son who they baptised Francis, and who gave every indication that he wanted to live.

"People like being in The Grapes, they feel they're really welcome. In fact a lot of them tell me it's better than their own home, nice and peaceful and that they'd rather be here than there," William said, lifting the piece of meat skewered on his knife up to his mouth.

"I can believe that," the corners of John's eyes crinkled with laughter, "our little Francis has a pair of lungs on him and that's for sure. He's only a month old and can bring the house down!"

The friends were sitting together at a quiet table set in the corner of the dining room, tucking into one of Mrs Jackson's famous beef steaks, liberally seasoned with pepper and accompanied by a honey sauce and potatoes. William looked around and agreed to himself. It was a very satisfying room despite, or maybe because of, the low, smoke stained ceiling and the mismatched tables and chairs. There was a roaring fire in the large, open hearth, rows of shining pewter mugs, jars and bottles lined up behind the long, solid oak bar at the end of the room and the delicious smell of home cooked food wafting in from the kitchen at the back. The gentle murmur of friendly conversation and laughter, joined from time to time by the squawk of the hen who had taken up her residence on the window sill, filled the air. "I shall be sorry to leave, I know this sounds sentimental but I feel a lot of these customers are my family."

"Let's hope they follow you to their new home then," John grinned at his friend, "you'll need all of them and a good many more and you'll need the gentry with their money to spend if you intend being anything more than a lowly bottle-shop owner using a fancy name."

They were interrupted by Ruth coming to their table, "Shall I take your plates Sir? I've got orders from Mrs J to say it's plum pudding next and there's extra sugar for you and your sweet tooth."

Ruth was a pleasant country girl, well trained and more than capable of looking after all the diners by herself now that Mary was so busy with the children. She was friendly with the customers but never too friendly, listened patiently to their confidences and jokes and whilst she was a plain, woefully thin girl, there was often one drunken customer who chanced pressing unwanted advances on her when in his cups on a Saturday night. Ruth loved working for William, she thought him handsome, clever and kind and spent a lot of her life thinking how to please him and anticipate his every request. John guessed she might be half in love with him, but William dismissing this as a fanciful idea, wondered out loud, "Well, what do you think John? She's a bright young thing and learned the job here quickly and by goodness she's loyal to me. Maybe I can find something for her at the vintners."

The vintners shop was his project ripe for the picking. He had thought about, talked about, dreamt about and learned about the wine and spirit trade at every possible opportunity over the past years and he knew he should start it now.

"I was looking at an old house on Weekday Cross just up from you, past where your mother lives. Mrs Wordsworth's, it's on the other side of the road next to Dales the druggist's place, up by Blowbladder Street. The poor old dear is selling up and going to live with her daughter in Leicester. I think she's sad to go but it's good news for me as the house is just the right size for us. Can you come and have a look at it with me later?"

The house William had set his mind on was a large, half timber house, a little like The Grapes but with the panels newly filled with red brick. The ground floor had previously been the pawnbrokers shop run by Mrs Wordsworth's late husband and was now empty, showing no trace of artefacts, precious or otherwise. The frontage had two large, square paned windows and as well as a main door in the centre, which gave the building a pleasing sense of symmetry, there was a second entrance on the western side, and to the rear, a small yard and a wooden shed which William hoped would provide sufficient space to store his barrels. Inside, a counting house led off the main shop and stairs rose up to the first floor where there was a kitchen, a generous space which could be divided into a parlour and separate dining room and three good bed chambers. In the attic, there was more than enough space for Fanny and the servants. William looked at John, the enthusiasm glowing on his smiling face, "Mary will love to have all this space after the cramped rooms in The Grapes"

"You're right she will, and I can see her and Sarah having a fine time at the shops looking for furnishings. It will make a very welcome change for my wife to be helping spend your money instead of mine! Not that she's extravagant, she just has an acute awareness that our social standing is increasing - I'm sure she'll be able to instruct Mary in this too!"

"That's my only stumbling block John. Mr Stephenson at Valentine & Reave's is getting the paperwork together but I've got to go to Smith's Bank for a loan, and I'm not sure that I'll get it."

"How much are you looking to borrow?"

"Well, I'll be able to manage the rent but I need more working capital. I can't run a shop without keeping a good stock and I know they won't be the gentry, I'm not grand enough for them, but a lot of my customers are likely to be folk who are used to having a bit of credit," he looked around the room one last time and made towards the door, "I'm really worried about the Bank, I don't know what I shall do if they refuse me. I'm going to ask for £200 but I suppose I could manage with a bit less, and if they do let me have it I bet they'll charge five per cent, what do you think?"

"I should think you'll be offered the money, but as you say, at five per cent. When I took out my loan the other month to invest with the wool stapler I told you about, I saw Abel Smith himself, but my situation was a bit different, and also he and Knowles are acquainted."

They went back downstairs and John standing by the window, looking out at the folk walking by, gave his friend a huge grin, "Between us, we'll take over the town at this rate!"

"This," William said as his eyes swept the room, "is a very good step on that path!"

The morning of William's appointment at Smith's Bank dawned cold and drizzly, reflecting William's own mood. Mary watched him with sympathy in her heart, taking him in her arms she tried to reassure him, "Please don't worry so my love, you'll see, you'll convince them that you are a good prospect without any effort at all. Just remember how well you improved the tavern and how well you have made your plans for the shop. The bankers will be very silly to turn you down, especially as Fanny has sponged and brushed your breeches till they look like new, your coat too and I have turned the cuffs on your best shirt to hide the frayed edges."

Mary's remarks made William smile, albeit a nervous smile, and having checked and checked again the clock on the mantle above the fireplace, he decided to set off early rather than risk being late. Not wanting to take the certain chance of being splashed with the morning debris which flowed like a river down Middle Pavement, he turned sharp left and walked briskly up Drury Hill, left onto High Pavement, across Weekday Cross into Market Street and arrived in Market Place outside Abel Smith & Co. with time to spare. If bank buildings were designed to intimidate the mere mortals going through their doors to ask for money, then this handsome building did just that to William.

"What on earth am I doing here. They'll take one look at me and throw me out," he thought, and then at the back of his mind he could hear Mary's voice urging him, "Don't be such a fool, go on, knock on the door!" So he knocked.

Less than an hour later he was striding back along the road with his head high, his spirits restored and the prospect of £200 in a new fangled account at Abel Smith & Co.

He rushed home to give Mary the news, his excitement tempered just for a moment when he said sadly, "I just wish my Father was here to see this day. I'm thirty five years old and I own my own Vintners. I shall call the shop Severns, that was his name too and it will make him part of the adventure. Maybe John is right, this really is the start of our dynasty and we will take over the town!"

CHAPTER FOUR
Nottingham 1758 - 1766
1760 George III accedes to the throne : 1763 the Seven Years
War ends

William gave up The Grapes in April and the family moved into
their new house and shop in Weekday Cross. Whilst Mary, with
the help of Fanny, and a new scullery maid Clara, had set about
turning the upstairs rooms into a comfortable home for them all,
William spent his waking hours planning, stocking and opening
up Severns. He brought Ruth from The Grapes with him and she
was engaged not only to work in the shop, but also to help Mary
in the house. Ruth had willingly left the overcrowded, damp
house where her mother lived in Narrow Marsh and was quite
content in the cramped attic together with Fanny and Clara. She
was proving just as dedicated to William as she had been before.

William took the advice of James Ashby to engage the
services of a wine merchant based in London called Charles Jubb
and there had been great excitement when early one May
morning, Suttons Wagon arrived back in Nottingham from the
four day round trip to London and soon afterwards, a local carter
pulled up outside Severns to unload the first casks of port and
madeira for William's stock room.

There was just enough space left to set up a small bottling
station and William had acquired a stock of glass bottles, large,
round and with bulbous bottoms, explaining to Mary, "The wine
won't keep long in these, the cork dries out too quickly and lets
in air which spoils the taste of the wine, so our customers will be
coming to the shop to refill them over and over." He would draw
off the dark red, fortified wine from the Douro or the sweet

madeira from the exotic island off Africa, with as much pride as a father presenting his first born son!

Being a naturally gregarious, jovial man with a fund of stories and anecdotes, who made sure that his prices were keen and service excellent, William's shop became a popular place to be. There had been a saying during the first half of the century, 'one penny bought enough gin to get drunk on and two pennies bought enough gin to get dead drunk on', and in an attempt to address the debilitating effects of fifty years of this cheap gin, the government had brought in the Gin Act which, whilst stopping rogue producers, had also increased the taxes for licensed merchants like William. Luckily, the increase in price had hardly dampened the lucrative demand in local inns and taverns, which meant that Severns wines were stored alongside plentiful barrels of gin, beers, brandy, rum and Scottish lowland whisky. William had worked hard to gain the custom of nearby hostelries and one of his first patrons was Walter, the new landlord of his own old tavern, the name now changed to The Golden Fleece.

Mary was very happy in her new home. Helped by Sarah they had arranged and then rearranged the pieces of old furniture brought with them from the tavern and Mary had diligently cut, sewed and adapted coverings for their chairs and beds. William had insisted on bringing the old frayed rug and of course his favourite chair, the tapestry now bald in places and the stuffing lumpy, "I find it most comfortable Mary, I don't want you to fancy it up, I like it just as it is. It reminds me of where I began and spurs me on to do the best for you all."

She had staunchly resisted her friend's entreaties to purchase what she, Mary, regarded as extravagant luxuries. "Sarah dear, we are not in such a fortunate position as yourselves yet and I must be prudent," she was furiously polishing an old copper coal scuttle, determined to make it shine like new, "I have good, warm bedding and a sturdy bedstead, an oak table to eat at and thanks to you, the most beautifully embroidered table cloth to cover it. We have enough chairs to sit on, Billy, Jack and Martha have clothes on their backs and shoes on their feet. That is enough for now and I am very grateful for it. Besides, the new baby will be here very soon and you know the expense that will bring, not to mention that during my lying in I will be unable to help in any way. There, that looks better, it will do very nicely now don't you think?"

Sarah took the scuttle from her and placed it to the side of the fireplace, "Very well my dear cousin, but as soon as this child is here and you are churched, I insist we go to the bazaar together and choose you a new set of cups and plates for afternoon tea. You cannot entertain the good ladies of Weekday Cross with these old brown earthenware ones. I saw the prettiest Derby Porcelain tea set in Bridlesmith Gate last week. It is decorated with delicate blue and pink flowers, with golden leaves and gold edging. I would love to have it for myself but I think John would say, enough!"

Picking up an old pewter candle stick, Mary began polishing again,"How is little Francis," she asked, "you've left him with your nursery maid so he must be well?"

"The little dear is thriving, growing fatter every day. Oh, Mary, I am so hopeful this time, I don't think I could bear to lose him too. Johnny is now three but so very prone to stomach ailments and fevers that I fear he will not live for me to see him breeched."

Mary was brought to bed again on 1st October and gave birth to a healthy, lusty baby girl. Named Polly she became, much to the puzzlement of two year old Martha, an instant and firm favourite of her father's.

The family's life was good, they were happy together and through William's hard work, Severns began to thrive. Babies continued to arrive and Benjamin was born in April '60, James in April '62 and George in November '63.

The same year as Benjamin was born, when Billy became seven, he started school. William had thought of sending him to the Bluecoats, but the opportunities at Widow Mellers free grammar school on Stoney Street offered a far better curriculum and certainly now with the teaching broadened out from Latin and Greek to include more literacy in English, mathematics and natural sciences, Billy's education was chosen with a life of commerce in mind. William's first born son was to become Severns heir.

The following year, when the time came for Jack to follow Billy to school, he had pleaded with his father to be allowed to attend Bluecoats, "It was good enough for you Father, so it will be good enough for me," he reasoned. All Jack wanted to do with his life was to work with 'Uncle' John, learn the butchery trade and have his own slaughter house and shop. William agreed that Jack could follow his chosen path but was adamant that he must have the best possible schooling first, Jack attended the grammar school where constant comparison with his studious brother and a lack of natural ability, resulted in long and tedious days for him.

Martha found Jack's attitude unfathomable. At five years old she was bright as a silver button and longed to go to school, constantly pestering her parents. "No man wants his wife to be schooled," Mary told her feisty daughter, "it will be enough for you that I will teach you to write your name, and you will learn to sew, cook and keep house and if you are dutiful to us, your parents, you will be practised to be dutiful to your husband."

Martha took the opposite view. "I will never marry," she told herself, " I am not going to wear myself out constantly tending to a man's needs and, worse, bringing forth child after child." Wise beyond her years, and unlike her father, she had noticed the toll bearing so many children had on her mother and whilst at this age she did not know the words to express her thoughts, she had a profound belief that life for a girl was not fair, life was unduly weighted in favour of her brothers.

Luckily she was very fortunate in Billy. Not only a pious and empathetic boy, he also had, for one of his sex and age, an unusual sense of justice in this regard and he took Martha aside when she was seven, "Don't be too sad, I have an idea. I can teach you to read when I am home from school and maybe you will be allowed your own Bible."

Martha was thrilled but worried, "Oh thank you Billy, thank you, but what should I do? If we tell Papa he will say no, but it is wrong not to tell him, he will think we are deceiving him."

"I will speak with Mama, I don't think she will be completely against you learning to read, after all you would be reading the Bible, and maybe she can persuade Papa."

Mary's view that the ability to read, of itself, would not lead to Martha's moral downfall sealed William's agreement and with Billy's patient tutoring, Martha began to read the Bible. This skill, once mastered however, created a further problem for her. Frustrated by the limitations of possessing only the Bible to read, no pamphlet or missive found within her boundaries was left unmolested, but was avidly deciphered, devoured and committed to her memory. As she grew older, this haphazard approach to reading material explained the range of topics on which she had a small amount of knowledge and her sometimes rather surprising opinions!

Billy was a very considerate child, he continued to adore his mother and was kind and patient with his younger siblings but of all the subjects he was learning, instead of relishing the mathematics or science, he was most interested in the classics and religion. Over the years he became very pious and took to reading the Bible every evening after the family had eaten, and would often request permission to read passages aloud to his mother, Jack and Martha.

As the children all grew older, during the service each Sunday morning at St Mary's, whilst the younger ones fidgeted, finding it hard to sit still on the unforgiving wooden benches and harder still to concentrate on the lengthy sermons, thinking only of the time later in the day when they would be free from their chores, Billy sat engrossed by both the doctrine and the melodramatic eloquence of the minister. That this minister had attended Cambridge University, put him at the zenith of Billy's esteem and made the boy all the more determined to study hard. At home after the service, when dinner had been finished and cleared away, the girls might want to find a stick to draw a hopscotch pattern in the dusty ground outside their house, or play their skipping games; Jack would take himself off to try and find Uncle Crosland to talk to; Ben would hope to meet up with Francis Crosland to rush around like small boys always have, running races, fighting battles or kicking a ball about, and the little ones would be settled to sleep or nursed at home with

Fanny and their mother; but Billy would engage his father in discourse on the day's sermon, questioning and commenting on the teachings raised that morning.

§

"Oh Sarah," Mary hugged herself and rocked back and forth in her chair, "I know it is God's will that I am blessed to bear these children and indeed I wish you could be just as fortunate, I know how much you would like another child, but I am so afraid."

As soon as Mary had realised she was expecting again, her eighth pregnancy in thirteen years, she could not curtail this overwhelming fear, "George's birth was very difficult and I am still so tired and I have such pains."

Sarah was brushing Mary's hair, long soothing strokes, the brush straightening the greying curls just for a moment before they were released and sprang back into shape, "Please try not to worry my dearest cousin, I shall pray that the Lord looks after you. Remember, all your babies have been strong and healthy and maybe you will have another daughter this time, you have five sons and I'm sure Martha and Polly would like a little sister for a change. Besides," she began to pin the hair back up under Mary's cap, "I need you to have a good selection of daughters for my Francis to choose from in the future!"

In June her labour was hard and much too long. Mary knew in her heart all was wrong. Fanny would not leave her side except to call Ruth from time to time to bring a glass of wine with a dram of borax, sugar and cinnamon for her mistress. Mrs Adams, the midwife, kept up the encouragement and William was instructed to keep the children away from the bedchamber and to demand their silence. On the second day of Mary's dreadful suffering, Josiah was born. His body frail and whimpering led William to fear the worst and he called for the priest to baptise him straight away. However, fate having a reputation for being mischievous and contrary, baby Josiah lived on and it was tragically, Mary who declined.

Her body, so weakened by the birth, deteriorated day by day. She was unable to nurse little Josiah herself and a wet nurse was found. A local tanner's wife who lived in Narrow Marsh was willing for the money paid to her by William, to come up to Weekday Cross to feed the baby. Even in her feeble state Mary insisted the baby would not be taken away to any filthy home and to those around her, observing, it seemed that as Josiah slowly gained his strength, Mary's was draining away. She could not rise from her bed and it broke her heart to be so weak, unable to hold and comfort her little ones when they cried for her. Billy was inconsolable, spending every waking moment when not at school or church, sitting at his mother's bedside, quietly reading his Bible and frequently praying together with her. Fanny and Ruth made nourishing broths and sweet barley water to tempt her appetite, but it was to no avail, Mary lost her struggle to live in November, she had a massive seizure and then her pain was over.

Fanny washed and laid out her beloved mistress, dressing her in her shroud. William, in a trance, dealt with the clergy, engaged the grave digger and hired a pall and bier. He would never recall having done all this and when the mourners had left the house, Mary was taken on her final journey, to St Mary's Church.

"Ashes to ashes, dust to dust". William could hear the words but he seemed to be wandering in a thick, white, November fog. He thought he knew where he was, he had after all walked to the churchyard, but his mind was confused, he couldn't be there. How could he have lost his Mary? He could see her in his mind now, coming towards him wearing the pale blue dress with the tiny flowers, her dark red curls framing her face and her green eyes and lips smiling at him. Over the years he had never seen, never noticed, the stout woman she had become. He had not seen the grey streaks in her dulling hair tucked, as it always was, under her little white linen cap. He had not noticed the careworn look on her face, the tell tale little lines that showed her constant nagging pain. He had always looked at her and seen what he wanted to see, his young bride. How could she be gone? He could understand the Good Lord wanting her, she was after all, an angel, but she was his angel and William still needed her.

"Papa, Papa". He looked down at Billy his eldest son, thirteen years old, standing at the grave beside him.

"What about the children," he thought, "motherless. Jack, Martha, Benjamin and dear little Polly, they were here with him. Dressed in their best clothes, bewildered, looking anxiously at their father's blank face and having to turn to Billy instead. But what about the babies, too young to ever remember their mother, James and George still in petticoats and Josiah whose arrival in the world just six months ago had heralded the departure of his beloved wife. What will become of them."

William knew these things happened. He had been around death and the dying all his life. His parents long before their time, Mary's parents, and children died too. His little sister gone, his dear friend John's unborn babies and last year their little John who managed to struggle through less than four years of life. William knew it was to be expected that a woman's life of lying in and providing children for the future could be cut cruelly short, but he did not expect it to be Mary. It was November 1766, she had lived only forty one years and now he would have to manage without her.

"Papa, Papa we should go," entreated Billy, "the minister is waiting for us." William turned to his son and with an unfamiliar action, put his arm around Billy's shoulders. His other arm, in a much more practised movement, went around his darling Polly. "Yes son," not much more than a whisper, "let's go home.".

CHAPTER FIVE
Nottingham 1766 - 1770
*The "Great Cheese Riot' took place in Nottingham, infantry
and cavalry were brought in to keep the peace after the Mayor
was knocked down by a large rolling cheese !*

When her mother died, any vain hope Martha had harboured of having a life free of domestic drudgery, faded overnight. Together with Fanny, she was now expected to take over the household for her father and to step into her mother's shoes caring for her younger siblings. She knew there was no recourse to rebellion, there was no other option. Aware of other girls, some younger than herself, who were in the same position she resigned herself to the task, with sorrow but no outward resentment.

Martha was a gangling girl, her long arms and legs as ungainly and uncoordinated as a new born foal's. Her face was round and plain, her button nose smothered with cinnamon coloured freckles, her chin slightly jutting and all this was topped with shockingly, ginger hair in such turbulent, tight little curls that she seldom resembled anything but a bird's nest. Polly, her sister, was a very different child. Pretty, quiet and obedient, William doted on her, petted her and held her up as an example to the others of a perfect child. At eight years old she was a smaller version of her mother and had inherited Mary's stature, her soft pink skin, pointed chin and rosebud lips. Even her eyes were flecked with green and she too had a lustrous crown of dark red, soft curls.

It was to the younger girl's credit that her older sister loved her with all her heart. Polly possessed such a sweet and loving nature it was impossible to bear her any grudges and aware now that changes would have to take place, hiding her own distress, she bravely promised to help Martha as much as she was able by looking after her young brothers.

Benjamin was sent off to school with Billy and Jack a little earlier than might have been, but he was a clever little boy, eager and ready to learn and his absence from home all day relieved a little of the pressure. School hours were long, seven in the morning until six in the evening everyday but Sunday, and Ben was thrilled to go. Unlike Billy, his favourite subjects were arithmetic, geography and Latin and although he would never admit this to his father or older brother, if he could have ignored the long and tedious religious instruction, he would have done so. This left little James, breeched soon after his mother's death, and three year old George at home with the baby Josiah. These older two, quite understandably, had no time for the sickly baby, he held no interest for them at all being too young to join in their games and so they ignored him. The boys spent their days together, they shared their toys, their meals, their bed. The infant George grew to rely on his bigger brother, he became James's shadow, he worshipped him, his life was lived for 'Jay, Jay'.

Martha's distress at finding herself in the position of home maker was mitigated a little by her elevation in the eyes of the family and her slightly greater degree of freedom. William had arranged within a week or two to 'borrow' Mrs Jackson from the Golden Fleece for a morning, to accompany Martha and Fanny to the market and, with the benefit of her long experience, help them in their shopping. On this Wednesday morning, Martha was anticipating a pleasant hour amid the smells, sounds and sights of the Weekday Market stalls. They would not, she had been told quite categorically, go near The Shambles.

"That's where the meat market is. A filthy place, you wouldn't want to put your feet anywhere near the ground it's just a morass of mud and muck," Mrs Jackson turned her nose up as if the stench was somehow reaching her nostrils whilst still at home, "ugh! the air is foul with the steam rising off the cattle, and the place is packed so tight with people you can't move. Mind you, it's not just the countrymen, but thieves and vagabonds, pickpockets and street hawkers, all pushing and clamouring. It's all together a dirty, noisy, unwholesome affair. Dear Lord, you'd not believe it if you hadn't seen it for yourself. No, us ladies will only go to the civil stalls of the Weekday."

Martha was rather dismayed, "I'd like to see it for myself," she whispered to Fanny, "then maybe I could believe it!"

"Sshhh!," Fanny was appalled, "it really is not a place for a woman, let alone a child."

She soon forgot about The Shambles, completely seduced by the atmosphere of the Weekday market, Martha was determined to show her readiness to take charge of the family shopping. Having been warned of the unscrupulous ways some market traders would try to take advantage of her, buying a pound of butter, she told the vendor, "Make sure you cut it from the centre of the block please, I don't want those tainted outer edges." When they stopped at the egg stall, she scrutinised the rows of brown, white and mottled shells and chose the longest, oval eggs. "That's right isn't it Mrs Jackson, they'll be the best and freshest?" and after a short reference with the cook, she spoke up loudly to the fowl seller, "A brace of wild duck please, those two with the bright yellow beaks," she looked at Fanny who nodded, "and a pair of pigeons and a woodcock, the plump ones. Can I check that their noses are dry?" Fanny would help her make some pies which they could eat with a range of Crosland roasted meats over the next few days. They chose some dried and salted meats for the evening suppers and when Mrs Jackson was obliged to leave and return to the tavern, not wanting the outing to end, Martha pleaded, "Please Fanny, we've got plenty of time, please can we go to Kings?"

It was her favourite place in Nottingham, Kings the Grocers. Boasting wonderful sash windows it was housed in a stately, gothic style building in Wheeler Gate. Inside, the ceiling of the shop was of magnificent plaster work, elaborate trails of foliage joined with curlicues sprouting hops, pears, pomegranates, apples and flowers and the spaces in between were filled with birds and butterflies. Martha would spend almost as much time marvelling up at the ceiling, each visit showing up something new for her delight, as she did browsing the vast array of goods, the different aromas delighting or repulsing her. "We need tea Fanny, from the East India Company, not the smuggled Dutch tea, and for father's sweet, spicy puddings, sugar, dried fruit and spices."

Their life settled into a routine, the wet nurse was dismissed and Fanny took over the main caring of Josiah, who with her careful attention, began to increase his hold on life. Sadly the happy atmosphere seemed to have left the house when Mary left, William could not shake off his grief. Overwhelmed, he was no longer always amiable and when he could muster up his previous cheery demeanour, it was mostly reserved for his customers. He spent less and less time talking with his children, except for Polly whom he cherished, loving to sit her on his knee in the evenings where she would smile and chatter away, happy to see that she could make her dearest papa smile, letting him put his sorrow aside for just a little while.

When Billy's home lessons began again, this time mainly for Polly and incorporating some arithmetic for Martha, James clamoured to join in, he was so keen to learn and longing to go to school with his brothers. George was not at all interested in reading, he was a boisterous child who found it difficult to sit still and concentrate. His sulky demands for Jay Jay to continue playing were gently denied and even for those few hours a week, it became plain that George was lost without his brother, he could not amuse himself, he was angry and would creep away to hide in their bedchamber. When James began to find his few precious possessions damaged, the heads broken from his prized pewter soldiers, the feathers pulled from a shuttlecock and his favourite ball went missing, George denied all knowledge and James would shrug his shoulders and give in to George's pleas to play.

It was in the weeks leading up to Billy's fourteenth birthday that William proudly confirmed his intentions for his eldest son. "Well son, the time has come for you to leave school and come and work with me here, in Severns. Your mother would be so proud of you and the business will be yours to run in the future."

Billy was devastated. "Father, I cannot do that. I have never taken a moment's interest in commerce, I cannot believe you would wish me to. Surely you understand, surely you must have seen I have a calling to God and my only wish in life is to be ordained a minister in the church? I need to go to university," his voice breaking, "Father I beg you, please let me continue my studies at school. Two more years of Greek and Latin and I can apply to Oxford, I am told that Jesus College is admitting more and more students from families such as ours and I am sure I would be offered a place."

"University! Where do you think the money will come from to keep you there, and besides, even if I found the money, Oxford is no place for a son of mine. It offers a world of temptation and idleness, with drinking and debauchery at the top of their curriculum."

"Father, I am certain I have been called by God himself to enter the ministry, and you must know me well enough, you must know how hard I study and as your son you cannot believe I would waste such an opportunity. I have no interest in idleness, I live to work and I must study divinity or my life will be worthless."

William relented, speaking with him after school the next day, without a word of explanation he told Billy, "I have considered what you have said, you may stay on at school, but I shall have nothing to do with your desire for Oxford, that will be your own responsibility. I cannot support you there and provide for your brothers and sisters too."

Billy was almost overcome with relief, "Thank you father, thank you. I shall dedicate my life to the service of the Lord and to helping my fellow man. I'm sure mother would be proud of me in this way too, I promise I will not let you down."

It was during the next year, at school, that he heard of John Wesley the Methodist preacher and although he was not spoken of in any favourable light, Billy was curious to learn more of this man. He went along to the weekly gathering held in the Methodist headquarters, a cottage in an alley off Narrow Marsh. This chapel had come into being after John Wesley had been asked to preach there and so many people attended, upstairs was used too and a hole knocked through the floor so that Wesley could be seen and heard by everyone. Already known by locals as Crosland Place as John owned several of the homes in the row, renting them out to tanners, the name was now official.

After his first meeting, Billy was keen to discuss the ideas he heard there, "Father, Mr Wesley and some friends of his at Oxford have formed a group for Bible study and prayer but what is more exciting is Mr Wesley preaches to crowds of ordinary men and women, just like us, he teaches that there is salvation if only we repent our sins. Why does our Church lack this compassion and ignore the spiritual needs of the poor. The Methodists are addressing this void."

He was baffled when William would not listen, "But Papa, Mr Wesley is still an Anglican and insists that his followers continue to worship at their local parish church. Why can we not talk about it?"

William's hands were clenched into fists, his face contorted and puce with anger, he spoke through gritted teeth, "His views are heresy, that's why. I'll not have it spoken of under my roof. Heresy!"

Billy sadly kept his views to himself, discussing them only with the folk attending Bagshaw's cottage, but father and son's disagreement came to a dramatic and calamitous end just before Billy's sixteenth birthday. His life revolving around reading the Bible, Methodist tracts and papers, Billy approached William one evening. Lifting his chin and looking him straight in the eyes he breathed deeply, "Father, I have examined my conscience and prayed for guidance, I have not come to this decision lightly, but I am now firmly of the opinion that I cannot devote my life to the Anglican church. I am destined to be a preacher, I have no other choice but to spread the word of our Lord to help the poor and underprivileged learn their scriptures. If they do, they can save their own souls, I truly believe that God will grant people salvation if they repent and go on to lead honest, moral lives. They are not damned forever as our Church tells us, I know man can be spiritually reborn and saved. Mr Wesley is doing so much good work all over the country, I wish to join him." He looked beseechingly into his father's cold, grey eyes, "I cannot ignore the injustices in this world. Only this January I witnessed for myself some poor woman, whose only crime was to steal a loaf of bread for her starving children, tied to a cart and whipped soundly as they dragged her from the Weekday Cross to Market Place. We should be helping end such poverty and teaching these ignorant people that God will forgive them and save their souls if they atone and live in his ways, not degrading them along the streets."

"So these are your Wesleyan ideas are they boy?" William spat out the words, "What right have you to question the teachings of our Church. These miserable sinners cannot be saved, only the righteous, those who have always lived a proper Christian life will be chosen for God's heaven," he crossed to the window, his anger cutting Billy as sharply as any knife could, "I have told you before, I will not have your heresy spoken in my home. Unless you recant, you will leave my house tomorrow. You can make your own way in the world with your dangerous doctrines. Ever since you were born I have strived to make sure you have the best possible chance in life, and this is how you repay me? I will not have you here another day."

The next morning, William's resolve was not weakened, his son must leave, but Mary's voice had spoken to him in his sleepless night and he pressed a canvas purse into Billy's hand. The boy was standing ready by the door, grasping an old leather bag containing a few meagre possessions and his precious Bible, "Here is a guinea, I will not have my son destitute whatever his views. Keep it safe for it must last you until you can find work, and you are as like to have it stolen or give it to the first beggar you see if it is not concealed beneath your clothes." He looked sadly at this gentle son, Mary's favourite son, "Send word to your brother Jack as to how you fare, but I will not see you again. May God forgive you and keep you."

With that he turned away and retreated to his work, not wanting to hear Billy take farewell of his siblings or for them to see him raise his hand to wipe away the tears welling in his eyes.

CHAPTER SIX
Nottingham 1772
*James Hargreaves has settled in Nottingham and built the
world's first cotton mill.*

George looked down transfixed at the dark red pool growing around and over his feet. Fascinated he watched the little rivulets escaping towards the edges of the room, winding their way around the bases of the barrels, setting off in new directions as if on secret missions. "George, what on earth happened? What have you done?" James stood in the doorway.

George looked up, realisation dawning on his face, "Nothing!" and he darted past his brother, out of the room, across the shop, through the front door and began to run in the direction of the school.

James crossed quickly to the large wooden keg, spotted the cork bung on the floor and with shaking fingers, fumbled it back into place stemming the flow of his father's best vintage port. Breathing a sigh of relief to have stopped the flood, he was racking his ten year old brain as to how he could clean the mess up, and he was stumped. The problem was solved for him as William chose that very moment to arrive in the bottling room, "James, what the devil's going on here?"

"I'm sorry father, I'm so sorry. I just wanted to help and thought I could fill a few bottles for you, but I dropped the bung and then …"

"Get out of my way," he pushed James aside roughly, slammed his hand on the top of the barrel and turned to face him, "I don't ever want to see you in here again, do you know how much this has cost me? I thought I could trust you, I thought you might be the one of my sons to come into Severns, but I'm obviously wrong, you're a disappointment like the others. Get off to school right now, you'll be late, even George has just rushed past me and it's a very bad day if you are later than him."

James left the room, sick at heart. He wanted so much to work with his father and it had been his favourite treat these past couple of years to help William with the bottling. With his tongue clamped tightly between his teeth and lips, he would concentrate hard and rarely spilled any of the precious, velvety liquid. He ran towards Stoney Street, not wishing to be late for school, but for the first time in three years, he felt no excitement for the day ahead. His mind going over and over what had happened and wondering why George had done it.

§

Later that March morning it seemed winter had been ousted for a day and as the watery sun warmed the sodden ground and it's warmth penetrated Severns, so it had warmed William's mood. He left the shop and made his way through the streets towards Wheeler Gate to meet his cronies where, like many men before him and, he surmised, generations of men to come, they would sit and 'put the world to rights'. Most often, their conversations centred on the parlous performance of the politicians, their lack of foresight or their corruption and very occasionally, should they happen to agree with a policy, on their wisdom. Unlike the nobility and the ragged poor, these men had not been drawn to war, they and their sons had not rushed to sign up for the King's shilling to fight, and die, for the glory of their country, these middling sorts just got on with their parochial lives, and paid their taxes.

"What news Sir?" the cry went up as William walked into Kings Coffee Shop situated in the house next to the Grocers. Looking through the fog of tobacco smoke at the tables surrounded by Nottingham's finest traders and merchants, he spotted John Crosland together with some friends, and being beckoned over joined them, sat down, ordered a penny cup of the dark, gritty, black coffee and lit his pipe.

"It's good to see you William, it's been an age since you were last here," Henry King welcomed him, "how do you do?"

"I'm afraid I've been besieged with family problems, not much time to remember there's a wider world outside of Weekday Cross."

The table was littered with the latest news pamphlets and papers but the friends eagerly picked up William's theme.

"Well, there's one less worry for you, your Jack," John Crosland slapped his friend on the back, "he's a fine, hard working lad, and he's picking up the trade well. Got a lot to learn but he's keen, so keen he's not above thinking he knows it all already, and only three years into his apprenticeship with me!"

"Sounds like a good son to me," Walter Chapman, lamented, "I've got four boys and not one of them with an ounce of intelligence or gumption. I'm sure they are expecting me to provide for them, and any family they might have, for the rest of their lives!"

The friends' voices rose in agreement, the youth of today, how easy they wanted their lives to be, and William agreed, "I was adamant my six sons would each have a decent trade. All I ever wanted in life was my wife Mary and for my eldest son to carry on the business when I'm gone, was that too much to ask? The Lord has taken one and the devil, the other."

"Come old friend," John waved his pipe at William, "all is not lost, you have many other sons, what about them?"

"I should count my blessings, I know. Our Jack is well settled with you and I thank you for that, he has only ever wanted to be a butcher. But then there's Ben, he's an adventurous boy and he's not going to be content to stay and run the shop, he wants to travel somewhere, anywhere he says, outside the confines of Nottingham. He's now declaring, over and over, that he wants to be a grocer, and more to the point, a grocer in London."

"My youngest son is going to his brother in London, the eldest will take over next door," Henry nodded towards the grocers shop, "so I sent Fred, the second boy, down as an apprentice to a grocer, what, it must be ten years ago now, and with a bit of my help he and a partner are out on their own and doing very well. It's all Robert talks about, wanting to follow him so I'll send him in due course," Henry turned to William "Isn't your son Benjamin a great pal of his at school?"

"He is that and it's your Robert that's convinced Ben the future is not just in grocery but in sugar refining and now Ben has his heart set on it."

"Well, I can help when the time comes, if we agree terms that is, he could go to Fred's too, better be a formal apprenticeship I think."

"That's three sons down but you've still got three more Will, and three's plenty!" laughed John, "you can choose one of them to carry on for you."

"Young George finds it impossible to apply himself to just about anything but I'll be setting our Jack up on his own in a few years and when George has grasped enough arithmetic I'll put the rascal with him, in the butchery. He looks up to his brother so I'm hoping that will steady him," William looked around gloomily, "Josiah the little one is too young to think about yet, and I'm not sure his brain isn't feeble, he's so small. Doesn't grow a jot. I can't really see him doing anything much with his life. I don't have much to do with him, he reminds me of Mary's death, but I'll send him to school next year."

"So that leaves James doesn't it?"

"Yes and I can tell you I'm a mightily disappointed man. I'd been relieved to find that James was interested and wanted to be in the shop with me, but even he has let me down. He's only young at the moment, still got a few more years at school, but it seems he can be reckless and disobedient too, so now I'm not so sure. I don't know what I've done to deserve this, all my sons are determined to confound me." Murmurs of sympathy rose from the table, "And you've got two daughters to marry off as well ain't you?" asked Henry, "seems to me you should be looking for a new mother for the lot of 'em. Make life easier for you."

"Since when has a wife made life easier?" Walter asked, "Damn sure mine doesn't!"

As the companions laughed, William stood to go, "Well, I guess I had better get back, see if I've still got a vintners shop, it's been in female hands all morning!" He left the coffee shop to the sound of his friends still chuckling, his mood reverted to despondency.

Martha was aware of the jealousy between George and James but had not realised it's extent until she saw the look of glee on the younger boy's face when James had been castigated that evening, humiliatingly, in front of his family for his wilful behaviour in the bottling shop. Fighting back his tears, James had apologised to his father again and begged forgiveness. George had not, and did not, say a word.

Later in the evening, realising James was not in the house, Martha went out into the yard and saw him, sitting on the low wall to the side of the bottling shed, kicking his heels in the dirt. She didn't think she had ever seen him look so unhappy.

"James my dear," she said as she sat down next to him, "please don't take it so to heart. Father was angry but he will not stay that way. What happened, did you drop the bung and couldn't find it?"

"No Martha, it wasn't like that."

"Well, I'm sure it was an unfortunate accident and I don't really understand why you were there instead of on your way to school."

"I thought I heard a noise," and James, bravely biting his lip, could not help a quiet sob, "so I went to look."

"Well, that still doesn't explain why you decided to fill a bottle of port James, why did you do that?"

He began to cry, Martha put her arm around him and asked gently, "tell me what really happened James, none of this makes sense."

James confided the truth, "but Martha, please don't say anything. We are brothers and I've always been told we should stand up for one another, look after each other. George is always in trouble and I don't want to be the one to make things worse between him and Father. Why is George so mean to me Martha? I don't think I've ever done anything to hurt him the way he is so spiteful to me. He used to break my toys you know, it wasn't me being careless."

"I think he is jealous of you, you used to be so very close when you were young and he feels that you have moved on without him. You are clever and working hard at school and he is rather a naughty boy and won't try to learn anything. He will soon change, as he grows older and realises how silly he is. If you really don't want me to tell Father I won't, but I will give George another chance to confess. Come on in now, it's getting very cold out here, it will soon be time for bed and maybe George will say sorry to you when you are alone."

They went into the house and Ruth, who had been quietly working in the shed, followed a few minutes later. Earlier that evening when she had been asked to clean the wine stains from George's shoes, he had remained silent, and now, agonising over what she should do with this new information, her sense of justice came to the fore, and she determined to tell William the truth.

"You deceitful, untrustworthy boy! Why would you betray your brother like that?

George was standing the next evening on the frayed end of the old rug, looking at his feet as his father railed at him. He could, if he was very careful, get the toe of his shoe underneath another thread and gently pull … "pay attention to me boy, when we are all together you will apologise to James later this evening, and you will apologise to me too. I cannot understand your actions in the first place but it is unforgivable that you let your brother take the blame. James is a hardworking, loyal boy, he would not have told me the truth, he was prepared to give up his privileges for you, but now it will be you giving up yours. Why did you do it?"

George shrugged his shoulders, "He could have told you, but he didn't, so I didn't."

"Isn't it enough that you are idle and good for nothing? Your school master has told me so on more than one occasion, I've a good mind to take you out of school already. You and James are family and family is everything. Integrity is everything".

CHAPTER SEVEN
Nottingham 1775 - 1776
The American War of Independence begins

Jack had received another letter from Billy. The first had come a few weeks after his expulsion from home when he was able to assure his sisters and brothers that he was safe and well having gone immediately that dreadful morning to the Methodists, and from there he had been offered a home with a Dr Wright in Rotherham where he could continue to study and follow the teachings of Mr Wesley.

He had sent news each year since then and William, as unswerving as the day his son had left, refused to read the letter or stay whilst Jack read it aloud to his siblings. Sitting in the parlour, following their evening meal, all thoughts of chess or backgammon gone, they listened for the slamming of the door as William left the house to spend the next few hours in the Golden Fleece.

From his previous letters, they knew that whilst in Rotherham, their brother had become a lay preacher, frequenting the iron foundries and preaching to crowds of workers in that grimy, industrial town. It was here that Mr Wesley heard him and greatly admiring Billy's zeal and commitment had invited him to join him as a trainee. At first Billy had been stationed in Sheffield where they had a congregation of over seven hundred and the following year he had travelled to Gloucester to take up the station there and to reach out over the next few months to the people of the towns and impoverished villages of that county. Travelling between stations as an itinerant preacher he would address the locals along his route, staying where he was offered food and accommodation and in '74, Billy had moved into North Wiltshire, living in Bristol. The cause of the letter's greater excitement was the information that he was to come to Nottingham the following year.

Bristol, October 1775

My dearest brother Jack,

I am writing today to tell you of my life this past year and to advise you of the happy anticipation I feel at being chosen by Mr Wesley to stay in Nottingham for the most part of '76. He wrote to me in June of this year to put forward the notion and since then we have made arrangements such that it can happen.

I am pleased to tell you that my life is still very busy and I am fulfilled to be carrying out God's work in this way. My days here in Bristol are long even when we are not travelling, and here I must break off and give you an aside to say, I agree with Mr Wesley himself that it is perfectly possible to sit astride a horse and read a book, my horse being perfectly placid and content to follow my servant patiently.

We are instructed to be always diligent and to never be unemployed for a moment, but dear brother, I do not need to be cajoled, I need every minute of the day to carry out my work. In the early mornings before breakfast I read my Bible and now also have the opportunity to read it in Latin, and this not being sufficient alone, there are many other theological books to read. After breakfast, if I do not need to travel far afield, I will read again for some hours and then I like to visit the sick and pray with them.

Next I will go to wheresoever we can gather the people together, maybe a farmer's kitchen or the back parlour of a shopkeeper. I can preach five or six sermons a day, all of which must be thoroughly prepared and have meaning for the particular audience.

My special joy is in meeting with the children. I think it must remind me of those times when we were young and were able to put aside the sorrow of losing our dear mother for a moment and be happy. I try to gather the children together for at least an hour a week where their chatter, laughter and their open minds to our teaching is a delight. They are extolled to learn the "Instructions for Children" and the following week I will test them on the understanding of the passage they have learned by heart. If I can persuade the parents to accompany them to my meeting, then I feel I have really achieved something.

After our evening preaching there is most often a meeting of The Society, and then we will eat again and afterwards, what little is left of my time that day, is spent in quiet contemplation, a little more reading and writing down what has occurred since the previous night. Of course, this routine can easily be broken should anyone come to me for advice or in distress.

On the subject of distress, but before relating this I must first assure you that this letter comes to you from your brother who is in fine health and condition, I had an experience the other day, the like of which I had never had before. I was on the road going to preach in an area of this town where the docks are situated and riding through a crowded and insanitary area, encouraging my horse to pick his way carefully through the rubbish and muck in the dreadful road, I was accosted by a mob, a small mob I am pleased to say, of anti-clerical men, women and children. The abuse they shouted at me was unpleasant enough but when one or two began to throw stones, I became quite worried. A large stone hit my forehead and I was bound to retreat with the blood running down my face and find another way through to my appointed destination. I count myself lucky that the injury was not serious, I have heard of colleagues being set upon by very angry mobs and even by highwaymen.

The knowledge that there is so much drunkenness and cursing, even from the children, makes me convinced even more so that these are the places where God, and therefore I, am needed most and it makes me more determined than ever to teach these people that if they repent, believe in God and are born again, the Lord will offer them salvation.

I need to carry on my work helping to relieve poverty and ignorance. The appalling conditions in which so many of the poor are living, in our industrial towns in particular, cannot but breed immorality and degradation.

My dear brother, I have enjoyed my letters sent from Martha and carry them close to my breast, reading the news

again and again. I wish that I would hear that our father has relented and would allow me to visit home when I am in Nottingham, but I fear that is not to be. I pray for him, and of course for you my dear family, each day. I am hopeful that I will see you all again very soon. I trust that all is well with you and our brothers and sisters. Please kiss them all for me and remind them that I am,
Your loving brother
Billy

§

Billy had been delayed leaving Bristol and their patience to meet up with him again had to last almost a full year, until the following September. The reunion when it did happen, was emotional, joyous and, because of their father's absence, sad, all in one moment.

"Come in my dear Martha, come in, come in all of you. It is splendid to see you, you have all grown up whilst I have been away, even you Josiah, you are a young man and you were but a baby when I left. Polly, you are as lovely as I remember and you two curly haired rascals, how good it is to see you. Jack," he shook his brother's hand, "how goes it with you, I could not have relinquished the role of eldest son to a better man, and you must be George, come in, take your coats off and let us sit and talk. There is some tea coming. Sit please, I am eager to hear all your news."

The weather being a little too cool to meet and stroll in Nottingham Park, they had all arrived at the White Lion where Billy had organised a private parlour and they arranged themselves in the various chairs, some placed at the edge of the room and some around a large oval table set with cups and plates. Tea arrived very soon, was poured from the large china pot and Billy explained his setback, "It was in part due to the escalation of the revolutionary war in America, and the issuing of the Declaration of Independence," he began, "Mr Wesley has been very vocal in his opinions on America and whilst in Bristol last year, he took the opportunity to publish a lengthy tract entitled 'A Calm Address to our American Colonies'. Having hitherto been very much against the British oppression of the Americans, this tract rather reversed his opinion."

"I have read in the papers about our treatment of the American people," Martha spoke up quickly, "and it cannot be right for Mr Wesley to support our government imposing such heavy taxes on them when, as I understand it, they have no right to vote for our parliament. What is it they are saying, 'it is wrong to have taxation without representation'."

"You see how little Martha has become a firebrand in your absence Billy? Who would have thought she could be so political, and comment on such important matters."

Martha glared at her brother Jack, her eyes blazing and replied tartly, "At least I have an opinion because I take the interest to read about the world, you, with every advantage, ignore everything and think the world begins and ends with a butchers shop in Nottingham."

"Martha, I'm very pleased that you have read about these affairs, but you are repeating the popular view, a view not necessarily shared by people with the best interests of our Empire at heart," Billy tried to calm the waters, "Mr Wesley has been at great pains to educate the working people during his preaching as to whose doors the blame for this unrest should be laid at fairly and squarely."

"And who is that then," asked James, "I'm with Martha on this, I thought the trouble was caused by King George imposing taxes on the colonists as retribution for the tea traders rebelling in Boston and all that tea going into the briny? It seemed obvious to me that punishing them like that wasn't going to have the desired effect, no wonder there's to be a revolution. Why ever should they want to be under our throne any longer. Mind you, George would have looked a pretty impotent King if he hadn't set up any reprisals."

"What I wanted to say," Martha stood her ground, "is Father and Uncle John were discussing it at the time and I heard them say it was all because King George was trying to shore up the East India Company, and because that company was given a monopoly of the tea trade and they had a huge surplus, it was sold off direct to the Americans at a much lower price. No wonder the merchants were so angry, they were out of a job. Is that not so Billy?"

"As usual, I don't believe the politicians thought their moves through properly. I'm not convinced they intended to burden the Americans with such a level of taxation, but my Ministry is firmly of the view that there is a body of powerful men in England who are quite against our King, and who have fuelled the flames of hatred abroad with letters and petitions to this end. Mr Wesley has seen much of this feeling throughout that country and that is why he wrote as he did, to try and bring about a 'calm' again."

"But why did this mean you couldn't come to Nottingham before now, what had it to do with you Billy?" George having sat, half listening, bored, to his elders thought he'd just get to the point, "we've been waiting a long time since your last letter."

"Well spoken, George. I had to wait for Mr Wesley's replacement for me at Bristol to come, and he was travelling with the Minister himself and could not be spared until now. However, now that I am here, I will be around for a good few months and I hope to make plenty of time in between my duties to talk with you all. It will have to be in my lodgings or as today, if we are to be all together, in the Inn, as I fear I must not come to Weekday Cross. How does our father regard your coming to meet with me?"

"Well," answered Polly looking with awe at her brother, "he hasn't said anything much really but he has such a sad look on his face ever since he sent you away, I'm sure he will relent in time. We must pray that he sees things differently soon."

"Or you could change your views Sir," a voice from the corner, "you could come back to our Church completely and then Papa would be happy. I have been looking forward to meeting you for so long, I don't remember you of course, I only know what my brothers and sisters have told me and I hope I will have some time to sit with you to talk? My favourite subject is geography and I'm interested in what's going on in America."

"Josiah," smiled Billy, "I had forgotten you were here, what are you doing? Oh, I see, you have your tin soldiers lined up. No, Josiah, I cannot change my beliefs, I know the way forward to salvation is to have Faith. Faith is all we need. But whilst we are getting to know each other, I should be glad to help you with your next battle - are we fighting the French, or the Americans?"

CHAPTER EIGHT
Nottingham 1776
The American Declaration of Independence is signed on 4th July

Thanks to Sarah's patient teaching, Polly had become very accomplished with her needle and was kept busy assisting Fanny in making, mending, cutting down or letting out, her brothers' clothes as they all grew, but her main love was to make the best of the few dresses she owned. She loved to shop for remnants of ribbons or lace and would painstakingly undo existing bows and trimmings, replacing them with different colours or placing them in a slightly different position. She took such pleasure in this and her head was full of plans for parties and dancing, places she could wear her dresses and be seen. In this quest she had luckily found Aunt Sarah was her ally.

Sarah was troubled to see the changes in William, he had aged badly since his wife's death and even more so since he had expelled Billy from home. Mary would have been worried about her 'bear', his thinning hair was white, often not as tidily drawn back as it should be, his jowls had become lose and flabby and his girth, well, he was getting very fat.

"John, is there nothing you can do to shake him out of this lethargy," more than once Sarah approached her husband, "his lack of interest in life is not good for those children, especially not for Martha and Polly. The boys at least are apprenticed or at school, the girls have no life outside of that house and they are not children anymore, they are young women. Surely you can see this, William hardly bothers with his shop and James tries to help but he is far too young to know how to deal with everything, he tells me he spends most of his time badgering his father to show him what should be done. It's a rare day that William goes along with you to Kings or sees his friends."

"I do try Sarah, I've even suggested he finds a new wife, what more can I do?"

"Well, I think you can insist that we all start going to the Assemblies together again, there's one this Thursday, that would be a good start."

This wasn't an altogether altruistic move on Sarah's part as she loved, if not to dance herself, to watch those who were dancing. With a faraway look in her eyes she would remember the excitement of being young, when she would long for the precious moments to touch and be close to John as they danced. Now it was with Francis in mind, not just the girls, that she thought Thurland Hall the ideal place for them to mingle and for courtships to begin. That William steadfastly refused to join them was disheartening, but at least he allowed the rest of the family to come and content, Sarah would sit as chaperone to Martha and Polly, chattering with her friends and glad that, with no daughters of her own, she was doing the best she could for Mary's.

Polly revelled in these evenings and whilst Martha grumbled about all the fussing over hair and dresses, she too appreciated being away from the bounds of the house. Miss Polly, who was always in demand, would sometimes deny her beaux if they did not approach with a friend in tow who had been fiercely instructed to request the pleasure of a dance with her sister, Miss Severn. Thanks to her, Martha took to the floor from time to time, the contrived manner of the invitation not spoiling the occasion at all, she was an accomplished dancer and rather enjoyed it! However, for her the pleasure wasn't the thrill of dancing and romance but the thought that, with Sarah's discrete presence, she might be lucky enough to sit with someone, preferably not too ancient a man, with whom she could have a serious conversation. She sometimes thought if the next words she heard were from arguing boys or comments on the latest fashion, she would go mad. She longed for more in her life, she wanted to make a difference in the world, or at least in her own world, but was confined to watching her brothers forge their way whilst she could only watch from the side lines.

"Martha, do hurry up, we will be late," Polly trilled as she pirouetted, "doesn't my dress look divine. I knew these blue ribbons would be so much better than the green. Do you think Francis will be there tonight, do you think he will notice, oh, I do hope so. I'm sure he admires me and I love to see his eyes following me around the room when I dance with the other boys. Is that bad of me Martha?" and not waiting for the answer, she skipped out of the room, put on her cloak, smoothed it down one last time, and waited with her brothers, as impatiently as ever one could wait, for her sister.

Polly was determined to find love, and these dances were the best place to find it. Sitting for a moment at the side of the ballroom, she swooned, "Martha, don't you think it is the most heavenly feeling to be in love. I want to marry as soon as I can, I'm sure I am in love with at least three boys already and if they ask me, I don't know who I shall choose."

"Polly, you are much too young. You are only eighteen, please don't think about marrying yet," Martha frowned, "besides, you are underage and your father would never allow it!"

Polly danced and danced, flirted with many of the boys and was thrilled that Francis was there. Her brother Jack, torn away for the evening from his plans, emptied his mind of thoughts of cattle and sheep and danced as many times as was seemly with his favourite girl, Ann. In between dancing, he tried to no avail to speak seriously with George about starting his apprenticeship early next year, but George was too distracted by the sight of so many pretty little girls of his own age, and Jack had to let him go. Watching from the side with Ben, he laughed out loud when George's bold request for the next dance, caused one girl to blush bright scarlet, turn to her friends, burst into giggles and rush away.

Martha's evening was a tremendous success. Sitting, watching and dreaming, her reverie was interrupted in a most gratifying manner when Edmund Brown, the new curate of St Mary's came up to her and asked diffidently, "May I be so bold as to sit and talk with you, Miss Severn. I care little for dancing and I know you can be relied upon for interesting and stimulating conversation."

§

One benefit of Billy's late arrival meant he was still in Nottingham in April when Jack and Ann were married. He could not of course attend the ceremony or the party afterwards but he was able to meet Jack's bride and to wish them happiness in person. It was a short service with just the two families and a few friends present, and as soon as the register had been signed, the guests made their way from St Nicholas's Church, along Castle Gate and up Low Pavement to the Golden Fleece for a wedding breakfast, prepared by Mrs Jackson who was still working there and delighted to prepare her finest for William. He had arranged it with Walter the landlord, and Thomas Gadsby, Ann's father, had provided a fine feast for his daughter. Her mother had sewn and trimmed Ann's Sunday best dress ready for the day, a new blue ribbon round the hem; blue for purity. Ann's dark hair was high on the crown of her head with cleverly engineered curls and ringlets softening her square jaw and large, slightly crooked nose, the blue bows pinned into her hair, matching her dress. She managed to look, as all brides do, radiant, and when glancing covertly at her new husband Jack from time to time, allowed herself just a little feeling of self congratulation.

At the end of the wedding breakfast, when the time came to serve Mrs Jackson's special wedding cake of sweet minced meats, herbs and spices, it was Polly who found the glass ring hidden inside it. "It's me, it's me," she squealed, "I have the ring, I shall be the next to marry," she lowered her head and quite artfully, looked from under her long eye lashes, down the table at Francis sitting there, twenty years old, his face crimson as she caught his eye.

Jack and Ann left the wedding feast after the dancing and walked arm in arm along Lister Gate, down towards the river Leen and Finkhill Street, to their new home. William had been as good as his word and the new bridegroom was now Jack Severn, Butcher of the Town of Nottingham, and his mind, lately singularly set on his shop, was very much elsewhere this evening as he ushered his new wife through the front door and immediately up the stairs to the recently furnished bedchamber.

John Crosland became a godsend to the new young butcher. With his guidance and advice Jack purchased his first few sheep, grazing them on land out at Langar where his Uncle, Richard Cramp was controlling the family concerns following the death of Jack's grandfather. Now that George was thirteen, William apprenticed him to Jack and he began to learn the skills of a butcher but most of his time he found himself responsible for deliveries, errands and taking orders. He had to admit he was rather enjoying the work, he had a good deal of freedom but initially he had complained bitterly to William when told of this decision, "Why do I have to run around for Jack as a butcher's boy," he glowered, "why should James be allowed to work with you Father, why can't I? I want to be a vintner too, butchers are always covered in blood and mess."

"James is older than you and that would be reason enough," William answered and continued, not unkindly, "but add to that the fact that he applied himself to his lessons and is able to add up more than two plus two, and that makes it an even more sensible decision on my part. Come George, you have always looked up to your brother Jack and he will teach you well, you will make a good butcher. Why do you speak this way about James still, you are brothers, I do my best for both of you."

"James always gets what he wants, I never do, but alright, I'll work with Jack it will keep me away from him!"

George began to love working with Jack and he was happy being with him. These two brothers looked alike, they were taller and leaner than Billy but without the handsome features of their brothers Benjamin and James. Their noses were a little thin, their skin quite pale, and straight hair the uninteresting colour of a brown mouse, but their eyes had enough warmth in them to make up for any deficiencies, real or imagined. When they were not sporting their bloodied aprons, but dressed in best linen shirts and stocks, the shortened waistcoat and slimmed down coats revealing their breeches smart and tight around their form, they cut a fine dash and it was no wonder that at twenty four Jack was already safely married. George on the other hand had a natural, and at fifteen somewhat expected, healthy lust for life. They were known for their quick wit and ready smiles, and were a great favourite, not only with the servant girls but with many of the housewives too who shopped with them in Finkhill Street or at their weekly stall in the Shambles. It was strikingly apparent to the family that when he was away from James, George's nature was to be a cheerful, sociable, charming young man. That he was often cunning, idle and cruel was alas, also sometimes apparent.

CHAPTER NINE
Nottingham 1778
In the American Wars, France opens hostilities with Britain

John was pleased to help young Jack in this way, but he wished he could help his old friend William more. They still met up most weeks and one fine February morning he had managed to persuade William to stroll to Kings with him where they were sitting enjoying their coffee, soaking up the urgent sound of the men's conversations all around them. Knocking the ash out of his pipe on his heel and cleaning out the dottle, he surprised William, "I think I should hand over to Francis as soon as I can, my health is not good, not good at all. Sarah keeps threatening to call in the doctor to see me but they're all quacks. The truth of the matter is that I'm too old and we should expect problems at our age shouldn't we? It's no good thinking pills and potions can stem the tide of time. No, I'm prepared for the future and I want to be here for a while just to watch from the side lines, see how Francis gets on."

William looked wistfully out of the window at the street heaving with people and life, "It comes to us all, I'd like to hand over to James but he's not ready yet, he's only been in with me for three years and needs a lot more experience."

"I thought he was bursting with new ideas for you," laughed John, "you're always telling me you can't keep the young whipper snapper under control. He's got a sensible head on his shoulders mind you, maybe you should take notice of his ideas, you haven't done much with the business since ..." he hesitated, "well, for a long time, and what happened to us taking over the whole town together?"

John undid the drawstring on his leather tobacco pouch, took out a pinch and put it in the bowl of his pipe, pressed in another pinch and tamped it down, then after the third pinch, lit his match, put the pipe to his mouth and drew the flame over the strands. Four matches later, the tobacco was alight properly and he could speak again. William continued to stare, morosely, out of the window.

"He told me you turned down the opportunity to take over Ernest Hunt's vintners shop? It would make sense to me to take it on, he's giving up next month and you could keep the premises in Market Place, two shops in different areas is a good idea. I think you're giving up a golden opportunity to expand, you would keep all his customers too."

"I don't need the extra worry, I've still got enough of my old customers and we have enough money to live, not extravagantly, but we don't go hungry. James doesn't realise the uncertainty there is in business, I don't want what we already have to be put in jeopardy. He'll be able to do what he likes when I'm gone, that's if they keep the shop. It's a lot of them to share it, eight children. I mean seven," his gloom spreading like a cloak around his shoulders, "I sometimes long to just go and be with Mary again."

John puffed slowly on his pipe, "You're having a bad day, you don't think this way when Walter or somebody comes into the shop and you're sitting there with your glasses of port, pontificating on what the town Aldermen or the government should be doing better! You've got enough life in you then, haven't you? Anyway," John went on, "haven't you got young Josiah to get settled, before you pop off, to join Mary I mean!"

John's good humour could usually lift William's spirits but today he remained despondent, "That's true. I still think Josiah is a bit simple minded although I don't have bad reports of him from his school master. It must be because he is so small and so quiet, I'm never sure if he's in the room or not, which makes a pleasant change from having our George around. He was always so boisterous that it's quite a relief he's over with Jack most of the time. Anyway, going back to Josiah, I don't think there's any point in keeping him at school any longer and you've met Ambrose Cook, he's a glazier over at Barker Gate, one of my best rum customers? He's suggested that I send Josiah over to him. I haven't mentioned it to the boy yet but I think it could work out. We certainly don't need any more butchers in this area, that's for sure!"

§

"Please hold your plate towards me and hold it still George," Martha was spooning out some potatoes onto his pewter plate, already laden with beef and turnips, "this will end up all over the table."

"A few more please Martha, it's winter and I'm always starving in winter. Is this our beef or Uncle John's?"

"Yours I'm pleased to say, I brought it back this afternoon after I left Ann. Jack is so delighted to have his first baby, she's to be called Mary after her grandmother."

"How is Ann now?" asked Polly, "I couldn't bear to stay with you, she appeared to be having such a terrible time, her screams were awful and when you think how tiny mother was compared to her, you'd have thought it would have been easy."

Martha stole a look at William, Polly's remark had make him wince, "She's fine now the baby is in her arms but I shall visit every day for a while to help, you know for someone who looks so robust, Ann is a little bit giddy."

"Can I come with you tomorrow," asked Polly, "I have sewn a very pretty little linen bedgown and matching cap for Mary, trimmed with bobbin lace. I do hope Ann will like them, and I do so want to see the baby."

"No more talk of babies and lace please," James rolled his eyes, "we seem to have heard nothing else for days. It's putting me off my dinner, and I need to ask you Father, do you think we should go to London to meet up with Charles Jubb?"

"What do we want to do that for? Everything is running along smoothly, he never lets us down," William finished eating and pushed his plate away, "thank you Martha, that was very tasty."

" It seems to me that without going over all the details of our arrangement with him, we might not be getting the best deal and I think we should talk with him about expanding our range of wines, he'll know what is becoming popular," James continued, "you haven't introduced any new ones for at least three years and it's always best to try and stay ahead of the fashion, in wine as much as anything else. What do you say?"

"You could meet up with Benjamin too," Martha looked at William, "it would be so good for him to see someone from home. I write to him but he's no correspondent, I can't remember the last time he wrote back."

"If Lizzie King didn't tell me from time to time what was going on we wouldn't even know if he was alive or dead, she hears from her brother Frederick quite often." Polly gave a long sigh, " Oh I wish I could come with you, I would so love to visit London"

"You say you'd like to go anywhere that wasn't Nottingham, but you know very well it's not for women to travel about, you are to stay at home and make sure your menfolk are looked after. I don't know where you get your ideas from," George wiped his mouth on his sleeve and rocked back on his chair, grinning, "did you hear about that man who sold his wife and two children in Market Place the other day, fetched £2 7s 6d. Maybe we should sell you Martha, although I can't imagine who'd want to buy you, every time I see you, you've got your head in a book!"

"That's enough George, don't speak to your sisters like that, not even in jest, and no, James, I am not going to London so do not ask me again." William's words were final on the matter and he turned to Josiah, "I do have some news for you though Josiah. I have arranged for you to go and learn the glazing trade with Ambrose Cook in Barker Gate. You are twelve now and your health is good enough for you to be out earning."

"Please Father, could I not stay on at school for just one or two more years like my brothers have? I enjoy learning and my master thinks I am doing well? I am very interested in geography and thought I might be able to become a teacher."

"I have made my decision, you are to go to Mr Smith, I cannot see the advantage of you staying at school, you need to start earning your living."

"Of course I will do as you wish Father," Joe's bitter disappointment plainly visible on his face, "I am much stronger than you think just looking at me. I know I'm a bit of a sorry specimen.

Polly rushed to his defence, "No you're not Joe, you are the most handsome of all my brothers and what you lack in height you make up for in kindness. You would never say those horrible things to Martha as George does, and you James, you are so wrapped up in your own world, you rarely have time for the rest of us."

Just as both boys started to disagree, Jack arrived unexpectedly. Alarmed, Martha rose quickly from the table, "Is anything wrong with Ann and the baby? Should I go to her?"

"No, no, all is well and it would only be news of a very important nature that would cause me to leave my wife and baby this evening, but I felt I should share the little I know at present with you straight away," he nodded his thanks to Fanny for the glass of wine she had brought him, "please father, I must beg that you do not stop me or leave the room, but I have had a short letter from Billy."

William pushed back his chair so violently it fell as he stood up, "You know I will not have his name mentioned in my presence. Stop now or I shall have to ask you leave."

"But father, the news is that he has left Mr Wesley, he has given up following the Methodists. I thought you would like to hear that," the silence in the room was deafening, "I have no real details but he wrote from Oxfordshire to say that for some time now his mind has been ill at ease and something in his situation was proving very irksome to him. He tells us that he is praying every day for more faith and for a firmer conviction, hoping that God could give him more assistance in his duties. He did not write where he would be staying but he was hoping to enter Edinburgh university to study divinity and he would write again soon."

" Can he come home father, can we write to say that?" Martha's answer from William was the door creaking shut after him.

CHAPTER TEN
Nottingham 1779
The world's first Iron Bridge is built in Shropshire

Nature overtook John Crosland the following spring and before he could begin to enjoy his retirement, he took to his bed, dying within three weeks. William was shaken to the core at the loss of his friend. Through all his joys and sorrows John had been there at his side, his comfort and support, his true brother in life. He mourned his friend and in spite of Polly's entreaties, withdrew more and more from life outside of Severns.

It had come as a great surprise when Francis, just twenty one and with all the new obligations landed on him, had approached William to ask for Polly's hand in marriage. They were both, he assured him, sure of their own minds, had loved each other since childhood and in spite of being young had no doubts that they would be together. In addition he reminded William that, most importantly, he could provide for his daughter handsomely.

"If you would only say 'Yes' Sir, maybe we could marry in August, on Polly's twenty first birthday. I know she would love that, and she's so very excited about planning a wedding party."

William, sadly aware that Polly would come of age in a matter of months, had bowed to the inevitable, relinquished his favourite without demur, given the happy couple his blessing, and promised Polly a modest dowry.

"The world is changing too fast," William lamented often "and not for the better. The old ways are important and should not just be thrown aside when anyone has the fancy."

"But father, that is how the country moves on, things must change, we cannot stand still," masking his exasperation James began to sharpen a quill, the shavings falling to the floor, "and not all changes are bad, look at the machines we have now, they produce more goods than we could ever have done by hand. With the population increasing so fast, we need all the help we can get to keep them fed and clothed, and you know we should be moving forward with Severns too if we are to survive. I have been studying your accounting ledgers and our business is not growing, and some months it has dropped alarmingly. We are losing customers, not gaining them. Don't forget we have the girls to support, not just ourselves."

"They'll be married soon and not our responsibility anymore," William looked dolefully over at Polly and Martha who had joined them in the counting house, "what good is there in that change?"

"Papa," Polly came over to his table and took his hand "please don't talk this way. It's only natural for me to fall in love and want to have my own family. Remember how you felt when you met Mama and all you wanted was to be married and be with her. I love Francis so very much and we will be happy together, but I'm not going to abandon you, of course not, how could you think I would?"

"Well, you needn't worry about me father, I will not marry, I made that promise to myself years ago," Martha placed a glass of port in front of him, "so I will be able to look after you. The world will not let me do anything else or be more useful."

He gave a long, sad sigh, picked up his glass of port, "Come James, back to work, I need to look at the orders from Goosegate, I'm not sure they are right and I'd like you to go over there this afternoon."

The ladies returned to the parlour and the conversation had only just turned, as it did so often now, to the forthcoming marriage when James came in ushering Francis before him. After the customary greetings, the rearranging of chairs and the request to

Clara for tea, James said with more than a touch of relief in his voice, "I'll not be staying, but Francis here insisted on coming up to see you Polly, goodness knows why, he's going to have quite enough of you after August!"

"Very funny James, you wait until cupid's arrow hits you fairly and squarely, you'll eat your words."

To James's confusion, everyone laughed out loud. It was a not very well hidden secret that he was entirely enamoured by a certain young lady, Lizzie King, and could often be found 'accidentally' calling on his own sisters if he had heard she was to be present.

Feeling awkward, he tugged at his shirt collar, "Anyway, now that I have done my duty by my friend and brought him here, I will get back to the shop. I really want to work on father about a visit to London."

August was not many months away and the wedding preparations were consuming the sisters' waking hours. Martha had written to Billy in Edinburgh and Ben in London to tell them of the date and for some days now, Polly had been listening out for old Tom Croft's bell as he made his postal rounds, waiting impatiently for their replies.

When she did hear, the news was rather disappointing. William was deeply engrossed in his studies at Edinburgh and feared he could not, in all conscience, leave at that time and besides, he pointed out, their father would not allow him to attend the wedding and festivities themselves. He sent the couple his love and assured Polly he would pray for them. Ben scribbled a note to say he would not be present either, he was very sorry but Frederick could not spare him for that amount of time, so he wished Polly and Francis well, and gave no indication of when, if ever, he might see them again. The major part of his note was to ask when James was going to London.

"Well, that is just too bad," cried Polly, "I do think he might have come. Lizzie was telling me that the stage would only take two days from London as it is summer and the roads are drier, or he could even have come post and that would have saved time."

Martha was probably the most disappointed of them all to not to see Ben, but understood, "Post is far too expensive Polly and I don't suppose he has much money in his pockets yet. Even the stage fare is almost £2 and he would have to put up overnight somewhere both on the way here and back. Don't be cross, I'm sure we will see him soon, Frederick says he is doing very well and talks about having his own grocery before long."

"That's as maybe, but this is my only wedding day and it would have been good to have him here. Ben is such a rogue, he still never writes to tell us his news."

Polly's frustration about her brothers was short lived as the excitement of the wedding plans escalated. Although it wasn't strictly necessary, as William would never have denied his favourite anything, she had put on her most appealing and tender smiles and exhorted him to allow her to have a wedding that would look and feel as good as any genteel occasion,

"Please Papa, instead of making over my best dress, please may I have a new and special dress for the day, it is all the fashion now."

William wasn't really sure what this entailed but agreed, with only one, half hearted warning, "Don't forget, I'm not made of money!"

Fanny was enrolled to help with sewing the wedding dress. Polly had spent hours looking carefully at the dresses in the shops in Bridlesmith Gate. "They are much too expensive", she reported back to Martha, "I can easily make my own, and then it will be exactly as I want it." She sketched out a pattern using many of the details of the designs she'd seen. "The dress itself will be quite straightforward Fanny, it's known as a 'polonaise' style, and can you see, "she said following all the lines on the drawings with her finger, "really it just consists of three parts. The long robe which has these three swags holding up the skirt at the back and sides, a petticoat which will have pleats all round from the waist to give it a fullness and because the robe joins at the neckline here, and then slopes away to the waist like an upside down letter V, I shall need a matching bodice to go under it."

"My goodness," mumbled Fanny, rather bemused as Polly continued, " the sleeves will be to my elbow with a little ruffled lace to act as a cuff and I shall add some gathered ruffles of the same fabric all along the edges of the robe which will look so pretty. I have my eye on a very sweet, cornflower blue cotton which I think will do very well for the robe and then, very daring, I will have the petticoat in white. If I have my hair dressed high with ringlets to the sides I can put little blue ribbons to match and fresh flowers pinned in it. Oh, Fanny, it will be so wonderful and I must not forget, I will need some little high heeled shoes too, oh, and maybe a new reticule ?"

Whilst the ladies were preoccupied with the wedding, Jack arranged a trip to Langar to speak with his Uncle Cramp and Francis, thinking he might invest in land in that area, agreed to accompany him .

"I was thinking of asking young George along, it would be an adventure for him, something different and might make him think it's worthwhile buckling down and learning," Jack told Francis, "what do you think?"

"Good idea, and I know what we could do, ask James along too. Maybe some time out in the countryside would help those two boys sort out their differences. I have to say I don't understand George and his envy of James at all."

George was overjoyed at the prospect, James less so, "Just make sure I have a docile old nag to ride, I'm not at all keen on horses, dangerous beasts in my view, how Billy spent all those hours on the back of one I don't know!"

They met up at Bennetts Livery just after dawn on a dry, warm May morning. James was last to arrive and found his travelling companions ready mounted and waiting patiently.

"Morning Caleb," he called to Mr Bennett, "did my brother tell you I need the slowest, gentlest horse you've got?"

They set off walking slowly, some of Martha's pies and beer in their saddle bags, the early sun rising in front of their eyes, heading south east out of the town. As they reached the open fields, the air became fresher and cleaner and they stopped and, as one, breathed deeply, "My, this is a tonic, it will do the soul good to be out here for the day away from the smoke and grime," Francis threw back his head smiling, "this will clear our minds."

They followed the track, making their way carefully over the ruts ploughed up over the winter by the wagons and carts, the churned mud from the passage of horses, cattle and sheep, hardened in the recent dryness, and the miry patches and lingering puddles creating an obstacle course to be negotiated slowly or if possible, avoided. Taking short cuts across fields they talked together easily and there was no sign of any animosity from George, he was friendly and civil. Jack felt the outing was a success. By the time they reached the end of the Stragglethorpe Road they stopped for their refreshments, enjoying the camaraderie of the open air eating, their mood happy and united. When they had regained their saddles, Francis moved away and James was leaning toward Jack, "Sorry brother, I could not hear what you said?" when his horse gave an ear piercing whinny, and reared up then immediately bucked and kicked out it's back legs. Caught off balance, James could do nothing to save himself, he was thrown violently to the ground, landing with a sickening thud on his left shoulder. Jack leapt down from his horse and bent down to James. "Are you hurt?

James groaned and with his help, sat up gingerly, shaking his head he answered," I don't think I've broken anything, but God's blood, my shoulder hurts. What the devil happened, why did that damned horse do that?"

Francis had turned back, he caught hold of the jittery horse's harness and seeing James, white as a sheet, clutching his arm to his chest, said, "I will go back home with James. Jack, you and George go on to Langar," looking at James, concerned for his friend, "I will hold your reins too, that way you can support your shoulder and you will be safe."

George had said nothing, his face impassive, but as they went on their own way, a small smile escaped his lips and his eyes shone.

Caleb Bennett was perplexed when he tended to his horses later that day, "That's a strange thing, looks like this old nag's flank has been stabbed," he thought as he cleaned the trickle of dried blood discharged from a small puncture wound. A hole about the size a butchers hook.

CHAPTER ELEVEN
Nottingham 1779
There are significant riots by framework knitters in June

"I can hear the shouting from here," Martha stood at the window smoothing her apron over and over, "oh, where is Josiah. I can't make out where the mob might be. Come on Joe, come home!"

"Try not to worry so my dear, I'm sure there is an innocent explanation why he is delayed," joining her, Edmund Brown leant again the window and cupped his hand to his ear, "it sounds to me that all the noise is coming from down by the river, I can hear the church bells ringing. Josiah need not go anywhere near there, from Barker Gate he can walk down past St Mary's and round. He'll be quite safe."

Edmund had thoroughly enjoyed his late afternoon visit to Weekday Cross, taking tea and conversation with Martha and Polly. He was never happier than when he was there, but for Martha, even the excitement of Polly's wedding had not changed her opinion of married life and this was, she had to admit to herself, causing a slight difficulty. She and Edmund had developed an agreeable relationship and when they met at Thurland Hall or when he called, at her express wish only, they found their natures well suited. Edmund was rather shy, an insignificant man to both his peers and his superiors in the Church, and he relished his position as teacher and mentor to Martha who was interesting, interested and intelligent. This modicum of self importance helped improve his confidence in the world at large and they shared the same views on what they considered social injustice. Both had a vehement dislike of cruelty whether to their fellow man or to animals, and maybe surprisingly for a curate in the Anglican church, he was as enthusiastic about the idea of elevating the standing of women in society as she was. And he was, Martha realised, in love with her.

"It's late and father is asking for his supper. Edmund would you stay and eat with us, Fanny is nearly ready to serve. I don't think you should venture home until we are sure the streets are safe," Martha turned back to the window, anxious, "Joe, where are you?"

The family had just, at William's insistence, gathered at the dining table when the door burst open and Josiah rushed in, his eyes bright, his face visibly pulsing with emotion, "This has been the most exhilarating evening of my life!"

"Joe, you are bleeding!" Polly rushed to him, "your arm, what has happened? Your clothes - they're torn and you are filthy, whatever have you been doing?"

"I'm fine Polly, please don't fuss, it's just a scratch. I met up with Tad and we went down to the Leen to watch the riots. Father, it was unbelievable, there were hundreds there, women and children too, all shouting and struggling with the constables, and then we saw a group of men break down the door of a house and drag out the knitting frame. They smashed it to pieces there, right in front of our eyes. I didn't know men could look so wild, and they'd beaten the poor frame owner, his head was covered in blood."

He stopped to draw breath and took the cup of milk George handed him, who said angrily, "What the devil were you thinking of Joe, Martha's been tearing her hair out with worry, she was convinced you were dead in a ditch somewhere, and what's happened to your arm?"

"The dragoons came to clear the mob away, we heard them charge down Narrow Marsh and then they swept along the river, it was a magnificent sight. Their uniforms and their sabres held high, the noise and smell of the horses, it was terrifying but spectacular too. But then it all became dreadful, the crowds were trapped in a bottle neck, too many of them to get out and it was carnage. I saw a child trampled under a horse and women were trying to grab the horses' reins and drag the soldiers off...."

"Stop talking for one minute," Martha roared, her worry turned to impatience, "what happened to your arm? Take your coat and shirt off right now and let me look!"

"It's nothing, I can't feel a thing, it doesn't hurt at all, but I'm sorry for the mess and my coat will need your needle Polly dearest! A sabre just nicked me that's all, I couldn't get out of the way quickly enough. Tad and I were on the edge of the crowd but we'd stepped back into a doorway to avoid the dragoons and just waited a minute too long to watch instead of getting out first. My word though, we had to run full pelt, you wouldn't believe how fast we went!"

"That's enough Josiah," William's voice was icy cold, "let Martha clean and dress your arm then sit down and get on with your supper. I am ashamed of you that you gave so little thought to the rest of us and put yourself in such danger."

The conversation during the meal remained on the riots. Josiah apologised, "I'm sorry father, I should have thought first, but I needed to see for myself, surely the knitters deserve better treatment. I know I'm still young but I can still see it all around me, people with not enough to eat."

"This anger has been brewing for some time, many years in fact," Edmund was emboldened, proud to be the one to share information, "and the fact that Parliament has thrown out, again I might add, a Bill to regulate the knitting industry, was the final straw."

"But why would you break up the only means you have of earning a living, it doesn't make sense," Polly looked at Edmund.

"It wasn't necessarily those same men breaking the frames, the mob is more likely to be the hundreds who have been put out of work by the Masters who've taken on children as apprentices, at a much lower wage of course," Edmund grimaced, "and what is worse, I have heard that the Parish has actually been selling children to them."

"That is slavery and the slave trade, just by another name," Martha was outraged, "it cannot be right to put men off like that, they have their families to support. Who will feed them?"

"It's all their own fault!" Martha looked at James in horror, "I was taught at school there are three things which stop people

74

falling into the depths of poverty. Belief in the Lord, education and most importantly that you must work hard. You've always said that too Father, it's what your father told you. If they worked harder they would still be in jobs."

George stabbed his knife towards James, "What would you know, how could you understand what it's like to be poor and have no family to support you? You've had it too easy all your life, and even now father's still looking after you!"

James gripped the arms of his chair, flinching as the bolt of pain shot through his still sore shoulder, and was about to launch an attack on George, when William answered him, "What you say is true James, I too have always believed in those three tenets but a little compassion never went awry. You know my parents died in poverty, I've taken you to see where they were living in such dreadful conditions and they certainly worked all the hours that God sends, and what about my sister, your little aunt who was just a child and almost certainly starved to death. I was so very fortunate, my father sent me to school and then Mr Partridge found me. I was able to escape that appalling life."

The family went quiet for a moment and then Edmund filled the awkward gap, "I agree with the knitters and their demands, and I think Martha, you do too? The industry needs regulating to stop such abuses by the manufacturers and it's difficult for them to get organised because so many still work from home. When they tried to get a national charter back in '53 it wasn't successful, now the Associated Knitters, which is what they call themselves these days, are desperate to have rights put in place and that's been turned down again."

"I'd like to help them organise themselves," Josiah said, "Tad and I agree, we're going to do something. We just don't know what yet! These people have no justice, no rights."

"Hundreds of frames have been broken up and thrown into the streets already, how much longer can this go on? This is day five of the troubles," George goaded his brother, "what would you suggest they do James. No use saying work hard when they have no work to do, no use saying they should have had an education, that was out of their hands, no use saying pray, that doesn't put food on the table!"

" I just don't understand why they feel the only way open to them is to riot and smash things up." James's heart was not really in this argument but he would not lose face to his brother, "and don't forget, the frames belong to the Masters, so they will be suffering financially."   "Well, only in the short term, I fear the knitters will suffer harder and longer. I agree with Joe, it does seem to me that the poor have no power at all over their own lives, in spite of what you may say James," Martha looked into his eyes, "and I don't think you really believe that, you are just so absorbed in your own world, getting on and becoming successful, it has coloured your judgement. Edmund and I are sure there will be greater trouble to come from the knitters, and in the not too distant future"

§

It was in the aftermath of the riots, in early August just three weeks before Polly's wedding that, unknown to her when she had woken that morning, Martha's life changed for ever.

There had been huge excitement when a package arrived from London. Thinking that he was indifferent to his sister's celebration, Ben had astonished the family by sending three pounds of chocolate as a gift for the feast. Martha was delighted, it had long been her ambition to enjoy this expensive luxury and she had looked through her book and settled on a recipe involving a lot of cream, egg yolks and sugar which she felt would make a wonderfully good, hot chocolate drink for later in the wedding afternoon. She was, that day, on her way to Kings to decide on other sweets to accompany the meal and to purchase plenty of sugar.

Just after she turned off Market Street into Byard Lane she was aware of a young girl sitting in a door way crying, dressed in filthy rags and her face covered in sores. Martha would not ordinarily have stopped at such a common sight, but there was something unusually pathetic about this little beggar, and she reached into her apron pocket, brought out her purse and was almost knocked off her feet when the girl sprang up, snatched it out of her hand and darted away. Looking around for assistance but seeing no-one close by, Martha followed as fast as she could, knowing full well that once the child reached Bridlesmith Gate she would disappear into the crowds and be lost forever. Martha was no match for her speed but caught up due to a moment's carelessness on the thief's part, when looking round to see if she was being gained on, the girl ran full pelt into the arms of a local constable and came to a full stop.

When Martha reached them he had her by the shoulders, was shaking her and threatening her with actions which sounded to young ears much worse than death. "Constable," panted Martha in a voice she hoped still sounded composed and authoritarian, "thank you for stopping her. She is the daughter of my washer woman and all I wanted to do was speak with her. I'm afraid I appear to have frightened her into running away."

"Are you sure you know her," he looked down at the girl, "empty your pockets," he snapped.

"That's quite alright officer, I can take over from you now," she looked the constable firmly in the eye, gripped the girl's wrist and dragged her away, "now Annie, you've got some explaining to do."

Why she had done this on the spur of the moment Martha would never really know, but the sight of this ragged child had so moved her that when the constable had gone, still holding the wrist very tightly, she bent down to speak, "What is your name?" The child looked at her, her large blue eyes peering out from the grimy face, with disbelief and fear, "What you gonna do wiv me Missus, I never took money before. Don't tell me Pa, he'll beat me, I was only suppos'd to beg."

"I'm not going to hurt you, I want to know your name and where you live and I would like my purse back, now."

"Me name's not Annie, it's Grace, and I'm not telling you where I live, me Pa'll kill me."

"No he won't, not if I don't tell him you are a thief."

"I'm not a fief Missus, I'm just hungry and so is my little brother and me Mam's dead and me Pa's not got any work and he's hurt. It's only me what can help and no-one will give me a job neither."

"So tell me where you live and I will see what I can do," Martha thought it must be fate that brought this desperate child to her, "but you have to prove that I can trust you."

"Oh you can, Missus. I never stole before. I know it's not right but I'm so hungry and so is Tommy and I didn't know what else I could do."

All thoughts of sugar and chocolate vanished from Martha's mind, this little child was the incentive she had needed all along to do something, something practical, something real, "Here, we will buy a loaf of bread and some salted meat and you will take me to your home."

It was even more grim than Martha expected. In the middle of a row of three storey, typical, frame work knitters houses on Leenside, an area damp and stinking from the river, overcrowded and sordid. The child pushed through an open door and Martha followed, the bread and meat in her basket. She looked around, it was squalid, the rank smell almost causing her to retch, she wanted to leave. From the dross on the floor she thought more than one family might live here, but there was a complete absence of furniture save for a battered, oily table in one corner. The child, it was difficult for Martha to think of her by name, saw her horrified look, "Me Pa burnt the chairs last winter, we were so cold, they made a good fire, but we have to sit on the floor now."

"Is that you Gracie," from the hallway, a man's voice was followed by a high pitched wailing from an infant, "where've you been all this time. Did you get anything today? What the …," he stopped the oath just in time, "who are you and what are you doing with our Gracie? Come over here girl." His voice was not rough or uncouth as Martha had expected, in spite of his unshaved face and filthy clothes, he had, and she thought it very strange, an air of dignity about him. "I'm sorry I can't offer you a chair and a cup of tea."

Martha bristled at the sarcasm but stood her ground, "I found your daughter begging on the street, distressed and obviously starving and took it upon myself to accost her. Having heard her story, I bought a loaf of bread and a little meat for her and her brother. I expect there is enough for you should you wish."

"Why would you do that then, what do you want? You don't look like the missionaries who say they want to help, but only really want to steal your soul."

Martha smiled, "No, I'm not a missionary, and you'll not hear any doctrines at all from me, I just wanted to help this child. Were you put out of work during the riots in June?"

"Yes, my frame was up in the attic with another chap's, we worked for the same Master, but the mob came, threw them out on the street and broke them up, broke my head too," and he turned to show Martha an angry wound, still not healed, behind his right ear, "don't know why I tried to stop them, the owner had already decided he was going to open up in a bigger place and take on children to learn the job, they're much cheaper you know. Don't have to pay them half as much. God help their little fingers though," he held out his left hand. There were no fingers, just ugly, angry looking red stumps, "I've been trying to get work these past weeks but I've given up hope, nobody wants a one handed knitter. It was alright working from home with Gracie to help but I'm too slow for a group. We try to make do on the pennies from the Poor Relief and the church, but it's not enough to pay the rent and feed the three of us."

Thank goodness the infant Tommy had stopped his wailing. Martha looked down and saw why, the girl had torn off a piece of the bread and was stuffing it into his mouth, he was ravenous. She didn't know what to say or do. She realised she had come here with no idea of the next move and standing there in that wretched room she felt completely helpless, but somehow she couldn't leave without giving out some hope to this destitute family, "I will come again tomorrow," she murmured and turned to go.

"What's your name Missus?" the girl looked up into her face, "I want to say thank you."

"It's Miss, not Mrs, Miss Severn. I will see you tomorrow, same time. Stay off the streets and that's an order.

CHAPTER TWELVE
Nottingham 1779-1780
Lord George Gordon leads anti-Catholic riots in London

For the rest of that day and during a sleepless night, Martha contemplated what she should do. With luck, Edmund had been able to call during the afternoon and she put her dilemma to him, describing the morning in great detail. They sat in a corner of the parlour so that they would not be overheard by Polly, Lizzie and Sarah who sat sewing by the window. "I must do something, I have said I will go again tomorrow but providing a loaf of bread and some meat each day is not the answer. What should we do Edmund?"

Edmund could only suggest, "Well, the church does provide some relief to the needy, but I think as the father said, it is often conditional, and anyway like the bread and meat, it's not really solving the problem, just treating a symptom. Until he gets another job they are in danger of ending up in the workhouse, or worse."

"I don't think he will ever be able to work again, could you speak to your Minister about getting him a place in The White Rents at the bottom of Houndsgate. It's rather awful but he's too young for the Collin's Almshouses and White Rents takes poor of any age. It will mean they'll at least have a roof over their heads as he must be evicted from Leenside any day now, the other families have left and he can't find any rent by himself."

"I'll see what I can do but getting a place there is a case of waiting for one of the existing residents to die. I have just remembered one thing though, I heard Mrs Green the housekeeper at the Marchant's house on High Pavement say the other day that they were thinking they should take on another girl to help with the laundry, I can certainly put in a word there. I was in the fortunate position to help her out with another matter last year. Laundry is hard, unpleasant work for a young girl, but it's better than most alternatives," he was thinking, Martha knew, of the child prostitutes found only too frequently out on the evening streets or in the town brothels, "yes, I can certainly try to help there."

By Polly's wedding day, Martha had placed Grace, cleaned, tidied, her hair under a new white cap and with a new brown work dress, in the employment of Mrs Green and Grace's father and brother were on the waiting list for a White Rents property. Until that became available, the girl's wages were helping to keep body and soul together for the three of them and Martha had promised to go and see her as often as she could.

Martha had also decided that she would look for other opportunities to help individuals, "My mistake Edmund," she told him firmly, "was thinking that the problems were so enormous that I could do nothing to help, but now I realise I can do a little and a little is what I must do."

§

These embryonic ideas put to one side for a while, Martha concentrated on Polly. All the planning and hard work for the wedding was worth it. The day dawned bright, dry and sunny. The menfolk were dressed in their best, the ladies were wearing their Sunday dresses, and Polly looked so beautiful she took their breath away. Francis wore a superb, midnight blue, silk suit, his ivory waistcoat having exquisite embroidery, golden leaves and foliage that had taken Sarah many weeks, each stitch containing love for her only son.

"I'm sure I'm happier even than the couple, I just so wish my darling John was here to see his son safely married, and married to his dear friend's daughter too," she confided in Martha, "I fear I shall cry but my tears will be of both joy and sadness."

William had insisted that the wedding breakfast would be held at the Golden Fleece, "We need to support our friends Polly, Walter is a good man and deserves our custom. I know you are going up in the world, but don't forget those you meet on the way."

"Of course not Papa, and it will be lovely to have Mrs Jackson prepare the food, we know she is such a good cook and I've always been fond of her. Please don't worry, I will be perfectly content with the Fleece."

If Jack and Ann, when they sat down to the sumptuous feast, made any comparisons to their own wedding breakfast just two years before, they said nothing. Sitting with baby Mary on Ann's lap, they too were amazed and delighted as the tables began to fill and groan under the weight of dish after dish as Mrs Jackson and her girl brought out the food. Jack's gift to Polly, though how he came about it he would not say, was a haunch of venison, roasted to perfection with wild garlic, rosemary and thyme. There was a saddle of mutton with black pepper, mace and a crunchy oatmeal crust and caper gravy. Chickens spit roasted, their gravy flavoured with anchovies, wine, oysters, mushrooms, celery and mace. A succulent saddle of lamb, roasted suckling pigs, potted salmon spread thickly on slices of bread and butter, whiting pies accompanied by artichokes and green beans fried in flour and butter. Pigeons stuffed with parsley were made into pies, and brought from Melton Mowbray especially, juicy pork and bone jelly pies with their bow shaped, crusty pastry cases. Stilton and cheddar cheeses, bread in beautiful shapes and patterns and to follow, syllabubs sweet with nutmeg and cream, plum puddings with William in mind, sweets and nuts. The family and friends talked, laughed and drank as much sweet red wine from Portugal, madeira, sweet brown sherries from Spain, and porter as anyone could wish to drink. Later in the evening, Martha brought the wonderful meal to a climax with her rich, unctuous, hot chocolate.

When the guests got up to dance, James, overjoyed that Lizzie King was there, was in danger of commandeering her all evening; George preened and showed off to the young country cousins; Martha discussed her growing charity plans with the ever attentive Edmund; Jack payed great attention to Ann, their next child being due in two months' time and they both fussed over baby Mary making sure she did not crawl under the dancing feet. Only William and Josiah, watching from the side lines were a little pensive.

William was thinking of his Mary, how much she would have enjoyed seeing her daughter wed and of his best friend John, dead too, missing the pleasure of witnessing their two families joined together for the future. He was also torturing himself, questioning over and over again in his mind, his actions those years ago when he banished Billy from this happy family home.

Josiah's mind was dwelling on the world outside. He had come to the unhappy realisation that he was a disappointment to his father, his stature, his nature, his very presence perceived as the cause of his mother's death. He had become a very serious child and as he grew older and saw the injustices in the world around him, he determined to follow his instincts and fight for those who found themselves powerless and oppressed. He would continue to pursue his interest in the politics of his country, and with no real education, if he did not have the words to fight with, he would fight with his fists.

Much later, time came when the sedan chairs arrived to carry the new Mr and Mrs Crosland to their home and life together. Their way lit by the flaming torches of the link-boys, the chairmen took them to their new, commanding house in St Mary Gate.

In the absence of her own mother, the task of speaking to Polly earlier that week on the expectations of her wedding night, fell to Aunt Sarah. She was happy to fulfil this obligation but when the time came, even she faltered at passing on the all important details of the night.

"Polly," she started, "you will be wondering of course about the mystery that surrounds a wedding night and I want to say that you should forget anything you may have heard that it is an ordeal for you to suffer. It need not be so at all."

"Why no," exclaimed Polly, "I have a little understanding. I am aware of my body and how it feels when Francis kisses me, it is just heavenly."

"Well there is a little more to it than that my dear," Sarah floundered, "I just wish you to know that there is no reason, if

Francis is kind and patient with you, and I'm sure he will be, why you should not enjoy your wedding night. This first night may be a little painful but that should not be repeated."

It was on arriving at St Mary Gate that Sarah's words came back to Polly and it was with a mixture of adventure and apprehension, her new maid Alice dismissed for the night, that she sat shyly in the marital bed, clothed in her new linen nightgown with blue ribbons at the neck and cuffs, her hair brushed until it shone the curls hanging loose around her shoulders, waiting for her husband. Had she but known it, Francis was waiting with his own contradiction of emotions, great anticipation and anxiety!

Later, Polly lay awake feeling as sufficiently pleased with her initiation into womanhood that she began to wish the following night was not so far away. Blissfully, she did not, after all, have to wait that long as in the early hours of the morning, Francis turned to her, took her in his arms and confirmed her first impression, that making love was wonderful. She and Francis were intoxicated with each other.

These first heady months of marriage were the happiest of Polly's life. Crosland trade was prosperous and Francis had insisted that Polly engage a cook, thus each day she consulted with Mrs Morley to ensure Francis had his favourite foods prepared. When he returned to St Mary Gate, she fussed over him asking for every detail of his day and when he answered, "Well, just the same as yesterday really, you know life as a butcher is not that exciting," she delighted in telling him in minute detail of her own day, where she had been and who she had seen, who she had spoken to and what she had heard. Becoming accustomed rapidly to her new status, she spent part of most days strolling around the shops in Bridlesmith Gate acquiring many possessions for their new home, some necessary and some bought very much on a whim.

§

One afternoon, they'd been married almost a year by then, she and Francis had gathered James and Lizzie, Martha, Edmund and Josiah together at the theatre in St Mary Gate where they were appreciating a light meal during the performance of a play called

'The Discovery'. Polly loved the theatre as a place to see and be seen rather than for the plays and this afternoon was no exception. Finding the performance less than captivating she was fidgeting a little whilst looking around at the clamour of happy people strolling and talking behind her.

"Concentrate, Polly," admonished Martha kindly, "if you listen to the players you would be able to follow what is going on. It is a comedy by Mrs Sheridan and there are so few women who write plays, we really should take notice."

"Well, perhaps it's because it is written by a woman that I'm not finding it particularly riveting," her eyes twinkled, "shouldn't she be at home looking after her husband and children, not sitting writing all day!" Polly loved the opportunity to tease her older sister and was firmly of the opinion that Martha was far too solemn and if only she would allow herself be in love with Edmund, she could be truly happy, "besides, this company of actors is not very inspiring, I cannot believe in a single one of them. I don't know where the troupe has come from."

"I think the only Discovery we have made is that we could probably do a better job ourselves than most of these so called professionals," James smiled at Lizzie, "I'm afraid I'm getting very bored with the actor playing Sir Anthony Branville, who they say here in the programme, is a notorious bore!"

"Well, we should have paid to sit on the stage itself with the big wigs and then you could have joined in very easily, I'm sure you wouldn't bore me," Lizzie fluttered her eyelashes at him and then turning to Josiah said, "I'm looking forward to the interlude, I understand there will be musicians and also some little dancing dogs who can perform amazing tricks."

Martha joined in with their laughter, "I must admit I am looking forward to the entertainment too."

It was good, the music was rousing, the little dogs both clever and hilarious, and thankfully, the second part of the play was a great improvement on the first. At the end, no one was in a hurry to leave and looking around, Martha tugged on Edmund's sleeve, "Look, I can see Mrs Smith over there, I would like to speak with her, come, let me introduce you. Elizabeth and Thaddeus are with them Josiah, why don't you come over too."

Josiah followed Martha over quickly and having greeted the Smiths and Bessie their daughter, turned aside with his friend Thaddeus. They had met at school and continued to be friends, sharing a fierce interest in politics, "Hey Tad, how are you? Sorry I haven't seen you much since the riots, I had to promise my father I'd stay away from any trouble and it's been difficult for me to get out so much. It was great though wasn't it?"

"Have you been keeping up with the war?" Tad asked, "I heard that we've captured Charleston in South Carolina? I've got hold of a new map of America, it's much better than my old one, I'll bring it next time we meet."

"We needed that win," said Josiah, "nothing much has been happening for ages. The last big battle was when we beat back the French at Rhode Island."

"Well we've got a bit of excitement here at home. Have you seen about the protestant riots last month in London? I read a pamphlet my father brought home and he says rumours are going around that it's a plot by the French, stirring up the anti-Catholic feeling over here so that the country gets in a mess and the French can invade."

"That would be a good fight Tad but I don't believe it. What I heard is the trouble's been going on for a year or more, since the government said the papists could have more freedom, and in return, the army could recruit Catholic soldiers to fight in America."

"That sounds more like it I suppose. Did you hear when Lord Gordon handed in his anti-Catholic petition to the House of Commons, the mobs attacked some of the nobs arriving in their carriages, throwing stones and all sorts and later in the day, hundreds of protesters went on the rampage"

"It was one of the biggest riots ever seen in London, before the army was brought in the mob destroyed churches and homes and nearly burnt down Newgate Prison. There's still a lot of prisoners who haven't been caught," Tad threw a look over to his mother, "it sounds a fantastic battle, the army shot over two hundred people and arrested loads more, including Gordon,"

"Nottingham is so boring, our uprisings are nothing in comparison, no wonder nothing changes. We could do with some real excitement here, I need more than one sabre scratch on an arm!" decided Josiah grinning.

At the same time, once Martha had introduced Edmund to Eleanor Smith, the wife of a prominent baker, she came straight to the point, "I am so pleased to have bumped into you Mrs Smith, I have a project in mind and you are just the person I need to help me. I want to set up a charity to work with the poor wretches who are finding themselves out of work and depending on the Town to support them. Well, I know for a fact that it is impossible to live decently on the Poor Relief, especially if the family is large and I want to do something practical for them and as it is difficult to decide what exactly to do for the best, I thought the first step was to form a little committee of like minded women. I hoped you would be interested in joining, Edmund here is very supportive of the idea and has promised," here she turned to smile at him, "to give as much help from the Church as possible."

"My goodness Martha, you have quite taken me by surprise," Mrs Smith answered somewhat flummoxed, "I will have to speak with Mr Smith of course and let you know what he says but I think it might be a commendable idea. Oh, I think Mr Smith is waiting to go," and with this she turned smartly back to her husband and Bessie.

"Well, having to ask her husband for permission to do something on her own, that's a good enough reason never to get married." Martha was too exasperated to see the crestfallen look appear on Edmund's face. Would he ever be able to summon up the courage to tell Martha how he felt about her and ask her to marry him.

CHAPTER THIRTEEN
Nottingham 1780
The Industrial Revolution is beginning to transform Britain

Martha's mind was far from romance. She had kept her promise to Grace Woods to visit from time to time and see how she was faring at the Marchant's house. Learning that the girl's afternoon off was on Thursdays they sometimes met, as this afternoon in question, to take a short stroll in the park. The day was bright and warm and Martha saw an amazing change in the little waif she had rescued. The patches on her skin were clearing, her straight blond hair was clean and pinned tidily under her white cap, her deep blue eyes had lost their wild stare and the stark, emaciated look she'd had when they first met had been replaced by an open friendly smile. She was a very pretty little girl. So far her father and Tommy had not been found a place in White Rents, but with Grace's wages and the offerings of food from Martha, they were keeping their heads above water.

"How are you getting on with the laundry work? Are your hands any better than when I last saw you?"

Grace held her hands up for Martha to see, "I think they are a bit better, I'm getting used to having them in the lye. It really burns me but Hannah told me the skin on my hands will get tougher."

Martha could see the child's hands were bright red, angry and sore, and thought alas she had not so much faith in Grace's new authority, a child called Hannah, who at twelve years old, appeared to have an opinion on everything, "Here, I have a pot of lanolin with some calendula flower oil for you, I think it will help speed up the healing process."

"Oh, thank you Miss Martha," Grace looked with wonder at the pot. This was the first present she had ever had, the first little personal treat she had ever owned, "I'll be ever so careful with it, I'll only use a tiny bit and make it last."

Martha smiled, "Don't be silly, I want you to use it every night. I will bring you another pot when that one is gone, so when it is empty bring it with you when we meet and I will take it and ask Clara to fill it up again for you. Is there anything new happening for you at the House?"

"Well Miss Martha, it's really hard work still. I'm lucky that there's a boy to bring the wood for the fire to heat the copper but I still have to pour in so many buckets of water that my arms nearly drop off. Then when it's all boiling I have to stir so much that it makes me really tired, if it wasn't for the steam and fumes in my eyes I'm sure I'd fall asleep on me feet," she was quite the little actress taking a theatrical stance, her hand held dramatically to her forehead and eyes rolling backwards, laughing, "but at least they can see I'm too small to lift the linen out of the copper and rinse it, and I can't be trusted yet to hang it out to dry. I have all that to look forward to when I've grown an inch or two." She looked up, "but Miss Martha, I'm not complaining, I love you so much for getting this place for me, I don't know where we'd be without you. I won't let you down, I promise."

Sadness clouded Martha's face, this little girl, aged not much more than ten, 'what an old head on such young shoulders she thought,' and as if she had been heard speaking out loud, Grace exclaimed, "Bless my soul, Miss Martha, don't look at me like that, you're giving me the shivers!" The mood was broken and they both roared with laughter.

"Let's sit for a while here, there's a little step in the wall which makes a good seat," Martha stopped, "then I'll walk with you to Leenside to see your father and Tommy, I have a few things in my basket for the family.

§

Martha was in the kitchen helping Fanny with the weekly baking when Ruth came rushing into the room, "Martha, come quickly, your father wants you. He has a visitor, come quickly."

Alarmed, she wiped her hands on her apron and hurried down to the counting house. Next to her father stood an old man in shabby country clothes. His labourers smock barely covered by an old and worn jacket, his breeches long and tucked into boots, dust filling the cracks in the old leather. He was grasping a brown felt hat with a magnificent pheasant's tail feather fixed in the brim and he had a very familiar look to his face. She looked, puzzled, at her father. He was grinning and introduced his visitor, "Martha, this is my brother Gabriel. I wouldn't have known him had his face not reminded me so much of my own !"

"Well, praise the Lord," she exclaimed, "what brings you to Nottingham? Why don't you come upstairs to the parlour Father, you will be more comfortable. I can offer you some coffee Uncle Gabriel if you would prefer that to beer?"

They settled themselves at the table, Martha chattering non-stop, "I knew father had two brothers but had lost touch with them. Are you married, do you have a family? Is your brother with you still in the village? How did you find us?"

"Whoa, Martha, give the man a chance," chuckled William, "I'm sure Gabriel will tell us his story in good time. It's what, fifty two years since I left for the town, since I saw you last."

Gabriel began to speak. He was the younger of the two brothers left in Kimberley and had been married, his wife now gone, his children grown and all but one son moved away. Their elder brother John, who never married, had died only a few months ago. "I've come about our older sister, Eliza."

"My Aunt," cried Mary, "how marvellous, I had forgotten you had a sister Father. Oh, but it is so sad, your baby sister died here in Nottingham many years ago when she was still a child. I never met her of course. Your parents had such a hard life here in Nottingham Uncle, it is difficult to believe it was any easier than the misery they left behind. Has Father told you his story?"

"Not yet girl, give me a moment, perhaps I should tell it over a plate of bread and cheese?"

Gabriel nodded and when the food arrived, he tucked in as if he had not eaten for a week. "I'm sorry," he looked a little embarrassed, "I have been in town for three days now and with very little money, just enough to pay for a lodging, I've not been eating as well as I do at home. Let me hear of your lives whilst I eat and then I will tell you why I am here."

He settled back, Fanny bringing some extra meats and ale to the table, and listened to William talk. When William finished and Gabriel's hunger was sated, he began.

"It's a complicated story so I'll start at the beginning. Our sister Eliza married, must have been the year before you left the farm William, and moved away with her husband. I didn't take much notice of such things in those days, I was about fifteen and only interested in myself. The two brothers born between you and me and two older sisters had already died as children, but I don't suppose you remember anything about all that, so there was just John and me and we were tied to the local landowner when father brought you to Nottingham. We just got on with our lives out there, didn't expect to hear from our parents and didn't hear from Eliza either until about six months ago when a pedlar came to Kimberley and he searched brother John out to give him a message from her."

"A message, do you have it?" asked Martha.

"No, she couldn't write so the pedlar had been paid to remember what she said. Good job he had a vast memory, there was quite a lot of it! I've learned a bit more since then so what I'll relate to you is more than we knew then. Eliza had a daughter, her name was Charity and she married a man, here in Nottingham called Thomas Woods."

Martha gasped, "I know a Thomas Woods!"

"Well Eliza was widowed and went to live with the Woods somewhere in Nottingham and was sending word to her brother to say that her daughter Charity had died and she, Eliza, was looking after her two children. Their father Thomas had a crippled hand, he'd caught it in a machine and it went poisoned and he lost the fingers. So he couldn't get much work. Now, she said, she herself was very ill and worried about her grandchildren, wanted to know if John could take them onto the farm."

"Did you say this was six months ago? What has happened to Eliza?" William leaned across and topped up Gabriel's beer pot, "is she still alive? Did you find her?"

"No, the pedlar arrived just as John himself was dying and it's taken me these months to find the time, and the money, to get into Nottingham to look for them. It wasn't easy but yesterday I was steered towards Leenside where I found Thomas Woods and he had this most astonishing tale to tell, and here I am!"

"It is the same Thomas Woods, it has to be, the crippled hand could not be just a coincidence. So Grace must be Eliza's grand daughter. She is your great niece! I cannot believe it! Uncle, you know she is settled with a family in the town?"

"More than that, I know it is all because of you Martha, I know you are the one who saved her and saved her family."

"It must have been fate that August day, I felt such a drawing towards her, it must have been the Lord bringing her to me. What do you wish to do now? I am sure she will fare better here than going back into the countryside and you know, I have a group of ladies who help feed the family?"

"Yes, ma'am, Mr Woods sang your praises to me and I can leave Nottingham with my conscience clear, I found Eliza's family and there is nothing better I can do for them. I shall be glad to get away from this hellish place now, back to the peace and quiet of my fields."

"We should bring the girl here, do you think?" William looked at his children gathered round the table, "she is after all my own blood." He and Martha had recounted Gabriel's visit over supper that evening.

"Yes," replied Martha immediately, "you've seen for yourselves how Fanny tires so easily. The lion's share of the work has been done by Ruth and Clara for months, and now Clara is walking out with her young man it won't be long before she wants to leave us to be married."

"For heaven's sake," William put his finger to his lips, "Fanny's only in the kitchen, don't let her hear you. She will be mortified!"

"Oh dear, yes, but we could bring Grace here from the Marchant's house, Fanny can take her under her wing, teach her how to cook and sew. She's a very bright girl and will learn fast and I am already extraordinarily fond of her. She must be more than eleven now and then when Clara leaves, I'll look for someone to take her place and Fanny can start to sit back completely."

"It's a splendid idea Martha," Polly beamed, "we can't help but like little Grace, cheeky though she is, and I'm sure father that you'll find she'll be quiet and obedient!"

Grace was delighted to leave the laundry, "Mind you, Miss Martha, I was looking forward to being allowed to use the iron one day. It looks good fun," and putting a look of disapproving disdain on her face, she lowered her voice an octave and said, "Grace Woods you have much to learn before you will be allowed to even wash the young ladies' linens, you cannot think you would be allowed near them with a hot iron do you?" She made a perfect impersonation of Miss Shaw the senior laundry maid, and finished with an abrupt twist on her heels.

Martha smiled, "Are you going to mimic me and my family too," she asked, "you'd better watch out for my brothers, if they catch you they'll box your ears!"

"Oh Miss, I can't help it. It just happens! I want to be an actress, Hannah and me have been to the theatre on our days off and they look so lovely on the stage in their fine frocks, and I can sing and dance really well already. I know I'm not old enough yet, but I really want to join a troupe." She caught sight of Martha's face, "Please Miss Martha, I'm sorry, I don't mean that I'm not ever so happy to come to you, I'll do my very best I promise, I shall be so obedient you won't even realise it's me."

"You must try to remember to call me Aunt Martha from now on, we are family."

Grace was as good as her word and with Fanny's teaching blossomed, learning their ways as quickly and easily as Martha had thought she would. She was always cheerful and had a habit of singing the latest songs from the musical plays whilst she worked in the house. The boys thought her a joy to have around and even William was completely won over. When Clara left the house to be married and young Dolly joined to take her place, Grace assumed her natural position as leader.

CHAPTER FOURTEEN
Nottingham 1780
The American Revolutionary War continues

William's low spirits and lethargy started to lift once Grace joined the household, he loved to tease her and complained jokingly about her singing, but the little girl brought a ray of sunshine into the house. He spoke to her of his childhood and told her the little he had learned of her grandparents life too. He visited her father Thomas and was cheered to have met his brother once again.

Polly was especially pleased, "I am so happy Grace is cheering poor father up," she told Francis, "it is lovely to see him smiling again. I feel he is becoming the dear man we used to know and I do so wish for that. He has had far too much sorrow, even I could not comfort him, and I know he still misses having me at home."

Polly's wish for her father came true within the month and not entirely due to Grace. William was jolted back into life by a most unexpected miracle. He received a letter directly from Billy.

Weedon Beck, September, 1780
My dearest father,

I beg your forgiveness in disobeying your command not to contact you directly, but my desire to communicate this to you is greater than the perceived consequence of your wrath.

I wish to throw myself on your mercy and beg that you receive me back into the family circle. You may ask yourself,

94

'what has altered, why should you have a change of mind?' well, I will try to explain.

When we first parted I was a young, naive boy but over the past ten years I have experienced life and learned enough to make me, not regret, but mourn the aftermath of my impetuousness.

As you may know, I have finished with the Wesleyans completely. It is too long a narrative to write to you here in this letter, but I would relish the opportunity to speak with you face to face about my reasons. I cherish the memories of our debates all those years ago before we were so at odds with our beliefs. I cannot inform you that I have returned to the Anglican church, I fear that is still impossible for me. I can never accept the present relationship of the Church and State, for me the Church must, in essence, be autonomous. As for the doctrines I follow, yes, I shall remain a dissenter, a non-conformist. I must be honest with you here father, I would not wish to persuade you with half truths. I do not believe in the Trinity, God is one entity and Jesus Christ his son. Nor can I believe in pre-destination, I am fervent in my conviction that all of God's people can be saved and enter into heaven.

I have these past eighteen months been attending Edinburgh University where I have had the privilege to study moral philosophy under an inspiring professor, Adam Ferguson, together with Rhetoric and English Literature with a Mr Hugh Blair. It has been the most empowering and enjoyable time and whilst I was sorry to leave, I came away re-energised and enthusiastic for the next chapter of my life.

This next chapter is beginning here in Northamptonshire where I have come under the tutelage of Mr William Hextal, a non-conformist minister from Market Harborough, a town not that far from here. My intention, should I be deemed acceptable, is to enter his church and become a minister myself. I have no other desire in life but to preach the word of our Lord and to be his instrument in teaching his peoples how to live a good and Christian life. Should I save some souls along the way, this will be ample reward for me.

Father, I have other, more temporal news of great joy and happiness. I am to be married. My betrothed is Elizabeth Hextal, the daughter of my mentor William, and we have set a date for April of next year. It is a little way off as Elizabeth lost her dear mother this year and wishes to stay in mourning until then.

My revered Father, it would give me great comfort to know that I may be received by your good self, back into the bosom of my family. I crave your forgiveness but I know that this is only for you to bestow and that our beliefs may always come between us, but my life is incomplete without your acknowledgement. My future wife joins me in imploring you to reconcile and restore harmony between us for the future.

We have spent too many years apart Father, but I have never stopped praying for you or being your loving son,
Billy

William did not have to think twice. It was as if a huge tun boulder had been lifted from his shoulders. He had wanted so many times over the interceding years to embrace his son and consign this madness to the past, that he clutched the olive branch Billy offered, with all haste and gratitude. "My stupid pride," he admitted to Ruth, "has denied me ten years of this kind and generous man, how could I have been so stubborn?"

"Well Sir, you do disagree with his religious doctrine and that is no light matter," Ruth defended him, "many people before us have gone to their early graves rather than change their beliefs."

"I am not going to change my views, dear Ruth," William's eyes glistened as he looked at this loyal servant, now his friend, "I will believe as I have always been taught but I have learned my lesson, I will now accept that others may believe differently. I must write to Billy immediately."

"Well, I hope we get to meet Elizabeth before April," Martha spoke for them all, "I'm sure we will like her, Billy is such a good and gentle man, I can't think that he would marry someone who was not of the same nature."

"Father will you let us go to a non-conformist wedding," asked Polly, "I do hope so, I have an idea already about my gown and bonnet. George, you will be excited to go on the stage coach won't you, and I know the London stage stops at

Northampton, Lizzie told me, and that it starts at five in the morning on Tuesdays. Billy's letter says he is living in Northamptonshire so I'm certain it would be convenient."

"You don't know anything about it Polly," scoffed George, "the wedding could be held anywhere. Mind you, father, if we do go, I shall sit outside up top on the stage."

"Let's wait to hear more details," William took off the spectacles he had recently started wearing and taking out a large kerchief began polishing the lens vigorously, his actions designed to draw attention away from the welling up in his eyes, "but I'm not sure my old bones could stand such a long journey, I know the coaches are very uncomfortable and the roads are appalling."

At the beginning of October Billy made the journey to Nottingham to seal the reconciliation with his father. It was a joyful occasion, for the first time in so many years they were all seated round the large table in the house on Weekday Cross enjoying a family dinner, fashionably late at 3pm to please Polly, but Billy had come without Elizabeth, "I fear she is a little too delicate to make the journey, the weather being so unpredictable at this time of the year," he explained. "The wedding will be a very quiet affair, a simple ceremony as Elizabeth and I feel very strongly that we do not wish to do as many other non conformists do, and marry in the Anglican church. I know because of this, our marriage will not be recognised in law, and any child of our union would be base born. We have decided therefore not to have the blessing of our own children as neither Elizabeth nor I would ever consider bringing a child into the world to be unlawful and discriminated against."

"How?" Polly questioned, "how will you prevent a baby? Francis and I are hoping very much to have a family, I'm really impatient now as we have been married for ages."

"My dear sister," answered Billy, "Elizabeth and I will concentrate on higher matters of life and dedicate ourselves to the Lord's work. We shall manage quite well, and you will understand more when you meet her. She is a wonderful woman, a truly generous nature and solicitous in her thoughts for others. She was thinking only of you all when she suggested, and I thoroughly agree, that we cannot expect you to travel to Lutterworth for the marriage next year and that we shall come, as man and wife, to visit you here in Nottingham in April."

"Well, that will be marvellous," William said cheerfully, not seeing the raised eyebrows around the table.

The change that came over William was as startling as it was rapid. The first thing he did was visit Mr Valentine's office, "I would like you to change my Last Will and Testament to include all of my eight sons and daughters. I can die easy now," he told the aged solicitor, "my conscience is clear, my family is united again."

He began to take more interest both in his own life and of those around him. His face lost the haggard, melancholy look it had carried so often in the past, his pale eyes looked brighter, his jowls less flabby and his revitalised posture gave the illusion of a reduction in girth even if in reality it stayed the same. Most importantly, he was ready to discuss the future.

Having decided to walk together through the park one morning, Martha canvassed his views on her plans. "Father, I've got my committee of ladies together now and we want to set up a small foundlings home along the lines of the one I've read about in London."

"My dear Martha, that is a huge institution costing many thousands of pounds, I don't want to dampen your enthusiasm but I think you are setting your sights too high."

"I know we can only do it on a very, very small scale and even that is proving hard to establish. We have a handful of traders willing to subscribe but they wish to provide goods rather than money, so whilst we are striving to achieve the home, all my ladies have agreed we will provide food two or three times a week to families most in need. We have a rota set up and good, wholesome food given to us, so we are doing something. Just not enough. And all this is very gratifying Father," she linked her arm through his, "but I am determined to set up the little home for these desperate waifs and strays, the death rate amongst them is dreadfully high and the numbers I see on the streets makes me ashamed sometimes that I have such an easy life."

"The London Hospital had very influential people raising the money, I rather fear you will find this a stumbling block here in Nottingham. People are being asked to subscribe to so many things, we were only talking about the new general hospital the other day."

"James has warned us a home will cost a fortune, rent for the property, money to kit it out, wages for the staff and to buy medicines and food, and a million things we haven't thought of yet, but we can do it. We will start small, just half a dozen children maybe. It's exciting, we've already got an appointment with Mr Marchant, his housekeeper who took on Grace has opened the way for us there. I don't know if he will help, but he might send us in the right direction. It will happen, we will make it happen."

"Well Martha, I don't know what the world is coming to, women wanting to make their own way. It will certainly be an uphill task, but yes, if you are that determined, I cannot say no, you can count on me for a small subscription, it won't be much but it will be something."

"Oh Father," she threw her arms around him, "thank you, thank you. It means so much to me."

William, unaccustomed to such a display of affection from this rather austere daughter, disengaged himself, mumbled something about work to do and took his farewell, leaving Martha to make her own way home.

She was eager to give Ruth the good news. Having much less to do in the vintners now that James was working in Severns, she had gradually become involved in the project and was now Martha's indispensable right hand. Thankful for a new challenge, she excelled in persuading butchers, bakers and grocers to donate the food which was then delivered to the good ladies' cooks, turned into prepared meals and delivered in the ladies' baskets to the families on Martha's 'list'. Their eyes and ears on the street to determine the genuinely needy from the work shy or scroungers, was Grace's father, Thomas. Thanks to Edmund, he had just moved with his boy into a White Rent's property and felt so indebted to Martha for saving his daughter from the streets and for his own improved situation, that he became a steadfast member of what was now commonly called 'Miss Martha's Missions'.

The far more complex question of James and James's ambition was the next thorny problem for William to tackle and he had a sleepless night before meeting to discuss it with him.

"What about our existing customers, most of them have become friends, we can't turn them away just because we want to go all 'la di da'," father and son were sitting at the small round table placed by the window in Severns, "and aren't most of the newcomers to the town that you talk about, the poor, come to work in the factories? They won't have the money for fancy wines, they'll be sticking to gin and beer like they always have done."

"I'm not suggesting for a minute that we turn away any of our customers Father, we will need every one of them but we need to do something to build Severns back up again. We are losing pace instead of gaining it and I'm quite positive that we could open a decent Wine Merchants shop, a step up from the vintners here." James persevered, "We'll have to concentrate on the new monied men, manufacturers and the like. I know we can do it Father, and the first step is for us to go and meet with Charles Jubb."

William crossed his arms and sat back in his chair,, "I can see you will not rest until this happens, but I shall not go to London. You can go, make plans for April, after Billy's wedding. The roads should be dryer by then and less hazardous. Write to Benjamin and decide how long you will stay."

"I can't believe it," James said over and over to the others, "Father has agreed I can go to London. This is the beginning for Severns to really grow, you wait and see."

George did his best to spoil James's moment, "That's you all over, always getting your own way, always thinking of yourself," he flung the abuse at James, who, so bewildered by his brother's accusation, was stumped for words.

CHAPTER FIFTEEN
Nottingham 1781
The Foundation Stone is laid for Nottingham's new hospital

Thinking the winter would drag by slowly as he waited for the spring and his trip to London, James found the opposite to be true. So much happened in the family that the months flew by.

November brought sadness, Jack and Ann's baby Mary died from whooping cough. Going to raise her from her afternoon nap, Ann found the little girl fighting for breath. She nursed her, helplessly listening to the dreadful whoop of her breathing until Mary gave up her struggle and passed away in Ann's arms. It was hard to believe that bright little baby, just testing out her attempts at first words, her unsteady legs tottering around the home, full of curiosity and love had gone from their lives. Whether it was a blessing that their second child, Jon, was born within two weeks of Mary's death, they were not sure. Their grief tempered their joy.

§

In December all attention turned on Polly. She and Francis were expecting their first child. "I am so thrilled," she told Martha, "Francis has been reading the latest medical advice to me and I am to keep active and take gentle exercise to keep both the baby and me healthy.

Sarah, when she heard the news, put her doubts and fears to the back of her mind, "that was me," she told herself sternly, "this is Polly, and there is no earthly reason why she should lose her child," and she began to sew a layette at once, "The months go so quickly, it will be June before we know it. How I wish John were here to share the excitement."

The fact that he was to become a father, propelled Francis to consider the future, and he went to speak with James. "You remember my father invested with Jeremiah Knowles, and Knowles' son John took over when the old man died, well John himself is not at all well now. I've just signed an Indenture with him to buy the Middle Pavement properties from his Estate when the time comes," he was helping James move some barrels in his store room, "and I was thinking of you and Severns, and now that I'm in here, I think it's an even better idea. The town house, the one next to the old timber framed building, would suit you really well as a wine merchant's. It's got so much more room than here and more storage and there are several buildings in the yard behind, the yard at the back of The Fleece. You'd only need the ground floor of the house, not the rest of it."

"It sounds a marvellous idea, just help me shove this beer into the corner, that's good, thank you. It's certainly true, we do need more space, especially now that father might be coming round to my ideas for expansion. He's in the shop with Henry," James straightened his back, grimacing as he stretched, "come over and tell him about it, he might listen better to you."

They sat at the other two chairs round the table and taking a cup of coffee each, joined in the conversation.

"My eldest son is very ill with tuberculosis," Henry was saying, "he's not likely to live much longer I'm afraid, and I need young Robert to come back from London to take over. Frederick's too well established to want to come to Nottingham even if I asked him. I know it's all too common, but God it's unfair, the boy had always been so strong and healthy. His mother's devastated."

"He's got a wife and half a dozen children hasn't he?" asked William, "she'll have to find a new husband. I've never wanted to marry again since Mary died but everyone spent years telling me I should get the children a new mother, I just couldn't bring myself to do it. I doubt she'll get a choice in the matter though, she'll need supporting ."

"That's true enough," sympathised Francis. "How long before Robert will be ready to take over Kings do you think? Has he finished his apprenticeship?"

"Well, he and Benjamin went down to Fred in '74 so their seven years are up next year but he'll still need my input for a while after that I should think," Henry sighed, "let's hope the Lord spares me."

§

The Lord did not, alas, spare William's household. After spending a joyous Christmas Day at Weekday Cross, Sarah Crosland and Ruth retired to their respective beds that night feeling a little unwell. Within the week, the two ladies were fighting for their lives, victims of an outbreak of influenza, a fight they both lost.

"It's so unfair Martha," Polly's face was stained with tears, "Sarah was so looking forward to her first grandchild, it's too cruel for her to be taken. Now our baby will have no grandmother to know and with Uncle John gone too, there is only father to be grandparent."

"It does seem horribly cruel, and I am lost without poor Ruth too. I felt she had really found her purpose with the Missions, she had wasted far too much time mooning after father for so many years," Polly's eyes widened when she heard this, and her sister smiled, "didn't you ever notice? Well, I don't think Father did either, anyway, I don't want to appear heartless but with her gone I've got quite a problem."

"I'm sorry Martha, I quite forgot to call Alice for tea." The sisters were seated on elegant, walnut easy chairs in the Crosland's beautiful drawing room at St Mary Gate. When Polly got up and crossed to the bell pull hanging just inside the door, Martha looked around her. The wall panels were painted a muted grey, setting off the crimson fabric on the chairs and two plump couches perfectly. Covering the centre of the scrubbed wooden floor was a large carpet square in a darker tone of grey with the floral border a mix of crimson and blue and draped to either side of the two large, sash windows, were long crimson curtains falling to the floor.

"I see you have hung the portrait of Grandfather Martin at last, it looks tolerably well in that corner. You are a good girl."

"It is a pity it's not a very good likeness, nor I'm afraid, very good quality," Polly moved to stand in front of it and nibbled her lower lip, "but he was our dear Mama's ancestor and I have it there for her."

Alice brought in the tea tray, and as with everything else in the room except the portrait, the china was of the very highest quality, the silver teapot and bowls, impeccable. Polly asked, "Now that poor Ruth has gone, can't you work with one of the other committee ladies?"

"It's not just with the charity but at home too, I don't really want to take on another girl, but it will mean expecting Grace to do more, or me." Martha walked to the fireplace and was about to put a shovel of coal on the burning embers, when she caught Polly's look out the side of her eye, and said, "You should call Alice, the fire will go out." Returning to her chair deep in thought, she decided, "I think I will wait and see how it progresses."

§

Martha had been pleased when Edmund sent a note asking if she would be free to join him in the new Tea Room recently opened within Kings the Grocers. As she walked up Wheeler Gate she could see him waiting outside, he was obviously agitated, shifting from foot to foot, pulling at his coat sleeves and fidgeting with the fancy pin holding his stock. She raised her hand in greeting and as she drew level, before she had a chance to speak a word, he opened the door and ushered her inside saying, "Martha, I have something I wish to speak with you about."

"Have you found a new girl for the Marchant's laundry," interrupted Martha unbuttoning her overcoat, "since we took Grace away I've been looking for someone suitable and you were going to speak with the family Thomas Woods told us about?"

"No, Martha, I would like to talk about a personal matter, please could we sit a little while, over here in this corner where we will not be disturbed." With a hint of foreboding, she sat, not saying a word whilst he ordered their tea. Edmund continued, "Martha you must be aware that I hold you in the greatest esteem. I admire your dedication to charity and your kind and caring self. No, please let me continue," Martha had opened her mouth to speak, unhappily aware of what Edmund was about to say, "I am, as you know, just a curate at St Mary's and as such, my circumstances are so meagre that I would never have dreamt of speaking with you in this way had I not learned of some information last month which has changed my prospects completely. My uncle Sir Thomas Brown died in January and it appears I am his heir. I had no idea of this, he was my father's brother and he never spoke of him, only to say that there had been a family rift many years before when they were both children. Be that as it may, I now find myself a wealthy man and the owner of his country estate near a town called Woodbridge in Suffolk. I am, it seems, destined to become a gentleman of leisure and as such, my dear Martha, I am in a position to ask you to marry me. It would make my life complete. I have the greatest affection for you and together we could continue with your work in Suffolk."

Martha was lost for words, she had no real idea of Edmund's background and the knowledge of this new and privileged life came as a huge shock to her. Her mind was reeling and whilst she was taking time to try and form her words, it struck her that she would miss this man, her friend and support, miss him much more than she realised. It had never occurred to her that he would not always be there, in Nottingham, close by to speak with and to enjoy his company whenever she wanted.

"My dearest Edmund," she hesitated, "I am amazed and I am so very pleased for you. The inheritance is a bounty that could not be more deserved by any man and I know you will do so much good with it, but Edmund, I think you know in your heart what my answer to your proposal must be. I cannot marry you. I promised myself many years ago when I was very young that I would never marry. Edmund, I am not willing to be a wife to you in the fullest sense and no, before you say anything," she shook her head, "I would not ask you to forsake the very fundamental desire of a man to become a father. This is my choice and should be my choice only, I have no wish to impose my decision on another. Please forgive me, Edmund, I had hoped of course that we would remain friends and colleagues and I shall miss you very much in my life, but no, I cannot marry you and move away. My life is here in Nottingham, as Miss Severn.

§

Not many weeks later, the year that had started so sadly, took a devastating turn. Polly miscarried her baby. She was inconsolable, "Francis my love, I am so sorry, I have failed you," the tears were rolling down her cheeks, "it was all my fault, I so wanted to be married on my birthday I ignored that it was a Thursday and I've always known it was unlucky to marry on a Thursday. Oh why did I insist," she wailed, "and you were to have your first son in June."

Francis was worried for Polly's health, putting his own grief to one side, he begged her not to blame herself and to be calm, "There are many years ahead of us to make plenty of babies," he assured her, "I just want you to be strong and healthy again my darling. Rest and get better and no more of that nonsense about Thursdays, it's just an old superstition and it's rubbish. I'll send Alice to you, you are not to move from that bed until you are quite recovered."

Thankful to be able to leave the despair in the house behind and his wife in the more capable, female, hands of her sister, friends and maid, he retreated to the safety of his office, where his private thoughts dwelt on his own lost siblings.

CHAPTER SIXTEEN
1781 Nottingham
William Pitt the Younger enters parliament, age 21

When the day of Billy and Elizabeth's wedding arrived it caused a turmoil of emotions for the sisters and when the married couple arrived in Nottingham on the 26th April for the wedding party, it was to be the last time Martha and Edmund were together, and amidst the celebrating, they said their sad good-byes.

The married couple had arrived at the White Lion Inn by post-chaise. They clattered into the yard, swerving under the huge sign swinging from the great beam across Cow Lane, and on alighting at this great coaching inn, were shown to their rooms where the new Mrs Severn forsook all offers of refreshment and took to her bed with a fearsome headache.

The journey had been long and slow but far less unpleasant than coming by public stage coach. "Oh my dear husband," Elizabeth had protested when Billy was planning the trip, "no, I really feel you could not endure the stage coach. It would be most inconvenient for you to have to sit with strangers as I am sure they would wish to talk to you and I know you would prefer to think or read to yourself. Also, I have heard that the dreadful state of the roads, even the turnpikes, cause the coaches to be frightfully uncomfortable and I would worry about your poor back, and there is always the threat of highwaymen. No, husband, I think the expenditure for the chaise is quite necessary," and Billy, who had been thinking that they would travel by stage coach, agreed.   "Of course my dear, post-chaise it will be, but not for myself alone, I would not wish for the world that your journey should be any more unpleasant than is absolutely unavoidable."

Billy's finances were, as yet, to pick up and his rough calculations for the journey there and back, the driver's wages, the lodgings overnight at Loughborough, food and drink, tips for the ostlers and the days spent at the White Lion, warned him the trip was going to cost the best part of his savings. A far cry from his lengthy journeys on horseback with excellent hospitality provided free by his brothers in the church.

The day after their arrival, the whole family was to meet in the afternoon at the Golden Fleece for the wedding party and Polly arrived at the family home in Weekday Cross in good time. Her health now recovered, for Francis's sake she tried hard to put her grief behind her, and had been dressing and preparing for the party the whole morning. She looked quite exquisite in a butter yellow, silk taffeta dress, her modesty assured by a little tuft of lace tucked into the low cut décolletage, her sleeves trimmed with lace to match. Her dark red hair was piled fashionably high with a few soft curls left to frame her little face, and the excitement of the day removed any traces of sadness from her eyes. "I'm certainly not going to hide my hair under a cap today," she chattered away to Martha, "Francis likes to see it like this, look, with just these few ribbons. I wonder what Elizabeth will wear, Francis told me they have come by post-chaise so she must have money. Oh, I expect she will be in fine silk and put us all to shame."

"Well thank you Polly, that's made me feel a lot better," Martha raised her eyebrows, "I thought I was looking relatively grand wearing purple instead of my usual dark blue working dress!"

"Sorry dear Martha, I always say the wrong thing. You do, you look positively charming, the colour is more grape, I think, and is such a good choice with your hair. Francis is checking that the boys are looking their best. I tried to persuade him to wear a new fangled frock coat, I'm sure they must be much more comfortable to sit around in, but he won't. Anyway, I'm sure they will all look very handsome and Billy will approve. I've insisted that they all, including Josiah, have their hair powdered a little, and I've had to remind George he is not to scratch at his head. What would Elizabeth think."

When everyone was ready, cloaks and hoods were brought for the ladies, sedan chairs summoned and they made their way to the tavern.

When the carriage from the White Lion arrived bringing the newlyweds a buzz of excitement ran round the room and Billy strode in beaming with pleasure, leading his new wife on his arm, her air of dominance arising only partially from the fact that she towered over him. The introductions were made, baby Jon coo'ed over, outfits were scrutinised up and down and first impressions rapidly made. The wine began to flow, the guests were pressed to take their seats and the meal began.

Much later in the day Polly had the chance to speak with Martha, "I never would have believed it," she uttered with disbelief, "how could Billy have chosen her, he could have married anyone in the land. Her dress is so plain! I was sure she would wear silk not wool and that ochre colour over the brown petticoat is just so wrong for her. It has drained her cheeks so that she looks like a ghost and anyway, her face is so pinched and pious it would suit a nun's wimple! Did you see her kerchief warn as a shawl around her neck and the mob cap sitting on top of her hair? It looks so matronly and, so … so, tall! She looks as if she is, but I'm sure she cannot be much older than us."

"Stop, stop," Martha giggled, "we must not judge a woman on her sense of fashion. You can tell she is a very devout lady and obviously very kind."

"How can you tell that," asked Polly, "I can't see the kindness, only that she needs Billy to pander to her every minute and do you notice how she turns the words around such that she is concerned for him! 'oh, I think we should be seated by the fire if possible husband, you know how you feel the cold so!' I think she is of a very nervous disposition and she sounds quite waspish and so …so," Polly hesitated, a line forming between her brows, "so Holy! I can't imagine them having any fun together." At this she exploded into giggles, "I'll wager it was her who told Billy they would not be having any children, and not for the reasons he gave us!"

"Quiet Polly," Martha was trying to control herself, "that's an awful thing to say. Look, Billy has chosen her and we must make sure she feels welcome. John and Ann are doing very well, she does seem to be genuinely fond of children, and she and Josiah were speaking for ages, I could overhear them talking of the plight of the poor, so she can't be all bad."

"The good thing is, Father is so happy to have Billy here and they have been very careful not to mention anything to do with religion that might upset him," Polly turned as James and George joined them, "so how do you care for our new sister?"

"Billy says she is a little indisposed and needs to return to their lodgings." James said by way of an answer, "she looks to me as if she is permanently indisposed."

"Indisposed towards having a good time I think," George made no pretence, "but now that she's going, can we can start the dancing, those little country cousins are very enticing."

"That is enough you wicked boys, she is our sister, our brother's choice of wife and we must learn to love her." Martha wasn't really sure about that sentiment herself and gave a silent sigh of relief that their paths, given the distance between them, would not have to cross too often.

When Billy and Elizabeth returned to Market Harborough where he was to continue his instruction for the Ministry and Elizabeth was to start her life as a dutiful Minister's wife, it was only William who was genuinely sorry to see them go.

§

The visit over, at five in the morning on Tuesday 1st of May, James was standing outside the White Lion, the large round collar of his new surtout pulled up around his ears to keep out the rain dripping from the brim of his hat, checking for the dozenth time the straps on the pristine, dark brown leather portmanteau at his feet. At last, he was waiting for the stage coach to London.

Within an hour of James's departure, George had presented himself at William's counting house, "Father, I've been with Jack for years now and he just has me running around making deliveries and cleaning up, don't you think it's about time I had a bit more to do. I could deal with the livestock side for him but he won't hear of it, could you put in a word for me? Or set me up in my own shop, after all, you're letting James work with you in Severns, and he's even going to London on his own."

"George, I'm sorry but I have spoken with Jack and I agree with him, you're not ready to take on anything more yet. I sent you to him early as you were wasting time and money at school, but you've still two years of your apprenticeship to run. You must apply yourself better to what you are doing and learning right now, rather than starting new things. He says you daydream, take much longer out on the streets when you are supposed to be making deliveries and you spend far too much time talking with the girls who come into the shop. It's not professional and you would not have the first idea of how to run a business. Jack also tells me you are often late arriving at the shop in the mornings, yet I know Martha makes sure you leave home on time. If there was more room in the house in Finkhill Street I would insist you lived there. It is not right to treat your brother this way, I would find it hard to defend you if he says you have to leave."

"But it is because I have no responsibility, that I cannot take much interest Father. Sweeping out the yard and endless sharpening of knives is hardly important, I am much happier when I am allowed to practice cutting the carcasses but Jack only lets me do this under his gaze, and he's often too busy. James doesn't have to sweep the shop or clean your yard, and he's allowed to help with the running of Severns. It's not right that he has all the privileges and I don't, I'm just as much part of this family as he is."

No amount of pleading made any difference, William finished the conversation, " We'll talk again next year, so make sure I can agree to help you next time."

CHAPTER SEVENTEEN
London 1781
Sir William Herschel discovers the planet Uranus

Benjamin awoke to the cry of 'milk below' coming through the cracks around the window of his lodgings in Mrs Warner's house in Bermondsey. As he carefully tested opening his eyes, one at a time, not quite able to focus, he heard the bells of St Mary Magdalene calling the early risers to morning prayers. He'd had a great night at the ale house 'Simon the Tanner' in Long Lane where he and a group of friends had said goodbye to his best chum Robert. As anticipated, Henry King had called him back home, his brother now close to death. Benjamin would miss Robert, they had been inseparable at school and had come to London together to be apprenticed to his second brother, Frederick, a wholesale grocer in Stepney.

The boys had grown up with each other over the past seven years in London, always sharing a room, they had worked and played together, their lives were entwined and they were the greatest of friends. At first they had stayed in an attic room in Frederick's house, leaving for the premises of King & Bankes each morning, but at the beginning of this year they had moved out and taken up the room in Grange Walk. Mrs Warner was a young woman whose husband was serving in the Royal Navy, fighting, Ben thought, in the American war. She provided a good breakfast and a substantial supper, the bed was comfortable and the sheets tolerably clean.

This May morning, once his brain started to wake up, Ben leapt out of bed, cursed and dropped his aching head into his hands for a moment, carried out his ablutions quickly, greeted

Mrs Warner cheerfully, ate his bread and cheese, drank his coffee and sallied forth to greet his brother. James had arrived in London late the evening before and had slept the night at 'The Swan with Two Necks' in Lad Lane, across the river in Cheapside. Ben walked quickly as the daylight greeted the already busy, noisy streets. He passed the vendors at their customary stations and negotiated the early morning carters, wagons and scores of Hackney carriages cantering to and fro, the constant clattering of the iron hooped cart wheels bouncing along the granite setts of the road ringing in his ears. This morning he avoided Annie who stood on the corner of Long Lane selling her gingerbread and who had taken rather a liking to this handsome young man with the red brown hair who stopped by most days for a halfpenny slice, Ben didn't have time to stop and flirt today. He called "good day to you," to the penny pie man, "not this morning Simon, I've just eaten." The air thick with the smoke from hundreds of coal fires pulled at his chest, the loud creaking of the hanging shop signs seemed to scream in his ears, the smell from the excrement on the pathways invaded his nostrils but he was smiling to himself.

As he arrived, slightly out of breath, at the courtyard of The Swan, he heard a shout, "I'm heartily glad to see you brother, but you are late!"

Looking up at the second floor gallery, he saw James leaning over the handrail laughing. It was almost like looking at a reflection of himself, Ben had forgotten just how much they looked alike, "James you rascal, come on down or shall I come up to you?"

Before he finished speaking, James had disappeared from the gallery and minutes later rushed across to Ben and embraced him with all the force of a hurricane. "It's good to see you brother, and it's good to be here in London at last. The journey was an adventure in itself but I expect you remember that, I'll tell you all about it, we have so much to talk about and I want to hear all about your life down here, I'm sure it is much more exciting than mine in Nottingham."

"Let's hope three weeks is long enough then," Ben could not stop grinning, "let's settle up here and I'll take you home with me. Mrs Warner is happy for you to have Rob's bed and

Frederick has said I can spend some time with you this morning and then we'll come back to Cheapside to meet him and I'll introduce you to his partner Nathaniel Bankes. You can start learning all about the grocery trade. It's so good to have you here, I can't quite believe it, and you're right, I have loads of interesting stuff to tell you and to show you."

After an hour or so it was as if they had not spent the past seven years apart, they were easy in each other's company and they never stopped talking! "I had an outside seat on the stage," James told Ben, "they have only four seats inside on the Nottingham Times coach and at half the price too, I thought it better to be outside than stuck inside with goodness knows who. It was pretty awful though, I thought one time I was going to be pitched off, the bucking and rolling from the ruts in the road was so bad."

"Any highway men," asked Ben, "I remember when Rob and I came down we were really keen to be held up, it would have been so exciting. I wouldn't think that now and not just because I am older and wiser, the thieves are getting more and more daring and a lot more of them are happy to use their pistols. On the plus side, I think the coaches have better springs than they used to, so you probably had a very easy ride compared to mine!"

"Well, I'm not in any hurry to go back, that's for sure," he linked arms with Ben as they walked, "we stopped overnight at Northampton at the coaching inn there. It was good enough, but my room companion was a very rum chap, I'm hoping I haven't got his lice!"

"It will take us about thirty minutes to walk home so we could hire a cab if you like, there are some over there but given the amount of traffic over the bridge, it's just as quick to walk."

"I'd rather walk, I shall see so much more this way, the city is a thousand times busier than Nottingham and I must admit, the smell is a thousand times worse too, and I've never seen so much smoke, it's like huge black clouds hanging over us."

"You'll soon get used to it, just watch out that the carts don't splash that muck on you. Wait up," Ben pulled James into a side alley, "there's a line of cattle coming and we need to keep out of their way, they've been driven over London Bridge on their way to Smithfield Market. Luckily there's not that many of them at this time of the year, you should see it in the autumn, thousands, but the bridge will still be completely jammed, it's always packed with traffic and horses in the first place."

The noise from the cows and the drovers bellowing was deafening, Ben shouted, " God, the mess they make is unbelievable We'll take this little alley here and join the road again later, mind those cess puddles, I know you want to look around but here you really do have to look where you put your feet."

Talking all the way, James's eyes darting from one side to the other, upwards and downwards, the journey passed quickly, "Here we are, Grange Road, and home."

The house was a handsome two storey brick building and on entering by the front door, Ben called out, "How do you do Mrs Warner, here is my brother to meet you."

Kitty Warner was a graceful young woman, not too slight in stature, wearing a plain, dark blue wool robe, a white apron and a small white cap and she appeared comely rather than pretty. She greeted James with a welcoming smile, "It's good to meet you James, we have been looking forward to your arrival, I hope you will find the room to your liking," and she led the way upstairs to a room at the front of the house, "I see you do not have much baggage so there will be plenty of room for you both. I will leave you to arrange yourselves and see you at supper time."

It took only minutes for James to empty his bag and the two young men were out on the road again, making their way back towards London Bridge. "We'll stop at Button's for a cup of coffee on the way," said Ben, "and then cross the river to the City."

"Marvellous, I'm really looking forward to seeing the river and the Pool of London, it was dark when I arrived last night and I could only get an impression of the ships."

When he did get to the Thames, James was astonished. Nothing he had been told could have prepared him for the spectacle before his eyes. It reminded him of a forest, bare tree trunks crowded together reaching upwards to compete for the light above, but here, some of the trees were adorned with large white sails, some furled, some flapping, and everywhere, jangling shackles holding miles of tarry rope. Men were climbing and running through the rigging as nimble as any monkey and the ship's gilded figure heads were staring dead ahead, close enough to be whispering their secrets to each other.

"There must be hundreds of ships, maybe thousands, and all those small boats, are they taking the cargoes to the wharves?"

Before Ben could answer there was a thundering shout behind them, "Mind yer backs!" and a porter, bent double under the weight of two enormous sacks, struggled past causing James to stumble backwards into the path of a skinny sailor, his face burnt from months at sea, his pigtail gleaming with oil and an aura of salt and tar clinging to him like a second skin, "Watch out you idiot," and seeing the bemused look on the boy's face, he said, "don't worry, I haven't time to fight you today. I'm in a good mood, off to see the prettiest girl in all Wapping. Been away a good two years and she'll be waiting for me," and with an exaggerated wink, he rushed off.

James was in a daze, "How on earth do any of these ships manoeuvre in and out?"

"Somehow they manage," Ben was amused at James's face, "but it can take days or weeks to offload the cargoes, there's a good deal of damage to the ships and a huge amount of theft. All these little skiffs buzzing backwards and forwards are good camouflage and it's impossible for the Customs men to keep an eye on everyone and everything. There are river hackneys everywhere too just to add to the chaos. Let's walk on up here," and he pulled his brother's arm, "It won't be much longer before we have to have more and larger docks. We desperately need wharves where the bigger ships can moor easily, the East Indiamen have to stop and unload downriver at Blackwall and that of course means dozens more barges bringing the goods up here to their warehouses in the City."

"I guess if you could do away with so many lighters and all these little boats, everything would be safer and run faster and more smoothly but it's not just on the water," James wasn't going to get caught again and quickly side stepped a wagon laden high with bales of a fabric, tied up with rope, "I've never seen so many people in one place. That line of carts, it's a like hackney rank, is it the same? You just use the first one in the queue? It's amazing to me that anyone knows what is going on and where stuff is going. It's the most exciting place I've ever been to. Look, that's coal being landed over there, where has it come from?"

"Hundreds of coastal ships bring coal and grain from around England, and they all compete for space here with the East India's. Not to mention tuns of timber and hemp from Russia, and you'll be interested in the ships bringing wines from the Mediterranean countries. There's a much bigger world out there than I could ever have imagined when I was a boy in Nottingham."

"You're right, a much bigger world Ben, and I'm absolutely determined to be part of it, like you already are!"

The two young men finished making their way to King & Bankes in Cheapside. "Welcome to the City of London little brother," Ben held his arms out wide and bowed, "the hub of London, all the top commerce of the whole country is carried out here in just one square mile," and when they turned into Queen Street, "Here we are, this is us."

They had stopped outside a large brick warehouse with a very grand sign, golden letters announced "King & Bankes Grocers". "Come on in, I'll show you round and introduce you."

James tried hard to feign sophistication and stop his jaw from falling open onto his chin. The space they had entered was vast, three storeys high with loading bays giving access to each floor from the front. Windows were allowing the daylight to flood in and hoists dangling from beams, were being rapidly raised and lowered by several men in brown aprons, whilst the gaffer in charge shouted instructions to them. Every inch of the place was filled with sacks, butts, kegs and wooden crates. As they walked through the door, on the right were dozens of sacks containing grains and behind the sacks were counters. There stood the traders, dressed in the height of fashion, their tight coats cut away making curving tails, their waistcoats short above long, tight breeches atop silk stockings which themselves were placed inside costly, buckled, leather shoes. They were fingering the contents of small canvas bags filled with samples, and then dropping the grain to the floor.

"What are they doing?" asked James, "and why are they dropping it on the floor, it seems crazy."

"Checking the water content," Ben ushered him past, "and they can't put it back in the sample bag afterwards, their hands might have made it wetter or dryer and it wouldn't be fair to the next buyer."

"What a waste though, the floor is covered."

"Don't worry, we don't lose out. We sweep it up at the end of the day and sell it for horse feed, we look after our profits alright!"

They passed sacks and sacks of flour and moved along to the next section where James was staggered at the array of goods. The pungent aroma of spices from the East Indies, pepper, cloves, nutmeg, cinnamon and ginger filled his nostrils making it hard to breathe deeply for fear of sneezing. Tall cones of sugar wrapped in brown paper, some with a smart 'K&B' embossed label, stood like stately ladies or were packed into wooden crates alongside sacks of dried fruit, currants and raisins. There were tuns of salt, wooden boxes of cocoa, and an enormous area containing nothing but sacks of coffee beans and chests of tea leaves. "And what is this," James was examining a sack containing small, pale brown, slightly curved hard tubes, "it doesn't look as if you could eat it."

Ben laughed, "That's macaroni from Italy and it's what those awful men in their outlandish clothes and fancy speech are named after. They think they are mimicking the young gentlemen who've made the 'Grand Tour' to Italy and learned to love macaroni, but of course, most of them are just ridiculous fops. Have you not seen it before, it's made of tapioca flour, goes soft when it's cooked and is delicious with a meat sauce. Here it is in another shape, these long strands are called vermicelli, this is good with a sweet cream and sugar sauce."

"There are foods here I've never heard of, and I certainly haven't seen or eaten 'em at home. These kegs, soy sauce, whatever is that. Gosh, Martha and Polly would love to be here to see all this. I wouldn't let them come to London though, it all seems too busy and dangerous for women." James looked up, "Good Lord, is all that floor given over just to tobacco?"

All this time, the men in the aprons were bringing in more sacks and barrels from carts waiting outside, the hoists were constantly lifting crates up to be stacked on the higher floors and the whole warehouse was a mass of movement, noise and smells.

"It will happen all over again tomorrow James, and the next day, and the next day. We can only hold so much stock, and it's not just a question of room, we have to have it in peak condition so we can't hold it long. The demand for food is enormous, the population in London is growing so fast and this new class of merchants and tradesmen, the middling sorts, they want everything that our new overseas trading can offer. Everything they see the 'nobs' enjoying, they want for themselves, and lots of it. We have most of our customers in London but our goods go all over the country too, you'll see the wagons loading up first thing in the morning. We even supply Henry King, but you'd expect that as he's family," Ben laughed, " it would be a poor show if a father and son didn't support each other. What a pity we don't trade in wines, then you could buy from us too. It's a really exciting time James, all these new ideas and the world opening up. Profits couldn't be better. Ah, here's Frederick, come and meet him.

CHAPTER EIGHTEEN
1781 London
The American Revolutionary War continues to dominate the news

"My first appointment with Charles Jubb is next Friday," James munched his bread as they ate their breakfast, "I'd like to talk everything through with you Ben before then. Having seen the scale of K&B I'm a bit nervous that my basic ideas are just that, too basic. Before I came down here, we had no real notion of the size of your outfit and I'm a bit daunted."

"Well, don't forget I'm still learning too, a lot of the time I'm helping Frederick rather than dealing with anything on my own, but yes, of course I might have some new thoughts. Next Friday you say, that means we have a few days to knock the edges off your accent boy, these Londoners won't understand you if you don't start talking like them," the look of surprise on James's face was quite comical, "don't be offended old chap, you must have noticed how my voice has changed, no flat vowels anymore, you'll have to change yours too if you want to get on in this world."

They were ready to leave for Cheapside, "Today we'll stay at K&B and next Monday, Frederick says I can take you to the Corn Exchange. It's an unbelievable atmosphere and if you think we are booming at the grocers, you'll be stunned at what goes on over there."

Before then there was Saturday night and Ben was determined they should make the most of it. Frederick had allowed them the day off on Sunday and as long as they could surface in time for the mid morning service at St Mary's they could stay in bed a little longer and sleep off any excesses. "What do you say about going to 'Simon's', it's my local ale house and I can introduce you to some of the folk I've got to know," Ben had just got in from getting a late shave at the barbers nearby and was inspecting his face in the looking glass, "yes, that's better. Ready to wow the ladies! Good grief, you'd better get off round to Sauls right now, you look as whiskery as a rat!"

James returned, face smooth, hair tidy and the perfume of pomade around him, "I've been thinking," Ben said, "after Simon's, we should take a walk through the New Spring, best pleasure gardens in town, over at Vauxhall. They're worth a visit just to see the artificial lights when it gets dark, and it's always a relief to get away from the stench of these streets for a while. There'll be music, probably a concert, and singers performing all the latest songs everywhere and you get an interesting mix of people, all sorts from every walk of life. So what do you say, the gardens open at five, it's two shillings to get in and with luck we'll see fireworks later on. Of course, there will be plenty of food and drink and as your older brother I feel it's my duty to introduce you to the pleasures," his face broke into a huge grin, " or maybe the dangers, of being a young man about town."

Enjoying a pot or two of porter in the tavern, and in an exuberant mood, they were joined by a few of Ben's friends for their excursion to Vauxhall. One of the major dangers for a man about town was easily avoided as James was repelled by the brazen attitude of the painted girls parading in the dimly lit areas of the gardens, plying their trade alongside courting couples and clandestine couples seeking seclusion for a while. Another major danger was however, not avoided, and the two young men found themselves struggling to greet the Sunday morning. Those wonderful effects of beer which had made them so erudite, so amusing and so confident the night before were gone, and they were left with a sour taste in their mouths, splitting headaches and the frustration of not being able to clarify their thoughts. "My but it was a grand night, worth feeling like this." they agreed.

Ben was not yet qualified to deal at the Corn Market without Frederick but he had accompanied him many times and knew and was known by, several of the merchants there. Dressed smartly, James in fact in his very best clothes, Ben suggested they avoid the turmoil of London Bridge by walking to Horsleydown and taking a water cab across the river there. "We might get wet this way but there's less chance of being sprayed with muck by the carts, and you'll get a magnificent view of the Tower and Water Gate. That's the gate the traitors are taken through to be imprisoned in the Tower and then hanged, or worse. It makes me shiver just to see it and I'm not a traitor, goodness knows what they feel going under it."

Without mishap, the brothers arrived at Mark Lane in the heart of London's mercantile area, surrounded on all sides by warehouses crammed full of the freight brought up the Thames on each tide, alongside the offices of merchants and companies carrying out the distribution. Cranes fifty feet high, had pendulous bales and packages swinging from them, casks and barrels were being rolled down ramps into cellars and broad wheeled wagons were kicking up the mud and dust in the road, "It's a quagmire when it's wet James, all this dust in the nose is the lesser of the two evils," Ben stopped momentarily at the side of a cart to speak with the driver, the horse waiting patiently, blinkers forcing him to face forwards and a cloud of dust and flies swirling around his head. Other drivers staggered up and down stairs with heavy sacks on their backs, their legs buckling at the knees.

James had been overwhelmed during the past few days with the visions and wonders of London, and he was unprepared to be awestruck yet again by the hurly burly of these narrow streets. He ran after Ben up the steps of an unpretentious building, went through some iron gates and was confronted by a simple but elegant Doric colonnade, the eight pillars of which supported a two storey high building, with more stone steps leading up from either side to two coffee shops above. Around the whole market ranged stalls and counters covered in the little canvas bags and small wooden sample boxes of oats, rye, barley, corn and seeds, just as at King & Bankes, but in vastly greater numbers. The space was crowded with all manner of men creating an unceasing babble of sound. "Who are all these people?" asked James, "there are hundreds in here."

"Stand over here," Ben pulled James to an empty spot next to the stone steps, "and I'll try and point out who's who."

He identified the impassive faced city speculators. Smartly dressed, masking their eagerness with looks of disinterest, looking to buy future stocks at the keenest prices to sell on at the highest prices, never actually touching what they dealt in. "These are the money men pure and simple," Ben explained, "they deal internationally and, above all other traders, determine what price we all have to pay for grain here at home."

There were provincial merchants and millers, plain spoken countrymen, Kent farmers who produced so much of the grain and swarthy looking men, looking very much to James like sailors, "Why would the tars be in here?"

"They'll be some of the Kent hoymen, the hoys are the boats that bring the grain up the Thames from Kent and I don't know all the details, but there are some ancient rites which let some of them collect certain dues here. Apparently, their ancestors provided London with food during a famine or a plague or something, I can't remember, but that's why they are here. That man over there," Ben pointed to a smartly dressed man with a sheaf of papers in his hand and a young man trailing him taking notes, "I'm interested in men like him. They are the factors and supply bakers all over the country by funding the purchase of flour and grain in the first place. I want to be in that position once I've got my own shop up and running."

"I thought you wanted to be a wholesale grocer and open up a sugar refinery," James raised his eyebrows, "that's all you talked about when you were at school with Robert."

"All in good time. I'll need a good deal of cash to invest for that and the best way to make it quickly is to become a factor, so that's step two of my plan, my own shop first though!"

They moved away from the steps and manoeuvred their way through the press, foreign voices mingled with the English. "There'll be Greeks, Germans, French. Not all of them buying or selling, maybe just watching the prices here for their own firms abroad."

"There's no grain in here to supply all these people," James asked, "where is it stored?"

"That's the point of the Exchange, it's not here at all, they would need a space ten times this size, no, it's just the samples here, the grain is at the wharves and warehouses. That's why it's good to be a factor, with a network of connections I can buy and sell a huge amount and it's down to the original owners to deal physically with the transactions and make sure the orders are delivered."

"Sounds a perfect arrangement Ben, I'm wondering now how I'm going to make the most of being in the wine and spirits trade. Seems to me I should be cutting out my middle man as soon as possible, but as I haven't even met him yet, I'll not be telling Mr Jubb that on Friday!" James grinned from ear to ear.

"Don't be too impatient little brother, you've got a lot to grasp. Now, it's a pity I can't take you into Jacks Coffee House up there, I'm not qualified to go in on my own, only with Frederick, but it's an education in itself to see all the commerce that's transacted over those tables. The whole world takes note of the prices agreed here in London, like I said, the price of a loaf of bread is set in this building by these people and you know yourself the political implications of that. Too high and there's a good deal of trouble. Let's go and find something to eat and drink, all this talk of bread is making me starving," and with that they pushed their way back to the iron gates and strolled away down to the bustling streets."

James was inspired, his head whirring with new ideas of how he could translate all this information to his own future. A little respite came from this exhilaration when a letter arrived from home. Sitting at dinner in Mrs West's dining room, Ben opened it up, "Dear old Martha," he said, "she never fails to write and keep me up to date with what's going on in the family, I expect she's missing you too, you've been gone almost a week!"

This letter turned out to be somewhat different from the usual as Martha declared quite quickly that there was little news from home and that all was well. She was writing to remind James to visit the Foundlings Hospital in Bloomsbury and get an understanding of what was provided for the children and how.

"It is very difficult for me to find enough information here in Nottingham, and I suppose being a woman is not helping me either. I know the London Hospital is a very large institution and, without the help of the major gentlefolk I am only trying to set up a tiny home here, but I want to learn from the best in the country. I think in the beginning, we could only take up to six abandoned babies, but that is a start.

Polly has asked that you bring back any pamphlets or leaflets from the shops showing the latest fashions the ladies are wearing in London please and Joe would like any up to date political news you can gather. Finally, Grace has asked, if you go to the theatre would you be so good as to bring any leaflets about the play and the actors - and she is also sure you will meet the King! So you will be very busy on our behalf but I hope will have plenty of time to enjoy with Benjamin."

"Well, I must do this," groaned James, "I owe it to Martha to help, she has always been such a good sister to us and she is quite adamant that her foundlings home will happen. I'll go to the hospital one day next week, I'd like to spend the days with you at the moment, I don't want to make a fool of myself with Jubb on Friday."

"We are going to Covent Garden to the theatre this evening." It was Wednesday morning and the brothers sat drinking tea in Mrs Warner's dining room, "it won't interfere with your day so no worries there. Frederick suggested it and is making up a party with Mr Bankes and their wives. You'll be able to do your research for Grace and with luck get enough fashion ideas for Polly all in one go."

When they arrived outside the doors of the Theatre Royal in Drury Lane, the other members of their party were already waiting in the crowd. Frederick spied Ben as the boys sauntered up and came over, leading them back to where his group stood. "I'm so pleased you managed to persuade this young scamp to come tonight," he spoke to James as he put his arm round Ben's shoulders to give him a fierce hug, "he's a complete philistine, no culture at all. Here, let me introduce you," he turned to his companions, "James Severn, this is my partner Nathaniel Bankes whom I believe you met briefly in the office and this lovely lady is Augusta, his wife, whilst this equally lovely lady on my right, is my wife Ellen."

"My goodness, you are like two peas in a pod!" Augusta smiled, holding out her hand to James, "Please, call me Gussie, everyone does, even your brother. How do you do Benjamin."

Taking her hand he quipped, "His older and I rather think, more handsome brother!"

Ellen greeted James warmly, welcoming him to London, whilst Nathaniel shook hands with both boys and demanded, "What do you know about this play then? It's called The Rivals by that Sheridan chap, did you hear Fred, he owns this theatre outright now since Garrick died. It's supposed to be a comedy so that's an advantage, that last play we saw Gussie made me want to do away with myself it was so depressing. The only enjoyable bit was watching the audience throwing apples at the actors."

The doors of the House opened and the six of them pushed forward in the squeeze making their way to one of the Boxes on the right hand side of the Pit which had perfect views both of the stage and the rest of the auditorium. James had been often to the theatre in Nottingham but this was unlike anything he'd seen there, in the brilliance of hundreds of candles he could not believe the crowds.

"Good heavens Ben, this is a rung up from St Mary Gate, and should I tell Polly that she ought to have a fan if she wants to be in the height of fashion."

"The real reason for the fans is to signify that you have a Box rather than being down with the masses," Ben looked at his hosts, "Frederick and Nathaniel subscribe to the theatre and rent this one for the season."

Nathaniel pulled a face, "Don't remind me, that's why my wife forces me to sit through some truly awful productions," he held out glasses of wine, "here, I hope you enjoy this James, Ben has been telling me you are becoming something of an expert!"

The production began, the light supper was eaten, and the interval acts enjoyed. James laughed uproariously, thoroughly enjoying the play, and remarked afterwards, flushing a little with embarrassment, "Maybe it's my provincial ways that found it so funny?"

"I have to own up, we have seen it twice before, but each time it is as captivating as the first. My favourite character is Mrs Malaprop, she is so funny but doesn't know why," Ellen told him and seeing her husband's smile admitted, "Yes, I'm afraid I sometimes muddle my words like she does!"

"Our sister Polly has asked me to describe the latest fashions in London and I shall be able to do so very well now that I have met you both," James flattered the ladies, "but I think she would be completely won over with some illustrations. Where would be the best place to get hold of some?"

"Better than that," Gussie put her hand on his arm, "we will take you to our mantua maker in Oxford Street. I'm sure she will gladly let you have a fashion drawing or two won't she Ellen? I am due for a fitting next week and we had already thought we might go on Tuesday."

"That's a superb idea," Ben answered for his brother, "that way Polly will have completely up to the minute sketches. Nottingham is way behind London so she'll be tickled pink to be the first to know."

"How kind of you both, Tuesday would suit me well," torn between the frightening thought of a morning with these two refined ladies and the relief of having one of his assignments organised, James accepted gracefully, "and next Wednesday I shall visit the Foundlings Hospital on behalf of our other sister, Martha. She is quite intent on setting up a home for orphans in Nottingham, but on a very, very much smaller scale."

"How exciting and I'm thrilled to say we may be able to help there as well. I will ask my friend Arabella Henham to arrange your visit, she is on one of the committees there. In fact, Ellen, why don't you come too if you are free, Arabella is always trying to get us involved and this will be a good opportunity to see what we might like to do."

CHAPTER NINETEEN
London 1781
England have been at war with the Dutch since Dec 1780

Friday came, and James took a cab to the offices of Merriman & Jubb in Bow Lane, not at all far from King & Bankes. Charles Jubb was a distinguished looking gentleman, he had a long, pointed nose and enquiring grey eyes looked at James from under his immaculately powdered and dressed wig. Happy with what he saw, he spoke in a gentle, refined voice, "Good morning to you young man, I am very pleased to meet you at last and I trust your father is well and prospering. We have never met in person of course, but I like to think of him as a friend after all these years. Come, come, James, take a seat here. Can I call for some refreshment for you?"

By the time Charles drew breath, James had had the opportunity to calm his nerves and now sat relaxed and at ease.

"I am heartily glad to meet you Sir," he said, "I have a million questions. I am determined that my father's vintners will flourish when he hands it on and he may have told you also that it is our intention to open another shop in Nottingham in which to increase our range of wines. I will need your advice on that."

"First things first, you are an eager young pup! Let me start with some history my boy," Charles handed him a cup of the dark, strong, coffee that a young assistant had brought into the office, "it is always useful to start at the beginning and if you are to sell fine wines to educated gentlemen, it is essential that you know where it comes from and how it is produced." He settled back into his chair, a distant look in his eyes as he started to talk about his life's work.

"Just about all European wines come from the vine Vitis Vinifera," he began, "and this vine has been cultivated in Europe for centuries. All these years of propagation have resulted in many different varieties which produce very good quality grapes, the finest of which it is generally agreed, grow in France. So, dear boy, before we come onto the political reasons as to why you and most of your father's generation know nothing but Portuguese and maybe Spanish, wines, let me tell you about the best, let me tell you about French wine."

Pausing to take a sip of his coffee, he continued, "The same specie of grape can be grown in different countries of course or in different regions of the same country but it is the particular combination of soil and climate, what the French call the 'terroir', that will determine the taste and the quality of the wine. For example, the same vine can produce grapes in, say, Germany or Austria that I would find hard to recognise as the identical grapes grown in France. This is not to say that they are inferior, just different. Unsurprisingly, the wine growers have learned over the centuries which type of grape will flourish in which area of the country as there has to be perfect harmony between the species, the climate and the soil in order to produce fine wines."

He looked over to James and smiled, "You may have thought all you needed was sunshine. Well, heat and moisture are most necessary as well as sunshine but, just as important, is air. That is why practically all the best wines are grown on hillsides, often so steep that terraces must be formed and in this way the sun can bathe each vine individually and air can flow round them freely. In the Douro region of Portugal where you know the port wines you drink emanate, it is so hot that the vines must always be on terraces for this very reason."

Charles Jubb was now completely absorbed, his hands clasped together in front of him, fingers forming the shape of a cathedral spire, he continued as if giving a sermon in church on a Sunday. James sat listening carefully, fully engrossed as his 'minister' spoke of the differing weather patterns, the dangers of spring frosts, the damage occasioned by hail storms, the vital importance of the weather at each stage of the growth. The budding season in March and April, the fruiting season in September and October and the all important wood ripening time after the harvest, necessary for the vines to flourish the following year.

James felt little need to interrupt as he was sure his questions would be answered in due course. Much of the information was not entirely new to him, but this venerable expert sitting opposite held him spell bound as he talked on with a detailed account of how the cultivation, planting, pruning, hoeing, staking and treatment of the vines and then the fermentation of the perfectly ripe, sugar laden grapes produced the nectar known as 'good' wine.

When Jubb suddenly sat up straight and enquired, "What do you think about taking an early repast together, I can continue your education whilst we eat." James, taken aback, stuttered, "Absolutely Sir, that would be most agreeable."

"We might even try a few of the wines we are going to talk about next, our dining room here is where we entertain valued customers such as yourself," Charles granted himself the faint trace of a smile, "and allow them a tasting."

By the end of the afternoon James was very much wiser. He now knew that as a wine merchant he could rely on the consistent taste and quality of each specific wine, "Some year's harvests produce better or worse wine, more or less acidity, and by blending, the growers use their experience and judgement to produce a standard of quality and therefore, of price, each year."

"But I thought blending was only needed for inferior wines?"

"Not at all. Many French wines and our two most popular wines, port and champagne are always blended. It is only the very, very finest growths which are not."

They were seated, waiting to enjoy their meal when Jubb gave James some advice, "At this moment in history, I would not recommend a provincial wine merchant, and especially a young man such as yourself just setting out in the trade, to stock much French wine. As you already know, the generations who drank only French wine and believed it superior are gone and it will take a great deal of persuasion to capture a new clientele and indeed, until the government relents on the present pernicious taxation, only the more affluent can afford to drink it. But you have, I'm sure, a certain monied population in Nottingham and as their numbers are increasing rapidly amongst the merchant classes, I shall suggest you do carry a small amount of claret, in which case, we shall concentrate our discussion on this, the good red wine from Bordeaux, whilst we enjoy our dinner. We can meet again to discuss the Iberian wines."

The meal was served by two white gloved waiters and Jubb poured a little red wine from a bottle standing on a side table close to his elbow, into each of their glasses and carried on speaking, "The trade in claret has a very long history with England. Bordeaux together with some of the best vineyards in France have been under English rule at various times over the years and the merchants from there were encouraged to bring their wine across the water and, indeed, were even given a special status to sell it in London. These libations were called 'Gascon' wines for maybe three centuries, and the Gascon merchants became very rich and powerful. Eventually, and not unsurprisingly, they upset our City Aldermen and their privileges would be gradually denied they were told, if they did not agree to give up their nationality and settle in London permanently. One effect of so many of them choosing to leave our capital rather than become Englishmen, was that Bordeaux wines were then available to be imported into many of our other cities and it opened up the rest of the country to the wine's delights."

"So politics, taxes and wine have always gone hand in hand, not just recently?"

"Exactly, dear boy, since the time of King John, but it's not just one way, the government has also taken steps to protect the wine trade, the Vintners Company have the right to enter all establishments who sell wine, check the quality and destroy it if they see fit." Raising his glass to his lips, he looked James in the eye, "Now, what do you think of this wine? Tell me what you can smell and taste. Tell me what it makes you imagine or think of."

James raised the glass by its beautiful, twisted stem to his nose and breathed in deeply, then exhaling he took a mouthful of the inky, dark red wine, savouring the smooth liquid in his mouth, and answered, "It is delicious. It feels soft on my tongue, not astringent at all, perfumed and I'm sure I can taste plums."

"That's not bad my boy," Charles was pleased, "you appear to have the start of what we call a good palate. With more experience and a little guidance I hope you will have the makings of a first rate wine merchant. You will need to learn about all the different grapes and believe me, there is a great deal to know. I am still learning after all these years," Charles was back in his element, "I shall talk this afternoon about two particular clarets which I would anticipate recommending you to take, but first a little more history and geography for you."

The waiters were attentive and they were both served with more roasted lamb and vegetables.

"The name we use, claret, comes from the original French name for the wine of the Gironde region, 'clairette'. It was then a very much lighter wine both in colour and taste but now that we are able to age the wine longer, we mature it in the bottles, it develops into this more complex, dark red, sensuous liquid. In making claret it is said that man does not help or hinder nature, man just intervenes to remove any possible cause of imperfection. Nature produces this wine, perfectly in harmony, not too much or too little sugar, not too much or too little tannin or acid, a perfect balance. This variety we are drinking comes from the Médoc, one of the six principal districts where claret is produced, situated on the gravel banks above the Gironde estuary, north of Bordeaux. Luckily I thought to bring this Cassini map," he stopped to open out a large map of south west France and pointed to Bordeaux, "you see here, where these two rivers meet and flow to the sea, this is the Gironde. I will only mention today, two of the other districts, Graves and Sauternes," here he opened a large plan of the Bordeaux vineyards and laying it over the map, pointed to the areas, "as I must be careful not to overwhelm you with facts, and in any case, we will concentrate on Médoc, where the usual specie of Vitis Vinifera is the Malbec grape. These vines are grown on gentle hills, the soil being chiefly composed of gravel, rich in silicates and sometimes chalky."

James settled back, listening to the exotic names of the vineyards roll off Charles's tongue. Labarde, Cantenac and Margaux. St Julien and Pouillac and the celebrated Chateaux Lafite, Latour and Mouton. Almost immediately, he sat up again, just a little bit straighter, the wine and words were soporific.

Charles spoke of the quality of the wines from the different vineyards and finished by telling James, "This wine is from vines in the Margaux area, not the very best which is Chateau Margaux itself, but Chateau Ferrière, still a very good wine and one I believe would suit your potential clientele. The family Ferrière have been growing grapes in their vineyards situated behind stone walls in the centre of the village of Margaux for some fifty years now and their wines are becoming known and respected." Taking another sip and then a short respite to finish his meat, he continued, " I should interject here, you will hear all sorts of pronunciations of these places, Margoose, Margon or worse," he stopped to chuckle quietly, "the funniest to me is the famous Chateau Haut-Brion in the Graves district, often said as O'Brian such that people believe it to be owned by an Irishman!"

James laughed politely as Charles took out his handkerchief to dab at his eyes, and thanked God silently for not having, at least not yet, said anything to embarrass himself and cause Charles to laugh like this.

Taking two clean glasses, Charles poured from a second bottle, "This is the second claret I would recommend to you, even though, as I have been at pains to advise, I do not in any way suggest you should hold much in the way of French stock, however it is good to give your customers a choice so that they may dazzle you with their insights as to their preferences. Some men have a huge desire to impress, with or without foundation," and he chuckled again, "and this is also from the Médoc, but this time from the district of St Julien where the soil is just a little richer, still mainly gravel and the wines are very fine. St Julien lies between Margaux and Pauillac, where, amongst others, the finest vineyards of the Médoc are situated, perhaps you remember their names?"

James, being tested was pleased that he could remember, "Chateaux Lafite, Mouton and Latour" and breathed a sigh of relief.

"This is from Chateau Lagrange, part of a very picturesque estate owned by the Baron de Brane. I went there in '71, had a marvellous visit." His eyes held a distant look, James cleared his throat, and Charles focussed again abruptly, "The Baron also owns the Mouton vineyards, and here the terroir is typically gravelly but maybe a little more sand and traces of iron. Again, this is the Malbec grape and tastes very similar to our first wine. By the way, the Malbec grape is also called the Côt grape, so listen out for that. Can you taste any subtle differences?"

James wasn't sure how to put it into words but he tried, "Well, it seems a little more, I don't quite know how to describe it, maybe richer, but it is still fresh, smooth and maybe some blackcurrants added to the plums? Could there also be a hint of spice?" He felt sure he was blushing, "I'm sorry, this is all new to me to be talking this way, I feel a little foolish to be honest."

"Well that will soon change," Charles looked at him kindly, "the good thing is you can taste a difference and you will become very happy to try and describe this to your customers in time." Summoning yet two more clean glasses he went on, "our final wine of the day will be a sweet, white Sauternes. It is especially popular with the ladies, as is Champagne of course but we will address that another time, and I am quite partial to the Sauternes too, perhaps when eating sweet meats." He called for the waiter to remove their plates and requested dessert fruits.

"Sauternes is a relatively small region, south of Bordeaux, producing almost exclusively white wines. Here the soil is a mixture of clay and gravel or chalk and clay, and the wealth of sunshine ensures an excellent, naturally sweet grape. The best comes from Chateau Yquem, but that I believe will be too expensive for the provinces, so we are tasting a wine from a less well known vineyard, Chateau Roumieu, located on the chalk-clay plateau of Haut-Barsac. I will let you taste it before I continue," Charles had a smile on his face which James wondered at, but he picked up his glass and tasted the sweet nectar.

"My word but that is luscious," he exclaimed, "I can certainly see how it would be popular with the ladies, my sisters will love it. It is richer and sweeter than the Portuguese white wine that my father has tried in the past. I'm sure I can taste honey and ginger. Why are you smiling?"

"Well, I didn't want to tell you this before you drank it, but Sauternes is made from grapes which have, to put it mildly, become a little over ripe and are in fact beginning to rot. If the weather conditions are moist, the ripe grapes become infected with a grey fungus,the name of which is botrytis cinerea but I don't expect you to remember that, and although you would think that a grey rot would destroy the crop, because the grapes are perfectly ripe when infected and are then exposed to drier conditions, they become a little like raisins. That means they become partially dehydrated but retain all their sugar content and this necessitates more grapes to make the same amount of liquid. In this way they produce particularly fine and concentrated sweet wine. Now this I do expect you to remember, this infection is known as 'noble rot'"

The afternoon over, James left Merriman & Jubb his head buzzing, he had not realised how interesting his future career was going to be, he would never stop learning either, and he went back to Bermondsey full of enthusiasm, longing to talk with his brother.

CHAPTER TWENTY
London 1781
The French defeat the British at Chesapeake Bay in September

"Stop!" Ben cried, "you are exhausting me, and what's more, all this talk of wine has set my taste buds on fire, let's go and have a glass or two at Simon's if you must carry on."

James did continue, he tried to repeat everything he had learned that day, "and I'm to meet with Charles, yes, he asked me to call him Charles, and his partner Mr Merriman again next Friday to discuss the Iberian wines. He, that is, Charles, says we will not have dinner this time as he dining with Lord someone or other, which is a pity because did I tell you, he's explaining why the taste of a wine influences the taste of the food."

"Yes, my dear James, you did tell me, and more than once!" His eyes wide, making a grimace, he glanced over to the door "thank goodness, here are Samuel and Ned, let's go and join them. We will have plenty of time over the next two weeks to discuss your plans for Severns and can work out what you need, get an idea of the costs and figures and where you will get the money from to start up a merchants, but for now, it's drinking time. Sam, Ned, 'How do you do, are you both free for the evening?"

James spent as much time as he could with Ben during the next week, he was keen to understand K&B's systems and even donned a sack apron to join the men unloading, hoisting and stacking to see how stock maintenance and counting was handled. He shadowed Ben on the shop floor dealing with the customers and getting to know the ordering and distribution systems. He spent hours in the office with Frederick who showed him the financial ledgers and talked of Balance Sheets and Profit and Loss accounts.

"It makes father's vintners shop look very small fry," he confessed to Ben over supper one evening, "but Severns does just support the family and we have a pretty good life. The thing is, it's just not enough for me and now that father has finally come round, I want a much bigger, more profitable show. I see so many merchants rising up in the country around me and I want to be one of them. Thanks to you, Ben, I realise I must concentrate on the financial side of a business just as much as knowing my products, the wines and spirits."

Friday, he presented himself back at Merriman & Jubb and was shown to a large salon where Charles introduced him to Richard Merriman, his Partner. Over coffee and macaroons, Merriman recited the history of the Iberian wines. "You'll know some of this James, but as you found out from Charles last week, it is our practice to start at the beginning. There is everything to gain and nothing to lose by knowing a few elementary truths about wine."

"I am indebted to you Sir. I can say quite truthfully that it will be good for me to be reminded of what I have already learned and I am sure there will be much that you say that will be new to me,"

"Port has a very interesting history, just as the French wines do, and surprisingly, owes its existence chiefly to the industry of Englishmen," settling back in his chair, Merriman took on the air of an authoritarian school master, "back at the end of the sixteenth century some adventurous Devonshire men went to Lisbon and Oporto, their main purpose being to buy locally and send back to England the produce of Brazil, the country Portugal had lately discovered and closed to trade with all other nations, including England. Then, during the last century, our English fleets in the Atlantic were ordered to repair to Oporto or Lisbon to take up vast quantities of wine for the sailors. They now, as you know, have rum to stave off scurvy, but back then it was a daily ration of wine. Well, because of this great demand, the Englishmen devoted their spare time to planting more and more vineyards on the sun-baked hills of the Douro Valley."

"I think we should taste this," Charles poured them all mouthful of rich, dark vintage port and catching his Partner's frown, "sorry Richard, I didn't mean to interrupt!"

"The Portuguese wine growers were not a bit like the French, they had neither the knowledge nor the will to find foreign markets, they suffered from corrupt officials and did not improve their conditions or protect themselves. This left them at the mercy of our men who bought the wine at ridiculously low prices and sold it very profitably in England. Then politics came into play, old King William prohibited the import of French wines for a while and when trade finally resumed, as you know, we have taxed French wine grossly whilst encouraging the importation of Portuguese. These Portuguese concerns are still mainly in the hands of Englishmen, and that is why the country drinks port, but, make no mistake, port can be remarkably good!"

Taking a sip from his glass, Merriman glanced up and glowered, "It is, as you also know, a fortified wine," Charles who had been about to speak, closed his mouth rather sharply, "but it is not fortified as you may have thought in order to preserve it better in the shipping, it is a case of man intervening to improve nature."

"Ah, the exact opposite to the situation with a claret," James said.

His complacency was quietly dampened by Merriman's sardonic, "Quite. If I may continue!" He paused to emphasise his point, "you discussed with Charles the process of fermentation last week, and in the case of port, when a certain amount of the grape sugar has transformed to alcohol, brandy is added to the liquid which checks any further fermentation. Because this raises the alcohol level of the wine immediately, any remaining sugar is left as just that, sugar. No more alcohol is made."

He handed James another glass with a mouthful of a slightly paler, lighter liquid, "Now taste this one young sir, we will discuss it later. Once the wine is sent by barges down the river Douro to Oporto - have you seen the map? Charles, did we bring one?" Charles jumped up to open a map of the Iberian Peninsular which he placed in front of James, and Merriman pointed, "it is stored in vast warehouses or lodges and this is when the shippers have to make an extremely important decision. Shall they keep it bottled, in the lodge for two years and then allow it to come to England to be sold, the wine having improved over those two years to become the captivating and generous wine we know as vintage port? Or at that stage does it lack body, bouquet or the 'right' quality. If so, it must be kept in Oporto in large flasks with newer and better wines added frequently until the whole improves sufficiently in quality to become tawny port. Lighter in body and colour."

He reached forward and poured a third measure for them each, "Now, here is yet another type of port, you will taste an obvious difference I hope. Sometimes a vintage port - what is the definition?" he peered at James.

"A vintage port, Sir, is one fit to be bottled and shipped after being kept in the lodges, untouched, for two years."

"Exactly, well sometimes a lesser vintage port will be kept in the wooden flasks for an extended number of years before it is bottled. By letting the air in, unlike the sealed bottles, it takes on a little less colour and strength than a vintage port but more than a tawny port, and that is what makes a ruby port."

James was about to ask for a little more information about ruby port when Merriman barked, "What important fact have I not told you?" His momentary hesitation led to Merriman carrying straight on, "You will notice that I have not told you which specific grapes are used in the making of these ports and that is for a very good reason, I do not know. Many grape varieties are, rather randomly, planted together in the vineyards, sometimes even white grapes too."

The meeting was over without warning. Merriman got to his feet and announced, "Dinner with Lord Luscombe to discuss his cellar, come Charles, we must leave now. James, we will leave you in the capable hands of Matthew Thorpe, he is one of our senior apprentices and it will be good for him to tell you about sherry and madeira. I assure you he is very knowledgeable." With that they said goodbye and James was still thanking the gentlemen profusely for their time as they left the room.

The door reopened almost immediately, "How do you do, I'm Matthew and very pleased to be here. You've met Mr Merriman then? I can tell by the look on your face, he's as curt as Jubby is friendly don't you think? Was it a bit like being back at school?"

"I should say, but without the threat of a beating for not paying attention, although, I wasn't quite sure even about that!"

The two young men settled down to an enjoyable and relaxed meeting. Knowing that true sherry came from the Jerez district of Spain, James learned from Matthew, that, again, it was the mixture of the grape, the soil and the method of fermentation that determined it's unique taste. "At the beginning of the century trade was badly affected by the war with Spain, everyone arguing about everyone's claim to the throne after Charles II died - inconsiderate of him to die without any children don't you think?" he chuckled, "anyway, then the good old Methuen treaty was signed and that dampened the Spanish trade even further."

Just as his superiors had done, Matthew took some small glasses from the cabinet ranging along the side of the room, and poured a small amount of sherry into the first two. Handing one over he went on, "Strangely enough, the drop in trade helped the sherry makers. As they couldn't sell it, the sherry sat around in oak barrels in the Bodegas, and as smaller quantities were drawn off, they topped the barrels up with newer sherry and the air getting in gave the liquid more concentrated and nutty flavours. They still do this and call it the solera system and what makes sherry so different from other wines is that when the fermentation is taking place, a scum forms on the surface that is called the flor and it is this that gives the wine it's specific character." He paused dramatically to take an ostentatious sip from his glass, 'he's been watching Mr Merriman' James smiled to himself, "In addition, when our national taste moved so much towards sweet, strong wines, the producers decided to fortify it with brandy, and you know what that does?"

"Kills off the fermentation."

"Yes, and this made the wine oxidise, that's react with the air, even more and to develop a real deep perfume. This one is called Oloroso, it means pungent in Spanish. Some districts used less brandy and produced a lighter, more delicate sherry with a taste that reminded them of apples, Manzanilla, which means little apples."

"I didn't realise I would be learning a foreign language as well."

"There's more," Matthew had poured the second wine into new glasses, "taste this Manzanilla, you can really taste a difference from the first, can't you? Then there is this third style, made by limiting the number of times fresh wine is added to the solera, and it produces a wine that reminded them of a neighbouring wine from a place called Montilla, so it's called Amontillado. It's quite fragrant from the flor. Here, taste it."

"All three taste very different, I think at the moment I prefer this one," he gestured to the second glass, "Manzanilla, right? I'm pretty sure that the people likely to be my clients will be drinking Oloroso at the moment, I shall have to educate them!"

"Good luck with that," Matthew drained his glass, and looking at the bottle thought better of filling it again, "Politics took a toll as usual and in fact the Spanish growers had huge battles with the merchants, but the merchants have won. Of all the wines, sherry is testament to the triumph of the blenders art. Gosh, that sounds as if I've learned it off by heart from Mr Merriman, and I have!" he bellowed with laughter and James joined in until their sides hurt.

When he calmed down, Matthew continued, "Back to blending. Sometimes they add wine made from a very sweet grape, Pedro Ximénez or sometimes a dark brown Spanish wine to add colour. Sorry, I can't remember the name of that one, I only remember Pedro as it makes me think of a fisherman or something!" Which set them off laughing again.

"I'd better not have any more of this, I can't concentrate! Does the constant blending ensure a continuity of quality and taste for the buyers, is that right?" asked James.

"Absolutely, and another unique property of sherry is that it will not deteriorate if you leave it uncorked for a while. It remains just the same. You try doing that with champagne, ugh!"

Agreeing not to taste it, the two young men spoke finally of madeira, a sweet, thick wine from the Portuguese Madeira Islands. "It has to come here on ships making the long passage from the East Indies, and learning from the early port trade, the producers added brandy to stop the wine spoiling over the months. Remarkably, they also discovered that the intense heat in the ships holds changed the nature of the wine."

"Is this how it is produced still?"

"No, now that madeira wine has become so popular, ageing it on these long journeys costs too much, so the producers on the Island have worked out that they can store it out there, leaving it on trestles in estufas which are special rooms, and the tropical sun does the job for them."

He was sorry when the discussions came to an end, but James took his leave and with yet more notes written laboriously by the apprentices as part of their training, copies of which Charles had generously given to him, he took a hackney back to Grange Walk. There he picked up his pen and paper to add, in his neat and tidy writing, his own, copious comments.

§

"It's your last few days in the city James, we should do something after church on Sunday, something that will be interesting to tell the boys at home, after all, you've done your duty for the girls. I think we should go to Astley's circus, there's nothing like it been to Nottingham I'll be bound. Also, you've been studying practically non stop since you arrived and we don't want you becoming a dull chap. I know, I'll ask Mrs Warner if she would like to come along. She must be lonely without her husband, she hardly ever goes out and I'll see if she would like to bring a friend too, then it will be a jolly party."

After the Sunday service they gathered outside the church and the brothers looked at each other in surprise. Kitty Warner looked strikingly different. Out of her weekday clothes and dressed in a charming robe, the fabric covered in sprigs of flowers, it was as if she herself had blossomed too. Her dark, almost black hair was neatly curled and pinned up under a broad brimmed straw hat trimmed with blue ribbon and she wore a matching pale blue cloak to save her from the slight chill in the May air. She was arm in arm with an older lady, "Benjamin, James, this is Maria Shaw, we have been dear friends it seems for ever, indeed, Maria was a good friend to my mother before me. With Nathan being away she keeps me company most of the time and we are so looking forward to the circus."

"Don't remind me of my age young lady, I may look like an old goose but at heart I'm still a young duckling. Oh no, I don't mean that do I," and Maria convulsed with infectious laughter, "it must have been that deathly sermon, it's put my brain, or at least what's left of it, to sleep. But it's true, we are looking forward to Astley's. It's about time Kitty had some real fun with fun young people instead of with an old duck like me. I've got the right fowl this time!"

Maria felt it her role to entertain and the walk to Westminster Bridge passed quickly and without incident in spite of Maria's many entreaties to "mind that heap of muck dears, you'll disappear up to your armpits" or "I hope you boys have your money wallets deep in your trousers, there's nothing but pickpockets out here on a Sunday." She was an exuberant lady and her bright eyes, sparkling from within the lines and wrinkles of her face, exacerbated no doubt by the constant exclamations and laughter, gave her the air of a mischievous monkey.

Kitty revealed that Maria's late husband had owned one of the many tanneries in Bermondsey and that since his death some ten years before, two of their sons had taken over. "Smelly occupation tanning," Maria screwed up her nose, "but some beautiful end results. Look at Kitty's shoes, lovely aren't they, such fine leather. Watch out for that horse muck dear, they won't be so lovely if you kick that!"

"Mrs Warner, would you like to stop for refreshments, we have plenty of time and The Tabard Inn is on our way. It has a good reputation for a decent plate of ordinary, and at this time of day there shouldn't be too many rough necks around."

"Yes please Benjamin, what a lovely idea and please, call me Kitty. Maria has spoken already of age and being addressed so formally is making me feel ancient!"

The happy band arrived at The Tabard and were shown to an old oak table in the corner of the main dining room where not only could they sit and talk in comparative quiet, but the situation afforded the ladies an excellent view of the whole room. "Oh I do love to watch people," admitted Maria with a guilty smile, "it can often make me feel so much better about myself." Laughing and talking together they enjoyed a meal of chicken pies and roasted salmon with, at Kitty's insistence, cabbage and carrots. James tried to recommend some wines but Ben said quite firmly, "No, you and I are having ale and the ladies will have glasses of port wine."

By the time the four of them arrived at Westminster Bridge, spirits were high and anticipation higher. They were not disappointed and even though Mr Astley himself was not riding, his pupils put on an exhilarating show. Young men, dressed in colourful, skin tight breeches and waistcoats, wearing soft leather slippers, balanced precariously on the bare backs of the horses as they galloped at great speed around the circular arena, and as if that were not marvellous enough, they amazed the audience with acrobatics and feats of daring. Accompanied by the rousing sound of fifes and drums, the riders thrilled the adults and children alike.

"I loved the Little Military Horse," Kitty said dreamily, as they walked away after the show, "however could he learn to count? When they pretended to shoot him and he feigned death it looked so real I thought I was going to cry."

"At least they didn't shoot him for getting his arithmetic wrong," joked Ben, "but then why would he get it wrong, he's supposed to be able to read his trainer's mind too." Maria's laugh got them all going again, and Kitty was saying, "It was all so wonderful, the tumblers were so clever, did you count how many of them made that human tower, and I just adored the clown, he was such a fool. Maria, what did you think of the pantomime, I must admit I couldn't quite follow the story all the time."

"I don't think that mattered too much, it all looked suitably dramatic don't you agree James, I noticed you laughing at one point where I am certain it was supposed to be sad!" Maria collapsed again, howling.

"I thoroughly enjoyed the show even though I am not at all fond of horses," laughed James, "in fact I'd go so far as to say I thoroughly detest them, but that's if I have to actually get up on one of the dreadful beasts! Every time I have anything to do with one," he rubbed his left shoulder, " I end up getting hurt!"

"Oh, thank you Ben for asking us to join you," Kitty's face glowed, "I have had such a lovely day, it is a very long time since I enjoyed myself so much."

By the time they reached Grange Walk that evening, Ben realised that, because of Kitty, he too had enjoyed himself more than he had done for a very long time.

CHAPTER TWENTY ONE
London & Nottingham 1781
The British Surrender at Yorktown in September but the war
continues in Europe

James left London early the following Thursday morning with competing emotions. Not wanting to leave the intoxicating city but anxious to get home. Outside the 'Swan with Two Necks' he bid a heartfelt farewell to Ben, begging him to come to Nottingham before long to see everyone, climbed aboard the stage coach and settled himself onto one of the topmost outside seats. "All in all," he rationalised his thoughts, "it's better to be going home. I've done everything I planned to do and more, and I've really missed everyone and have so much to tell them."

The arrival of the stage coach at The White Lion on Friday night caused the customary commotion. The "halloo" of the coachman's horn heralding their approach, the clattering of hooves as the horses swept into the yard, the clinking of the harnesses, the calls of the ostlers as they ran to tend the horses and the rapid footsteps of the porters, anxious to earn their tips for unloading and carrying the baggage into the coaching inn. James climbed down warily from his seat, the long and slow journey had made him ache all over and the windblown rain that afternoon had penetrated down the collar of his coat leaving him cold and damp. The euphoria of the previous weeks had deserted him. He heard a call, "James my boy," and saw through the gloom of the lighted flares in the yard, a reception committee of smiling faces, "we have come to meet the prodigal son!"

James's mood was instantly restored and he hurried to greet and hug his father and brother Josiah, "How good of you to come, it is so good to see you," he was being ushered towards an old brown and white horse standing in the shafts of a small wagon, "Joe, be careful with those packages, try not to drop them. Here let me take my travel bag from you?"

"Francis has lent us Tom with his horse and wagon," William explained, "there is no moon to see by tonight and with all the rain, the roads are just a black mire." As if on cue, the old horse gave a great snort sending chaff flying from his nose bag as he stood contentedly munching away on his oats. They clambered aboard, Tom gee'd up and they set off along the dark streets, home to Weekday Cross. James felt the tiredness wash over him, "I have so much to tell you but I shall wait until we are all together, else having to tell it all many times I shall end up without a voice for at least a month," he punched Josiah playfully on the arm, "but this much I will say now, Benjamin is in fine fettle and I have had the most interesting and enjoyable visit. Father I am so grateful that you allowed me to go, I shall not disappoint you with all that I have learnt."

"We have heaps to tell you too James, they've laid the foundation stone for the new hospital you know, and Mr Cook put in his tender for the glass and we have won some of the glazing work. It's really exciting."

"All in good time Joe," his father opened the door and James breathed a contented sigh, it was good to be home again. Fanny brought ale, bread, some pickled meats and cheese and he realised he was ravenous, dinner had been hours ago and whilst he ate, Martha fussed around him, "We have missed you so much and are very glad you are home, safe and sound. I fear you look exhausted, we will not keep you long this evening."

"I shall be extremely pleased to sleep in my own bed again," admitted James, "and no noise from you two rogues," he pointed to his younger brothers, "but at least I do know you, my nights at the Northampton inn, sharing with strangers, has made me surprisingly fond of you both!"

The seductive aromas of beef steaks, roasted chicken and pastry roused James from his sleep, he stretched his legs, bounded out of bed wincing at the ache still in his back and prepared himself for the day. "Good morning Martha, Fanny," he said brightly, "or rather, good afternoon. I cannot believe I have slept so long. I didn't hear my brothers leave nor," he grinned as he saw Grace enter the room from the kitchen, "did I hear Gracie's caterwauling." Grace's face fell and James said kindly, "I've missed your singing, you're just as good as some of the flower sellers I heard in London. Mind you, I'm pleased to say your breath doesn't smell of brandy like most of theirs!"

"Am I truly?" her eyes lit up again, "do you think I'll be good enough to go on the stage when I'm older?"

"One thing at a time little miss, I'd like a jug of porter right now please."

Polly was able to join them for dinner, still held, to her chagrin, at one o'clock and James was eager to hand out the gifts he had brought. He passed Polly the sketches given to him by Madame Leclerc the mantua maker, "I don't reckon she's been any nearer to France in her life than I have, but Frederick King's wife Ellen, and Mr Bankes' wife Augusta, think her very talented and as they are both very fashionable ladies, who am I to argue," and he then presented her with another, larger packet, "and here is a length of fabric, sufficient I am assured, to make a matching robe and petticoat. I am also led to believe that these printed cottons are all the rage in London and when I described you, well I described the colour of your hair, I was assured this peach coloured print would be ideal."

Polly hugged and kissed James and moved to a seat nearer the window to pore over the drawings, small exclamations of pleasure escaping her lips from time to time.

"For you, Martha, I have some leaflets and information about the Foundlings Hospital. Mrs Bankes was very kind and introduced me to an Arabella Henham ..."

"Not LADY Arabella Henham," the squeal came from Polly, looking up from the drawings momentarily, "she is so well known in fashionable circles, oh James you are so lucky, I would love to meet her. What was she like?"

"Well I didn't know she was titled at first but she is very approachable and a down to earth lady for all that," he handed Martha a small brown packet, "and I have a little present for you, from Paternoster Street, the book buyers paradise!"

Even before all the wrapping was torn off she exclaimed, "Oh how wonderful, it is Mr Fielding's book, 'The Adventures of Tom Jones'. I have so wanted to read this, Tom is an orphan boy - just like those I wish to help. But James, it must have been so expensive, thank you dear brother, I could not be more pleased."

"For my popinjay, or as I have learnt recently to call you, macaroni, brother," he said mysteriously and watched as George drew from the wrappings, a set of matching shoe and breeches buckles, "only plated and paste I'm afraid, funds wouldn't run to precious gems - you'll have to wait a few years for them, and Joe, here I have brought you a copy of an engraving of the Map of the Known World. It is by a chap called Prinald, English although his name doesn't sound it, and according to Ben he is supposed to be one of the best. It's right up to date, drawn in '66 I think, so I'm hoping that it's newer than the one you pore over with Thaddeus."

"We're happy for you to go away more often if you bring back such presents each time," joked George, swallowing his usual resentment."

"I've not forgotten you Fanny, here is a lace kerchief which will look very fine on your Sunday dress and Grace, for you I have the leaflets from the Theatre Royal Drury Lane, and look, there are the words to some of the latest songs. I can't help with the music, but I bet you will hear someone singing in the street and I know you can pick the tunes up quickly. I hope you have been concentrating on your reading lessons with Aunt Martha, and here is a little fan, so you can pretend you are a great lady at the theatre. Only watching, not performing! Now, where is our Dolly, I have a box of candied fruit for her when she comes in and after dinner I will go along to Jack and Ann's, I have a box of sweetmeats for them and a pull along little horse for Jon."

Looking at the smiling faces around him, he turned to William, "So, as you can see Father, I have spent this year's profits all in one go, so for you I have only a head full of ideas and a whole sheaf of information from Merriman & Jubb to make sure we can bring them into being. Well, and just a little something else, a pound of Benjamin's finest tobacco."

William was overcome, the tobacco was presented to him in a magnificent box, made of mahogany and shaped like a sea chest. His voice close to breaking, he said, "Thank goodness it has a lock, I shall keep the key close to me so all you young villains cannot help yourselves."

As soon as he could, James met up with Francis, "I have so much to discuss with you, I had the best time in London with Ben," James took the jugs of ale from the landlady at The Crown & Cushion, "Thank you Mrs Else. Let's sit over here Francis and first, tell me how the Crosland empire is faring?"

"My latest interest is in these Enclosure Acts, I'm all in favour of them, it's far more efficient to work larger tracts of land where we can benefit from the machinery and knowledge that we now have. Crop yields are greater and that can only be to the benefit of everyone, rich and poor alike."

"Yes, there is so much resistance but I've heard a lot of tenants are in favour too, the compensation they get from the government has been good. I suppose it's hard on those that don't want to give up the old ways and hard for the small holders to lose the common land for grazing, but it's progress, it has to be done. They should try to come to an arrangement with the new land owners."

"It's good for English industry too, the tenants who haven't wanted to stay have taken their cash and moved to the towns where we are crying out for workers. If you think about it, it's not going to do you and me any harm either, more people in town means more customers at our shops. I'm taking advantage of it anyway," Francis downed his ale, "I've bought a few acres out at Langar, close to your Jack's land, but I'm not throwing the tenants out, as long as I can trust them I need to employ them to run the farm for me. I'm increasing my herd and going to build a bigger dairy to make butter and cheese for wholesale."

"Sounds exciting Francis," James was just a bit envious of his friend's progress, "have you had to borrow from the bank or have you found a factor?"

"A factor, it's all tied up with the Middle Pavement properties I'm after. Did you know John Knowles has died? He passed a few weeks ago now and his trustees are hanging onto the properties I have the option to buy and when we were talking, one of the trustees, a fellow called Tyson, said he was looking for investments and well, it's all agreed now, just waiting for the paperwork from Dudley Reave to be finished and we can sign. A lot can happen if you go away for the best part of a month James! Oh and just whilst I think of it, I hear that there's a new landlord at 'The Shepherd and Shepherdess', Sam Morley I think his name is, so you might want to go and introduce yourself, I know you could never persuade old Foster to deal with you."

"Thanks for that, I will. Hope you're not expecting commission though!"

Francis having brought the conversation round to Severns, James rushed on to talk about his visit to London, "Ben is determined to have his grocers shop by next year, then reckons he'll become a factor and make some money so he can open up as a wholesaler. I'm sure he'll do it too, he's very single minded and hard working."

"I wonder who that reminds me of! Another pint," and Francis beckoned over Mrs Else.

"The best news is, I've got father round to seeing the sense in having another shop and starting up as a merchant. It will take Severns to the next level but keen as I am to get going, I have to buckle down for a while longer and really get to grips with the financial side of things. If we are to expand we'll need capital and not just for the stock, the gentry are demanding longer and longer credit, and if I want the Bank to lend it to me, we'll need to show a good profit and a healthy balance sheet."

"Maybe you can persuade your father to let you take over running the current shop completely, he's not a young man anymore is he? More to the point, he just about gave up on it for all those years, after your mother died and he had all that trouble with Billy and it rather went downhill. You'll never get on if he's always there holding you back."

"Don't let him hear you say he's getting old, or he'll never retire. But you're right, I have to run things my way, I have so many ideas but he's a bit too cautious."

The beers gone, Francis stood up, "Well, I'd best be going, I told Polly I'd be back for dinner with her today at three and I need to check on a few things first. She's a bit anxious at the moment as you can imagine."

"Anxious, why?"

"Well, what with losing the first one she's terrified she'll do something to lose this one too."

"Good Lord, congratulations, she didn't say a word when we all met up the other day so I'm sure I'm not supposed to know yet. Good luck my friend, I won't say a word and when she tells us all, I'll put on the best show of surprise you've ever seen."

§

When James had sat down again with William to discuss his visits to Merriman & Jubb, it was very apparent that his father was content with things the way they were. He was however pragmatic and agreed, "Yes, I get tired now at my age, maybe it makes sense for you to take over the greater role of running the shop. You are certainly right that you must understand all the aspects better if you want to have your own business when I am gone."

"You remember we told you Francis is buying some of the properties in the yard behind the Golden Fleece, the ones John Knowles owned, well he should finalise the deal early next year. It includes that old timber house and the newer brick one next to it. You know which ones I mean?"

"Yes lad, I used to live there remember, and I don't go around with my eyes shut even if you youngsters think us old men do!"

"Well I don't think the timber building is right for me, I mean us, at the moment, but Francis and I have talked about us renting the ground floor of the newer one, it would make a fine merchant's shop, plenty of room and Francis has agreed that we could share the caves underneath the old house, they are really extensive. I can take you to see them, they will be perfect for keeping the butts at a good temperature. Also, there are some smaller sheds at the rear if we need any more space for storage or bottling. Then, once the shop is going well, I think we should import our wine directly, old Jubb makes good money from us and we could keep that for ourselves," seeing the look on his father's face he quickly added, "that's well in the future of course, but I do think we should."

"It's good to have ambition at your age but be careful you don't try to do too much too quickly," William had a distant look in his eyes, "and from what you have told me about Benjamin's plans, I think the world's moving too fast for me." Then looking at James directly, "I'm glad to hand over the running to you, and I will agree to us starting the new shop when the premises become available. You will be responsible for talking with the bank for the investment, but you will have my backing. I know you will do well, but just always remember you have a responsibility and an obligation to your family, all of you, to and for each other, and particularly for Martha until she marries. Polly is her husband's responsibility now but you must always make sure that she too is looked after." He poured another glass of port and smiled, "I shall enjoy sitting here in my shop, talking to my old customers and tasting your new wines and maybe I shall find more time to put the world to rights."

James was surprised at such a quick capitulation but grasped the opportunity with both hands. He knew he had to gain more customers, not just more taverns or ale houses who made up the larger part of his present income, but the individuals, and specifically the wealthy individuals of the town, who would be willing to pay the high prices for his French wines.

CHAPTER TWENTY TWO
Nottingham 1781
The British defeat the French in the Bay of Biscay

There was one cloud on James's horizon, "I haven't seen Lizzie for an age," he told Polly one afternoon when they had found time to join Martha for tea at Weekday Cross, "have you any idea what is going on there?"

A look passed between the two sisters, "Come on, tell me what's happening? I used to meet her here with you so often and now that I come to think back, she's not been here for weeks. Has she gone away?"

"Polly, I think you should tell James … what Lizzie came to tell you," said Martha, "it's only fair and," looking at James, "I'm surprised you haven't heard from Frederick."

"Heard what Polly?"

Polly was unable to meet his eyes, "Lizzie came to see me a month or so ago. She said she didn't know how to face you herself but her father has arranged for her to marry Alexander Quincy, you know Charles Quincy the silk merchant's son," she looked up, "obviously a strategic move for Mr King, financial reasons. Lizzie was so upset at the beginning … but I've heard she's a lot happier now. She's going around with a different circle of friends and is full of how wealthy she will be, telling anyone who'll listen that she'll have her own carriage and fine silks to wear. You are better off without someone that shallow James, don't let it upset you." Polly had been furious with her friend when she'd heard the news and she was not about to relent now, "I've cut her before she has the chance to cut me!"

154

James was stunned, "I thought you might say she'd had to go and visit a maiden aunt in the north or something, and that would have been bad enough, but I wasn't expecting this. Why hasn't she tried to speak with me, you'd have thought she would given how close we've been for so long. I thought we had a bit of an understanding." He was struggling to know what to feel and what to say, " Can you invite her here for tea Martha and I could speak with her then? Don't say I'll be here in case she doesn't come. Why would she be worried to talk to me, I don't understand. Do you think she might change her mind?"

"No James, she will not go against her father, and I daresay her brothers are all in favour of the match too, it will be quite advantageous for them. I expect that's why Frederick kept quiet. But I will invite Lizzie to come later this week, I think you deserve an explanation from her direct."

Tea was over and James left feeling downhearted, "Well, I've nothing to distract me from work now," he thought to himself, "onwards and upwards."

"James my dear, I am so sorry I did not tell you myself," Lizzie was flustered, "I was afraid. You know I have always been so fond of you and had even imagined that one day we would be together, but I cannot go against my father's wishes and he had already agreed with Alexander's, I mean Mr Quincy's, father, the terms of the arrangement. I was mortified when he told me and not at all prepared to accept the situation, I had not thought my father so old fashioned. Then, well, when I had met Mr Quincy and saw that he is very handsome and appears to be very well bred, well, it seemed that I should make the best of it and, well, that is why I pretended at first to be happy, and, well, now I feel I truly am in love and am so happy. Oh James, do say you understand and will forgive me, I hate to see you looking cross."

"I'm not cross, I'm sad Lizzie, but more than that, I cannot understand you. Not so much for obeying your father, I realise you feel there is no alternative, but I thought there was enough affection between us since we were children that you would have come to tell me before now. I know that I cannot compete with the wealthy Mr Quincy, it will be many years before I can afford a personal carriage or silk dresses for a wife."

Suddenly he wanted to leave, right that instant, and in his haste he jerked the table violently causing the tea cups and plates to rattle and wobble dangerously. In his embarrassed confusion, he managed to mumble, "I hope you will both be very happy together and that he will treat you kindly, but I will miss you Lizzie, and should you ever need my help, I shall be here." He left the room without a backward glance.

§

Martha was feeling nervous and because of this, she was feeling cross with herself. This was her cause and she knew full well she was quite up to the job, but this was also the first real committee meeting for her charity and she was to address the eleven ladies who had been invited, and accepted, to serve on it with her.

With Ruth gone, Eleanor Smith had become her stalwart second in command and between them they had cajoled and persuaded the other ten ladies that a small home for foundlings, whilst addressing only the tip of the iceberg of the town's social problems, would nonetheless, be a worthwhile endeavour. They had chosen ladies they thought could bring, mainly through their husbands of course, practical help and at the same time as finding committee members, Martha and Eleanor were tirelessly seeking financial benefactors. Now the time had come to set the project in motion and she was excited as they had some very positive plans, but anxious as it was to be a very great undertaking for them.

Her knees shaking a little, she stood and looked at the ladies seated around her in the tea room at Kings, mainly traders' wives, all dressed finely for this inaugural meeting. Smoothing her robe down for the hundredth time, quite unbidden, the thought popped into her head, 'It would give us all a good deal more room if the fashion wasn't for these ridiculous hoops under our skirts, and we could sit more comfortably. Her mind was now relaxed, and she began, "Welcome ladies to our inaugural committee meeting and my very first pleasure, indeed my honour, is to welcome especially Mrs Margery Foxcroft who has graciously agreed, together with her husband, Alderman

Foxcroft to be our patrons. Perhaps we could show our appreciation."

A small ripple of applause from gloved hands circled the group and all faces turned towards the plump, satisfied countenance of Mrs Foxcroft, who, rather regally, inclined her head to acknowledge her new position.

"Alderman and Mrs Foxcroft have very generously allowed us the use of a sufficiently substantial house in Narrow Marsh for our home, at a peppercorn rent for the first three years and it is with great pleasure that I have their permission to name the house 'The Foxcroft Home for Waifs and Strays'.

Another round of muted applause, and another regal nod.

"We have discussed our aims and ambitions before but I would like to take this opportunity to clarify our major intentions. One, to provide a home, food, clothing and access to education for six orphans of the town of Nottingham. Two, our priority is to take in the babies of unmarried girls who have got themselves into trouble and having no support, abandon these waifs on the steps of the workhouse or church, or worse, leave them in alleyways to die. Three, to place these children at an appropriate age into gainful employment. Girls into domestic service and boys into formal apprenticeships." Martha looked up and there was another round of applause and another regal nod. "I am also very proud to announce that we have to date, annual pledges sufficient for at least three years of running costs of the home. These marvellous benefactors have many calls on their generosity at this time and we are extremely grateful to them. I shall hand over now to Mrs Smith to whom I am also extremely grateful and who has worked tirelessly with me on this aspect."

More muted applause and another regal nod.

Eleanor Smith stood and nervously read out various figures and who, or mostly, whose husbands, had promised their help to the project, each name eliciting a round of applause and Marjorie Foxcroft's regal nod. Worryingly for Martha, she advised her colleagues that Mrs Polly Crossland was unable to attend, being indisposed.

Relieved, Eleanor sat down again and Martha got to her feet. "I shall not keep you much longer ladies, this is the last item of the day. In the first instance, when we are quite sure all legal and financial matters are in place, I suggest we take two slightly older children, about two years of age, into the house immediately, and the next four as babies when they come along. The babies will need to stay with the wet nurses for the first year of their lives at least and therefore the house would be empty. Mr Woods who lives in a White Rents house and whom some of you have met, has become an invaluable contact for us and he told me of a very sad situation where a recently widowed young woman has herself just died and her two small children are temporarily lodging at the mercy of a neighbour. I propose that we give a home to these two as soon as possible and in the interim, make a small payment to these neighbours to continue providing for them until we are ready."

The meeting over, all remaining tea was drunk and the room was singing with the general twitter of ladies gossiping. Martha was able to take her leave. It had been a very warm summer and now, towards the end of September, the sun was beating down on her as she hurried along the streets, the hot dust in her throat and nose and her anxiety over Polly's indisposition, the first she had heard of it from Mrs Smith, causing her to perspire uncomfortably.

"Polly dearest, please stop crying, that will really not help at all," pleaded Martha, "just tell me calmly what Dr Bayley said."

"He said," Polly mumbled in-between her sobs, "that he didn't think I would keep the baby but to try by staying here in bed, maybe for weeks. I'd be happy to do that, Alice can manage quite well without me, but he still thinks the baby will die." Her sobs reached a crescendo and then, suddenly, she shuddered and they stopped. "Martha, I had missed three of my monthly flows, I really thought it would be alright this time."

What has Francis said," asked Martha.

"He is heartbroken, I know, but he says not to worry, there is plenty more time. I told him last time too, it's all my fault wanting to marry on a Thursday."

"And he told you it is superstitious nonsense Polly, you must stop thinking such rubbish, it will not help you stay calm and pray for the baby," she settled Polly's counterpane and called for Alice, "Please go to my brother at the vintners, he has had a delivery of some new sweet white wine, ask him to draw you a bottle and then mix half a glassful with a spoonful of warm brandy and bring it to your mistress." She turned again to Polly, "James has told me that the London ladies drink this or sweet champagne to build up their strength, so I suggest you ask Alice to prepare it for you three times a day, and please dearest, stay calm. No more tears, it is not good for either of you."

It was all to no avail, Polly lost her second baby. "I am a failure," she wept in Francis's arms, "it would be better if I died too so you can marry again and have the son you desire."

"I'll not listen to any more of this silliness," he answered kindly, "you are my wife and I love you, I could not dream of a life without you. Please don't torture yourself in this way, you are all I need to keep me the happiest man in England."

He confided to James later, "I am loathe to put Polly through all this again despite telling her we shall have plenty more opportunities. In my heart I believe there should be no more pregnancies, however, she is adamant that we try again and so I suspect we will, I cannot resist her."

"It's the will of God Francis and He has decreed it is your duty to beget children with your wife, or at least to try to, and anyway, there's no reason to suppose that you will never have a child. Many women lose a baby, look at your own mother, and Polly is still young. As you yourself have told her, there is plenty of time."

§

Listen to this Edward, I want to put this in the Nottingham Journal. I have spoken with old Cresswell and he has given me the cost and I think it's good value, so what do you think of the words,

"Messrs W and J Severn wish to inform the good townsfolk of Nottingham that they now stock a superior Sauternes wine from France. Full and sweet, this luscious white wine will suit the sensibilities of the delicate, fairer sex admirably. Messrs Severn are also delighted to offer sweet Champagne, a perfect 'pick me up' for the ladies after lying in and a delicious drink at any time. They will continue to offer you superior Port Wines, Brandy and all usual manner of beverage. Please be advised that you can

find them at Weekday Cross, open for your convenience everyday but the Sabbath."

"It sounds mighty grand James," Edward replied, "should appeal to the nobs no end. Then you'll become very grand yourself and have nothing to do with the likes of me!"

Edward Langford was a friend from school days, now finishing his own apprenticeship to his father, a linen draper and mercer, "I'll be having to bow and scrape to you like my father would have me do to the nobs who come in our shop, they're always trying for a special deal and asking for longer credit than they have any right to. I don't of course, bow and scrape that is."

"No, I can't imagine you do," laughed James, "come with me, I'm going over to the Journal offices so it can go in the next edition. It will be interesting to see what happens, advertising is quite the done thing in London, I saw ...",

"If you tell me one more thing about how bloody marvellous London is, I'll, well I don't know what I'll do but it might involve a lot of pain on your behalf Severn, I'm jealous enough that you've been and I haven't, without having to hear about it non stop. Come on, lets drop that note off and go on to Kings, I was really sorry to hear about Lizzie.

§

December arrived and the nature of the town changed, people hurried around wrapped up against the cold, scuttling indoors out of the chill winds and off the wet, boggy streets. Great excitement came for James just before Christmas. Sitting at his desk in the little counting house off the main shop floor, which was now, Jack said ostentatiously, called the Office, he heard the door open and hurrying to greet the entrant, stopped dead in his tracks, it was Robert Foxcroft, the Alderman.

He recovered his composure quickly, "Good day to you Sir, it is an honour to have you visit Severns," then instantly dismayed he added, "or have you come to see my sister Martha on Foxcroft House affairs?"

"No, young man, I have come to see you but certainly your sister has been instrumental in my coming," he sat on the proffered chair, wrapping the tails of his coat to the front of his corpulent girth as he did so and then fussily arranging them once settled, "she has managed to persuade my lady wife of the virtues of a white wine from the damn Frenchies, called 'Sotuns'. What do you have to say about it?"

James could not believe his luck, "I'm sure the best way to discuss this Sir, would be to sit with a glass of our finest vintage port and when the talking is over, perhaps you would like to taste the Sauternes."

James's words flowed as fluently as did the Alderman's wine. It was a success, Alderman Foxcroft left two hours later, happy in his decision to purchase a dozen bottles of the 'Sotuns' immediately for the little lady, with the promise of a monthly order if she so wished and, the real bonus, an order for a dozen bottles of Severns finest port.

"Let's hope you have a good stock, I'm sure Mrs F will boast about it to her intimates, you'll have a queue to your door, I'll be bound."

James was thrilled and related the whole encounter at dinner, "It couldn't have been a better customer, Mrs F is a doyen of the ladies circles and old Mr F himself is sure to let on that he has changed from Huthwaites to us. I must get new premises soon, we shall run out of space, oh good Lord, I must send my order to Jubb immediately."

"Seems like he kept up with Foxcroft glass for glass," commented William wryly as James rushed off, "he'd better not get into that habit. But my, I'm pleased for the boy, and well done Martha, it seems it's all thanks to you.

CHAPTER TWENTY THREE
London 1782
England has the last "hanged, drawn and quartered" execution for treason

The street outside had an eerie, muffled sound, 'more snow in the night' was the drowsy thought that came to Ben as he roused from a deep and dream filled sleep, 'it will be freezing today'. He turned over in bed and drew Kitty closer into his arms, she snuggled her head onto his shoulder and they lay, content, awaiting the new day, their thoughts for this short while only of themselves and their love. Day break and reality would overtake them all too soon.

Ben couldn't believe it had come to this, he only knew that since that day at the circus last May he had found himself thinking about Kitty constantly, found himself wanting to see her, making odd excuses to call on her when he arrived or left the house, found himself dreaming of her, found himself wanting more than anything else, to touch her, to kiss her, to cherish her.

"Good heavens Ben," pontificated his friend Ned when he was mooning about her in 'Simon's' one evening, "sounds to me like you've got a bad case of lust for the woman. Does she know? She's married though ain't she, didn't you say there was a husband in the Navy?"

"I doubt she's aware I'm alive even," sighed Ben, "she probably thinks I'm just a boy and hasn't noticed how I adore her."

"That's just as well I should think, you don't want to get mixed up with a tar's wife, he'll likely beat you to a pulp when he comes back and finds out."

Ben tried hard to heed this advice," Yes, I know you are right, it's a hopeless case, she's a married woman, she loves her husband," he tried to convince himself, but he couldn't stop his heart racing when she came into the room or his eyes from following her every move.

In the week before Christmas he had agreed to meet his friends in the tavern for a Christmas Day dinner. Frederick King was taking his family home to Nottingham to stay with his father, and for the first time, Ben was going to spend the holiday alone.

"We'll make our own celebration all right," Ned had assured him, "they do a splendid dinner in 'Simon's' and if we should just happen to have a glass of port or two too many, the good news is, we don't have to get up for work the next day."

On Christmas Eve, Kitty had cleared away after supper and her other lodgers having gone their separate ways for the festivities, she found herself alone in the dining room with Ben. "Benjamin," he was too agitated himself to notice the nervousness in her voice, "would you like to have Christmas dinner here with me tomorrow? Maria has had to go to visit a cousin in the country who is unwell and asked for her and I thought as you are alone and I shall be alone that maybe we could ... well, it's just that I feel a little sad and lonely ... but, no, it's silly of me to ask, you are bound to have made arrangements. I'm sorry to have troubled you."

"I cannot think of anything that would give me greater pleasure Mrs Warner," Ben burst out, his heart carrying out double somersaults, distraught to think his beloved was lonely and at the same time exalted to think he would spend this special day with her, "I had only thought to join the boys at 'Simon's' but to be with you would be infinitely more enjoyable."

The day began with ecstasy for Ben, whilst walking together to church, "Please Benjamin, you must call me Kitty, we are friends are we not?" changing too soon to agony as he realised how impossible his love for her was. After the service they arrived back at Grange Walk where Kitty allowed Ada, her servant, to go home to her parents for the rest of the day. "I will not have much to do before we can eat," she told Ben, "so maybe we could share a glass of wine together now."

As soon as they sat and began to talk, the ease they had found with each other all those months ago returned, and by the time Kitty served the meal, she had bewitched Ben. When asked, she told him about her life. "I was brought up by my mother alone, my father, whoever he was, had disappeared before I was born," there was no self pity in her words, it was just the truth, "and although it was tough for mother with no support, she worked hard and we managed." She hesitated and sat looking at Ben.

"Please go on, is your mother still living?"

"Yes, she lives in Woolwich and I see her from time to time, she doesn't work now as I can help her out. She used to be a cook at The Ship and Anchor which is where I first met my husband, Nathan. I had gone to the tavern that day to help as they were expecting the Fleet into Woolwich and Nathan arrived with some of the men from HMS Terrible. He looked so handsome, jet black hair but a pale, almost translucent skin, not tanned from the sun at all and he stood looking around with such confidence, I thought he looked quite aristocratic."

Ben felt a little insecure but he took another draught of his wine and carried on gazing at Kitty as she extolled the physical virtues of his arch rival.

"He was dazzling in his Lieutenant's uniform, his blue frock coat and white waistcoat seemed to light up the room and my head was completely turned, I thought him the most exotic man I had ever seen."

Ben tried to eat but his throat was dry with jealousy. "I'm sorry," Kitty was contrite and looking directly into his eyes, "it is wrong of me to neglect you and talk of Nathan, do you wish for something different to eat, have you tired of the goose."

"Not at all, this goose is delicious," he was chewing a piece of the rich, dark meat infused with herbs, "this is an outstanding Christmas dinner," then, managing to swallow his mouthful, added shyly, "it is an outstanding day all round, please continue with your story. How did you come to marry this Greek god?"

"Ha, ha! yes, I have rather painted that picture for you but I fear the story has no happy ending. I would like to tell you about it Benjamin, I feel close to you and there is only Maria who knows the whole sorry tale, but I am afraid it will shock you."

Ben's curiosity aroused, his response was genuine this time, "I'm sure it won't Kitty, please do go on."

"Well as I said, my head was turned and I cannot begin to describe the joy I felt when he spoke kindly to me and smiled, making me feel I was the only person in the room. I was almost seventeen and I found out later that he was twenty five. Looking back I can see how foolish I was, but he declared his love for me by the end of the evening and I believed him. I was so happy I couldn't sleep that night, and the next day he arrived at our home in Woolwich bringing little gifts of sugared almonds and a lace handkerchief," she hesitated again, "please Benjamin, please do pour some more wine, I think I should like some too, to give me courage, it is not easy to tell you this, even though you are such a very good listener."

Her glass filled, she took a sip and rose to move to the window, turning her face away from Ben's gaze, "Nathan asked me to marry him two days later and applied for a special licence from the Bishop. By this time I knew that he came from a station in life far, far above mine but I fancied myself so in love that this difference did not matter. My mother was only too pleased to give her consent and in her presence and that of Mrs Warner, Nathan's mother, we were married in the church at Woolwich," she looked round at Ben, "his mother was extremely superior and half frightened me to death. She hardly said a word to me, but when she did, she was not unduly unkind, and then she left Woolwich immediately after the formalities. I now know she was there solely in order to make sure Nathan went through with the marriage." Here she faltered, "It is hard for me to admit how foolish I have been, I am ashamed, I do so hope you will not feel any the less of me because of what I am about to tell you Benjamin."

"My dear Kitty, I hold you in the highest esteem and whatever you are about to say, whatever misfortune has befallen you will never change that," and without thinking he blurted out, "I love you."

Kitty was startled, her neck blushed a deep red and she stammered, "You do not know what is yet to come," and turning to the window again, "I must continue before I lose my resolve. As soon as we were married, Nathan told me his story. He had been obliged to take a wife very quickly in order to scotch certain rumours that were circulating about him and a young man from Kensington, and his mother had insisted that he was not to wed a girl from their own social circle as the gossip would have been unbearable. Hence me! Well Nathan was very apologetic and indeed over the next week when we were together he was kind and considerate, never of course consummating our union. Then he brought me here to Grange Walk where he told me that this house is his and that he would ensure I could live in it always and, subject to certain costs or taxes or whatever that his agent would deal with, I was at liberty to regard the income from lodgers as my own." Kitty was looking at Ben, "and that's how it has been for the past five years. I am neither one thing nor another, not a wife nor a widow."

"Have you heard from him in all this time?" asked Ben, "does he write, does his mother enquire after your wellbeing? Did the scandal cease?"

"One question at a time," smiled Kitty, "yes, he has written, sometimes with information about the dealings with his agent and he told me of his journeys. I know that his ship was involved in a battle off the coast of Portugal in '78, and also that they took a privateer. Next I heard that he was still aboard HMS Terrible when under the command of Captain Finch it was deployed in the American war. The very last I know, and not from him but from the daily journals, was about the battle at Chesapeake, I think that is the name, last September. The English themselves sunk the Terrible afterwards as it was so badly damaged. What Nathan's fate was I do not know, although I am assured should he have been killed or taken prisoner, the Admiralty would have informed me. I can only think he has completely deserted me, but of that I have no real proof either." Here, Kitty's composure faltered and she broke down into quiet sobs.

"What a dreadful situation for you my dear Kitty, please don't cry. I am here with you now and I will do anything I can to ease your pain, only do not sob, you will make me cry with you," and being in such a quandary, he got up from his chair, went to the window, put his arms around her and, not being rebuffed, kissed her gently on her cheek where the salty tears were falling.

Since Christmas Day they had spent every possible moment together. Waiting until after the other lodgers went to their rooms for the night, Ben would join Kitty in her private parlour where they would talk and his desire for her had grown ever stronger. As time passed, the strength of their feelings overcame the recklessness of such an illicit relationship and he took her to his bed.

One thing really puzzled Ben and when the time was right, he asked, "Why have you not denounced this vile man, as a pervert, he's unnatural and wicked and should be punished. It cannot be right that he continues as an officer in our magnificent Navy."

"No Benjamin," Kitty wanted Ben to understand, "I'm sure Nathan is at heart a good man and he does not deserve to be punished just for being different, he cannot help how he is. In that first week we talked at length about his feelings, he wanted me to know the truth and it is as natural for him to love another man as it is for me to love you and you to love me. The young man in question is not a naval man, he is a childhood friend, an artist now, and they have loved each other almost all their lives."

"Well loving your friend is one thing, but the bestial acts these men commit are sins in the eyes of God and should be stopped."

"Nathan has been at sea these last five years, do you not think it punishment enough to be away from the one you love for so long? He is an honourable man Benjamin," she looked earnestly into his eyes, "he could so easily have left me ruined. The scandal was over, his family were able to show he was a married man, he now had a wife, but he did not desert me completely. I have had financial security all these years and I have no reason to suppose he will suddenly renege on his part and evict me from the house. His only crime was to leave me lonely and now I have involved you in this mess, do you regret it?"

"My sweet, how can I regret anything, I had thought my love for you was hopeless, to know that you feel the same for me in return makes me the happiest man alive."

The euphoria of this new love did not distract Ben from his ambitions for more than a few days, such is the way of youth that his enthusiasm was increased fourfold and he longed even more for success. He would need to be financially sound if he wanted to claim Kitty for his own.

By October of that year, with Frederick's backing, 'Benj.n Severn Grocer' was established in a charming, double bay fronted house in Oxford Street and Ben was relishing his introduction to the world of a shop keeper.

CHAPTER TWENTY FOUR
Nottingham 1782
Britain continues to be at war with France

Jack and Ann brought another daughter into the world in January '82, named Mary Elizabeth for the little girl they had lost, she was known as Beth, and Martha, who wore the mantle of chief correspondent for the family, wrote to her two absent brothers to tell them of the happy news. She enjoyed writing letters and it was no hardship even now that her life was, thankfully, so busy, and it pleased her that Elizabeth would respond regularly.

Towards the end of spring, Martha had gathered the family together to hear the latest from Elizabeth, "I have news from Billy, but as usual, no word from London. Benjamin is just hopeless and," Martha glanced over to where James sat by the window, his finger running down a column of shipping figures printed in the Journal, "now that we do not see Lizzie, we get no news through Frederick either. We must suppose all is well or we might have heard."

"I'm sure Ben is just too busy," James defended his brother, "I know how much work there is to do to set up a new shop. What news from our saintly sister."

"Don't be unkind James, I'm sure she is much nicer than the impression she gave us when we met her, she says here that, *"I am relishing the role of supporting The Reverend who works so hard in his Ministry..."* Martha stopped mid sentence and looked up, "I'm not sure you were here George when the news came that Billy has now been ordained and is a Minister of a congregationalist church in Hinckley. Were you? Did anyone remember to tell you?"

"No," George grumbled, "that's so typical, nobody ever thinks to tell me anything. I am obviously the least important member of this family. What does it mean anyway, will his life be any different. I thought a non conformist was a non conformist."

"Well, I'm sure there is a subtle difference," replied Josiah, "but I think we'll have to wait to speak with Billy himself. The one thing I do know is that his congregation will run the church, not any 'official' body, or the state, and that was always very important to him. What does Elizabeth say about it?"

"Well, she doesn't really address that, let me carry on reading this passage. *"When The Reverend is not busy preaching or visiting the sick and poor of the parish, he loves to sit and talk with some of the intellectuals of the town. They have long philosophical conversations and I am privileged to be allowed to sit and listen from time to time. He is especially fond of speaking with young people, he likes to guide them in their views for later life, he speaks with such fluency and verve, he is very popular with them. Our congregation is growing quickly and this is very fortunate as our income depends on the numbers and I am happy to tell you, with The Reverend's permission of course, that he has now begun to invest in one or two properties and thus we shall be able to gather rents. We have settled into our new house in Hinckley very well. Thank you Martha for your suggestions as to the bed hangings. I have found an emporium selling the wool Harrateen and can accept the high price of £5 as I feel my husband's comfort and warmth is worth any price."*

"Elizabeth wrote to tell me that the house is old and how cold their room is," Martha explained, "apparently the windows are not a good fit. I thought I should tell her to get in a good glazier, Joe," she smiled, "but, instead, as they have a four poster bed, I suggested some thick hangings to keep out the draught. I didn't suggest anything that cost that much money though."

"Well, I'm glad it's all for your brother's comfort," William raised his eyebrows, "I'm sure your sister Elizabeth would be more than prepared to put up with the cold!"

"Father, you noticed too," Polly was laughing, "I thought it was just me! And how formally she refers to Billy, 'The Reverend'!"

"Well, I agree with that," George stood up and bowed, "now that he is a minister in the church, he must have a little more gravitas, 'Billy' just will not do!"

One letter Martha did not read out to the family was from Edmund Brown, but she told them of the contents,. "I had a letter from Edmund this week, or should I say, Sir Edmund. He is settled well in Woodbridge and remains interested in Foxcroft House, encouraging me to continue with the work. He is helping his local rector organise some ladies of his own parish to do more for the poor and out of work, but he writes to tell me he is getting married shortly. He feels he has a duty to produce an heir to the title and land and so he needs a wife. He has chosen the daughter of a local squire. She is twenty four and very pretty apparently."

There was no response, and, looking at the expressionless faces before her, she said emphatically, "I am very happy for him, I have not changed my views on marriage and would not deny anyone else the opportunity."

When she left the room, William spoke alone with James, "I don't understand that girl, she could have been Lady Brown of the manor and yet she chooses to stay here and work herself to death with this charity stuff. You really will have to look after her when I am gone."

§

"It seems I shall find myself in the role of favourite Aunt," Polly said, the smile on her lips not quite reaching her eyes, "looking after my nephews and nieces. Beth is a beautiful baby, dear Ann," Polly was struggling, this bitter sweet meeting was too soon after her own loss, "here, I have made this little bed dress and embroidered some tiny blue flowers on the bodice. I think it will look very sweet with her fair hair."

It was one of those infrequent fine, warm days in April and they had come to Foxcroft House to visit Martha, keen to see the progress she had made. Polly had resumed her life, putting her melancholy aside and was showing her support, James had been cajoled to come along too, to look at the books for his sister.

He was studying a large, as yet crease free, accounts book. Martha's careful writing filled only a few of the columns, her letters and numbers precise and not an ink blot in sight. "This is looking all in order Martha, I'm very impressed."

"We have more pledges of subscriptions and are nearly at our target. I do need more donations for our contingency fund but I am so happy we now have our first innocents, we're starting to give them a better life."

"I am very happy to help making clothes and furnishings as I have promised you Martha dear, but I am really not able to help in any other, shall we say, more direct, manner." Polly looked a little uncomfortable, "I do not wish to look after the children and nor do I want to risk my health going into those rather nasty dwellings that you seem to have no compunction about."

Martha did not mind at all, "Of course not my love, your talents lie with your needle and design, and you have such a gift of knowing exactly what can be done to clothe these children. They are apt to grow constantly," she laughed, "and it will take all your charm to find and persuade some seamstresses to help."

"Edward's father is a linen draper isn't he?" Polly put her arm through James's and gave him a nudge, "we need a draper to donate any off cuts of fabric they have. I have only hosiery bits to work with at the moment which are fine for blankets and shawls but I need wool or linen to make the girl a dress and pinafore and the boy will need shirts and breeches and they will both need a winter cape or coat. Can you speak with him about it James? Oh," she turned her head to Martha, "the other draper I thought you might approach is Olivia Martin. She is running the emporium in Warser Gate now that her husband has died. I think she is somehow related to grandmother Cramp, and also to Francis's mother Sarah, but it's quite a distant connection and you might not want to use it."

"Thank you Polly and thank you also for arranging for Dolly's sister Eliza to come as our servant. I told you we hired Agnes Adams, didn't I? We call her Matron although she's not really a nurse and her role is to be housekeeper and look after the children. She's very capable, widowed, her own children are long gone, and because her husband's mother was Mrs Adams the midwife who delivered all of us, it sort of keeps it in the family."

Martha had taken in the two young children to Foxcroft House in February and routines were starting to settle down. The staff were getting to know exactly what to do and Martha loved being there, talking with matron and considering how things could be done or done better and there were always a dozen queries to be dealt with or people to chase for promises given and not yet fulfilled. Foxcroft also had their first baby. Left on the doorstep within the second week of opening. A tiny mite, she was wrapped in a filthy piece of blanket and a scrap of paper with just the name 'Ann' written on it in feint, shaky letters, was pinned to it. Clutched in the baby girl's hand was her keepsake, all that her mother had to give her in life, a token promise that she would return one day to claim her daughter. It was a small mother of pearl button.

Agnes had sent for Martha straight away and within the hour she and the baby were on their way to the first of the wet nurses. Mrs Tebbutt was a boisterous woman and when she answered the door to her home in Pell Alley, she had a baby at her breast, "Don't mind me Miss," she said brightly, "this is Jonathon, my tenth. Betsey, come and move these things so the lady can get in. That's better," a girl of about twelve or thirteen came to the door and moved some boots, "come on in and take a seat."

Martha was pleased, Mrs Barratt had been right when she said Frances Tebbutt would be ideal. The house, though cramped and full of children, appeared clean and Martha liked the open friendliness of the woman immediately. "Here is Ann for you," and she placed the baby into Mrs Tebbutt's free arm, "we only have her name and a tiny button. We shall keep that with her records at Foxcroft House. Here also are two bedgowns and a new, clean blanket but I have not put them on her as I was hoping you would clean her first and she must be hungry. So hungry I fear she cannot cry."

"That's marvellous Miss, you leave her with me now and I'll get her sorted out. Why don't you pop in tomorrow or the next day if you can, you'll see a big difference in her by then."

"That is kind of you Mrs Tebbutt and here is the first week's payment. 1/6d was agreed with Mrs Twells I believe?"

"Yes, yes, thank you very much. Betsey, take this money and put it in the pot on the mantle, and then open the door for Miss Severn to leave. Good bye, we'll see you again soon," and looking down coo-ing at the baby, her attention focussed, "come along then my little love, let's have some milk."

Martha went back to visit a few days later and, as promised, Ann was looking as if she would survive her first week of life.

"My dear Edmund," she wrote later that evening, " I cannot begin to tell you the fulfilment I feel having saved my first three children. It is worth, to me, all the riches in the world."

"Polly, I don't want the children dressed in dark blue. Blue is the colour of charity and I see no reason to always remind them of their unfortunate start in life. We need brown fabric and I am going this week to see Olivia Martin. I sent a note to her, pointing out that we are very distantly related by marriage and setting out my needs and she has kindly agreed to meet with me to see what she can do to help. James's friend Edward hasn't come up with anything, although I cannot be certain that James has remembered to mention it to him."

Martha had brought a bundle of hosiery off cuts to Polly to see if they would be of use, "I think Mr Hornbuckle has been generous, I cannot see that these large pieces would be useless for him, how kind."

"I went to see the children yesterday," Polly said as she held up one of the pieces and looked at it thoughtfully, "they are very engaging and in petticoats for some time yet. When old enough, you are right, a little brown, not blue, dress and a white pinafore for Martha, and brown breeches and white shirt for Zachary. I didn't know the girl's name was the same as yours, it could not be more propitious for you dear sister, it is truly a good omen."

"Yes, such a coincidence, but she is known as Patty," beamed Martha, "and we know their surname, Green, but the foundling baby only had her name Ann. We have called her Ann Marsh as she was left in Narrow Marsh."

"What will you do if more babies are left on your doorstep than you are able to take in?" Polly opened her sewing chest and took out a box of pins, "it is very likely, and once you have six in all, there will be many years before the oldest leave and you can take in another. Will you have to take them to the workhouse?"

"It will be very hard and I'm sure you are right. Once word gets around, we will be first choice for the poor wretches. It would be good to find we might accommodate more than six but I must be sensible and be ruled by my head and not my heart."

Polly smiled at her, "That will be hard for you dear Martha."

CHAPTER TWENTY FIVE
Nottingham 1782
Building work was completed on Nottingham's new General Hospital

Josiah and Tad first met Luke when they heard him speaking in the market square one September Saturday morning. Standing on his upturned box, quite a crowd had gathered around to listen and agree or disagree with his views on the latest enclosures of common pasture land. Captivated by his charisma, the boys were dazzled with how he answered the sceptics, put down the hecklers and roused his supporters. "This is just what we should be doing Joe," Tad said eagerly, "let's ask him how we can help. What we can do."

"I know who you are lad," Luke said to Josiah when they approached him. "your father is a decent man. Many's the time he helped my family out when he was landlord of The Grapes, a decent man indeed. Does he know you're here talking with us rebels?"

"No, but we're sixteen and we know our own minds. The country needs changing, there is no justice for the poor. See here?" and Joe pulled back his sleeve, "this is from one of the dragoons' sabres during the knitters riots."

"My, that's a badge of honour for one so young? Why were you rioting?"

"Well, actually, we'd just gone to watch and the dragoons came and we didn't get out of the way quickly enough. But if we'd been older, we'd have been fighting."

"We certainly will next time," put in Tad, "it was so exciting wasn't it Joe!"

"What can we do to help? That's the worst part about still being young, we don't know where to go or what to do. We just know we want to make the politicians listen, we want to make things better for the poor."

"I hear your sister is helping without having to take to the streets and fight. I admire the lady, and you can tell her so from me, my name's Luke," and he held out his hand, "she'll likely have heard of me. I'll not be leading you into trouble boys, I've too much respect for your family, and you're still too young, apprenticed are you? I've got a small group together which meet on Tuesdays in Bone Alley, the third house on the left along from Narrow Marsh. You can come to our meetings if you like, we are always looking for people to deliver our pamphlets. That will be a start."

"Watch out," Josiah grabbed Tad's sleeve and dragged him round the corner of a ramshackle house into the alley way. They stood, their backs pressed against the wall, hardly daring to breath and watched as two men continued on their way past. After what seemed an age, peering cautiously round the corner and checking the street, they darted to a house deep in the heart of the labyrinth of lanes down by the River Leen. They pushed open the door and slipped inside.

"Sit down lads, we've not been going long," a burly man pushed them towards the last remaining upturned vegetable boxes arranged in two concentric circles in the otherwise bare room. In the centre of the circle was the man they knew only as Luke, and he was about to speak.

"This new hospital up at the Park is opening on the 27th and I've got the leaflets here for us to distribute. It's a damned disgrace to call it a hospital for the poor when if you've no money you can't be let in unless you've been recommended by a subscriber. In other words, a man who does have money."

"Even then it's not a certainty," said the burly man, "no smallpox or the itch, no infectious diseases and no disorders of the mind, oh, and if you are lucky enough to have a sponsor, they'll not take more than two of his recommendations at any one time."

"There'll need to be an awful lot of 'em to recommend us then," another man cut in, "when you think how many of us there are without any money, thousands!"

"There's to be a grand opening and celebrations for the burgers of the town," Josiah stood up from his box, "my employer is letting those of us who worked on the building go and stand at the side of the road to watch the mayor and his cronies parade up to St Marys."

"That's not right either, they're charging 2/6d a ticket to prevent us people turning up at the church door," Luke fumed, "the church should be open to all of us."

"What else can we do Luke to make our protest?" asked another of the men, "is it worth a major turnout? Should we march on them?"

"I shall certainly never stand and bow and scrape to these people," Josiah spoke up again, "but I can be in the crowd and hand out your pamphlets and if you march, you can count on us."

"I'll get the pamphlets ready for the morning," the burly man, obviously Luke's second in command, said, "so you can collect them before the parade."

"We'll not march," Luke said, nodding to his comrade, "no point starting a riot over this, it's not important enough, but we are going to join with two of our other groups next Sunday and march to Langar. They've enclosed nearly all that land now and we're planning to tear down some fences. There'll be a few bloody heads at the end of the day, that's for sure!"

As the men began to leave, one by one, silently into the night, Luke went up to Josiah and Tad, "I don't want you boys getting involved in the march, there's enough of us out of work already and we'd have your fathers chasing us down if you were caught and lost your apprenticeships because of it."

"Well, we can hand out the leaflets about the hospital though, can't we?" asked Tad, "we must do something and as soon as we've finished our seven years, we'll be with you on the streets."

Not at all satisfied with that they left the house, "I'm not going to sit back and do nothing Joe, apprenticeship or not, I say we join up with them on Sunday and go and break some fences, will you come? Right now though, I'd better get back home to sleep, as a baker's apprentice I've to be up at two to make sure all you revolutionaries have bread for your breakfast!" Tad roared with laughter.

On Sunday they caught up with Luke and his men on the outskirts of the town. "I had to go to church and I just hope my fidgeting didn't make anyone suspicious," Joe was feeling bad that he'd lied to his father, "I told them I would be poring over maps with you for the rest of the day and that your mother had offered me dinner. Don't like lying but I want to do this."

"I've said the same to my parents too," Tad stepped up the pace, "I can't imagine they will be checking. Hurry, I can see the mob ahead, a lot of them have sticks, pity we haven't."

It was a long walk, more than three hours, and when they reached the village Luke stopped and the men gathered round to listen for instructions, the two youngsters keeping out of sight at the rear of the crowd. "I don't want any violence today lads, it's enough that we pull up the fences, that will cause mayhem when the livestock moves around and cost 'em to put them back again. If their watchmen come for us, don't fight unless you have to fight back, they'll say we started any trouble whatever the case, but if we can avoid a ruck, so much the better. The watchmen are only doing their jobs, trying to earn a crust like the rest of us."

But there was a riot, the frenzy of men pulling up the stakes and trampling through the fields caused such a commotion, it was inevitable.

"Tad," called Josiah, "give me a hand here, I can't get this post out." With their hands bleeding from the splinters, they were working together when one of the Langar men came up behind them and with a vice like grip, knocked their heads together.

"You stupid young pups," he barked, "don't you realise what trouble you're going to be in, your lives will be ruined. Leave now and think yourself lucky it was me that caught you."

Just as they were wavering, turning to walk away, Luke came over, "What the devil? I told you two not to come here," looking at the retreating back of their captor, "you were damn fortunate there. Get off right now, run and join with that rabble making their way home," and he turned to follow the man.

Josiah managed to conceal his torn hands from Martha when he arrived home very late, tired, dirty and elated! He had gone straight to bed and rose early for work the next morning, avoiding any awkward questions, and thinking he had got away with it.

He could not believe his eyes when he walked into the parlour that evening, sitting there, drinking beer with his father was the huge shape of the Langar farmer.

"You don't recognise your uncle Richard then?" his father asked, "it's jolly lucky for you that he knew who you were yesterday!"

Lost for words, Josiah could only stare as his father vented his anger on him. He only half heard, "ruining your chances", "no regard for other people's property", "blatant lies". "What do you have to say for yourself boy?"

Shaken back into life, Josiah tried to defend himself, "We were doing what we think is right, the land has been enclosed and the poor tenants driven out or forced to work for even less wages. It is time the masses rose up and put an end to the injustices in this world."

"You're naive lad," Richard Cramp answered him, "you've got involved with Luke Fletcher and he's a bad lot, a trouble maker for sure. I've known him for years and when I thought it was you, he confirmed it for me. Your father has the right to know where you were and what you were doing, you're not of age yet."

"Do you know whose land you were on yesterday? Did you give it any thought?" William was fuming, "it was your brother Francis's land, Francis who does so much for us all, Francis who is married to your sister. You have cost him dearly and you know very well he has not treated his tenants badly, they have a good contract with him. I suggest if you want to be an activist you take the trouble to get to know the facts of the situation before you engage in mob rule. I never want to hear you are involved with Fletcher again, you will give me your promise."

That was not the end of the matter, after their uncle had left and William had retreated to the Fleece for a couple of hours, James took up the reins, "Joe, you need to stop reading the political clap trap that circulates and concentrate on learning how the country can move forward. We need to modernise, we have so many advantages, the factories are employing hundreds of men. On the land, combining the fields and using all these new machines that are available, makes farming more efficient, surely you can see that?"

Josiah did not get the chance to reply, George exploded at James, "Well, we certainly know who's talking now. You've had it easy all your life. You don't know what it's like to be overworked and still hungry, you think only of yourself."

"And you'd know would you George? I've had enough of your jealousy! When have you ever applied yourself to anything in your life, you didn't work at school, you are as dumb now as you were as an infant. You are a liar, deceitful, ungrateful and you say, I've had it easy? Look at you, living off the efforts of your brother. He does all the work and you just coast along, you think you will get by in life by being 'jack the lad' but it's Jack the butcher who's supporting you. Just stay away from me, I'm done with you!"

The room shuddered at the force of the slammed door. James left his siblings behind and seething with anger, left the house and walked down to Crosland's, their new butchers shop now on the ground floor of the timber framed house in Middle Pavement.

"I don't know what I've done to make George so bloody jealous of me," unable to sit still, James paced up and down in his friend's office, "all I do is try to make father's business pay so we can all enjoy a good life. George doesn't ever say a bad word about Benjamin, and he's doing much better than I am, he's already got his own shop in London. I'm still not out on my own. What have I done to deserve it?"

"Calm down James, I've got some good news for you. Here, sit down and have some coffee, this will take your mind off George. The tenants on the ground floor of the house next door are quitting in December and it can be yours if you are ready for it. You could get any alterations organised by the end of the year and start trading from there early '83."

His brother forgotten, James brightened immediately, "That's terrific news Francis, two months should be enough so I could be absolutely ready by the end of February, March at the latest. Since old Foxcroft came on board, word's got out and more Aldermen are on my books, and some of them are really interested in claret. It's damned expensive compared to port, but they want to be superior to the up and coming tradespeople, nothing like a bit of snobbery to help a wine merchant! If only this war with France was over, they'd forget their anti-French feelings. I was talking to Joe the other evening about it, he's only young but he takes a great interest and knows more about politics and world affairs than I do, and he thinks there's a good chance this American war will be over by next summer."

"My father told me he tried damned hard to encourage your father to have a little pragmatism when it came to dealing with the French. Glad to hear you don't have that problem." Francis smiled, he was about to leave the wine shop, "Speaking of your father, he was telling me that all the years he's known Alderman Hornbuckle, drinking coffee together almost every week, he'd never stepped foot inside here until Foxcroft switched to you! Goes to show it's 'who' you know that's important, not necessarily 'what' you know!"

"Oh good Lord, Francis, I'd forgotten why I came here, what started the row with George, we need to talk about Joe!"

CHAPTER TWENTY SIX
Nottingham 1783
The American War ends and Britain is at peace with France

James looked up with huge satisfaction at the wooden sign hanging above the door of the handsome, four storey house. "SEVERNS. Wine & Spirit Merchants. Purveyors of Fine Wines, Champagnes, Clarets & Port Wines. Finest Sherries, Brandies & Rums." written in beautiful, gold, copperplate script, topped with an ornamental letter "S", a vine entwined round it's body. It was a large sign, it needed to be seen.

He had worked hard to make the premises ready for the opening today and he ran up the three steps quickly, turned the heavy, brass key in the lock and walked into his new domain. He stood inside, splendid in his new Severns livery, dark green coat, gold waistcoat, white shirt and stock, khaki breeches and white stockings and gazed around the room, pride filling his heart. The walls had been lined with honey coloured oak panelling, opulent and warm. Standing, centre back, was an imposing, panelled, tall counter behind which were placed two high stools and abutting the side walls were two lower counters on which stood an array of different shaped and sized glass bottles. Each bottle proudly bearing a moulded stamp showing the same ornamental letter S as the sign.

To the sides of the room were placed a few wooden butts of port, sherry and madeira. "Only for show, they are just about empty," James had explained to the family when they had gone the previous day after church to admire the new premises, "drawing off the wines can be a very messy affair and we don't want the shop floor swimming in it. The bottling will be done in the room at the back, out of sight." He noted with pleasure that George had the rare good grace to look away, slightly shame faced.

"These glass bottles are also here for display but I have a decent stock of them in the back for filling. Things are looking up, I now have two customers who, like the nobs, have their own bottles for refilling, but most people will use mine. Or of course, buy the whole casks of wine like the taverns do, and fill them at home."

At the very beginning of the year William and James had decided they should both have an assistant. James dared to say to William that moving the barrels and casks was heavy work and they should take on two boys as formal apprentices. They had found two younger, distant cousins, Simon and Jacob Cramp, both of whom had just left school, had a basic knowledge of arithmetic, were fit, strong and keen to learn. Simon was to work with William and Jacob with James.

"I like the counter," Josiah sat up on one of the stools, "looks very professional. Will you sit behind it?"

"No, Jacob will sit there and keep the records up to date when he is not working in the cellars or the bottling room. I shall be in my office just over there," he pointed to another room to the left, and entertain the personal clients at the tables and chairs over here." Placed strategically in front of the square paned window to the right of the front door, was a very fine, round, mahogany table and four upholstered arm chairs, "Whilst he enjoys a glass of wine with me, it can impress anyone walking past."

"Good thinking, especially if it's one of your gentry clients. You'll need an extra chair though so that father can spend his days here too," Josiah grinned up at William and added, "just not that awful old Absalom Partridge chair you won't let Martha get rid of!

"It's a damn site grander than a butchers shop," George sniped, his moment of conscience forgotten, "I can't see you getting your hands messy."

"It's grand James," cut in William quickly, casting George a stern look, "but I can see all our customers wanting to come here rather than deal with me at Weekday Cross."

"No, Father, that will not happen. I have explained to the tavern owners that you are still their supplier and there will be many other customers coming to you rather than trekking down to me, after all, most of them are your friends. I want this shop to attract new, and hopefully, wealthier people and you will of course be welcome to sit here whenever you wish."

"Well, let's hope young Simon learns the job quickly then I can leave him to it in Weekday Cross and come down every day!"

As James stood, that first morning, surveying the scene, the door opened and Jacob came in. He was a fresh faced boy, his dark hair tied back neatly and he was wearing a dark green, full length apron tied over his white shirt and khaki breeches and was finished off with gold stockings. "My we look a dapper pair," he slapped his thigh when James greeted him, "I reckon customers will flock here just to see us in our finery!"

The steady stream of visitors all morning, many coming purely out of curiosity, were greeted by Jacob handing round trays laden with glasses of port, sherry and madeira wines. Little dishes of macaroons, candied fruits and nuts were on the counters and a hum of voices filled the room. James relaxed a little, he had a good feeling, this place would succeed. His plans put forward to Mr Carruthers at the bank had been convincing enough for him to walk away with a substantial loan but James knew there was no time to rest on his laurels, he must sell, sell, sell.

§

"James my old friend, we haven't seen you for an age, where have you been hiding away?" He had just walked into the Shepherd ale house in Weekday Cross and was greeted by the grinning face of his friend Edward, sitting enjoying a glass of ale with Francis and two other young men. James slapped him on the back, greeted Francis and as he turned to the other two, Edward asked, "you know James Dale and John Vezey of course? We've been talking about going to the Assembly tonight, we feel like a dance or two and hopefully there'll be some interesting girls there. Can you come along?"

"Not sure I shall come," Francis gave a sheepish smile, "I'm an old married man, and Polly is not feeling too well so it won't be appreciated if I come out for the evening and leave her at home alone."

"It sounds a grand idea," James had gestured to the barman for a glass of porter and he brought it to the table, "thank you Simon. I've been doing nothing but working these past weeks, but I'm very pleased to say my efforts are paying off, sales are good."

"I walked past the other day and you were sitting drinking with old Foxcroft, it's such a hard life for you," the young men laughed as James Dale bemoaned, "you should try being a druggist, it's not half as much fun and my mother is breathing down my neck all day checking I'm not going to kill anybody!"

"Well if you do, my old man's an attorney, I'll ask him to do a deal on the fees to defend you," John Vezey drank up, "another one gentlemen?"

James sat back and enjoyed the company of his friends, he had been so serious recently, ever since he came back from London, that he thought an evening out would do him good. Since Lizzie had broken her news to him he had not thought of romance, burying his feelings and concentrating on keeping busy but Polly had told him earlier that week the Quincy wedding had taken place and it had woken up the hurt he felt.

Later that evening, standing at the side of the salon in Thurland Hall, forgoing the current dance, Martha came up to him accompanied by an elegant lady in, he guessed, her middle thirties. "James, I wasn't sure if you would turn up this evening, it's been so many weeks since you've joined us here. Let me introduce you to Mrs Olivia Martin, you remember we spoke about her at home a while ago, she is a distant cousin of ours and I am very grateful to her as she has agreed to help with our venture at Foxcroft House." Turning to her companion, "Olivia, this is my brother James. I have six brothers which is, only sometimes, fortunate," she laughed, " and James is the bourgeoning wine merchant."

James took Olivia's hand, "How do you do cousin, I am pleased to meet you and hope you are enjoying the evening. I don't recall seeing you here before?" When he released her hand he wondered, had she left it in his just a few seconds longer than necessary? He looked into her eyes as they exchanged the polite small talk and studied her face. She had none of the expected features of a classical beauty, her nose was not quite tilted enough, her eyes were more pale than cerulean blue and her face in repose was as if she was enjoying a secret joke, such that a little smile played on her full, sensuous lips. James was intrigued, the shallow crease above her eyebrows was testament to pain in her life and yet her eyes twinkled. An enigmatic face. When he took her hand and led her onto the dance floor, an unfamiliar dart of pleasure surged through his body and as he watched her poised grace performing the steps for the cotillion perfectly, he felt himself the clumsiest fool in the room.

"What did you think of Mrs Martin then," Martha had been concerned for a few days and now had the courage to broach the subject, "she is very handsome don't you think?"

James was unsophisticated when it came to women, he had thought himself in love with Lizzie since childhood and not given a thought to anyone else, but even in his naivety he realised that Olivia Martin was likely to be a trouble to him, "I think her the most exciting woman I have ever met, but don't worry, I shall give her a wide berth," he assured his sister, "she has quite a dangerous air about her. She must be at least ten years older and I think she was toying with me, trying to disarm me. I must have seemed like an innocent schoolboy and she thought it good sport! I'm not sure I want to meet her again thank you, but I hope she keeps her word and helps with the orphanage."

"I'm glad you feel that way James, I was worried for you, she is a very charismatic woman, even I could see that. I rather hope you will have no more contact with her, she is a widow running that store on her own and, I have now learned, has earned herself quite a reputation. Unhappily, enough people saw you dancing together last week so there is bound to be gossip, whether there is good cause or not. I think I shall try to distance myself from her too and not call on her help too often, I do wish I had asked around about her first before diving in."

CHAPTER TWENTY SEVEN
Nottingham 1783
The Trent Navigation Company is formed

Towards the end of the month, whether he saw Olivia again or not was taken out of his control. James was sitting in his office, nibbling the end of his quill feather, trying hard to concentrate on a budget he was drawing up, when he heard the tinkle of the little bell above the shop door. He stood and made his way quickly to see who had come in and there she was, looking dazzling, the little smile playing at the corners of her mouth, "Good morning James, my spies tell me you have some superior white wine that the ladies have fallen in love with. I thought I must come and try some for myself," and she held out her hand in greeting.

An hour later, James was intoxicated, not with wine but with Olivia and had readily agreed to oversee, in person, her first delivery of wines the next day. "I think we should keep this little arrangement to ourselves for the moment," she had told him, "there are a lot of loose tongues in this town," and she took her leave.

He arrived the next morning, heart pounding and palms clammy, at her house in the most fashionable area of Castle Gate. His delivery wagon turned the corner and drew up just minutes later as he stood, fidgeting with his hat, rocking from foot to foot and debating with himself quite seriously whether to flee. The driver was dispatched to the basement to deal with a servant and James was shown underneath the ornamental fan light, through the narrow, high front door, across the hall and up a curving staircase into an elegant, high ceilinged drawing room. Olivia was sitting by a small table on which stood a silver tray, the perfect size for the two dainty Worcester coffee cups, the matching hexagonal coffee pot, a silver cream jug and sugar pot. An ornate, chased silver urn of hot water stood on a separate stand to the side. "Good morning James," Olivia held out her hand, "please do sit down, I hope you will take coffee with me."

James took her hand and found himself bending to kiss it, "Oh good Lord," he cringed, "what on earth am I doing, you will think me crazy!" Standing straight, trying to recover his composure, "Good morning cousin Olivia."

"What a gallant greeting," whether the smile was the usual one playing on her lips or the stifling of a giggle, James was not to know, "we will make a gentleman of you yet. Firstly though, you must call me Livy, I fully intend being your good friend and that is how I like to be known by my…" and looking at him from under her lowered eyelashes, she finished, "intimates."

She poured the coffee and enquired about cream and sugar, "I am of course, as you well know, in trade, and as such regarded as being quite vulgar by many of those professing to be superior, landed sorts, but I am a firm believer in equality in our society and I do not care to take notice of such opinions. I hope you will take this same view, but I fear that as you become more successful, you will need to comport yourself differently. I understand your sister Polly is adapting herself very well to her new middling status, certainly she is fulfilling her main role in this social rising, shopping and spending as much of her husband's money as is possible acquiring the trappings of gentility!"

"That's certainly true, and they have moved house too."

"Yes, Martha told me they are living in St Mary Gate which is, of course, a more acceptable address, but even though she is desperate to join them, it is not likely that she will ever be properly accepted by the gentry. Membership of that club must be facilitated by her husband, and I'm afraid Francis does not have the right approach. You however will, with my tuition, be as close to becoming a member of their elite group as is possible without the benefit of birth. You too must think soon about a larger house in a better position and you will have to take a wife at some time, although maybe your finances are not yet strong enough, but you will need someone to fill your home with paintings and carpets and of course, a piano," her secret smile, not laughing at him but at the absurdity of the social system.

Before James could stop himself, the story of Lizzie King spilled out, and Livy's reaction was suitably acerbic, "Well, she certainly is looking to move up the ladder a rung or two, Alexander Quincy is a snob of the highest order, but don't fret over her James, there are far better matches for you out there and you will soon agree with me."

James bit his tongue and sat back in his chair. Drinking his coffee he wondered if he should pinch himself. Was he really sitting here mesmerised by this astonishing woman regaling him with the myriad of social rules for meeting people, greeting people, seating people, dancing with people and generally just being with people.

"It's a wonder the world keeps turning with all these rules," he was laughing out loud, "and my brother Benjamin has already told me to lose my Nottingham accent."

"I'm glad he told you that my dear little cousin, you must hurry up and stop sounding like a country bumpkin!" Stopping for a moment to place her coffee cup back on the saucer, she looked him in the eye and this time there was no ambiguity about the mischievous smile, "and I shall also teach you to become an accomplished and thoughtful lover!"

The rattle of the china as James fought to control his shaking hands made Livy give a throaty laugh, "Don't worry, I am not about to seduce you here and now, you have first to learn manners, etiquette and the art of conversation. You will need to become accomplished in making love to a woman with words before using your body. But do not fret, the culmination of your education will come, I promise you, all in good time."

James felt this was the moment his real life began, he was hypnotised, could not tear his eyes away from her face, he was lost! It seemed from this point on, his free will had been erased, he felt he would be this ravishing creature's slave for ever - her very willing slave.

He came whenever she called which, he agonised, was not often enough. Over the ensuing weeks, her servant would come to the shop from time to time, to order wines and request that he oversee the deliveries himself. Instructed to keep the meetings clandestine, James became adept at secrecy, not breathing a word to his family or staff whilst wanting to shout from the rooftops that he was enthralled by the most exciting woman in the town.

Livy was fun. Their conversations never faltered, they shared the same sense of humour and now that James's gauche attempts at pleasing her had become more refined, they laughed and talked and there never seemed enough time for James before she would stand and say, "I think that is all for today my little one. I will look forward to our next afternoon."

Their conversations were not, of course, solely concerned with James's rise through the social rankings, they shared an interest in many things and being relaxed in his company, Livy would talk about drapery, her problems and her desire to modernise and expand, "It is twice as hard for me I am sure," she said without rancour, "the world is run by men and they do not take me seriously enough."

"You and Martha are kindred spirits in that regard," James agreed, "I have been brought up in a house with her singing from that very same song sheet."

Livy spoke little about her own life, save to tell James that her father was an unusual man, "Papa was a draper and I was his only child. He was determined that I should have a proper education, as equal as possible as if I had been a son. I had a governess and he insisted I was taught arithmetic, geography and a little science, not just how to sew a sampler, dance, sing and catch a husband!"

"But you did catch a husband?"

"Papa arranged it, Mr Martin was a draper in Newark but Papa was adamant that I should inherit his own concerns when he died, and whilst he lived, I would keep the major interest in it. Quite opposite to the law that would have given whatever was mine to my husband, and so it was written by the lawyers into my marriage settlement. Not long after I married, Papa died and Mr Martin and I ran the two shops. When Mr Martin died, I found myself in sole charge and I have loved every minute, commerce is, as you are finding out, so stimulating and exciting."

If James's mind dwelt on the anticipation of the second part of Livy's promise of education, he could be forgiven. He was a young man and sometimes, riddled with anxiety at the prospect, he would lie awake in the middle of the night imagining horrific embarrassment for himself and disappointment, or even worse, amusement, for Livy. When the time came, she proved as patient and expert a teacher in this regard as in social manners.

He had arrived that Thursday, summoned to call a little later than usual in the day, and Livy had greeted him in her drawing room dressed in a white silk day robe, the fabric clinging to her curves and the lace bordering the deep décolletage managing to reveal, rather than conceal, the tops of her breasts. James caught his breath, his terror replaced almost at once by an overwhelming desire to kiss and caress her, as he stammered, "Livy, you look wonderful, you are so beautiful."

She took his hand and led him to her bedchamber, "I shall teach you how to please a woman James and in pleasing her, you yourself will enjoy much more pleasure than with a quick and thoughtless encounter," her voice was husky, she purred like a cat, "but first you must relax, we will have a glass of champagne. The look of fright on your face puts me in mind of one about to be hanged, drawn and quartered, whereas in truth, I am sure you will find this afternoon a much more enjoyable occasion!"

They drank their wine and taking one of the tiny candied fruits from a silver filigree dish, Livy held it to James's lips and bid him take it, "Gently, my little one, slowly and gently. That is my instruction for you this afternoon."

James had very little experience of sex, he had once or twice joined his friends when they visited a bawdy house and had left afterwards feeling slightly ashamed and far from fulfilled by the brief, sordid skirmish. Mostly, he had been content to wait until he and Lizzie were married when, he imagined, everything would miraculously feel different. It amused Livy that he was so innocent and she told him many times how glad she was to be the woman to initiate him into the world of love. "You need never again know disappointment my little one," she caressed his chest as they lay together much later, in the afterglow of loving, "and when you tire of me, you will be a confident, and believe me, a perfect, lover."

James couldn't imagine ever tiring of her. He was besotted, he longed to see her and wanted much more than these secret trysts with her. He knew he loved her but as he was getting to know her so well, he realised he must bide his time, to declare his feelings now would be a disaster. As the months passed, he was dumfounded no one guessed from his face that he was in love, in love with the most ravishing and provocative woman.

CHAPTER TWENTY EIGHT
Nottingham 1784 - 1786
Mail coaches begin to run between Nottingham and London

Martha was able to look back on the first two years of her Home for Waifs and Strays with a great deal of pride and satisfaction. She was finally living a life she had craved whilst growing up. She was stretching her mind and capabilities, doing good work to help others and she felt she was making a difference in the world, maybe only in a small way, but making a huge improvement to the lives of these babies. Foxcroft House was now home to four resident infants. The original two children, Patty and Zachary, who had been joined by little Ann and a baby boy Agnes Adams had found on the doorstep, having been alerted to his existence by what she thought was the mewling of a kitten. They called him John Baptist after the Home's parish church, and being a hale and hearty baby, he had thrived and was now more than a year old.

Foxcroft also sheltered two more babies, living with their wet nurses until the end of the year, given up by heartbroken, ruined, servant girls, unable to care for themselves let alone a child. Martha and Eleanor Smith kept up their relentless fund raising for the orphanage, and Martha had ambition, she was determined to help a greater number of children in the future but for that they needed much more money.

Agnes was grateful to have a new girl to help in the house, Frances Tebbutt's daughter Betsey, who as the oldest of ten children had plenty of experience with babies. Frances had been keen to keep her at home, she needed help with her own brood, but Betsey had begged to be allowed to work for Martha and eventually the promise of an extra income to the household had swayed the decision. Betsey's desire to be working with Martha was certainly influenced by her crush on George and her hope that she would be able to see him more often. For the year her mother was employed as wet nurse, Betsey had often been a visitor to the house in Weekday Cross to collect the weekly pay and here she had met George, and at thirteen, developed a huge crush on the high spirited, handsome boy. He teased her unmercifully as if he were an older brother with every right to taunt a younger sister, but this only caused her blushes to deepen and her adoration to increase! Now, at fifteen she spent many a waking hour planning how to run into him, her most obvious ploy being to volunteer to go to the butchers shop for the Foxcroft House supplies, and her plan was bearing fruit. As Betsey ripened into a buxom, comely young woman, George's interest was aroused and his teasing took on a rather more flirtatious nature. Betsey was delighted with George and Agnes was delighted to have a happy, willing, Betsey.

Busy as she was, Martha never quite relinquished her mothering role and worried for, or rejoiced with, her siblings as appropriate.

From Jack she had gained a new little nephew Thomas, who was flourishing and who Ann, having had a difficult pregnancy and a gruelling delivery, was hoping would complete their own small family.

For Polly, Martha worried. She had lost another baby, this little embryo only managing to cling tenuously to life for a few weeks and it seemed motherhood wasn't to be.

"I thought it might be easier to accept the third time," Polly had sobbed in her sister's arms, "I know it was silly of me but I could not help but believe the baby would live. Dr Bayley thinks now I may be spared any more miscarries, he takes the view that I will not conceive again because he has seen how it has been with me in other women and thinks too much damage has been done. I don't know whether to be glad I will not have to grieve like this again or have it break my heart that I will not give Francis his son."

Martha also had to worry about her father. By the spring William's health began to fail. His joints ached, his bowels began to act unexpectedly and worst of all, in his view, he suffered dreadful toothache. Several of his teeth had fallen out and the remaining ones were causing him distress.

"All I can eat is the pap you feed babies with," he complained bitterly, "we weren't designed to live this long."

"Nonsense Father," Martha tried to reassure him, "you are much fitter than most of your old friends, and you do not have pap, Grace takes great care to cook you dishes you love and which are gentle on your teeth. You should have gone to see Mr Berdmore the dentist, he made a fortune from pulling teeth because people said he was so very good, hardly painful at all and you could have had new ones made of ivory or bone. But you've left it too late and I fear that troublesome tooth is going to fall out without his help. In his book, Mr Berdmore wrote that sugar is the cause of bad teeth, but you won't heed this advice and give it up."

William chose to ignore her, "Fanny was a better cook than that forward hussy, she would have looked after me better," he grumbled. Fanny had died peacefully that last winter and William had found the loss hard to bear, she had been one last link to his dead wife and they had passed many an evening playing cards or backgammon and reminiscing about the early days of his marriage. By then, Grace had taken control of the house, with Dolly, Anne and a new youngster, Maria, under her control, but William was right, she was not as good a cook as Fanny. "She doesn't know her place either," he carped, "she's here by our charity but instead of being quiet and grateful, she goes around singing all day and talking fit to bust. You are far too soft on her Martha, and have you heard how she mimics everyone. She mimics you, you know. Disrespectful I call it. It's just as well she is good at cards or I would have sent her up to Gabriel long before now."

Grace had a great affection for William, she was indebted to him, and cheerful without fail whatever befell her, she took all William's complaining in good part. It was true, she did love to impersonate the family and their visitors, she regarded it as good practice for when she became an actress, "But Aunt Martha," she would argue, "I don't have to be a loose woman to be an actress. Just 'cos others are, it ain't compulsory. I'll be alright and I'll be famous one day and you can come and watch me in London, in Drury Lane."

It was lucky for James that Simon Cramp was not only a fast learner but also a hard working boy as William found himself spending less and less time in the vintners shop. Simon filled the regular orders coming into Weekday Cross and organised deliveries to the taverns each week but James was still compelled to spend a great deal of his time attending to the ordering and accounting and not enough time canvassing for new customers. He was well aware that a direct approach to merchants and tradesmen proved more productive than his regular advertisements in the Nottingham Journal, and although young Jacob was a great help, he was no more ready to take on any of the financial side of Severns than Simon was. James was in a quandary and his discussions with Francis, and privately with Livy, drew him to a conclusion.

Wondering why, after all these years, he should feel like a recalcitrant schoolboy waiting to meet with his headmaster, James knocked on the office door, went in and confronted William, "Father, I think we should combine our two shops," he spoke rapidly, afraid to pause, "we are not getting any new customers here at Weekday Cross and I don't have time to develop new business as the boys are not ready yet to look after things completely on their own. Middle Pavement has plenty of room and if we rent out the shop downstairs here, the income from a tenant will help build up capital to invest in the future, and as soon as possible I think we should take on more space next to Severns, there are miles of caves under all those buildings which I know we can rent from Francis. It makes sense for us to expand now, since the end of the war in '83 trade is really picking up with France again and we can earn a good name for ourselves amongst the better off folk."

Seeing the look on his father's face, he hurried to say, "We can carry on living here in mother's home, you will not have to uproot after all these years."

"You can stop to take a breath now boy, you've taken my breath away too!"

So it was, against William's better judgement, as he was at great pains to say to anyone who would listen, that in March '86, all their business was transferred to Severns on Middle Pavement. The two young apprentices worked well together, enjoying each other's company and Simon learned, as Jacob had done some years before, to keep any suspicions about James's absences following the 'Martin' orders, to himself. Gratitude for their unexpected positions, ensured a deep and abiding loyalty to their master.

Not long after the amalgamation, word reached Nottingham that Charles Jubb had died and James seized the opportunity. "This is an ideal time father, the Trent Navigation has improved so much over the past few years it makes bringing heavy goods from Hull direct to Nottingham much easier. I think I should go to Hull to meet with Geoffrey Hadley, the importer I told you about who is looking for an investor, the chap Francis told us about. If he's as good as we hear, I think we should raise the money to go into partnership with him as soon as possible and import our own wines directly. At the moment it costs us dear to bring it up from London and very often it is shipped up the coast and through Hull to get to us as it is. We would become wholesalers here in Nottingham, and that is where the profits will lie."

"You go too fast young man, I will not have my family's future put to so much risk, we have already shut one shop down after your insistence that we open a second in the first place."

"But Father, it makes sense to have the premises in Middle Pavement, I thought you understood, it is more prestigious and it has all the capacity for expansion in the future. What I am suggesting now will make the expansion happen much more quickly."

William's temper, slow to emerge, now erupted, "Now I see my mistake letting you have your head before you were ready, but that is going to change. Whilst I am still alive I will go back to making the major decisions about my business. Don't you forget who started Severns. When I'm gone, you can do what you like with your share and take all the risks you want." He got up to leave the room, " Now, you will go to London and meet with Jubb's partner Merriman and arrange for things to continue as they have been. The mail coach does the journey in one day so you needn't stay long, but stay long enough to see Benjamin so you can tell us his news. He's another one trying to do too much too quickly."

CHAPTER TWENTY NINE
London 1786
Mozart's opera The Marriage of Figaro premières in Vienna

The night before James arrived in London, Ben and Kitty were alone in Kitty's parlour when Ada scratched at the door and came in, "I'm sorry to interrupt Madam but there's a gentleman at the door insisting he sees you. He says his visit is very urgent and in connection with Mr Warner. Here he gave me his card," and she handed it to Kitty.

"Daniel Dalvey? I don't know that name at all, it certainly isn't Nathan's agent here in London" she looked at Ben, "but I suppose I should see him, he may have news."

"Well you cannot receive him in here alone at this time of the evening, I shall stay," and he nodded to Ada to show the visitor in.

If his card had not stated the caller was a 'Gentleman Artist' it is certain his hosts would have guessed from his appearance. Beneath his chin length wig, powdered and precisely curled at either side, was a lean face, the hawkish nose reminding one of an eagle and his bright, jet black eyes added to the impression. He wore a pristine white stock, tied in an elaborate bow at the neck of his royal blue satin waistcoat, itself revealed beneath a fine cut away coat of umber wool. The lace ruffles on the cuffs of his white linen shirt framed his elegant, long fingered hands and oyster, tightly fitting breeches, white silk stockings and black leather shoes fastened with larger versions of the intricately engraved and bejewelled breeches buckles, completed his ensemble.

"My dear madam," he was speaking even as he crossed the threshold, returning his silver fob watch to the little pocket in his waistcoat, "I beg your forgiveness for visiting you uninvited at so late an hour but I have just this minute arrived in the City from Dover where I landed from the Continent early this morning and my errand is of such a pressing nature that I crave a few minutes of your time and apologise again unreservedly."

"How do you do Mr Dalvey," Kitty tried not to giggle at the sight of this flamboyant and flustered fop, "please do take a seat. You come on matters to do with my husband?"

"Dear madam, I would ask that I speak with you alone, some of that which I have to say is of a very personal nature and I am sure Mr Warner would wish me to only speak with you."

"This is Mr Benjamin Severn, my … cousin," Kitty hoped the pause did not register, "and you may speak freely in front of him. Indeed, if you do not wish to, I have no recourse other than to ask you to leave and make an appointment to see me at a more appropriate hour."

"My dear lady, I have endured the most dreadful passage from Calais in order to speak with you today, and I cannot therefore wait another minute. If you wish your cousin to stay then it is my pleasure."

"Would you care for some refreshment before you begin Mr Dalvey, if your journey has been so arduous I can offer you a light supper."

"That would be extraordinarily kind, and so gracious of you my dear Mrs Warner. I may call you Mrs Warner mayn't I? I feel I know you from our dear Mr Warner's letters. I am indeed quite famished, it seems an age since I dined at the coaching inn en route to London," and he sank into an armchair with a huge sigh.

When Ada had brought his food and left the room, he came straight to the point, "I have news for you directly from my dear friend Nathan. He is such a consistent writer and his letters have always been so full of interest that it healed some of the pain of separation," he paused and gazed at the ceiling, "I thought maybe they could be published one day as they hold such engaging accounts of the places and events the dear man has experienced these past years. Dear me, I digress," and as he paused again for breath and to take a bite of bread and cheese,

Kitty took the opportunity to say, "Alas, I fear Mr Dalvey, that I have had no news at all for these past near on five years. I have been worried, wondering where my husband is and how he is faring. The last I did hear, he was aboard HMS Terrible just before the campaign at Chesapeake Bay in the American War. I was unable to learn how many lives were lost or what happened to the officers. I have not heard from the Admiralty and I am assured that should he have been killed or badly wounded, I would most certainly have been given notice of that fact."

"But that battle was long ago, in September '81 and peace signed back in '83," Dalvey was puzzled, "I am surprised you have not heard his news since then, he certainly did not tell me he had ceased your correspondence. But to the point, I have, as I said, been travelling in Europe these last months and his most recent letter caught up with me whilst I was in Italy. I was in Vicenza admiring the great architecture of the genius Palladio, it is so very worthwhile visiting that town when you have the opportunity," he paused again, the faraway look in his eyes, then jolted and continued, "Well, the urgency of the letter he has enclosed for your good self and, because of the likely discomfort it might cause you, he, in his usual most thoughtful way, requested me to bring it to you personally. This caused me to leave straight for Calais, make the channel crossing, and here I am." He handed Kitty an unsealed note which she opened and read,

'I have asked my friend Daniel Dalvey to instruct my agent in London in the matter of the sale of the property wherein you now reside at Grange Walk, Bermondsey. I regret that I must ask you to vacate by the end of July '86, which gives you some six months to make alternative arrangements. I am sorry that I must do this to you Mrs Warner, but as Mr Dalvey will have told you, my circumstances are so much changed that I have no alternative.'

"The end of July," cried Kitty, "that is two weeks from now. This cannot be right, tell me what has happened."

"Your husband's letter is dated at the beginning of January of this year, but as I told you, I was on the continent and it only came into my possession recently," Dalvey began.

"Tell me, what has changed for Nathan, where is he, what is he doing. Is he in England, why has he not come to tell me this himself." Kitty's voice rose as did her anger.

"No, he is remaining in America. Some few months ago he resigned his commission in His Majesty's Navy and has taken up residence in Rhode Island and I am travelling to join him there at the earliest opportunity. He is saddened that he must incommode you in this way Mrs Warner, but he needs the funds made available from the sale of this house in order to finance a suitable dwelling in Providence. Don't you think that is the most appropriate name for the town we will live in? Rhode Island has a reputation as a sanctuary for religious and intellectual freedom and we are hoping we will live a more open life there," he smiled again, "Mr Warner has asked that I provide you with the sum of £100 once the sale is effected, and hopes that this will go some way to lessen your grievances."

"My grievances would be considerably lessened if he had not had the dishonesty to marry me in the first place," screeched Kitty, "and I see no decency at all in his years of silence, having deserted me, leaving me in a position where I am neither wife nor widow, and now rendering me homeless without notice. No thoughtfulness at all."

Ben could stay quiet no longer, he got to his feet, "No, Mr Dalvey," he bellowed, "£100 is an insult. Is it not enough that your friend," he sneered, "is a degenerate, that he must also be completely dishonourable through and through. The pair of you should be horse whipped, no, you should be hanged. Leave this house immediately," Ben physically pushed the man to the door, "and rest assured, Mrs Warner shall be gone from here by the end of the month and will have nothing more to do, ever, with either of you debauched creatures."

Collecting his overcoat and tall, broad brimmed hat from Ada, Mr Dalvey took as agitated an exit from the Grange Walk house as he had made his entrance.

"What shall I do," Kitty was weeping and Ben stood with his arms around her, his anger simmering underneath as he tried to console her, "and especially now", she whimpered in between sobs, "I had plucked up the courage and planned to tell you this evening Benjamin, I am expecting your child and I have been so worried as to your reaction and what on earth I shall do, and now this," and she howled into Ben's shoulder.

Ben's anger turned to surprise and then to delight all in a split second, "My precious love, a child? How marvellous, stop your crying right now and dry your beautiful eyes, we shall take this opportunity to live together as man and wife. I have long wanted to ask you, we will live in Oxford Street and you will take my name. I will arrange this week for the apartment over the shop to be made perfect for you, for us, for our family. Oh Kitty dearest, this will be a marvellous beginning, I shall provide for you and our child and care for you for the rest of our lives."

§

That next morning, James stood looking at the Trade Card in his hand. A fine line drawing of an East Indiaman, set against a backdrop of snow capped mountain peaks, a brilliant sun radiating from the left hand corner and underneath the image, a comprehensive list of goods that Benj. Severn - Grocer, could provide.

"The point of the picture," Ben said smiling, "is to send the message that all these products which now seem so essential and every day to us, are actually still utterly exotic and come from faraway places. It makes the consumer feel good."

"I can see that, they're excellent. I think I should have some made for Severns. The newspaper advertisements I run seem very mundane compared, and there's no place for an illustration in them either."

"There's no earthly reason the same thinking can't apply to you, wine is a necessity but like tea and spices, it is still exotic. You need a drawing of vines heavy with bunches of grapes - and sunshine of course. Not much of that here in England even in July!"

James had come straight away to meet with his brother in Oxford Street and he studied the floor space. It was a grocers shop, but unlike any he had been into in Nottingham, including Kings. Benjamin's premises seemed to exude a delicious air of extravagance. Pairs of candles hung by their wicks from beams in the ceiling, dangling above rows of tea chests and sacks of coffee beans, flours and grains, watched over by a mountain of artfully stacked sugar loaves, powdered sugar, muscovado sugar, sugar candy and candied citrons. A long run of counters on three sides of the room held baskets full of spices, peppers, almonds, dried fruits, anchovies, capers, olives and more. There were kegs of olive oil, vinegars and exotic looking sauces that James could not recognise and, under the shelves and counters, were drawers. Drawers filled with perfectly arranged merchandise, hair powders, rosin, beeswax, soaps, snuff and tobacco. It was splendid.

"I have a lot of individuals come into the shop to browse and choose their goods, ladies and gentlemen as well as their servants and they are all very discerning," Ben's excitement showed in his voice, "so it's important to make sure that we all know everything there is to know about our stock. There's a bit of a feeling going around that it's a waste of seven years to be apprenticed to a grocer and that after a few months, you can easily buy and sell all this, but it's not true, there's much more to it than just going to the wharves or the corn exchange. If you want to be successful, you have to be sure of what you are buying and selling so that you can advise and recommend. You must find it the same, your customers have confidence in you and trust you. Excuse me a moment," and he left James going quickly to greet a rather grand lady being ushered through the door by one of his white aproned staff.

James took the opportunity to stroll around, taking in the details of the design and looking for ideas. He noticed certain goods had already been weighed out and were in canvas bags or boxes, each with a personal hand written label attached, giving a description, weight and in one or two cases, a price.

"Sorry about that," Ben was back, "but it's always politic to make a fuss of your customers."

"I was looking around, it's a good idea to get away from the never ending bargaining on price, and also cash sales instead of credit. That's the way to go," James commented wryly, "when it's possible, of course."

"Some of my dealings are wholesale, not much yet, and although there is quite a lot of stock out the back here, the majority of the commodities are in bulk and I never even see it, I negotiate with the importers and it gets sent direct. We supply a few provincial grocers in the country and even in the short time I've been trading things have changed so much. The world is getting smaller and retailers have learned to be quite canny. Add in the fact that transport gets easier year by year and that there are so many more outlets to choose from, they don't have to just go blindly to one wholesaler anymore, they can pick and choose for different items. We have to be at the top of our game to attract and then keep our customers." He moved to the tea chests, "I've developed a bit of a name for top quality oils, vinegars and things like capers and olives but best of all, I'm getting a reputation for supplying very fine quality teas. Since Pitt lowered the taxes on it a couple of years ago after all that bother with the East India and Americans, there's been a twofold benefit for me, just about everybody in the land wants to drink tea and the smugglers of cheap Dutch tea have been put out of business.

"And you have a tea room right here in the main shop too. That's a clever idea, see and be seen, that's what society folk like. I have a lovely round table and chairs in front of my window, it helps that folk walking past can see us and more importantly, see who is in. Can you picture the house on Middle Pavement? I don't suppose you can, it's next to the old timber house which Francis owns, with the yard behind it, next to father's old tavern. You should come home one day soon and see for yourself."

"Maybe," Ben looked James full in the eyes, opened his mouth to speak but then gestured to one of his assistants, apologised to James again and rushed over to the other end of the shop. Later that day, he refused James's offer of taking him to supper at the Chop House in Thomas Simpson's and insisted that they go back to his lodgings for dinner instead.

CHAPTER THIRTY
London & Nottingham 1786
The Great Mace is stolen from the Nottingham Mayor

"Well that's a bombshell and no mistake about it," James was looking flabbergasted, "I'm not sure which aspect of the story is most confounding. I'm speechless!"

The trio were sitting in the parlour after dinner, a glass of James's special brandy in glasses before them. Kitty was in tears again and pleaded, "It is all my fault, please do not blame your brother, he has been nothing but a kind and loving friend to me these past years. I love him dearly and if you think our plan will harm him in any way, I can go to the country. My friend Maria has a cousin who I know would be prepared to take me in should she know of my desperate circumstances."

"I'll never let you go Kitty, and I'm sure James will agree with me. Moving away from here and setting up as man and wife in Oxford Street will do me no harm at all. We shall say we were married two years hence and as we are very unlikely to hear from that depraved husband of yours again or his family, our secret will be safe. We will have our own life together my love, you, me and our child." He had gone to Kitty and put his arm around her and now turning to look at James he asked, "How do you think I should deal with father? Not forgetting Martha, she will have an opinion I'll be bound!"

James had recovered a little by now, "I'm not too sure at the moment," he started, "but I'm damn certain you must say nothing about Mr Warner and his perversion, that would be a great mistake. We will keep that strictly between ourselves. I think you should say Kitty is a widow and you fell in love and got married and apart from being disappointed not to have known before, I can't believe anyone at home will have any suspicion that that is not the true story. As far as I'm concerned, Kitty, Ben, I am glad for you both. No one chooses who to lose one's heart to and only God can judge what is right and wrong and on that score Kitty, I wouldn't worry at all, it is that blackguard Warner who will burn in Hell, not you."

"Thank you James," Ben threw his arms around his brother and hugged him tightly, "I knew I could count on you, that's why we wanted to tell you the truth. It's a hard secret to live with and the only other soul we've told is Kitty's friend Maria and she can be trusted to take the knowledge to the grave. I know I can rely on you to help smooth things over with father too and we will come to Nottingham soon, but it's just not possible at the moment."

§

"What a wretched life that poor girl has had," Livy was lying raised up on one elbow peering into James's eyes as he finished telling her Ben's story, "I'm really pleased that she and your brother are going to live together and I see no reason anyone should question it. London is a big place and full of strangers, it's really not likely that anyone will ever know the truth when they move district."

"It's quite exciting for them I suppose, but Kitty is more worried about what God might think than being found out here on earth," James sat up and plumped up the cushions behind his head in Livy's sumptuous feather bed, "She's a very engaging woman," and grinning he took Livy's face in his hands, "but not beautiful and witty and cultured and sensuous like you my wicked mistress. How wonderfully we make love together."

Livy pulled away from his embrace, "Stop, I want to know more. What did you tell your family and what did they say?"

"Well it caused a bit of a stir naturally. We had agreed the story that Kitty is a widow, her husband died in one of the battles in America, and as they already knew that she was Ben's landlady, all we had to say was that the house reverted to his family in London when he died. It didn't seem unreasonable and as for getting married without any notice, well, just the usual thing, the child was on the way and they didn't want to wait. In fact, it all seems a perfectly normal tale of perfectly normal people!"

"So, another baby in your family," Livy mused, "don't you think it's time you started looking for a wife and got on with breeding? You know you should," she finished mischievously.

"You know perfectly well I have no intention of doing so. You are all, and more, than I need in a woman. My life is perfect as it is, I can concentrate on making money and then," he smirked, "when you are so gracious as to allow me, I can concentrate on you." he stopped to kiss her, "What more could I ask for? Certainly not what my friends are going through. Ed, got married earlier this year and they've just had a son and he says his life is not his own any more. John Barratt the builders' son married his Martha last Christmas Day and their child is arriving soon and even John Vezey who I never thought would marry, has up and done it." He pulled Livy towards him again, his body delighting in the feel of her smooth, fragrant, naked skin on his, "All I want is you. Not the henpecked life of a husband and father," nibbling her shoulder, "just you."

The arrangement he and Livy had suited them both. James's thoughts of marriage which he harboured when they first met had faded, he now understood that she was right to keep the relationship as it was. They were the greatest of friends and the best of lovers and neither saw the need to change things. They often talked of commerce and James came to appreciate her acumen and to rely a little on her views. She had expanded her own drapers, adding a silk mercer's shop to her holdings in the town.

"I have a good man running it for me," she told him, "he was with the previous owner for many years. I can trust him to do well for me too, so it seems I am more of a factor these days, not running the shops myself. You must hurry up my little one if you wish to rival me," she teased him as they finished their champagne, relaxed and sated after making love, "especially as you will need to provide for your wife and children one day, whereas I have no real family to consider, only my late husband's nephews and nieces, so I can indulge my own extravagances."

James pulled her, roughly, closer to him, "I hate to hear you say that my love, I am your family. I wish so much you could share in mine too, my only regret is that we must remain secret. Benjamin and I seem to have parallel lives, both of us with secrets."

"I'm afraid we must my little one, or you will ruin my reputation! As if I cared too much, and it would more likely ruin yours, but it would not help me in my drapers to have it known that we are lovers, a woman in business is looked upon so differently. We must be content with what we have."

It could not have been worse. James was taking his leave of Livy at her door in Castle Gate, they exchanged a fond hug and lingering finger tips, just as George was drawing away in the butcher's cart from a neighbouring house. Their eyes met, George gave a malicious grin and reined in the old piebald to remain in step with James, following him along the street, challenging him to speak, daring him to a public row.

George harboured his knowledge like a smouldering fuse creeping towards the gunpowder, he chose not to denounce his brother there and then, savouring the information and biding his time. As the days went by, James endured his brother's innuendo and veiled threats with silence, he wanted only to safeguard Livy from gossip and censure, and with no one, and certainly not Livy, to share his burden, the tension he felt at home was difficult to endure.

CHAPTER THIRTY ONE
Nottingham 1788
John Wesley preaches his last sermon, in Nottingham

Ben's news had naturally come as a great surprise to the family. William had expressed despair that his third son should appear so impulsive in every way. Not just marriage and fatherhood but rushing ahead so fast with his business. "You boys," he looked at James, "you don't take time to consider things properly. You just jump right in and hope everything will work out, you should both slow down a bit."

The sisters were very happy for their brother. Martha wished she could have met her new sister, but she hoped now that by writing to her, Kitty would keep them all up to date with Ben's life in London. Polly was particularly excited about the news and decided to redouble her efforts to persuade Francis to take her to London. She longed to go, to see the great capital and to engage in her most popular pastime, shopping.

Following his meeting with Richard Merriman, James had returned to Nottingham more determined than ever to switch to an importer in Hull, but disheartened by his father's reaction both to his own plans and to the news from London, he decided reluctantly to defer any discussions for a while, Ben's wholehearted endorsement of his plans was not likely to help elicit the desired response.

It was therefore to James's increasing frustration, that Severns continued to operate much the same over the next twelve months or more, until, in the late summer of '88 everything changed, William died. He had taken to his bed some months before and

Martha, Grace and Dolly had borne the brunt of nursing him. He took a poor view of doctors, completely refused to go to the new hospital and had wanted to rely on only a tincture of rhubarb and liquorice for his stomach complaints, neither ingredient stopping the pain. Inevitably he had grown gradually weaker until his heart finally gave out. He was sixty five years old and at the end, died a peaceful enough death in his own bed with Martha and Polly at his side. His daughters recognised he was pleased to be on his way to see Mary again, it was twenty two years since she had gone before him and he was eager to join her.

The whole family gathered for his burial at St Mary's. It was not too sombre an occasion, William had had a good long life and the sorrow of his passing was alleviated by the joy the siblings felt at all being together again. Kitty had felt anxious when she, Ben and their son first arrived in Nottingham, but was soon at ease when the family welcomed her with open arms, doting aunts and boisterous cousins fussing over the baby. His grandfather's namesake, he was now almost eighteen months old and known as William Severn, even though he had been baptised William Severn Warner as Kitty had found herself unable to hide the truth from her old priest in Bermondsey. After the traumatic meeting with Dalvey, she and Ben had settled down in the apartment above the shop in Oxford Street and were certainly not aware of any gossip, Kitty was accepted by the neighbours with only courtesy and kindness. The arrival of baby William cemented friendships with other wives and mothers and the little Severn family was happy and contented.

In Nottingham, only Elizabeth had reservations about them, "Do you not think Kitty is hiding something from us?" she asked her husband during a quiet moment, "it is as if she is guarding her every word."

Billy had not noticed anything amiss, but was aware that his wife had an uncanny accuracy when judging human nature. He acquiesced, "Well, you may well be right my dear wife, but it cannot be anything serious I'm sure, it is the first time she has met all of us, so we should keep this feeling between ourselves."

The most important issue of the day was raised early in the evening of the day of the funeral after their father's Will had been read aloud. The eight siblings and Francis sat round the table in the house on Weekday Cross, glasses of ale or port in front of them, the poignancy of the old tapestry chair bringing a lump to more than one throat. Elizabeth, Ann and Kitty were busying themselves elsewhere with the children and the Reverend, as the eldest son, rose to his feet and moved to the head of the table.

"It is no surprise that Father has asked for all his possessions to be bequeathed equally amongst us." He clasped his hands behind his back, "Father was a very fair man who strived all his life to do his very best for us, his family, and I sincerely believe he regarded us all equally in his affections and would not have wished to be divisive. However, James and I have spoken together as we are firmly of the opinion that the vintners, Severns, should be regarded as an issue separate from Father's personal estate."

James looked round the room anxiously, scrutinising his brothers and sisters, trying to gauge their reactions from their faces, as Billy continued, "I am convinced that the family as a whole, and let me reiterate, the family as a whole, will benefit far more in the long run if the vintners remains as one entity and also, importantly, if James continues to run it on behalf of us all. James understands the commitment and responsibility he will undertake, but he is eager to do so. Maybe you would like to confirm this James?"

James's heart was racing, "I truly think that Severns can grow and become a very successful business. It will mean taking some risks of course, but they are calculated risks, and I have spent many hours carrying out research and understanding how to take the operation forward so that it will provide for all our needs in the future. We are all doing well at the moment," he looked at his siblings, "Billy you say you are becoming quite comfortable in Hinckley. Jack, your butchery is going well and you have George under your wing. As for you Ben, I shall have to strive very hard to catch up with you, and Francis, you and Polly are certainly not struggling. Martha, Severns provides for you already and Joe, I believe you are well fixed with Mr Cook and happy with your lot? I promise you all, here and now, I will work tirelessly to make sure we are a great success and Severns can be handed down to the next generation, and the next, and the next."

George was so outraged he was ready to explode, "That's the absolute limit," he shouted, "it's completely unacceptable. Why should James have everything handed to him on a plate again, I should have my share now and he can work up from nothing like the rest of us. Father did all the hard work and," pointing at his brother, his face contorted, "he will get all the benefit. I need my inheritance for a shop of my own, I can't work for Jack for ever, and Father wanted us all to share the vintners and that's what we should do." His anger rendering him close to tears, he appealed to Jack, "surely you need the money for your shop and for the family?"

"Sorry lad, I agree with Billy and James, what they are proposing makes a lot of sense to me. Ann and I don't necessarily need the cash right now, and don't forget George, father paid for your apprenticeship so you too have had a good start. You have to work hard to make your way in this life and if you would only buckle down and take it more seriously, there's no reason why you can't do as well as Uncle Crosland and Francis, but it takes time. If you showed us you were ready, we would help you have your own shop, but you are far too busy playing instead of working."

"But that's my point, James doesn't have to work his way up, it's all there, ready done for him, it's not justice," he looked directly at James, his face puce with anger, "and what about his whore? You don't know do you, he keeps a whore in Castle Gate, or maybe she is keeping him. Olivia Martin, old enough to be his mother, yes, our sanctimonious brother." All faces turned from George to James.

James, his heart pounding barked, "Just shut up. You don't know what you are talking about."

"So the rumours are true then. You are her lover! When I first heard about it I thought it couldn't be true, you are so pompous, why would she want to bed you?"

"Stop! Is this true James?" Martha clapped her hand over her mouth.

Looking at his sister's face and then at the shock on his brothers', James defended himself, "Yes, it is true and I am not ashamed. I love Livy, she is the most incredible woman and she makes me very happy. Why should we not be friends?"

"It's a dangerous path to walk, even if it is more commonplace these days to have a mistress," Billy was worried, "does she expect you to marry her?"

"More's the pity, she doesn't. I'd marry her tomorrow but she cares too much for me to demand it. She is a good woman and I'll not let you speak ill of her."

"Oh I wish I had never contacted her in the first place," Martha had left the table and was standing by the fireplace toying with her apron, "it's all my fault. It makes sense to me now, ever since she started to donate linen for the children I have felt ill at ease with her, it always seems as if she is laughing at me."

"She would certainly not be laughing at you Martha, she admires you enormously for what you are doing. If only you got to know her you would find you have so much in common and would undoubtedly be friends."

"James, it will do you harm." Martha was crying, "there is a great deal of talk about Mrs Martin since her husband died. I'd say you are not the first young man she has decided to befriend, and as your sister, I ask that you do not see her again."

"Why would you say that? She is clever, hardworking and successful, and has definitely done nobody any harm."

"That's not true," snarled George, "she's got everything for nothing too, just like you, she didn't start that business, she got it by marrying for it, not a lot of cleverness or hard work involved with that. Unless her husband was old and ugly and she still had to bed him!" George sniggered, "no wonder you like her, she's like you, you've had it easy all your life, you think only of yourself."

James' leapt to his feet, his face close to George's, his body shaking and his voice choking with anger, "What have I ever done George to make you so jealous? What started all this? Since I was a boy I've tried to do the best for all of us. Yes I have ambition and there's nothing wrong with that, I want to be successful, if you weren't such an idle waster and tried working hard for a change, you could have your own business too. As for this, I would never have thought even you could be so callous. I'm ashamed to call you my brother."

Billy, rose to his feet again, his calmness belied by a furious little tick at the left of his forehead, "I think you should both take a deep breath, sit down and compose yourselves. Nothing is to be gained by hurling abuse. We must leave these personal matters aside and continue to discuss Father's Will. Let me try to explain a little more George. If Severns continues to thrive, not only will it afford an annuity for Martha, as it seems she is determined not to marry," he smiled weakly over at his sister, "but I am also positive that in the fulness of time, James will be able to make an annual dividend payment, to each one of us, from the profits."

"What if it doesn't continue to thrive, what if James makes a hash of it, what if Severns goes bust, like that chap on Goose Gate the other day, what then? If that happens, I won't have had my money now and I won't have it in the future. Father was dead set against his plans, we all know that, and I'd trust Father over him any day, he always said James had ideas above his station."

"James will not make a hash of it," Ben, recovering from the revelation about his brother, came to his defence, "I've spoken for hours with him about the way forward and we agree on his strategy. You can't say I don't have a track record George, I've got this far on my own and I think it's best for all of us, your brother has a very good business head on his shoulders."

"Well, it's easy for me," Josiah said softly, " I have every faith in James to do well by us and I'm happy with my own life at the moment. Mr Cook not having a son of his own, I'm rather hoping to take on more responsibility as he gets older and I won't be getting married for years. I just wish we could spend more time discussing how to help the real poor and needy rather than squabbling over father's Will, we all have more than enough as it is. Martha, you have always been known for your fairness, what do you say?"

George pushed back his chair and got to his feet, "I can see you are all against me, James has poisoned your minds, and there's no reason to ask Martha and Polly, they are just women and have no say in the matter, it is up to us six to make the decision," he growled nastily.

Martha, agonising at the thought of James and Olivia, was now thrown all over again, she raised her eyebrows and spoke to Polly, "Well sister, understand this, apparently we have no say! If ever we needed proof that women are just pawns in men's lives, that's it I think. However, what would you say if you could, dearest sister, if we were indeed allowed a voice on the matter of our own future, are we happy to entrust our family's fortunes to James," and Polly, her mind dwelling on Olivia Martin, nodded, mystified, in assent.

There followed an embarrassed silence and Francis looked at Billy, "May I speak?" At Billy's nod he said, "Billy's right, we should keep emotions out of this and look at it from a purely commercial point of view. James's private life has nothing to do with the decision, and inflammatory insults to the ladies will not help either," he stared icily at George. "I share the opinion wholeheartedly that the business will benefit the family better if it stays as one and I have every confidence in James to achieve his ambitions. He will certainly have my support and you should all, in good time, enjoy a share, but that means not splitting the assets up now. As I hope you well know, I would not recommend any course of action that would not benefit your sister, my wife."

"Well George," Billy looked at him sadly, "I'm sorry you feel as you do but I believe the decision we have to make must be for all of us or none of us. Would you want to go against all your brothers and sisters?"

"What choice do I have," he answered sullenly, "you've all made up your minds. Do what you like, I'm going to The Fleece and I shall drink to father's memory, he would never have wanted this."

§

In spite of the sadness he felt at losing his father, the realisation of the depth of George's jealousy and the danger of the exposure of his relationship with Livy, James felt an overwhelming excitement at the thought of his future and was now, more than ever, determined to make Severns a success. The day had dawned grey and overcast just one week after the big row with

George, but James had a spring in his step as he set off for Messrs. Valentine & Reave, his mission of such import that nothing could quell his sense of eager anticipation and the butterflies in his stomach as he made his way to High Pavement, ran up the steps to the imposing front door of the elegant, three storied town house, lifted the polished, brass ring from the lion's mouth and knocked loudly on the front door.

Having announced himself to a clerk he was now in the ante room of Mr Dudley Reave's office, where, instead of taking a seat as he was bid, he continued to pace up and down the room like a caged lion.

James was twenty six years old. His solid, stocky frame went unregarded beneath a face thought of as fine and handsome, crowned by dark blond hair tinged with the red inherited from his mother, and which hard as he tried to tame it, broke forth in little curls around his face and escaped at every possible moment from the ribbon that valiantly tried to hold it back.

Tapping and twisting his hat in his hands, he spun round as he heard the door open and without hesitating rushed to grasp Mr Reave's hand in his own, "Good day to you Sir. I have come to instruct you to draw up a Form of Renunciation, the matter is settled with my brothers and sisters, I shall be the sole beneficiary of our father's will. Severns is to be mine alone."

CHAPTER THIRTY TWO
Nottingham and Hull 1789
The French Revolution begins with the Storming of the Bastille

James found himself unable to take Martha's advice to finish his relationship with Livy and equally unable to tell his love of the dreadful conversation. For her sake, he was more cautious making his way to and from her house, for his own sake, he wanted to see her more and more. Since the quarrel, apart from George who never missed the chance to sneer about her, Livy was not mentioned again at home and Martha chose to find herself unavailable, asking Agnes to meet their benefactor instead, when she called at Foxcroft to see the children and leave the lengths of fabric.

Before leaving for London, Ben had tried to rally George round, "Come on, between us this will give us so many opportunities for our sons. Grocers, butchers, wine merchants and maybe glaziers. The future is looking so good."

"Well I'd better get going and make some sons if we are to have a Severn dynasty. Jack's got two already, you've got one and by the time James has had half a dozen, not with that old whore though, my boys will be like Joe and me, way down at the bottom of the pecking order."

Billy tried too, but could do nothing to placate George, he left the town assuring him he would pray for him. His sisters put the outburst down to George's grief at losing his father and forgave their brother quickly, and the rift, with all but James, healed quickly.

James tried hard to put the hurt he felt at George to one side and immersed himself in work, spending the winter preoccupied with an impending trip to Hull. He was to wait until the spring, but in the short term, Francis had arranged a meeting for him with Joshua Hooper, a hosiery manufacturer who exported his goods through an agent there. This gentleman in turn, wrote to Geoffrey Hadley their merchant, to introduce James and advise of his personal visit.

"Francis, why don't you come with me?" James asked, "we could do this venture together."

"No James, thanks all the same, but I'll not come for two reasons. Firstly I've got enough to do with my farms and the dairy, not to mention the slaughterhouse and shop. Plus I have to keep an eye on the tannery I put money into and in my spare time," he chuckled, "deal with the properties on Middle Pavement and some of those tenants need a close eye I can tell you. Also, now that I've bought those extra acres out in Langar, I'm supplying more and more butchers here, in town and a lot of the villages too. I'm hoping Joe and his fellow protesters leave my fences alone out there now, I think he was suitably embarrassed when he came to apologise to me, but I know he feels so strongly about the enclosures. My next venture is to start sending beef down to London, the demand there is never ending. I'm already sending down cheese and looking to increase that too, so it's a lot to be going on with." Francis was as enthusiastic as ever about his life, "It's a good year for mutton this year, the prices are high and I've also got my tenant farmers looking after ten pigs for me as a start. Then as if that wasn't enough to keep me busy, I'm negotiating for some land out at Gedling, thought I should diversify into some arable - barley and oats, but I need to look into it a bit more first."

"That's only one reason old friend?" James raised his eyebrows, "I did go to school and I can count!"

"Well, the second and the real reason I'll not come to Hull, is that I've promised Polly we're going to London for a month in May, so I can't be away in April too," he laughed, "come on, let's go and have a jug of ale together, we hardly ever make the time to sit and chat these days."

§

A week before James was due to leave for Hull, George requested the family's presence at his marriage to Betsey Tebbutt. "St Mary's on the 7th and we'll have a bit of a feast and party afterwards," he told them, "it won't be a grand affair, her family can't afford much, and father's not here to help pay for anything. It will be at the Kings Head which is fine, Dick Turpin used to drink there - but it's only the landlord who's likely to rob us now!" George roared with laughter, "Betsey's not feeling too good at the moment, she's a couple of months or so gone, but we're looking forward to the bairn. I suppose we will have to live with her mother," he directed this barbed comment to James, "but at least one more brat in that house won't be noticed."

James looked at his younger brother and his heart softened a little, he would never understand the way George felt towards him, but in that moment he saw the little brother he'd loved to play with, the child he had grown up with, "Well done George, I'm sure we can help out with the wedding party, we can certainly provide the beer for you. Betsey is an honest girl and it will be good to have you settled down - the young maids of Nottingham will be all the safer for it too!"

George did not return his smile.

§

James had thought his first trip to London those years ago had been tedious and an ordeal, but it was as nothing compared to the journey to Kingston upon Hull. The Nottingham stage took him only as far Gainsborough where he spent a passably tolerable night, dining with congenial folk at the White Hart and the next day, took another stage along the desperate roads towards Hull. Having chosen to travel inside the coach, he was irritated as one of his fellow travellers became desperately anxious when James pulled back the leather curtains at the window. He quickly learned that this farmer was firmly of the opinion that fresh air was extremely detrimental to his health and insisted that the curtains be drawn across again. Inevitably, the hours were spent in semi darkness and a stifling, stuffy atmosphere. James was the only man to get down from the coach willingly at the start of each moderate hill, and walk in order to lessen the old horses' load. Conversation was sparse, and to James uninteresting. He was very glad to arrive at Barton upon Humber where he alighted and, his bones shaken to their very core by this old, unsprung carriage, he stood testing his limbs watching with relief as the red rimmed wheels of the torturous carrier disappeared. His relief was to be short lived, his ordeal was not yet over as he was compelled to clamber aboard an old ferry boat, his bags thrown on unceremoniously after him by a porter of sorts, and he was rocked and rolled the mile across the fast flowing, terrifying River Humber. From the ferry landing stage an equally unsprung wagon carried him the last part of his journey into town.

Crossing the empty marshes he saw before him the vista of Hull's long, defensive walls built over with a patchwork of warehouses and shacks, and towards the town, the bobbing grey-white sails of the hundreds of vessels beginning or ending their adventures there. Closer to he would see the familiar, chaotic forest of spars, masts and tangled ropes, the chaos being controlled more or less by the harbour master. It was a smaller version of the London docks.

As the wagon drew up to the southernmost end of the High Street, the landlord of the George and Dragon was waiting to greet him, extolling the virtues of his establishment and promising that Mr Hadley had suggested he stay. A hundred yards walk and James's fortunes changed dramatically, a good cup of tea, bread and butter and a well aired, clean bed. What more could he have asked for!

Geoffrey Hadley was almost dwarfed by the dark brown, button backed, leather easy chair placed in front of the window of his premises in Bishop Lane. In contrast, his foot, made immense by yards of white swaddling, dominated the matching leather stool on which it rested precariously. "Forgive me my boy if I don't get up, got an attack of gout. Damned painful it is, feels like there's a rat underneath all this padding gnawing away at my flesh. Still, gout's a good thing, the doctors say it should prolong my days here on this earth so I'm almost happy to put up with it. Don't do much for my temper though," and as if to demonstrate, he bellowed, "Master Philip, bring more of this claret and a glass for Mr Severn - and hurry up."

He motioned for James to take the other easy chair and as he sat down, James began to study his future ally. Hadley's bobbed, curled and freshly powdered wig had been knocked a little askew by the high back of the chair revealing a little of the white stubble of his own hair beneath. Tiny ears framed the perfectly round face, itself practically eclipsed by a pair of huge metal rimmed spectacles perching on his straight nose. His eyes regarded James through the top half of the lens and the papers on his lap through the bottom half.

"How do you do Sir, please do not concern yourself on my account. I have had a very pleasant walk this morning from the Inn, your town in bursting with activity and I have had a lot to look at," James had taken an instant liking to this little man, "I'm sure I shall enjoy my stay here and I hope that we may do business together."

As the clerk brought the wine and settled it on the table in front of them, James looked around Hadley's office. At the far end was a double sided desk, the tops slanted to hold large ledgers that three more industrious clerks were inscribing with their quill pens. A magnificent bookcase held many more leather bound books and the walls were adorned with maps. Some showing the world, some Europe and some individual countries. Two globes sat on a high shelf above the door and Hadley's own grand mahogany desk and chair was set to one side of the room. This was most certainly a mercantile establishment, everything indicated wealth and worldliness.

"I'd better tell you a bit about us then if you think we might venture together," the mellow, urbane voice seemed at odds with his stature, "Hadley Bros. has never been involved in the major import, export dealings with Scandinavia and the Baltic, that's only for the big boys such as the Sykes and Wilberforces. Stop me and ask questions anytime my boy, otherwise I'll rattle on like an out of control wagon!" He took a draught of his wine, "Damned pain, it's only the claret that makes it bearable - and that's only just. Where was I? Oh yes, Hull's major imports are traditionally timber, iron, pitch, tar, tobacco and stuff and you know we've all had quite a boom since the end of the war in '83 and now one of our biggest industries has become whaling. Seems there's an ever increasing demand for whalebone and oil.

It's a horrible, bloody trade to make sure our ladies have corsets to make 'em the right shape and oil lamps so we men can see to admire 'em!" and he threw back his head as far as the chair would allow and gave a loud, throaty laugh. "We ship out England's lead, ironmongery and a huge amount of cloth and of course, there's a lot more besides. Hadley Bros., well, we're just a middling sort of House, clutching at the coat tails of the big merchants."

"Mr Hooper and I have spoken, therefore I know that you export his hose and because of our introduction, I assume that you must deal in wines and spirits, but I'm afraid I know very little else about yourselves or Hull, so I am very interested to hear what you have to say."

"Well, when you walked up the High Street this morning you'll have noticed those splendid houses. They used to be the grand merchant's homes, the land to the rear leads down to their own staithes on the River Hull, but all that changed when the new Dock was opened on the Humber in '78. We all have a licensed quay up there now which makes life a bit more organised I suppose. Not so much bother for the customs men anyway as they had a devil's own job trying to collect the taxes when each boat was a quay and the lightermen were hither and thither unloading and loading."

"I believe Sir, that the very same problems had existed in the Thames before the regularisation of licensed quays. Your new dock must have stopped much of the enormous amount of theft here too?"

"It most certainly has and you'll have seen the miles of warehouses along the banks, makes everything more efficient and less open to stuff vanishing in the night! But to continue about us, Hadley Bros. has an agent in Amsterdam - you understand that?" he looked up at James who shook his head but had no time to respond before Hadley went on, "we all have a good relationship with the Dutch, Hull has always been concerned with exports to them, and it's through them that we arrange all the credit to pay for our imports."

James looked a bit blank which prompted Hadley to say, "But I get ahead of myself, we will return to this aspect later. Hull is not just an international port it's also very busy with coastal traffic, mainly to and from London but this trade tends to bypass us merchants so we, Hadley Bros. deal primarily in importing wines and cognac direct from France - well, when we are not at war with the devils," he gave another throaty chuckle, "and from Spain and mostly from Portugal of course. We also take Portuguese cork which has a very large market, a certain amount of olive oils but that trade is increasingly going to London, and sumac."

"What is sumac?" James had never heard of it.

"It's a dried plant, can be used as a spice in cooking but the tuns we bring in go to the tanners. You'll have seen all the red dye that makes the leather so soft in the tanneries in Nottingham? Well that's sumac. We also deal with exporting hosiery from your home town and Leicester too, cottons from Manchester and still a bit of the cheap kersies. Sorry to say that's the fabric of choice for slaves clothes, but it's a merchant's livelihood and if we don't send it out, someone else will. I expect you are aware that the Iberian colonies are prevented from buying anything direct from us so we have a large market selling to Spain and Portugal for them to export to south America? Rum old situation ain't it?"

James concurred with a nod and managed to ask, "So tell me more about how the merchant process works, I know you do not have to lay out large sums to cover any goods in transit but it would be interesting for me to hear how you deal with these Bills of Exchange."

An hour later, James was fully conversant with Hadley's examples. He had followed the trails of merchants A,B and C on the tablet before him on the table and he also knew, he thought, why so many ledgers were needed to keep track of 'who owed who' and when, if ever, money changed hands!

Hadley being indisposed was to dine in his rooms upstairs but suggested that James walk out and eat at the Chop House within Kings Ale House. 'Kings', James thought, 'home from home!' He set off along the High Street and passed through The Exchange, a handsome square where the Custom House stood. Milling around, talking and smoking their pipes, were smartly dressed merchants and weather beaten ships' captains, many of whom James could make out were speaking in foreign languages and his anticipation grew as he likened the scene to those he had witnessed in London.

Back at Hadley Bros. his body replenished with a splendid meal of mutton and vegetables and his mind racing ahead with his hopes and dreams, James wanted to talk about transferring to Hull for his supplies and to investigate the possibility, told to him by the Hoopers, of taking a part in the merchant's business itself. He had wondered over his dinner, why Hadley would be looking for outside investors rather than involving his own family, surely he thought, Bros. was short for Brothers, and in addition, there appeared to be four apprentices already on the scene, undergoing the convoluted training. When he broached the subject, rather awkwardly, not quite knowing the right words to use, it produced an unexpected response!

"No, no, dear boy. I am not looking for investors in Hadley Bros. Oh dear no," Hadley's laughing led to coughing and when he had finished spluttering, he returned his large, white kerchief up his sleeve and explained, "Why ever would I do that. No, let me start at the beginning, I must make myself clear. My father started Hadleys in '33, he's now gone and I'm the only remaining son. I had four brothers, all older than me and everyone of 'em dead too, so instead of going into the Church as I'd planned to do since I was a child, I've found myself running this show. I'm a non conformist I might add, a Unitarian if you know what that means?"

"I certainly do Sir, my older brother is a Unitarian Minister, he's based in Leicestershire at present. When he first left home years ago, he was only sixteen and followed John Wesley but soon after that, he says, he saw the 'error of his ways'! He's a good man and has tried to explain all the differences in the church's attitude to me, although I fear I have not been an attentive pupil, but I certainly have no disagreement with the matter."

"Good Lord, what a coincidence. I think this bodes very well for us, don't you? Will you take some Port and a little biscuit? I think you'll like it, a Sandeman, one of the best. Well, so here I am, with no brothers and I have been rather remiss in not managing to produce any children either. My dear wife is a little delicate I fear and has not been able to carry a child to term, a source of great sorrow as I'm sure you can understand."

"Quite, my sister Polly has suffered in the same way and it makes her very melancholy from time to time. The similarities between our families is becoming uncanny."

"In spite of this lack of kin, Hadley Bros. is in very good shape and if I wish to expand, I can visit Mr Smith's Bank for funding. No, my future venture is a deviation from this path and potentially far more exciting and rewarding. I wish to gather together a group of like minded wine merchants to join me in becoming our own wine and spirit shippers. I'm sure this is the right path to take for the coming years and I certainly have the requisite knowledge. Of course, being here in Hull I am in the business already so to speak and I have the contacts here in England, and in Portugal, Spain and France. I have already an agreement in place with the owners of a small cargo ship and what I need is the working capital to tackle the increased complexities and primarily, as you will understand, to share the risk of this enterprise. For this I need outside investors." It seemed his enthusiasm took his mind off the gout and his face had lost the frown, "I had thought to seek nine other gentlemen, I have agreed terms with seven and I should like to offer you the opportunity, subject of course to our reaching a mutually satisfactory agreement, to become the eighth. I envisage that you would hold an equal share but given the geographical distance between us, you would leave the day to day operation to those of us here in Hull."

The serious discussions then began. Severns would benefit from the direct purchase of their wines and the quantities would be such that James could start to trade as a major wholesaler in Nottingham too. By the time he left town, the bones of an agreement for him to take a share in the syndicate were ready to be drawn up by the solicitors and all James had to do was find the money!

§

"Francis, this could be a great opportunity for you too," James had hurried to meet up on his return and they were sipping coffee together, "there is still one member to be found. A courier has brought the draft agreement to me and I shall take it over to Dudley Reave to go through it with me. Would you like to join us, listen in and see what you think? It would help me to have you there as you might spot something we don't. I'd like to have the best possible deal that's for sure."

"James, I don't know that much about the wine trade, it would be a huge risk for me."

"But you do understand commerce Francis. Come with me to discuss it. At least you wouldn't have to borrow the money like I will, you've been looking for another investment, you told me. It can be this instead of buying more Trent Navigation shares!"

"Well, I'll come to the meeting with Reave, but I'm not promising anything. You well know my priority at the moment is getting Polly to London and more to the point, getting back again, still solvent!"

"This will be a welcome respite from those negotiations then old friend. Today at five o'clock. I'll meet you there."

CHAPTER THIRTY THREE
London 1789
George III is known to be very ill, possibly mad.

May arrived and brought with it the day Polly had been longing for. She and Francis set off early in a hired post-chaise, "I could not bear to think of you on the public stage coach being thrown around for hours on end," Francis had decided some weeks before, "this will still be deuced uncomfortable, but at least we will have it to ourselves. It will be a ghastly ordeal and I don't understand why you are so keen to go! But keen you are, and so I have booked the finest rooms to stay in and you shall go shopping every day if that is your wish." He smiled at his wife, he still adored her, his heart bleeding for her as she put on such a brave face when surrounded, as it seemed constantly, by new born babies.

"Thank you Francis. You are the kindest husband in the whole world and I will buy you beautiful presents and turn our house into the most fashionable in England and everyone will admire you. And, I am so impatient to see the latest fashions, my dresses are all, I'm sure, so dowdy and provincial. Do you think Ben will introduce us to Mrs Bankes and her friend? I liked Kitty very much but I'm not sure she is dressed in the best of fashion. I saw a broad sheet the other day which shows our dresses becoming slimmer."

"That's a jolly good thing then," Francis looked serious.

"Why ever would you say that my love, I wasn't sure you ever really noticed our clothes."

"Well, I was thinking if we have to pay for the muslin by the yard, a slimmer fashion will save us a fortune!" and before

Polly had time to pout, he pulled her into his arms and kissed her fiercely on the lips.

"I've arranged for us to stay the night at Towcester, that will be more than enough miles for us in one day. We should be comfortable at the White Horse, I have ordered a private parlour for our dinner and I have heard both the hospitality and the food is excellent. I want nothing but the best for my beautiful wife."

Polly certainly did look beautiful. She had on a new, perfectly tailored redingote of fine, deep honey coloured wool. The fitted jacket, set off with reveres and cuffs of chocolate brown, the edges lined with golden buttons, was open over an ivory silk waistcoat embroidered with honey gold flowers, which in turn was worn over a white high necked shirt. The skirt, perfectly plumped over the padded under roll tied around Polly's waist just skimmed her delicate leather high heeled shoes and the pièce de resistance, her dark auburn curls were peeping out from under a striking, matching brown, broad brimmed hat which was trimmed with three long feathers. Francis had caught his breath when he first saw her, she looked exquisite and even Polly had to agree that her fears of appearing a country bumpkin in the big city were quite without foundation.

The following evening they arrived, a little weary, at the rooms Francis had taken in Jermyn Street. The owner of the house was to provide a general servant and cook and Polly was almost beside herself with joy when she learned that, through Ben's good offices, Augusta Bankes was to provide her with a junior ladies maid for the duration of her stay. It was a charming brick built house of four storeys and the couple were to have the use of the second and third floors, to Polly's eyes, an enormous apartment of drawing room, dining room, morning room and above, a large bedroom, dressing room and boudoir. It was richly furnished with brocade curtains and bed coverings of the highest quality. Mercy, the ladies maid, would join the other servants in their room in the basement and Polly was ecstatic, "Dear Francis, this is wonderful, it is like stepping into a palace. I do hope Mercy will not think me unsophisticated, Mrs Bankes, remember, knows Lady Arabella Henham and although I have been training Alice at home we neither of us know the real ways of London. Oh, I am so excited. I may not ever wish to return to Nottingham.."

"Wait until you have heard the noise of London and smelt the smells," Francis laughed, "you may find you long to go home to your market town!"

"Phooey husband. It is no good, nothing you say can prevent me from having the most splendid time here."

Polly always remembered this month as the best of her life, subsequent visits to London never surpassed the joy she felt this first time. She had a childlike appreciation of everything she saw and everything they did. Kitty made a very able London guide and whilst not overtly fond herself of shopping, cheerfully accompanied Polly on the daily promenades along Oxford Street and Cheapside, amused by Polly's repeated comments on the fine, wide pavements which reduced the hazard of filth splatters on her dresses. They paused constantly to admire the shop windows. A watchmaker, a silversmith, a china and glass shop and maybe a silk store, a milliners. Polly marvelled at the displays of confectionary, foreign, exotic fruits behind the grand glass windows and when invited by smartly dressed, deferential proprietors, they graciously entered many, many of the stores.

Polly was true to her promise to Francis, she purchased beautiful air twist stemmed wine glasses, fine bone china coffee cups, a silver tea kettle, coffee pot and sugar bowl, spice boxes, tea caddy, an exquisite tea table from Mr Gillow and much, much, more. All, she knew, would make her house in St Mary Gate as fine as any in Nottingham.

Together with Benjamin and Francis, the ladies enjoyed a trip to the theatre in Drury Lane, to Ranelagh pleasure gardens and the Chinese pagoda, they listened to a concert of Mr Handel's music in the Rotunda, they danced at the assembly there and Polly was awestruck when visiting in the evening to find the gardens lit with hundreds of glass lamps and, just as in a theatre, a scene, an arrangement of a millers house complete with artificial cascade so life like that Polly fancied she saw the water wheel actually turning. They saw an exhibition of strange birds and animals in the Strand, they witnessed a hot air balloon take off and were later mesmerised by the sight of it rising above the

London rooftops and they even made a visit to the Mint at the Tower of London to see the new coins being made.

Francis spent many days with Ben who was proud to introduce him to his fellow businessmen, show him the operations at the London docks and the Corn Exchange and together with Frederick and Nathaniel, visit the warehouses and wharves of King & Bankes. The men talked at length of their future expansions, and in particular of Ben's, now imminent, departure from the day to day running of his grocers shop to become a factor, "I need to get down to making some serious money if I am to be able to have my own sugar factory," he told Francis, "and the way to get that is by investing and I shall invest in those enterprises that I understand. I shall have my factory before too long, I promised myself that when I was still a boy, when Robert and I first came down here."

They were introduced to many of Ben and Kitty's friends, they dined with the Kings and Bankes where Polly was charmed by Ellen and Gussie and she was completely enchanted by the infant Will, "Such a pretty child," she flattered Kitty, "and so obviously a Severn with that red hair!"

The ultimate joy for Polly was the large, white, gold edged, embossed invitation on the mantlepiece of their drawing room in Jermyn Street whereby, *"Sir Ambrose and Lady Arabella Henham request the pleasure of the company of Mr and Mrs Francis Crosland at a Charity Ball to be held at Almack's Assembly Rooms on King Street in St. James in aid of the Foundlings Hospital. Saturday 30th May 1789."*

Her euphoria was not at all dented by her husband's teasing, his mock horror "What on earth will this will cost me in a donation, I will have to sell my entire business when we return home if I am to meet my pledge and be able to pay for all your extravagant purchases. I fear there might be no money left for new clothes for the occasion!"

Polly was ecstatic and at dinner that evening, discussing the excitement of the invitation, they learned that Gussie Bankes was the daughter of a parliamentarian, she had fallen in love with Nathaniel and being of age had married against her family's wishes. To their narrow minds, she had married beneath her and worse still, into trade. Since then she had been shunned by her kin and most of her acquaintances except for her dearest friend Arabella, who at risk to her own reputation had never dropped her. "Arabella," said Gussie, "has no side and is the kindest, most generous woman and she is blessed that her husband Sir Ambrose admires and supports her too."

Polly was very much inclined to agree, as she found herself the following morning, Kitty having had to excuse herself as she had awoken with a frightful headache, with Ellen and Gussie in Lady Arabella's phaeton on their way to Grey's, the ladies' favoured draper, to choose silk for her new gown. As they drew up outside the shop Polly gasped with delight at the array of silk, satins and velvets, all hung behind the large windows, artfully displaying the effect of the fabrics flowing as a dress would flow. Mr Grey hurried forward, took their hands in turn to steady them as they stepped down from the carriage and then ushered them into the shop.

Whilst the others sat with coffee at a table to the side of the main salon, Polly was paraded through room after room of fine materials. With a look of wonder on her face, feeling slightly overwhelmed at the superior selection on offer, Mr Grey could see she was unused to such an experience and recommended certain silks, eventually agreeing wholeheartedly with her choice of deep cream, a colour absolutely guaranteed to look striking with her delicate features and dark red hair. "We will have the gown ready for you by tomorrow," he assured her, "but we will need to sit with our dressmaker now for a while to discuss the details and then I recommend you visit Mrs Marsh the milliner across the street, who I am sure will find you the perfect hat with ribbons to match."

The evening of the Ball arrived and Ben, Kitty, Francis and Polly arrived at Almack's by private carriage. "Can't turn up to this do in a Hackney," laughed Francis, "and given that the whole evening is going to bankrupt me, what's the extra cost matter!"

Polly's dress reflected the latest fashion, a rounded profile and cream silk, it was adorned solely at the edges by an embroidered band and the palest of lemon yellow ribbon. Round her slender neck was her husband's surprise. Just as they were about to leave, Francis had asked her to turn her back and he hooked around her, a beautiful gold and topaz necklace. A cross pendant hanging from the rivière nestled perfectly at the top of her cleavage and as she turned to smile at her husband and kiss him, he handed her two perfect drop earrings to match. She looked entrancing and Francis glowed with pride when heads turned to admire her as they entered the ballroom.

It was a huge room, of double height, with five magnificent crystal chandeliers, the glow from these added to by a host of candles hanging from the high ceiling and candles set in front of mirrored sconces on the walls. The light in the room was brilliant, brighter than Polly could ever have imagined. Benches were set around the walls and the quartet hurried to take their seats in the second tier as hundreds of guests arrived.

They watched the couples already dancing the minuets and then at eight o'clock the country dancing began. The musicians performed from their gallery and a convivial master of ceremonies ensured the friends had their opportunity to take to the floor. Refreshments were served at nine o'clock in a very crowded Tea Room and afterwards the party returned to the ballroom for more country dancing. At eleven o'clock sharp the music ceased, they retrieved their coats, found their carriage waiting outside and made their way back to Jermyn Street.

"By God," Ben groaned to Francis sitting in the drawing room when Kitty and Polly had withdrawn to drink tea, "I'm glad the ladies enjoyed the evening, it was like purgatory for me. The crush, the heat, that infernal music and my feet hurt from all that gallivanting."

"Not really my cup of tea either," sympathised Francis, "but it was worth it just to see Polly so happy. She thought it a shame that we couldn't dance a minuet, but we all managed a good few of the others didn't we, even though I do have two left feet. And it was all for a very good cause too, so a good night all round I think."

"Yes, you're right of course," agreed Ben, "I thought the Henhams did very well, very approachable and jolly decent folk. I know they were after our money but not all the aristos are as polite to those of us in trade! Let's have a glass or two of port shall we, then I'll call for a cab to take Kitty and me home. I'm a bit done for I don't mind telling you."

Polly lay in bed that night reliving every moment of the evening. She remembered every detail and she had an idea. "I shall wear that dress again when we organise a ball at home for Foxcroft House. If I can be a guest of Lady Arabella Henham at Almack's, then I'm surely good enough to invite the bon-ton of Nottingham and rival that awful Miss Kirby up at the castle with her elaborate breakfast and supper parties."

CHAPTER THIRTY FOUR
Nottingham 1789
George III averts the Regency Crisis by recovering

Whilst Polly was fulfilling her dreams in society, Martha had been fulfilling hers too, but rather differently, she was rethinking her strategy. One of the foundling babies had died of a fever whilst teething and although another baby had been taken in almost immediately, Martha realised that Foxcroft House could easily accommodate an additional two infants. As she explained to her committee at their regular meeting at Kings, "Whilst we will need to bear the cost of the wet nurses, the actual property is being under-utilised. Agnes and her staff are quite able to look after two more babies especially as now the oldest boy, Zachary, is attending the Blue Coat school each day and our financial situation is quite robust. Here, I have the annual accounting figures which you may wish to look at," and she handed the red leather bound ledger to Eleanor Smith to circulate, " I am hopeful that we will have some more fund raising ideas from you all later this afternoon. Thanks to Mrs Smith's hard work and tenacity, the musical concert we held at the Trade Assembly last July was such a success it has made a great difference to our reserves, and my sister's tea afternoons have also reaped rewards."

Martha's head was full of ideas, "Of course, it would be madness to compare ourselves to such a large organisation as the hospital in London, but I don't see why we cannot take on their governors' ethos, that industry is essential for the development of our children. Their operation is so large that they have been able to set up a sort of factory where the younger children prepare wool for spinning, others spin it and then the older children weave it into the cloth which is sent out to be made into their uniforms. Now I know we cannot possibly do the same and indeed we are so lucky to have the donations of fabrics from our benefactors, but there is no reason the girls cannot be taught to sew the more basic underwear, the shifts and shirts. In London the children start working at about four years old but I think that a little too young, we could start them at five years. The boys will be trained to do some of the heavier household duties, they can work before and after school as they get older. This will help both ourselves and the children, as if they learn the tasks necessary to run Foxcroft House, we can keep the number of domestic servants down to a minimum and maybe, in the future, be able to take in even more orphans."

"Could we also find someone, one of us perhaps," said Eleanor Smith, "to come to Foxcroft House and teach the girls. I know they cannot go to school like the boys and will have to be content with basic Sunday school lessons, but it would be encouraging for them to do something artistic or musical? Mrs Adams will be teaching them sewing and housekeeping, but something a little different might be good for them."

"Are you sure an accomplishment in music would not render them unsuitable for domestic service," asked another of the ladies, "it would be foolish to encourage them to think above their station in life."

"I don't think so at all and in fact my sister is an accomplished pianist," Mrs Twells said with her usual brusque manner, "I'm sure she would be willing to go along an hour or two a week, oh, but we will need a piano."

"I know exactly where to get one from, well a harpsichord, not a piano. My aunt Mrs Ellis of Goosegate has just passed away and I do not want hers as we have a new piano," Mrs Stanley's face was flushed with pleasure, "it would be so good for the girls."

"Thank you ladies, we can certainly take that idea forward and I have one final request please, this time for Mrs Barratt," Martha now had no reticence in asking for help, "We need a secure cupboard to store the keepsakes and a note of the little information, gleaned or provided, when the babies come in. We are building quite a sad collection of buttons and trinkets and we must be sure to keep them safe as identification should the mother return in the future, however far away, to claim her child. Do you think a cupboard is something your husband could arrange for us?"

When, business over, the ladies talk descended into their usual gossip, Martha looked round the room and a warmth of unaccustomed pride spread throughout her body, 'How lucky I am,' she thought, 'this was my doing. Me, an uneducated woman whose sole expectation and destiny in life was to become a wife and mother, and here I am, running a charity, giving hope and a future to a few young souls born with neither.' She might also have considered, that along the way, she was helping these wives and mothers enrich their own lives too.

§

Before the end of the summer of '79, Francis had declined to take up the offer of joining in the Hull venture but James, with a rather large loan from the bank had become an equal shareholder of "Hadley's Wine Shippers" and their first shipment of wine had arrived, before the winter set in, on the "Lady Isobelle" direct from Oporto.

"Congratulations brother," Francis raised his glass of wine to James, "here's to your success as importer and may your mistress bring you great pleasure for the future!"

"My mistress?" James's face paled, "what do you mean?"

"Sorry James, I meant Lady Isobelle of course. Bit insensitive of me."

The ship had docked in Hull on schedule and Severns' shipment of port had been sent down the river to the wharfinger in Gainsborough. So eager had James been to set eyes on it that he, Jacob and Simon had taken the stage coach to see it landed there.

"I think it was a very successful trip," he was telling Francis, "I'm really glad I took the boys. They were jolly company on the awful journey and it was good for them to see a little bit of how importing works." James was proud of his young cousins and had thought a treat like this was just the thing to maintain their interest. "Hadley uses a man called Flowers and we found my five tuns of port in one of his warehouses and then watched them load it onto the barges to bring it down to Nottingham. Since the Trent's been improved, the journey is a lot quicker and everything went well. I liked Mr Flowers, a good sort, and I feel sure I can trust him for the future."

"I guess those boys must have thought it a great adventure," Francis was even a little envious himself, "what's Gainsborough like as a town?"

"Very prosperous. A lot of shipbuilding, rope works and the like, but there is no Customs House so it can't be an official port. Flowers and his cronies have been campaigning hard for one but to no avail, it would really boost their river trade."

"So, did you have your load brought down to the dock in town as usual? Or did you bring it the last miles by wagon, the Leen is nearer to the cellars isn't it?

"Yes the river, and it's thanks to you that I have the space to keep this amount of stock and bottle it of course. I could never have done it on this scale if we were still back at Weekday Cross. Mind you, I only had a small shipment this time, enough to let me test the waters and check that I can sell it all in time to settle my Bill of Exchange. I have six months but I hope to increase the quantities if this goes well and then I should be able to negotiate the full twelve months to pay."

"Well, maybe you should buy me another bottle of wine then," Francis laughed, "you obviously owe me as much!"

The wine on the table, James changed the subject, "I've got a bit of a dilemma. Martha has asked me to be a subscriber to the new hospital, it would cost £5 a year in case she needs one of her foundlings to go. The trouble is Josiah, he's so against it, in fact he's against so many things. Anyway it caused quite a row, with him saying that if no one took the subscriptions up, then the town would have to let the poor come and go as they needed. I don't know what to do. I think it would be good for my position in the town, and I don't really see how Joe can be right. I can't see it working any other way."

"Josiah wants to change the whole face of our society James, and I'm not saying there's not a lot that should be changed, but he was going about it in the wrong way. I'm glad he seems to have calmed down a bit since the ruck at Langar, pulling fences down won't get us anywhere. We need to get change by debate, get the new money involved in parliament. Speaking of which, did you see old Stanford's house last night? Polly insisted we take a sedan to go and look, the whole town was lit up like a pleasure garden but his house outdid them all. She said the decorations were as gorgeous as the silks he produces."

"Yes, we all went. Martha wanted to see and I'd heard he was supplying a hogshead of ale for the locals to drink the King's health - I'm as pleased as the next man that King George has recovered but I think Stanford was a bit excessive."

"I must say I am surprised the King is well again, back in the summer the word was he had completely lost his mind. Apparently he shook hands with a tree - thought it was the King of Prussia!"

"Shouldn't believe everything you hear dear Francis. I heard back in the spring that Polly had said she should have six new dresses for the trip to London!"

"That, alas dear James" sighed Francis, "was perfectly true!"

§

Sometimes an event that has been anticipated for a long time, when it happens, actually comes as a great surprise. Grace, having spoken endlessly of becoming an actress, asked to leave the family that winter to follow her dream. Whilst Martha had cautioned her repeatedly over the years about such a perilous moral path, she could not when it came to it, really find it in her heart to remonstrate for long. She, of all people, knew what it was to want a life away from the ordinary. The rest of the family were universally against the move, such was the stigma attached to actresses, but Grace was determined and Martha spoke up for her with her brothers. In October, it was with Martha's blessing, but also with sorrow in their hearts, that Grace left Weekday Cross.

The girl had gone to the theatre in St Mary Gate whenever she had the time, tried always to meet and speak with the actors and was well known to the theatre manager. This day she had been biding her time and on overhearing Mr Earl's anxious consternation that Mrs Warrel, who was to provide a song during the interval between the two plays to be staged, had been taken ill suddenly, Grace thrust herself forward in a do or die moment and pleaded to be allowed to take the missing songstress's place.

Her rendition of Lavender Blue had captivated the audience and the panache with which she had performed, together with her silvery, pitch perfect voice had caught the attention of Mr Parnell the actors' manager. She was to join their little troupe within the week, initially as an understudy and general factotum, but as far as Grace was concerned, she was already a star in the making.

This left Martha with an employment problem until she remembered old Mrs Ellis had died and her housekeeper was looking for a new position. Mrs Esther Ridley proved an excellent choice, dispensing almost immediately with the youngest girl Maria, "Really Miss Severn, she is completely useless, we do not need her at all, Dolly and I will manage just fine."

Martha did not argue, with William gone and George living at the Tebbutts, leaving just James and Josiah at home, she also felt the two servants could manage alone, "Thank you Mrs Ridley, that will be most appreciated."

CHAPTER THIRTY FIVE
Nottingham 1790 - 1795
The French Revolution inspires radical societies to be set up in
Britain
From 1793 Britain is at war with France again

The last decade of the century opened with the prospect of happiness and prosperity for all the siblings. It had taken her almost two years to plan but Polly had finally organised her ball to raise funds for Foxcroft House. It had, by Nottingham standards, been a very grand affair at the Assembly Rooms and Polly had drawn on every ounce of her charm and persuasion to ensure the presence there of many of the town's fashionable residents. She had engaged the best musicians she could find to play for the dancing; she specified the music herself; chose an excellent Master of the Ceremonies who made sure he got to know all the guests, thus enabling him to pay every individual sufficient attention and ensure that all who wished to dance had the maximum opportunity to do so; she directed the Tea Room to provide refreshments far superior to their norm and she had cajoled many in advance of the evening to attend the Card Room to gamble if their inclination was not to dance. Polly was 'Queen' for the night and, as many commented, the role suited her admirably!

Martha was overjoyed with the monies raised, "I never thought so many people would pay the 3/6d to come. Polly my dearest, you are a marvel," she hugged her sister closely, "this is almost enough to keep us going for a full year, maybe we can give the children some extra treats. Oh, it is superb."

"I had the most wonderful time Martha," Polly glowed with pleasure, "and not just being able to raise money for your orphans but seeing the likes of the Williamson and Marchant families here! Who would have thought it, Lady Henham's name obviously works wonders!"

"You must come to Foxcroft House to visit us soon dear, you have been so busy making money for us that you haven't seen the children in an age and there are quite a few changes afoot."

James had taken great satisfaction when in '94 his two apprentices Jacob and Simon Cramp, having finished their time two years before, had come to him one day to discuss their plans for "Cramps", a vintners shop they wished to set up. "We have learned so much from you Uncle James and cannot thank you enough, but I'm sure we are ready to get out on our own now. There are premises available in Bridge Street which we reckon we can afford," Jacob told him, "and Simon and I think that with the influx of workers living in Narrow Marsh, there will certainly be the custom for us."

"Not the fine wines that we sell here of course," Simon was quick to say, "but we have to start somewhere!"

This left James with the opportunity to take on another apprentice, "I think I'll take on a pair again," he told the family, "a little bit of rivalry does their learning good and they are company for each other, any ideas?"

"I know my mother's niece has a boy, Isaac Towle, who is a very studious youngster longing to get into business," Betsey offered, "I think he's the right age and his parents can afford to pay you the fees. Shall I speak with my mother?"

The other boy had come through Martha's colleague, Eleanor Smith, "A boy as bright as a button and wasted out in the countryside, Joshua is just the lad for you! He is so keen to move on that he threatens to go to the Red Lion where they are recruiting for the navy, calling anyone from Nottingham, Robin Hood's men. Say yes, then at least we can save him from that!"

It had been arranged and James was enjoying the role of tutor and mentor again.

George had avoided contact with James since their father died but very soon after his marriage to Betsey, he had come to Middle Pavement and standing in James's office, a belligerent glower on his face, he looked around, "Father had agreed I would have my own shop and if he hadn't been ill I'd have that by now, and a house to live in. What are you going to do about it now that you have his money?"

James winced inwardly but said calmly, "I don't believe he would have wanted you to leave working with Jack yet, but if you find a house somewhere in Narrow Marsh to rent, we'll talk. It can be my first obligation as father's beneficiary."

By the middle of '95, George and Betsey were living in Marsh Farm, a half timbered house in Byron Yard which had not, as far as anyone knew, ever been associated with agriculture and was certainly one of the better houses in the Narrow Marsh area. They were rapidly filling it with children, their first born, John, and now four daughters Betsey, Martha, Mary and Ann who had followed quickly after, and another on the way. "Goodness Betsey," Polly was moved to say, "I scarcely have time to finish sewing one set of little bed gowns before it is time to start on the next! But they are delightful little girls and young John is growing into a fine child. I hear he is enjoying going to school very much and is learning fast." They were a jolly, noisy and busy family, much like Betsey's own when she was a child and it seemed, on the surface at least, to leave little time for George's bitterness towards James to manifest itself.

"George was so pleased we heard from The Reverend last week," Betsey retrieved baby Martha just as she was about to place her sticky fingers on Polly's dress, "but it is a shame they have moved so far away to Norwich. Sister Elizabeth is so conscientious, writing to hear about all the children, I haven't met her of course, but do you think maybe she is not as you all first thought? George can be quite harsh about her, says she is rather demanding and leads The Reverend a pretty dance."

"She is a very good aunt to Jack and Ann's children too," acknowledged Polly, "but I saw and heard for myself how difficult she can be. It was interesting to learn that she has inherited that house in Broughton, I wonder if they will ever go to live there. I should so like to have our brother closer by, it is a long time since we saw him."

§

Josiah too had married in '94 much to the surprise of the family, his life having revolved it seemed, entirely around his work and his political causes. He had kept his promise to his father not to continue his association with Luke Fletcher but he felt so strongly about the dreadful conditions for the poor that once he had finished his apprenticeship he became increasingly involved in campaigning for one cause or another in the town. When the news of the revolution in France reached Nottingham in '89, he, Tad and Tad's sister Bessie had joined the many townsfolk who took a very sympathetic view. They already belonged to a small group of political protesters and activists but the French events provided the impetus for the trio to join a formal campaign for the reform of the rights of the ordinary man.

"See," Josiah said, they were meeting at a sympathiser's house in Narrow Marsh, "not only does Thomas Paine assert the natural birth right of all men in his book, but look here in volume two, he advocates some sort of social welfare for the poor and sick."

"The government needs to take action to help," agreed Tad, he was one of the loudest voices in the town campaigning on behalf of the knitters in particular, "there's nothing Pitt hasn't stuck a tax on and taxes on commodities like soap, candles and salt just hurt the poor twice as hard. Then there's the county rates and the tithes for the priests, no wonder there is unrest. People can't live."

Straightening the piles of pamphlets she was folding on the table, Bessie spoke, "That's the real point, wages have not kept up with the rising price of food. The poorest can only just afford bread and beer so there's nothing left for meat or vegetables, and what's that doing to their health? The number of children you see in the street with bare feet and dressed in rags, it's scandalous."

"And what happens?" Tad raised his eyebrows, "We've had five bad harvests this decade so what does the government do to help the poor? The price of wheat has doubled and put the cost of real bread up so much that people can either eat bread made from barley or oats, which is animal fodder," he fumed, "or starve. No wonder we have to take to the streets to protest."

"It's a bad situation all round, and if you get into debt you're put into the town gaol and have no way of recovering. One of our neighbours is the Keeper there," Josiah leant across to take a leaflet, "and he says it's a real problem, and not just the overcrowding from the debtors, but that the crime rate is rising so fast, mostly people stealing to feed themselves."

"Thank goodness for people like Martha," Bessie went on, "her group of women are doing what they can to help but it's precious little in the overall scheme of things. I've been reading Mary Wollstonecraft's treatise on the rights of women and it's so true. If women were allowed a better education we could compete with men on equal terms and if we could hold some power maybe the world wouldn't be so unfair. I'm sure women would not let all these children go hungry and if they didn't have to go to war every two minutes, the fathers could be at home trying to provide for them. The country should have a democracy, ordinary people should be allowed to make their own decisions, and women should have a vote as well as men. But if the landed classes resist attempts by people like us to gain even a little power over our own lives, what hope is there for the poor?"

"Paine wants free education for everyone, including women, and a pension or payments for those of us who get too old or sick to work. I agree with him, and with you Bessie, our taxes all seem to be spent on fighting the French," Tad raised his hand, "I know, not just them! The Americans, the Spanish, the Dutch, just about anyone it seems. But this latest war with France has been going on for more than three years now. Wouldn't it be better to spend our money on looking after our own people?"

"It's even worse than that", Bessie said indignantly, "Parliament are using our taxes to pay off the Prince of Wales's enormous debts. I heard it was to the tune of £65,000 each year, they increased his allowance because he obeyed them, stopped his philandering and married an eligible princess, that fat, ugly Caroline woman from somewhere in Germany. It's not just unfair, it's downright wrong."

"What I can't understand is that for each of us who can see all this injustice in the country, there are just as many supporting the King, but they won't shut us up. I know we are right and we must bring about change. This," Josiah handed another pamphlet to his friends, "is information on our Constitutional Society, we should join."

"We must be careful Joe," warned Tad, "even if we are not actually starting riots in the street, the government is cracking down hard on anyone who suggests we need reform in England. It's William Pitt's Reign of Terror and there are all sorts of laws out there now to stop political meetings and there are spies and informers everywhere. How they can think we are traitors I cannot fathom, but they do, and I don't want Bessie getting caught up in any trouble. Well, actually, I don't want too much trouble for myself either!"

Whether Josiah had married Bessie for love or because of his huge admiration for her, the family never knew, but the couple were settled into a small house in Byard Lane, and now, just over a year later, were delighted that Bessie was expecting their first child in November.

CHAPTER THIRTY SIX
Nottingham 1795
The French Revolutionary Wars continue

In London, Ben's stars were in the ascendency too. The Oxford Street grocers shop had gone from strength to strength and his initial plan to become a factor of commerce had come to fruition, since when he had invested with Fred King in his own grocery warehouse in Queen Street, Cheapside. Ben had also been made a Freeman of the City of London and he, Kitty and Will were now living in a quite splendid apartment in Grace Church Street, almost within view of the new premises.

Kitty had written to Martha with this news and as was customary, she gathered the family for dinner in Weekday Cross. Jack's wife Ann had been given the privilege of reading the letter aloud and stopped, looking at James she asked, "What does Freedom of the City mean?"

"Just about all business is carried out within the square mile known as the City of London and you cannot trade legally within that square mile unless you have been made a Freeman of the City."

"What would happen if you did?" asked Betsey. George would not come to the house on these occasions but would quiz his wife on her return, "How would they know?"

"I believe it's all policed through the Livery companies, they have long arms and if you are found not to belong, then you get a hefty fine," explained James, "Ben joined the Merchant Taylors Company and was presented to the court along with another forty nine names. He had to pay two pounds, six shillings and eightpence for the privilege and is bound by the Merchant Taylor's laws, no gambling, swearing or fornication!"

"Well that won't be a hardship for him?" laughed Polly, "he and Kitty seem to have a very genteel life now!"

"That aside, it really is a privilege. Ben can not only trade freely but he is entitled to vote in the parliamentary elections, so it is a real achievement for him."

"I'm really pleased for Ben," Josiah was exasperated, "but we are all just as capable as him of choosing who we think would make a good politician and one that would serve us, the people, rather than just himself."

"That's as may be," replied James, "but this is how things are and all your protesting on the streets is not going to change anything. It's not the way to go about it…"

Martha stopped him short, "Please, no politics now Joe, we are hearing about Ben."

"We are very lucky," Ann was ever ready to be the peace maker when the brothers started to argue, but James snapped at her, "That's because we work harder, it's our class that keeps the country going. The landed gentry are idle and feckless and if we keep helping the poor it will just encourage their bad habits …."

Martha banged her hand on the table and said sharply, "That is enough, this is my dinner table and not a political meeting. We should just be very happy that Benjamin and Kitty are doing so well. There is more good news from him too, would you carry on reading please Ann."

The extra news was that Ben was about to sign an agreement to go into partnership with Messrs. Smith and Cox to buy their own sugar refinery in White Horse Lane in Stepney. "My word," exclaimed Polly, "how grand. A factory! I'm so proud of him," and looking round the table added quickly, "I am so proud of all my family. Together we really are a force to be reckoned with aren't we? James is right, we shall become a dynasty!"

Fate however has a nasty way of bringing people back down to earth and after the happiness of the previous years, November brought tragedy. In Byard Lane, Bessie gave birth to a fine baby daughter but immediately after the delivery she began to haemorrhage, and in spite of the best efforts of the midwife and Dr Bayley, little Mary Ann was left motherless the next day. It was a terrible time. Martha was able to help with the practicalities and a wet nurse was engaged immediately for the baby but none of the siblings seemed able to comfort Josiah in his grief. It was as if he lost his mind and no amount of comforting stopped him repeating, "I have always known father blamed me for killing my mother and this is my punishment, my daughter has killed her mother too."

He took no interest in the baby save to remark that she reminded him too much of Bessie and he spent as many hours as possible, when not at work, with his political comrades. Mary Ann was cared for by her aunts and after a few weeks, she just stayed on with George and Betsey at Marsh Farm. As in Betsey's own childhood, one more baby in the house seemed to make no difference.

His brothers spoke forcefully, sometimes harshly, with Josiah reminding him of his responsibilities and his sisters begged him to take time with his daughter, "Really Joe," pleaded Polly, "if you hold her in your arms you will grow to love her." There was no persuading him and he began to take more and more risks, being out on the streets whenever there was a rally or protest, giving no thought to his own safety or future.

"He will come round eventually," Martha tried to understand him, "we all have to deal with mourning in our own way."

Josiah never did come round. Nine months after Bessie's death, on a June evening in '96, it was Martha who heard the insistent knocking and opened the door at Weekday Cross. Standing before her in the dusk was Tad and two men she had never seen before, holding her little brother up in their arms. His face untouched, serene and calm, his chest black with his spilled blood.

"I wasn't right there Martha, I wasn't with him," sobbed Tad, "I didn't see what happened but they told me he just stood there and let the Dragoon strike him down!"

"Where was he, what was he doing?"

"We had all arranged to plant a Tree of Liberty in the Market Square, dozens of us turned out and formed a barrier around the men with the spades, but the troops were sent to stop us and charged with their sabres drawn."

"Josiah had taken his shirt off and was holding up his arm," said one of the other men, "shouting to them to try again, we didn't know what he meant. He wouldn't move. He fell right there, he was dead within the instant."

Polly was devastated, "My precious little brother, it was Bessie's death that addled his brain and how he has suffered these past months and now this," and she sobbed into Francis's arms, "at least he will be at peace now."

Josiah was buried without delay, his house left empty. "It is as if he never existed," wailed Polly. "No my love, he will always be in our hearts," comforted Martha, "and we have little Mary Ann to remind us of him every day."

"And what is to happen to her?"

"We will not need to worry about Mary Ann, I have a plan."

CHAPTER THIRTY SEVEN
Nottingham 1797 – 1799
Jenner publishes his works on smallpox vaccination

The door to Marsh Farm was open when Martha arrived and she stepped carefully over two infant nieces who were sitting on the step dressing an old rag doll, noticing as she did, the odd white smudges on their faces. Betsey was in the kitchen, her own face speckled with white flour, her hands deep in a large bowl where she was kneading pastry.

"This explains your daughter's white face paint then," Martha laughed, "I'm sorry to call unannounced, I hope it's not too inconvenient."

"Welcome to the chaos that is my life," answered Betsey, wiping her hands on her apron and turning towards the fireplace, "Betsey, let Aunt Martha have that chair, you can take baby Sarah out into the yard, she could do with some air."

With a shy smile at her aunt, Betsey hitched the crusty nosed baby onto her hip and slipped out of the room. Martha spotted another little girl under the large, oak table playing with a wooden spoon and her own bowl of flour, "Hello, little Martha. Are you making a cake too?"

"What can I do for you Sister, would you like a cup of coffee, there's been a pot brewing all morning, it should still be hot?"

"I'm sorry I don't come here more often, it's so good to be in your happy home and it's on a matter of happy families that I want to speak with you."

Betsey said cheerfully, "I know what you are going to ask, and yes, Little Mary Ann should stay with us permanently. I wouldn't have it any other way, she is a little sweetheart and is already settled in with us. George will be fine to have her, no worries there."

Betsey had made it easy for them and as soon as she had agreed to keep Mary Ann, James put the idea forward to the rest of the family, at the same time promising that Severns would provide for her future. Everyone, including George, readily agreed and James was therefore more than surprised when George burst into his office later in the week, angry and aggressive, "It's not right that I have no shop of my own and I'm only renting Marsh Farm, my house should belong to me. You robbed me, I will not let you rob my son as well."

"George, I don't know what you mean? How can I rob your son? It doesn't make sense."

"You haven't got a son yet, and nor will you have if you keep on with that immoral, old woman. Jack's son Jon is too daft to take over from you and Ben's son William will be apprenticed to him in London. It should be my John next in line, he's a clever scholar and will be wasted having to be a butcher like me, he should take over the wine merchants, but you've brought those cousins in as apprentices so I can see what you're planning."

"You're wrong George, you've got it all wrong as usual. It's much too early to make a decision about who takes over. Your John is a fine boy but he's still got years of schooling to go."

"Well I don't trust you not to hand Severns over to one of those boys and my sons should have an inheritance when I die. They should have a property, I'll not let you squeeze them out like you did me, I want you to buy Marsh Farm in my name, it's no more than I deserve."

James dealt with his emotions in his usual manner, he redoubled his efforts with Severns and over the next year his wholesale business was flourishing. Lady Isobelle had brought home many cargos, his cellars were full, his customers plenty and life was positive. It was only George who ruffled his feathers. He had begun to visit Weekday Cross again when the family gathered together and since James had finally agreed to buy Marsh Farm outright for him, and had made the first of his annual dividends to them all, an uneasy truce prevailed.

One such evening, James broached the subject of moving home to Martha, "The tenants above Severns are moving out at the end of the month and as business is going very well now, it could be a new start for us for the new century. I think we could make the top three floors into a very good sized home which would do us admirably. There's plenty of room for the apprentices, Dolly and Mrs Ridley, and whilst it is a much smarter address for us than here, we can live in comfort without seeming ostentatious. Our customers won't think we have it too easy!"George quite predictably had not been pleased, "A smarter address," he scoffed, "just who do you think you are, Lord High and Mighty? You'll be too grand to even speak to the likes of us before long. Father would say you're taking too many risks, however much money have you borrowed from the bank? Jack told me that ship brings wine in every few months, how are you selling all that? Even he worries that you are taking on too much, without proper consideration. Now you want to pay rent in Middle Pavement when you've a perfectly good house here. You're just getting above yourself. Come on Betsey, I'm going home, I can't stay here and listen to this reckless talk."

James, as so often after a meeting with his brother was left both troubled and angry. He had thought George might appreciate the benefit of keeping Severns together since he had been provided with his own home and this latest outburst really upset him.

Livy had done her best to comfort him, "Please try not to dwell on it my little one, there is no reason for your brother's jealousy, everyone knows you do your best not just for yourself but for your whole family."

"I don't understand him, I thought it must be because of father's Will," James was perplexed, "look at Benjamin, he's successful and George just admires him. When I think back, he started to be resentful of me when we were young, I could never prove it but I'm sure he used to break my toys. I have no idea why and you'd think he'd be pleased I can help him out, he never worked at school and it seems he prefers making babies to working even now! Why would he say that Jack is concerned about Severns too, he's not said a word to me about it. I don't know what I should do."

"Well right now you can sit and eat dinner with me," Livy answered with a melancholy smile, "I have some news to tell you."

At Livy's behest, the nature of their meetings had changed over the past year, "James, listen to me," she had spoken firmly, "I am an old woman and it is unbecoming that we should continue as lovers. I do not wish to see one day, the look of distaste on your face when you too realise my body is sinking into decay. It is better to stop now and let me keep my dignity."

James's protests could not move her, "My love," he pleaded, "you are still the most enchanting woman and old, never! I adore you and want you just as much now as I did all those years ago when I was an innocent boy, still wet behind my ears."

"Well hopefully your ears are now dry and I have taught you enough to know when to desist," Livy looked into his eyes and took his hands in her own, "but I do fervently wish you will continue to visit me, we can dine together and you will always be the one I wish to talk to. I do love you so, and what I am asking is out of this love for you, not malice."

James had failed to see how thin Livy was becoming. She took great pains with her dress to disguise it and she wore more rouge to brighten her cheeks than before, but his love for her blinded him. At fifty four, she was still his beautiful, exciting mistress.

That particular day during dinner in Livy's sumptuous dining room, she looked up at him with a mixture of sadness and love in her eyes, "I have decided to sell my shops."

"Good heavens, why my dear? You love being in business, it has always been your life's blood," he spluttered through a mouthful of beef, "I never thought you would sell."

"I have no heirs to leave the business to James, my husband's nephews all work on the land up near Newark and I have been made a very generous offer by Roderick Thorne. He is a Welshman of all things, but a successful draper by all accounts."

"A Welshman, what's he doing in Nottingham?"

"He married Catherine Chettle, Alfred's daughter and has taken over their drapers in Lutterworth and now he wants to expand into Nottinghamshire. How they met I don't know," she laughed, "you seem unusually curious!"

"Well I'm not really curious about the Welshman," James smiled, "but are you sure you want to relinquish the reins just yet? I know you think you are old, but you most certainly are not!"

"Yes James, I am sure. None of us can go on forever. You should be thinking of who is going to carry on your dynasty too. As you have been obstinate so far and not married or produced a son, you had better get on with that quickly or you will have to look to your nephews - and you now know that's going to cause ructions!"

Deep in thought, he was unaware of the pain on Livy's brave, smiling face.

§

By the time the end of '99 was drawing near, James was very happy with his progress. Yet again the country was at war with France and this was having a significant, but not yet too damaging, effect on his trading. Leaning against his polished counter, he was discussing the problems with Francis, "It's just not as easy to do business with the negociants in Bordeaux now that both governments have put extra restrictions in place, and it's so galling when I've built up a pretty good wholesale network and even though it's still only a tiny percentage of my sales, I'd persuaded a lot of folk of the superiority of French wine."

"We'll have to go back to drinking nothing but port again, which is a shame because thanks to you I've developed quite a liking for claret," Francis grinned at his brother in law and James carried on, "Well, we can still get some through but not nearly enough so I'm having to appeal to my customers' tenuously held patriotism to forgo our enemies' produce at this time, of course I shall forget all that immediately if and when the damn war is over and normal trade resumes." He threw his head back and roared with laughter.

"Another example of pragmatism gained with age, I taught you well all those years ago!"

"Yes, I should thank you for that and I know I've thanked you before Francis, but it's a real bonus having your cellars. It's not just my stock, I keep barrels on behalf of several clients too. They buy their port by the pipe usually, a tun is too much, but even a pipe at over a hundred gallons needs a lot of space. We keep some to mature in glass with the rest being bottled as the year goes on. I'm turning quite a good profit on it at about £60 a pipe and I make a small charge for the storage. Claret is very good for me, but with the tax being so heavy I have to sell it at least twice the price, a hogshead - that's about half a pipe - can fetch £50. It's amazing there are those willing to pay that much, especially the clergy, they seem to know what they like! I just hope I can still get hold of some."

"How are you faring with Hadley's then, I know the shipments are getting through from Portugal, even since the Spanish jumped sides and joined the French, but it makes the channel a more dangerous place."

"We are only shipping port at present, I get my other wines through Hadley Bros. the wholesalers, just as before. Those bigger ships can usually avoid trouble, probably because they are armed and not such an easy target for capture. I'm sure you know it's not the navies that are the worry, it's the privateers. The French and Spanish crown give them authority to take our ships and then the seized vessels, complete with cargo, are sold at auction. With the privateer's captain entitled to a cut of the proceeds, it's not surprising that the navies aren't at all happy about it, the profits for a successful privateer are a much stronger inducement for men than service for the King. I know we sponsor English privateers too, but it's scandalous."

"Are you insured against being taken," Francis was concerned, "the premiums must be sky high."

"You've hit the nail on the head there," James exhaled loudly, "we're not responsible for the ship's insurance, we don't own it, just take space on her and our cargos are insured for the usual losses but not if the ship is seized. We found the price too great, we're taking the chance. Lady Isobelle is due in again just before Christmas and we have each got thirty of her three hundred tuns this time, thirty tuns of port with each of us exposed for £3,000. With so many celebrations planned for the New Year, my cellars will be just about emptied so a larger than usual consignment was necessary."

"Good God, that's a major commitment alright James, I'd really scale down again after this delivery. That's a huge amount of risk, I wish you'd spoken with me before you took it on, I'd have warned you against it."

"Well, I'll not lie to you, I'm a bit worried, the ship should be arriving next week but we've not had word from London, and Lloyd's information is usually pretty reliable."

"It's a bit early to worry old friend," Francis tried not to temper his own concern, "it's not an exact science calculating the time she'll take to get here, especially if there's bad weather in the Bay of Biscay, which is more than likely at this time of year. There could be any one of a thousand reasons to delay her and she could be sitting pretty in London waiting to make safe passage up our coastal waters to Hull any day now."

CHAPTER THIRTY EIGHT
Nottingham, December 1799
Income Tax is introduced to pay for the war against France

His worry about the Lady Isobelle, foremost in his mind for days, was instantly eclipsed by the devastating pain that descended on James on the 20th December when Livy died. Her maid sent word to him to come to Castle Gate early that morning and when he arrived, he was shown immediately to her bedchamber. His darling Livy, her face grey, her breathing shallow, took his hand in hers, "I'm so sorry to leave you my love, I tried to stay for you, but I'm too tired. I just hope I have taught you well my little one."

James was stunned, choking back his tears, he kissed her forehead, "My dearest Livy, why did you not tell me you were so ill? Why was I so blind I couldn't see you suffering. Oh my love I'm so sorry? What will I do without you, you are my best friend in all the world. How can I live without you?"

"Please do not be too sad James, remember the wonderful times we have had together, and smile when you think of me. No listen," she pushed his face gently away from her lips, "I cannot speak for much longer and I want you to know, I have left a little money to your sister Martha, for her foundlings. I know she became cold towards me, but I admire her so much for what she has done. Please will you tell her that for me, and tell her I understand. She loves you just as much as I do, she did not want you harmed for loving me."

James held her in his arms, gently stroking her face, telling her over and over how much he loved her and how much she had meant to him. He watched as her life faded away, he was bereft, his sorrow all the greater as there was no-one to share it with. His brave, exciting mistress. Gone.

He spent the next days in a trance, dealing with his customers whose excitement for Christmas and New Year celebrations failed to penetrate his misery. He tried hard to join in with Martha's plans to celebrate the end of the old century and the beginning of the new, but his heart was broken. His grief for Livy consumed him, putting his concern for the shipment with Hadleys to the back of his mind. Martha was full of remorse, "My poor brother, how I wish I had been kinder and now it is too late. I will accept the money for my orphans gladly, for myself I deserve nothing. May God forgive me."

§

The move to Middle Pavement had not yet happened and they were still living in Weekday Cross where, on New Year's Eve the whole family would be together. The Reverend and Elizabeth were travelling from Kidderminster where they were now living in a new ministry, the Norwich posting having proved temporary, and Ben, Kitty and Will were to come up from London.

"I know it is very hard for everyone to travel at this time of the year," Martha had agonised when deciding to write and ask if they would all come, "but it is such an auspicious New Year, we are so lucky to be alive to rejoice in it, I do hope they will all manage."

They did and there was so much news to catch up on. Billy and Elizabeth were enjoying their new home, "The Reverend works tirelessly campaigning for better conditions for the factory workers," Elizabeth told them, "Kidderminster is a centre for carpet manufacturing and we now rival Wilton for superiority, but the circumstances are very bad, especially for the women and children. With all his other campaigns too, I am fearful sometimes that my husband will leave the Church to enter politics, he is so supportive of the Whigs and their quest for religious freedom, not to mention Mr Fox's anti-slavery movement"

Billy looked lovingly at Elizabeth, "We are fortunate that our Church is a great advocate for women's independence as I find my wife very much involved in committees for many causes. She is so busy," he chuckled, "that I am surprised we recognise each other, we spend such active lives in different directions."

"Certainly no bother for them not to have children then," giggled Polly to Martha sotto voce, "but why does she sound so disapproving and censorious when she speaks and yet I believe she is really a very kind and caring woman. Look how she loves all the children. I don't understand."

Elizabeth did show a great fondness for her nephews and nieces, and was genuinely sad for little Mary Ann. "She is so like her dear father," she sighed, "such fine and delicate features. I am very pleased she is with you Betsey, you are a splendid mother hen, caring for all your chicks."

"You should hear her squawk at the brood when they are not behaving," laughed George, "then she can show them her sharp beak right enough!" He looked at his wife, nursing their latest son, Georgie, on her lap, "but I wouldn't ever change her."

"I must say I admire you, bringing up seven children of your own and your niece too. I found it demanding enough with just one child, and Will has always been such an obedient boy," Kitty smiled indulgently at her son, "it is good for him to spend time with his cousins and get to know them."

Elizabeth's favourite niece was her namesake, Jack and Ann's daughter. "Beth my dear," they were speaking together later in the day, "I have inherited a little house in Upper Broughton which is a village not far from here and although I have tenants in it at the moment, I wish you to know that it is yours to live in when and if you should ever so desire. It is somewhat removed from town, where the air is much fresher and the pace of life a little slower."

"Well thank you Aunt, that is extraordinarily kind of you," Beth was quite overcome, "but I think I am too young to move away on my own at present and especially as I have just started with Aunt Martha to learn the workings of Foxcroft House. She thinks I could take over from her when I am older, but I am very grateful to you and I will most certainly bear your kind offer in mind."

Will Severn charmed the whole family. He looked very much like his father and Uncle James, the same colouring and curls and he had a kind, empathetic way about him. At thirteen he was a pupil at the Merchant Taylors School, having passed a very stiff examination the previous year, and he was well aware that Ben was paying a significant fee to keep him there.

"I very much enjoy Latin and Greek," he told his Uncles, "and as long as I behave, I do not often feel Mr Bishop's knuckles rapping on my head like a bag of marbles."

To his little cousin Mary, six years old and immediately besotted with him, he confided, "Although I like my lessons, I hate my school, it is a barbaric place. The masters are cruel tyrants who love their canes and the boys are no better, but it would all be worth it if I could have gone to Oxford University."

"Why will you not go?"

" My father is dissatisfied that I am not learning the subjects to help me in commerce, he says I shall have to leave after one more year."

"Ask your Mama to speak for you. Surely she would want you to be happy?"

"I don't think she will and I would hate to upset her by asking. She never disagrees with Papa and somehow always tries to shield me from the outside world. I think she would rather I had stayed in Cheapside, but she does enjoy the fact that I am at such a prestigious school."

Whilst Will was opening his heart to little Mary, his father was holding forth.

"The sugar factory is in Stepney and my partners have already had a few years' experience in running a similar place, so I need to learn fast to catch up with them. As refineries go it is quite small but we can still process enough raw sugarcane to make a good profit. We have big plans for the future and I hope to make a name for myself and at present I'm kept very busy, Fred King and I still have our wholesalers in Queen Street to run and now we have decided to buy our own stables and horses. There's a decent yard in Whitechapel, convenient for both businesses, and William Winning is an excellent servant who we can rely on to run them."

"What does it mean to refine sugar and how do you do it," at ten years old George's son John was hypnotised by the tale of his Uncle's life in London, "can you explain it all to me?"

"Not right now my boy, but I will do some time, I don't think everyone today is interested in a chemistry lesson!"

"Forgive my note of dissent amidst your enthusiasm Benjamin, but don't the ships that bring you the raw sugarcane also take the slaves from West Africa back to the plantations in the West Indies?" asked Billy, "but of course, that's not really a question as I know that the answer is 'yes', and do you not find that a hard truth to deal with?"

"Yes Billy they do, but I can't hold myself responsible, I'm just a businessman trying to provide what the customer wants. They don't like the unrefined brown sugar in their puddings, or coffee and tea anymore, they know they can have white."

"That's no answer Ben for the morality of the brutal trade in human suffering. We should all be trying to stop this."

That debate would have to wait, their conversation was brought to an abrupt halt at the call from Martha that their celebration dinner was about to be served.

It was a delicious meal enjoyed with some of Severns finest wines. "By Jove, this claret is excellent," approved Billy, "and I've tried quite a few in my time. I like nothing better than a philosophical discussion with an agreeable chap over a bottle or two, and this is one of the best I've tasted."

"I rarely have the opportunity to try it, being just a poor butcher...," George's surly comment was stifled midsentence by the glares of his wife and sisters, "...but it is jolly good. Would be nice to try it again from time to time, here Jack, can you fill my glass."

The feasting drew to a close and Betsey rose from the table, "Well I think the little ones should go to sleep now, we can pick them out of your beds later and they'll not wake up when we carry them home."

"I will help you," Polly got up and took the toddlers Sarah and Ann by the hand, "then we shall enjoy ourselves waiting for the new century to arrive."

The cards and backgammon were brought out for the adults and the older children played checkers, spillikins and marbles. More claret was opened for the gentlemen, the ladies drank the sweet Sauternes and the minutes rushed by until just before the clock showed midnight, Billy, glass in hand, led the family down the stairs, along the side of his father's old vintners shop to their front door. He opened it wide, the cold night air engulfing them, the sky inky black with a myriad of stars twinkling through the clear, frosty air.

"The church bells are ringing," cried Polly and as the twelfth stroke died away, her oldest brother, the head of the family, spoke,

"It is the first day of January in the year of our Lord, one thousand eight hundred. Happy New Year to us all, let us raise our glasses in a toast, may there be peace in the world and an end to suffering."

"Listen," Beth was teetering on the threshold, "people are out banging pots and pans, what a noise!" "Don't go out my girl," Betsey snatched hold of her sleeve, "nothing must leave the house before something is brought inside. If you do, you will carry our good luck out with you!"

The ladies hurried back to the warmth of the parlour, the brothers following more slowly. "It is a good omen, a new century," Billy called for more wine, "let us toast our success as a family, accomplishment and happiness for us all."

The glasses were raised, the toast drunk and James, putting aside his sadness, took to his feet, "I should like to say a few words too. May this new century bring with it the beginning of our family's real prosperity. The beginning of our dynasty. Father would be proud, he has done his duty by us and more. Here we have Billy, an educated man, a minister. Jack, a successful butcher, stock owner and family man. Martha, achieving remarkable things in this man's world, her childrens' home making a real change. Polly, our beautiful sister, rising in society, showing how the rules can change in this time of opportunity. Benjamin, going from strength to strength in business in London and with more to come, and George. George I want you to know that my first obligation to the family in this new century, is to ensure you are set up in your own business, in your own premises where you can forge the future you desire for yourself and your family."

As he finished speaking and the family raised their glasses, a loud knocking was heard on the door downstairs.

Martha jumped up, "I'll go, it will be a friend first footing, come to wish us good luck. Don't worry, I know only a man can come over the threshold, if it is a woman, manners or not, she will have to stay outside!" and with the room ringing with laughter, she ran down the stairs.

A few moments later she reappeared to her rejoicing family accompanied by a stout gentleman dressed in a heavy overcoat, his face tired and unshaven, his hat in his hand before him, "I have come directly from Mr Hadley in Hull with a message for Mr James Severn."

The room became still, the laughter stopped and all eyes turned to James who stood up and took a step forward, his face ashen, "Mr Severn Sir, I have to inform you that the Lady Isobelle has been captured by a French corsair in the English Channel and taken to St Malo in France, to be sold at auction."

The silence was broken only by George's voice, loud with hate, "See where your greed has got you James, you have ruined us. You stole our birthright with the renunciation of father's Will, you took everything and now you have lost it all."

James's anger erupted in him like a volcano coming to life, his hands clenched into fists he walked the few feet across the room to his brother and all the hurt, all the injustice he had felt over the years at his brother's jealousy put such force behind it, than when his right fist connected with his chin, George's feet left the ground and he landed spread-eagled on his back. James looked down at him, his face boiling with rage, "You need to learn some manners you idle, sponging fool."

Without another word, James left the house, walked out into the moonlit night and made his way through the revellers, down the street to Severns. He went into his office where he sat at his counter, put his head in his hands and for the first time since he was a ten year old child, cried. Cried as if he would never stop.

He would save Severns, he would save his father's legacy, he did not know how, but he knew he would, but he had lost his greatest love, he had lost Livy and now he had lost his brother.

Thank you for reading this book. If you enjoyed it, please return to Amazon and leave a few words as a Review. I'd really appreciate it.

Read on for an exclusive extract from

VINES OF PROMISE

the compelling
follow-up to Grapes of Fortune

Vines of Promise

CHAPTER 1
Nottingham, January 1800
George III is on the throne, Britain, Austria, Russia, Portugal,
Naples and the Ottoman Empire were combined in fighting
Revolutionary France

James Severn rose from his bed as exhausted as he had been just a few hours ago when his brother in law, Francis Crosland, had persuaded him to take to it. "There's nothing that can be done tonight, James, get some sleep and your thoughts will be clearer in the morning," he'd said. Well that was a joke, James's thoughts had remained an incoherent turmoil. Here he was, thirty eight years old, on the verge of ruin and with no possible plan in mind to prevent it.

Standing in front of the looking glass he expected to see scarlet horns growing out of his head. After all, his brother George had accused him of being Satan, the devil who had squandered their father's inheritance, the devil who had lost them the family business, Severns. James saw no horns, but his usual wholesome features were pasty and grey, as if he had grown old overnight. He lifted up his square jaw now bristling with the morning's coarse stubble, rubbed his red rimmed, bloodshot eyes and ran his fingers through his thick, dark blond hair. Even with it cut short, his fingers caught in the tangle of copper tinged curls. Raising his right hand to massage his aching shoulder, the stiff, bruised fingers reminded him with an awful clarity of his final action before he had left the house last night. Then wrapping his arms around himself, he trembled, his chest rising and falling with each rapid, anxious breath.

He dressed automatically, giving no thought to his choice of shirt, coat or breeches, went downstairs and into the dining room. An unusual silence greeted him and looking in the corner he saw his father's long case clock had stopped ticking. Last night was the first time, in all the years since it had become his responsibility, that he had forgotten to wind it before going to bed. The hands showed ten minutes past twelve, ten minutes into the new century, the first of January, 1800. It was a cruel portent of when his own life had crashed around him.

It had been at that very moment, that the caller his sister Martha hurried eagerly to bring into the house, believing it to be a well wisher with greetings for the New Year, had turned out to be a messenger from Hull. The devastating news he brought, the news that turned James's world upside down, was that the brig Lady Isobelle, carrying a cargo of wines from Oporto had been seized in the Channel by a French privateer and at that very moment was lying in St Malo, awaiting auction and the auction of her cargo. Three thousand pounds worth of that uninsured consignment was port wine that belonged to James.

Martha came into the room, lines of worry newly etched on her round, plain face, plates with eggs and bread in her hands. She started, "Oh my dearest James, I did not hear you come down. You must sit and eat, you must keep your strength up."

"I have no appetite Martha. George is right, I have been reckless and greedy. I promised you all I would make Severns a success, I would take our Father's legacy and provide for us all, and what have I done, I have lost everything ."

"Don't speak this way James, it is just the shock of this dreadful news, you will recover, you will fulfil our trust in you."

"I don't know how Martha, but you know I will try, it's just at this moment I cannot see a way through. How is George, have you heard?"

"He has only a sore chin and bruised pride. After you left last night Jack helped Betsey get him home with all the children, he had drunk too much wine and was angry but I am sure he will see things differently today."

"I'm not so sure, he has been jealous and resentful of me all our lives. He's not going to relent now, especially as I won't have the money to set him up in his own business as I promised last night. No, I think George actually wants to remain my enemy and I don't understand why, I have only ever tried to help him Martha. All my life, since I was old enough to understand, I have been driven by the three tenets taught to me by Father and the Church; belief in God, education and above all else, hard work. I believed that if I just followed these, I would be a good man, I could be successful and happy. But it is not enough. Whilst I lay awake last night I realised I have been living a lie all these years! I need love too. Livy taught me to love, she loved me and I loved her with all my heart and now she is gone and I am all alone. How will I get through this without her?"

Martha put her arms around her younger brother and held him close. She cradled him in silence, there were no words she could say, she could only hope the love of his family could help fill the void Livy's death, barely two weeks before, had left. Benjamin came into the room and shocked at his brother's haggard looks, he tried to hearten him, "Good morning James, let's eat and then Francis and I will come to your office, go through the figures with you and between our three brains we ought to come up with a plan," Benjamin smiled at Martha, "these eggs smell good, will you have breakfast with us?"

"Thank you but no, I promised I would go to The White Lion to speak with Billy and Elizabeth and I will have coffee there with them before they leave for Kidderminster, Billy must get back to his Ministry today. Do you have time to see George before you and Kitty go back to London? I am sure he is sorry for what he said, he was a little drunk last night."

"Yes, Martha, I'll go and call on him later, I expect he will turn up for work with Jack as usual, but if not, I'll go round to Marsh Farm," Benjamin was eating heartily whilst James watched vacantly, not touching his own food, "but I've told Kitty and Will that we'll not be leaving Nottingham now until tomorrow so I'll be able to spend some time with Polly tonight too. Francis told me she was deeply upset, she loves both her brothers and hates to see them at odds. It was three in the morning when he got back from here and she was still crying."

"So I have troubled everyone more than ever," James put his head in his hands, "It was good of Francis to come and find me at the shop and bring me home, but maybe he should have left me there."

"Nonsense, get on with your eggs and we shall get our heads together," Benjamin said with bravado, "we shall find a way forward. We raised our glasses last night to enjoy a bright, new future with the beginning of this new era and so we shall."

When the two brothers arrived, the apprentices were already waiting outside Severns wine merchants on Middle Pavement, standing under the large wooden sign adorned with the gilded, ornamental "S" that advertised their business. James mounted the three stone steps without enthusiasm, turned the key in the lock and gripped the solid brass door knob. Unlike every previous day, he felt no pleasure in the challenge of pushing open the heavy, wooden door and looking round the room at the honey coloured, oak panelled walls and the tall counter flanked by two high stools. The arrangement of bottles displaying the same intricate "S" as the shop sign brought none of his usual frisson of pride and satisfaction. He was trudging through a nightmare of fog.

Francis arrived a few moments later and the three of them went straight to the office, where James opened the large, leather bound ledgers and placed a quill pen and some paper in front of each of them. As his brothers began to read, the concentration of silence was broken only by the tapping and scratching of pens scribbling their notes, but James sat staring at the figures swimming before him, his eyes as unfocused as his mind.

"James, I asked you what the current wholesale price for port from Hadley's would be." Benjamin's question brought him back to life and the three men worked together. By the middle of the afternoon, their prudent calculations and circumspect debate had led them to the consensus that it just might, but only might, be possible to recover. Severns bank balance was healthy and there had been high demand in December for the Christmas and New Year celebrations but James was expected to, and did, give long credit to his customers. If James could negotiate a favourable deal with Geoffrey Hadley's wholesale operation in Hull to replenish the cellars, then there was a chance, but a only a slim chance, he could trade his way out of trouble. The major crisis was that James was honour bound to settle his bill of exchange with the Portuguese wine grower on or before the first of April. He needed to find the three thousand pounds in only three months, a Herculean task.

Printed in Great Britain
by Amazon

37035988R00158